SCHOOL OF ORGANIC DISTORTION
PROFESSOR: *Terry Evans*

CLASS: TAUGHT BY:

Contagion
~~Microbiology~~ .... Carla Crook

Mutation
~~Genetics~~ .... Terry Evans

SCHOOL OF DESTRUCTION
PROFESSOR: *Luther Lasco*

CLASS: TAUGHT BY:

Explosives
                                                aka Trigger
~~Applied Physics~~ .... Gary Brown

Assassination (including poisoning)
~~Basic Physiology~~ .... Luther Lasco

Power Channeling
~~Personal Growth~~ .... Hari Saravati
                                                aka the Guru

Guerrilla Skills
~~Ecosurvival Techniques~~ .... Adolf Hauser
                                                aka the Führer

Case Studies I
~~Self-Discipline~~* .... Luther Lasco

*Classes with an asterisk are compulsory.

EVIL GENIUS

EVI
GEN

CATHERINE JINKS

HARCOURT, INC.

ORLANDO   AUSTIN   NEW YORK   SAN DIEGO   TORONTO   LONDON

Acknowledgments

The author would like to thank the Spastic Centre, Anthony Jinks,
and Peter Dockrill (and Elijah Wood for the visual inspiration!).

www.HarcourtBooks.com

First published in 2005 by Allen & Unwin, Australia
First U.S. edition 2007

Library of Congress Cataloging-in-Publication Data
Jinks, Catherine.
Evil genius/Catherine Jinks.—1st ed.
p. cm.
Summary: Child prodigy Cadel Piggott, an antisocial computer genius, discovers
his true identity when he enrolls as a first-year student at an advanced crime academy.
[1. Genius—Fiction. 2. Identity—Fiction. 3. Crime—Fiction.
4. Good and evil—Fiction. 5. Schools—Fiction. 6. Australia—Fiction.
7. Science fiction.] I. Title.
PZ7.J5754Ev 2007
[Fic]—dc22 2006014476
ISBN 978-0-15-205988-0

Text set in Ehrhardt MT
Designed by April Ward

First U.S. edition
A C E G H F D B

Printed in the United States of America

ONE

Cadel Piggott was just seven years old when he first met Thaddeus Roth.

Dr. Roth worked in a row house near Sydney Harbor. The house was three stories high, its garden shrouded by a great many damp, dark trees. There was moss growing on its sandstone window ledges. Curtains drawn across all its windows gave it a secretive air. Its front fence was made of iron, with a spike on top of each post; beside the creaking gate was a brass sign bearing Dr. Roth's name and qualifications.

"That's it," said Mrs. Piggott. "Number twenty-nine."

"Well, we can't stop here," her husband replied. "No parking."

"I told you to park back there."

"It doesn't matter. We'll try down this street."

"Stuart, that's a one-way street."

"Dammit!"

"I knew we'd never find a space. Not around this area."

"Just shut up for a minute, will you?"

Mr. and Mrs. Piggott were not Cadel's real parents. They had adopted him when he was not quite two years old. Mrs. Piggott was thin and blond, Mr. Piggott fat and gray. They almost never agreed about anything, but that didn't matter because they almost never met. Their busy schedules kept them away from home, and one another, a good deal of the time.

At the suggestion of the police, however, they had both agreed to attend this interview.

"We're going to be late," Mrs. Piggott warned her husband after they had circled the block four times in Mr. Piggott's big, gleaming Mercedes-Benz. "Just let us out, for god's sake."

"I'll park here."

"Stuart, you'll never fit in there!"

"Watch me."

Cadel said nothing. He sat on the backseat, dressed in his good brown cords and a lamb's-wool sweater, staring out the window at Dr. Roth's house. He didn't like the look of it. He thought it had a murky, ominous appearance.

"I don't want to go," he said flatly when Mrs. Piggott got out and opened the door beside him.

"I know, honey, but we have to."

"No we don't," Cadel retorted.

"Yes we do."

"There were no formal charges," Cadel pointed out, in his high, clear voice. "It was just a suggestion."

"That's right," said Mr. Piggott, yanking Cadel out of the back of the car. "And when the police make a suggestion, you always follow it. Rule number one."

"Be careful, Stuart, you'll wreck his clothes."

Cadel was so small—even for a seven-year-old—that he didn't stand a chance against Mr. Piggott. Though he dragged his feet and hung off his adoptive parents' hands like a sack of melons, he was forced across the street and through the front gate of number twenty-nine. The path beyond the gate was mushy with wet leaves. There was a rich smell of decay. The door knocker was a ring in the mouth of a snarling lion's head, painted black, like the rest of the ironwork.

Cadel noted with interest the switchboard near the door. It was obviously ancient, full of porcelain fuses and dial meters. The Piggotts' own house was only three years old, with a state-of-the-art electrical system, so Cadel was fascinated by this dusty old relic.

But he was not permitted to gaze at it for long.

"Come on," Mr. Piggott barked. "The door's open." And he pushed against it, causing it to swing back and reveal a long, dark hallway carpeted with dingy Persian rugs. About halfway down this hallway, a staircase the color of walnut swept up to the next floor. There were several doors to the right of the front entrance, but only the closest stood ajar.

"Hello!" said Mr. Piggott, marching straight through it. He wasn't a man who normally waited for anything. "We've an appointment with Dr. Roth. For ten thirty."

Gripped firmly around the wrist, Cadel had no choice but to follow Mr. Piggott. He found himself in a reception area: two rooms divided by a pair of folding mahogany doors. There were two marble fireplaces and two chandeliers. Cadel noticed cobwebs on the chandeliers.

A woman sat behind an antique desk.

"Good morning," she said calmly. "What name, please?"

"Piggott," Mr. Piggott replied, in pompous tones. "Stuart, Lanna, and Cadel." He looked surprised when the woman rose, revealing herself to be almost as wide and as tall as he was. She had a broad, square face and small blue eyes. She was wearing a suit the color of dried blood.

"I'll just go and tell Dr. Roth that you've arrived," she declared, before lumbering out of the room. Cadel didn't watch her go. He was more interested in the computer that she'd left behind, with its alluring glow and contented hum. The screen saver was one that he'd never seen before: a pattern of falling dominoes.

"Don't even think about it," Stuart rasped when he realized what was attracting Cadel's attention. "Sit down. Over there."

"Look, honey, there are toys for you to play with," Lanna said, nudging a large basket with the toe of her expensive Italian shoe. Sulkily, Cadel eyed the basket's contents. He was used to the broken activity centers and torn books offered for the amusement of younger patients at his local doctor's office and wasn't hopeful about the distractions provided here.

But to his astonishment, he quickly spied an old voltmeter, together with a book on flies, a plastic human skull (life-sized), a Rubik's Cube, and a Frankenstein mask. Further investigation uncovered a dead spider embedded in a resin paperweight, a shark's tooth, a Galaxy Warrior complete with Thermopuncher torpedoes, and a very curious fragment of puzzle bearing the picture of a staring, bloodshot eye over a set of claw marks.

He was puzzling over this macabre image when the sound of heavy footsteps reached his ears. It seemed that Dr. Roth's receptionist was returning, clumping down the stairs like someone wearing ski boots. Lanna, who had flung herself onto an armchair, immediately jumped to her feet.

Stuart glared at the door.

"Dr. Roth will see you now," the receptionist announced when she finally appeared. "You can go straight up."

Stuart and Lanna exchanged glances.

"Are you sure?" Lanna objected. "I mean, does he want to discuss things in front of Cadel?"

"Oh yes," the receptionist declared firmly. Something about her voice made Cadel look up. He studied her with care, from the top of her permed head to the soles of her brown shoes. She smiled in response, and the Piggotts all recoiled.

Her mouth looked as if it belonged to an older, harsher century.

"Why are your teeth black?" Cadel wanted to know.

"Why are your teeth white?" the receptionist responded, wending her way back to her desk. Lanna snatched at Cadel's hand and hustled him out of the room. She and her husband whispered together as they climbed the stairs, which creaked and groaned beneath them.

"Stuart, what was the matter with . . . ?"

"I don't know."

"Do you think this is a good idea?"

"Course it is."

"But what about that woman? Her teeth?"

4

Stuart shrugged. They had reached a landing, but it wasn't the right one. From above their heads, a voice said, *"Up here."*

A man was draped over the second-floor banisters. He was tall and thin and wore a tweed jacket. His thick, dark hair was going gray.

"That's the bathroom," he remarked in a soothing voice with a cultured English accent. "I'm afraid my office is at the top, here."

"Dr. Roth?" said Stuart.

"Yes, indeed."

"We're a bit late," Lanna offered a trifle breathlessly. "No parking."

"You should turn that front yard of yours into a parking lot," Stuart added, climbing the last flight of stairs. Gracefully, Dr. Roth moved to push open the door of his office.

"I would," he said, "if the local council would let me. Heritage listing, I'm afraid."

Stuart grunted. Lanna smiled a meaningless social smile. They both passed into Dr. Roth's office ahead of Cadel, who stopped on the threshold. He gazed up at Thaddeus.

"Why does she have black teeth?" Cadel inquired.

"Wilfreda? I'm not sure," Thaddeus replied. "Poor dental hygiene, I should think. Her parents had very strange ideas about diet and doctors. Maybe they didn't believe in toothbrushes, either." He cocked his head. "So you're Cadel."

"Yes."

"Come in, Cadel."

Dr. Roth's office surprised Cadel, because it was full of modern furniture and computer equipment. There were a number of glossy cabinets, some full of filing drawers, some with cables running out of them. Cadel's eyes gleamed when he spotted those cables.

"Sit down, please." Dr. Roth gestured at a cluster of couches placed between his desk and a pair of French doors. Lanna chose the crimson couch, settling down onto it very carefully, her bare knees drawn together. Stuart dropped into his seat like a stone.

"We brought this referral . . . ," said his wife, passing an envelope to

5

Dr. Roth. Thaddeus opened it, removed a folded sheet of paper, and smoothed the paper flat without taking his eyes off Cadel, whose attention was fixed on a modem attached to an inline filter.

"The police suggested we arrange some counseling for Cadel," Stuart explained. "They also suggested that he shouldn't be allowed to use a computer except under supervision. *Responsible* supervision."

"He's far too young to understand," added Lanna, smoothing down her short skirt. "His emotional maturity hasn't caught up with his intellect."

"He has a genius IQ," said her husband gruffly. "We had him tested."

"It's not his fault. We would have said something if we'd known what he was up to."

"He's not a bad kid."

Thaddeus raised an eyebrow. By this time he was glancing through the referral, nodding to himself. When he had finished, he refolded the paper and tucked it into his jacket pocket. "Right," he said, then cleared his throat. "Cadel? Would you like to use my computer?"

Cadel whirled around. Stuart and Lanna both gasped.

"But he can't!" Stuart spluttered.

"He's not allowed!" Lanna cried.

"Oh, I think he'll be all right," said Dr. Roth. "I'll be interested to see if he *does* make a nuisance of himself. There's some very tough security software installed on that computer." He smiled indulgently at Cadel. "Knock yourself out, kid."

While Cadel scuttled over to the desk, his adoptive parents looked at each other in dismay. Dr. Roth sank into the couch opposite them, his long, bony hands pressed together under his beaky nose. "So," he began, "Cadel has been hacking into high-security computer networks, is that it?"

"The power grid," Stuart interrupted. "And a bill-paying service."

"He likes the challenge," said Lanna, sounding worried. "I'm sure that's it. He's bored at school."

"He knows he shouldn't have," Stuart growled, "but I don't think he's aware—"

"That it's against the law," his wife interjected, at which point Stuart turned on her.

"I was going to *say* that he's probably not aware of the full implications, if you'd let me get a word in edgewise," he snapped. "It's *not* against the law—not when you're seven years old. That's the whole point. You can't charge a kid of his age."

"But the police thought that measures ought to be taken in any case," Dr. Roth remarked smoothly. "I understand. And may I ask whether you've discussed these matters with the school he attends? What's it called?"

"Elphington Grammar," Lanna supplied. "We live on the North Shore, you see."

"They've expelled him," Stuart said flatly. "Don't want him there. Too much like hard work, designing special programs for a genius."

"So we've enrolled him in Jamboree Gardens. They believe in small classes, and they nurture potential on an individual basis."

"It's one of those tree-hugger schools," Stuart concluded, without much enthusiasm.

Again Thaddeus nodded. In the brief silence that followed, the *click-clack* of a hardworking computer keyboard filled the room. Cadel sat perched on Dr. Roth's chair, his small feet dangling, his gaze fixed.

"Can you tell me anything else about your son that might be useful?" Thaddeus said at last, and Lanna leaned forward.

"We're not his birth parents," she revealed in a low voice. "If that matters. He knows, of course."

"This wouldn't have happened if his nanny hadn't left." Stuart sighed. "No supervision."

"Why did his nanny leave?" Dr. Roth queried, whereupon Stuart rubbed the back of his neck in obvious discomfort.

This time Lanna's voice was so low that it was barely a whisper.

7

"He used to charge things to her credit card. She used it so much that *of course* he picked up on it."

"He's a funny kid," Stuart admitted. "He's not normal."

"Stuart!"

"Well, he's not. You can't pretend he is."

"Shhh!"

But Cadel didn't seem to be listening. He was peering at the computer screen, his lips pursed, his brow furrowed.

"You know what he said to me the other day?" Stuart continued. "Lanna and I had been arguing—"

"We don't often argue," his wife broke in, smiling nervously at Thaddeus. "You're giving Dr. Roth the wrong idea, honey."

Stuart snorted. "Yeah, well, whatever you say. Anyhow, he looked me straight in the eye, and he said, 'You're like a malfunctioning modem with her. You need to locate the right initialization string.'" Stuart blinked. "Can you believe that?"

His wife tittered. "Oh dear," she said. "That is *so* Cadel."

"He carries the strangest things around with him," Stuart went on. "Not yo-yos or rubber frogs or stuff like that. He carries circuit boards and thermostats and ignition coils. God knows where he gets them."

"Out of my computer." Lanna grimaced, her face falling suddenly. "That's where he gets them. Or he dismantles the security system."

"We have a circuitry room," Stuart confessed. "It controls the security system and the phone system and the air-conditioning—"

"We can never get him out of there."

"Half the time, when you turn on the television, the garage door opens."

"Whatever kind of lock you put on that damned circuitry room, he always cracks it sooner or later."

"Like you said, Lanna, he can't resist a challenge."

All three adults turned their heads to study Cadel, who ignored them. He looked just like a little angel, with his huge blue eyes, chestnut curls, and heart-shaped face.

"We were wondering if he was a bit autistic"—Lanna sighed—"but he's not. We checked it out. He's just not very interested in people."

"Especially other kids," said Stuart. "Well, what other kids anywhere near his age are going to be interested in information protocol settings?"

"Quite," said Thaddeus. "And what do you hope to *gain* from having Cadel visit me here, Mr. and Mrs. Piggott?"

"Well . . ." Lanna cast a hopeless glance at her husband, who shrugged.

"We're just doing what we're told," he mumbled. "So this whole business won't happen again."

"Perhaps you can teach Cadel some social skills?" Lanna proposed brightly. "Help him to understand that he can't do whatever he wants just because he's smarter than everyone else?"

"Because he *thinks* he's smarter than everyone else," Stuart amended. And he narrowed his eyes, his jaw muscles working.

Thaddeus surveyed him thoughtfully.

"Ye-e-es," said Thaddeus. "I see." All at once he surged to his feet, taking Mr. and Mrs. Piggott by surprise. "Well, thank you very much for that input," he remarked pleasantly. "You've been most helpful. I'll keep it in mind when I talk to your son—it might be interesting to have some more tests done, but I'll discuss that with you later. Could you give me, say, twenty minutes? Twenty minutes alone with Cadel? It should be enough for today."

"You mean *now*?" said Stuart.

"If that's all right with you."

"Well, I . . . I guess so."

"If it's all right with Cadel," said Lanna. "Cadel? Honey? Do you mind if we step outside for a few minutes? Dr. Roth wants to talk to you."

There was no reply. Cadel didn't appear to have registered the fact that Lanna was addressing him.

"He won't even notice we're gone," her husband muttered. "You watch."

"We'll be right downstairs, honey. We won't be far."

"You'd think he was deaf," Stuart complained. As he nudged his wife from the room, she threw Dr. Roth a toothy smile.

"He's not deaf, actually," she assured the psychologist. "We've had tests done . . ."

Bang! The door slammed shut. Thaddeus waited until he could no longer hear the tramp of feet on stairs before strolling over to where Cadel sat in the typist's chair. Cadel ignored him. Suddenly, Thaddeus yanked at the chair, making it spin around until it was pointing toward him. Then he grabbed each armrest and leaned into Cadel's face.

Cadel's hands jumped up in a startled reflex.

"I'll make a deal with you, Cadel," said Thaddeus. "Can you keep a secret?"

Solemnly, Cadel nodded.

"Good. Then this is what we'll do. If you don't tell your parents about it, I'll let you use my computer whenever you come here. Does that sound good?"

Again, Cadel nodded.

"And all I ask in return is this." The corner of Thaddeus's mouth rose, revealing one yellowish, pointed canine tooth. Through the lenses of his spectacles, his eyes were as black as a snake's. His voice dropped to a throaty whisper. "Next time," he murmured, "whatever you do, *don't get caught.*"

TWO

Cadel Piggott had a very special sort of mind. He could picture systems of all kinds in three dimensions, with perfect accuracy. He loved systems: phone systems, electrical systems, car engines, complicated traffic intersections. When he first saw a map of the Sydney rail system, pasted on the wall of a suburban train, he was enchanted.

At Jamboree Gardens, the teachers understood the scope of his intelligence. They moved him up to fourth grade but would not accelerate his learning program any further. They told Mrs. Piggott that although Cadel's intellect was highly developed, his social skills were no better (and in some respects were poorer) than those of any other child his age. They did not believe that he would be comfortable socializing with children older than nine.

"We've developed a series of additional math and literacy units that our teacher's assistant will take Cadel through," one of the teachers told Lanna. "We think they'll help to keep him happy and interested, along with our art and music programs. You know we place great emphasis on creativity in this school."

But Cadel was neither happy nor interested. He was impatient with silk-screen printing and books about riding bikes to the park. His obsession was with systems, and he tended to ignore everything else. So he sometimes scored badly on reading-and-comprehension tests, though at other times the teachers at Jamboree Gardens would find him poring over books like *From Eniac to Univac: An Appraisal of the Eckert-Mauchly Machines*.

It was very hard to keep him off the school computers.

"He'd spend all day on them, if we let him," the principal told Lanna. "And when we don't, he becomes quite uncooperative. To be frank, we don't like him messing around with them, because half the time no one here can understand what he's doing. We can't supervise him responsibly if we don't know what we're supervising. It's very difficult."

"I know," said Lanna in gloomy tones.

"I really think he should be encouraged to focus his energies away from computer science," the principal continued. "A fully rounded person must diversify, or his intellect becomes narrow and blinkered. I think we'll have to institute a very strict timetable for Cadel. Make him understand that there's more to this world than computers."

She was successful, to some degree. Forbidden computers both at home *and* at school, Cadel turned his attention to the Sydney Rail network. He obtained every timetable for the entire system. He rode every line, over and over again, though not unaccompanied: a part-time nanny usually came with him, because the Piggotts often employed nannies, none of whom stayed for very long.

Occasionally during his sessions with Thaddeus, Cadel would even abandon the psychologist's computer and acquaint Thaddeus with his latest discoveries about gauges and signal boxes. When that happened, Thaddeus would put aside his newspaper and listen intently.

One day he said: "Do you think you understand the system now?"

Cadel pondered this question for at least half a minute.

"Yes," he replied at last.

"Because there's only one way to find out if you do," Thaddeus went on. "You can only tell whether you've mastered a system if you isolate and identify its weakest point. If you knock that out and the whole system collapses, then you know you've got a handle on it."

Cadel absorbed this advice silently. Across the room, Thaddeus watched his pale little face grow perfectly still.

Satisfied, Thaddeus once again picked up his newspaper.

For the next five months, Cadel worked and waited. Every spare moment was spent riding the rails, and at last, one afternoon in May, he spied a particular signal light being repaired. He got out at the next stop, and while his nanny was buying mints at a newsstand, he phoned Sydney Rail with the news that there was a bomb planted in a certain subterranean station. Then he went home to watch TV, which was full of stories about terrible rail delays affecting the entire Sydney network. Though no one had been hurt, on some lines commuters had been forced to wait for up to five hours.

The next day, Thaddeus asked Cadel if the train chaos had had anything to do with him.

"No," said Cadel.

"Are you sure?"

"I'm sure." Cadel had a very small mouth and innocent eyes. Although he was now eight years old, he hadn't grown much. Thaddeus looked at him thoughtfully for a while before nodding.

"You should never admit to anything," he said. "Denial is the second rule after 'Don't get caught.' You must always remember that, Cadel."

Cadel didn't even nod. He was being cautious.

"One way of making sure you don't get caught is by leaving the scene of the crime," Thaddeus continued. "If you keep concentrating on the railways, somebody's going to make a connection one day. You realize that, don't you? You're going to have to get interested in something else."

Cadel blinked.

"After all, you've proved your mastery," Thaddeus pointed out. "What else can Sydney Rail possibly give you? Nothing. You should move on to another challenge. The road system, perhaps."

Cadel's eyes narrowed. Previously, he had accepted Thaddeus as being simply part of his life. Now, for the first time, he questioned the psychologist's motives. What exactly was he up to?

"Do you tell Stuart and Lanna about anything we say in here?" Cadel asked.

"Of course not." Thaddeus spoke dismissively. "Why should I?"

In response, Cadel gazed at him until Thaddeus uttered a short laugh.

"Of course, you're free to doubt me on that," Thaddeus conceded. "I wouldn't trust me, either, if I were you." Whereupon he resumed his reading, leaving Cadel to turn things over in his head.

The following week, after much thought, Cadel asked Thaddeus another question. "Are you really a psychiatrist?" he wanted to know.

"A psychologist," Thaddeus replied jovially. "Yes, I really am. Haven't you seen all my degrees? I specialize in 'troubled youth.'"

"Then why are you letting me use your computer when I'm not meant to?"

"Because I think it's good for you."

"Better than talking?"

At this, Thaddeus cast aside his newspaper. He was sitting on the crimson couch, his long legs stretched out in front of him. Folding his hands across his stomach, he fixed Cadel with a bright and curious look.

"Why? What do you want to talk about?" he inquired softly.

"I dunno." Cadel had watched enough television to understand that certain things were to be expected in a psychologist's office. "Shouldn't I talk about my parents?"

"Who aren't really your parents."

"No," Cadel agreed.

"Does that bother you?"

"No."

"Why not? Because you despise them?"

Cadel lowered his chin a fraction, as he always did when he was feeling defensive. He looked warily at Thaddeus from beneath his fringe of curls.

"I don't despise my parents," he said flatly.

Thaddeus smiled. With a cracking of joints, he rose to his full height, which was considerably more than Cadel's.

"Don't bother lying to me, Cadel."

"I'm not."

"Do you think I don't know contempt when I see it? I'm very, very familiar with contempt, believe me." Turning suddenly, Thaddeus crossed the room to the French doors, where he stood with his back to Cadel, gazing out over the treetops. "Have you ever wondered about your *real* parents?" he said at last.

"I guess . . . ," Cadel replied. He was growing extremely uncomfortable.

"You must have tried to find out who they are," said Thaddeus. "Someone like you. With the Net so close at hand."

"I tried," Cadel admitted. In fact, he had tried very hard. He had dug through the Piggotts' family archives (such as they were) and found a birth certificate that listed his father as Daryl Poynter-Chuffley and his mother as Susan Jones. Unfortunately, he had got no further. There were no Poynter-Chuffleys to be found on the Internet—not even on various births, deaths, and marriages sites—and as for Susan Jones, well, that was a name too common to be traced. He could find no hospital records, because his birth had apparently taken place at home. And the home in question no longer existed, according to his research. It had been torn down to make way for a shopping mall.

Furthermore, he could find no trace of *himself* on the Internet. No online birth certificates. No online adoption records. So far, the only thing Cadel had learned was that his first name meant "battle" in Welsh.

It was all very peculiar.

Thaddeus spun around. He walked slowly back to where Cadel was sitting, then stood with his hands clasped behind him, contemplating his young client.

"What if I told you who your father is?" he said at last.

Cadel gasped.

"My—my *real* father?" he stammered.

"That's right."

"You know who my real father is?"

"I've always known," Thaddeus said calmly. Placing his hands on the armrests of Cadel's chair, he bent at the waist until his head was almost level with his client's. "I work for him, you see. He employs me to keep an eye on you."

"But—"

"He can arrange these things. He has a lot of influence, despite the fact that he's been in prison for the last five years or so." Thaddeus's gaze bored into Cadel like an ebony drill-bit. "His name is Darkkon. Dr. Phineas Darkkon. You might have heard of him."

Mutely, Cadel shook his head. He was overwhelmed. For a long time, he had worked hard to suppress all interest in his real parents. Having been unable to trace them, he had come to the conclusion that fretting about them would be pointless; it would ultimately drive him mad.

And now, all of a sudden, he was being offered the truth. After so many years, he wasn't sure if he could handle it. He was almost afraid.

"Your father was sentenced to life imprisonment," Thaddeus explained. "You were taken away from him, but he swore that he would never lose sight of you and that you would come to know from whose blood you sprang. Therefore, despite the American government's best efforts to keep you ignorant and unaware, your father has triumphed. Once again." Thaddeus pushed himself upright, so forcefully that the back of Cadel's wheeled typist's chair struck the rim of Thaddeus's desktop. "The Piggotts know nothing of this, naturally."

Cadel drew his knees up under his chin. In a breathless voice, he said: "Are you lying?"

"No."

"Truly?"

"Truly." Thaddeus folded his arms. "Though you're right to doubt me, of course. You should always doubt everyone."

"What about my mother?"

"Ah." Thaddeus took a deep breath. His tone softened. "Your mother died, Cadel. I'm sorry."

Cadel swallowed. He didn't know if he was sorry or not. "How?" he croaked.

"It was an accident, I'm afraid. Very unfortunate." A pause. "Your father was devastated."

"What did he do?"

"Do?"

Cadel lifted his head and looked Thaddeus in the eye. "What did he do *wrong*? Why is he in jail?"

At that moment there was a knock on the door. Thaddeus glanced at his watch with a frown.

"Your next client is here," Wilfreda announced from out on the landing.

"Thank you," Thaddeus replied. He smiled at Cadel. "Time's up, I'm afraid."

"But—"

"Do some research, Cadel. Phineas Darkkon. Look him up and see what you can find before you visit me next. It shouldn't be hard." The smile widened until it became a jagged grin. "As long as you don't tell the Piggotts, of course."

THREE

The day after Thaddeus dropped his bombshell about Dr. Darkkon, Cadel went to the library with his current nanny, Linda. Linda was English. She had blond hair and a slouch, and she sighed every time she spoke. She sighed when she asked Cadel how long he was going to be. She sighed when he replied that he didn't know. "I'll wait over here, then," she sighed and slumped into a seat at one of the reading desks, where she sat noisily sighing, and flick-flick-flicking through magazines about movie stars and soap operas. (Her acrylic nails were so long that she had trouble getting a good grip on the shiny paper.)

Cadel went first to the computer catalog. From there he moved to the reference section, the biography section, and the shelves devoted to biochemistry. A few old news magazines, one or two scientific journals, a book called *Gene Crime,* and another book on famous fraudsters were all that he needed. After trawling through these, he had a pretty good idea of who his father was.

In fact, he couldn't believe that Phineas Darkkon had never attracted his notice before.

Phineas Darkkon hadn't always been Phineas Darkkon. He had been christened Vernon Bobrick and had kept the name until he was well into his sixties. By that time, he was a famous geneticist, who had made a great deal of money developing "synthogenes"—artificial genes cobbled together out of genetic material not already patented by big research companies. Vernon had bought himself several mansions, an island off the coast of Australia, and a huge laboratory complex in

California. He had used this complex to study what he called "human potentialities," namely, the possibility that some people possessed "supergenes."

According to Vernon, while most humans were the equivalent of junk DNA, a very few were genetic gold mines. He had been investigating something called "spontaneous combustion"—a concept widely regarded as a myth—and had come to believe that the strange phenomenon of people suddenly bursting into flame, for no apparent reason, was related to a rare childhood skin disorder. Vernon argued that an extremely small portion of the human race was pyrogenic. "Pyrogenes" (as he called them) allowed some people to light fires using only their body heat. Most of these people were unaware of their hidden talent. Indeed, most were unable to harness it properly, with the result that they spontaneously combusted.

Hmmm, thought Cadel.

"Hello, dear," said a female voice, shattering Cadel's concentration. It was one of the librarians. She knew Cadel because he was a regular at the library. She was always asking him questions about the books he borrowed. "How are you today?"

"Fine," said Cadel, cautiously.

"You didn't come on your own, did you?" she asked, and Cadel pointed at Linda, who had her feet on a chair and was unwrapping a stick of gum.

"Oh dear," said the librarian, before hurrying off to have a word with Linda about rules and regulations.

Cadel returned to his books.

It appeared that most respected scientists had laughed at Vernon's views. Then they had become alarmed when some of his experiments resulted in the deaths of two university students. Vernon's research was outlawed and driven underground. Meanwhile, Vernon was pursuing another theory about UFO sightings and alien abductions. It was Vernon's opinion that such experiences were hallucinations, accidentally caused by *other people*—people with psychic powers.

Once again, however, he wasn't taken seriously.

It angered Vernon Bobrick that so many of his fellow scientists were blinkered and stubborn. He wanted to prove his theories, but to do that, he required even more money. First he engineered a fake gene-patent scam, which robbed thousands of eager investors of their life savings. Then he quietly established a franchise of faulty vending machines, all of which swallowed money without vending anything. He was behind a handful of miracle cures that cured nothing at all. Finally, and most importantly, he started an organization called GenoME.

Very few people realized that Vernon had anything to do with GenoME, which claimed that its trained GenoME "potentializers" could map your exact genetic code and tell you where you were going wrong in life. By knowing exactly what potentials were contained in your genes, you could see where you were pointlessly fighting against your very nature. GenoME's motto was "Messages in matter are messages that matter."

It cost a lot of money to get your genes mapped, and even more money to have the map analyzed by experts. Soon GenoME was enormously successful, with offices and members all over the world. "GenoME changed my life" was a remark often bandied around in the GenoME advertising. It was almost like a religion.

If Vernon Bobrick had simply sat back and enjoyed the profits that rolled in from GenoME and his other business interests, he would have been left alone. But Vernon was a man with a vision—a vision that he intended to pursue at all costs. He changed his name to Phineas Darkkon, pointing out to everyone who would listen that it meant "Dark Lord." Then he produced from his secret laboratory a person he named Doel the Disruptor. Doel, he said, possessed the power to make other people hallucinate. To prove his point, Dr. Darkkon made Doel concentrate his disruptive energies on an English politician, who collapsed in a gibbering heap, screaming about giant spiders. Phineas warned that if a sum of $500 million wasn't paid directly to him, a whole army of disruptors would be unleashed on the world, at his command.

Actually, Phineas didn't have a whole army of disruptors at his disposal. He only had Doel. And when the world's politicians called his bluff, his entire plan collapsed. (A great many powerful people were convinced that the shrieking politician had simply been drunk.) When Doel was arrested, it was discovered that his powers—if they existed—only worked in controlled laboratory conditions. Poor Doel ended up in a mental hospital.

Meanwhile, Phineas Darkkon vanished. When Interpol began to pursue him, he moved from hideout to hideout, waging a very peculiar war against the scientists whose lack of vision, he thought, had condemned him to life on the fringes. He contaminated gas pipelines with a curious kind of molecule. He corrupted computer systems across the world with a new strain of computer virus called "Darkkon." And he developed a vicious little retrovirus, which he threatened to release so that he could wipe out all the "junk human beings" who had hijacked mankind's destiny. Only those with "supergenes," he said, would be immune to the effects of this retrovirus.

That was when he hit the top of Interpol's Most Wanted list.

Shortly afterward, he was arrested while buying a box of tissues at a gas station in Colorado. He received a life sentence, at his trial. After attempting a couple of jailbreaks, he was put in a top-security prison, where he seemed to lose his fighting spirit. No one had heard much about him for several years, though rumors continued to fly concerning the whereabouts of his multimillion-dollar fortune. While much of it had been traced and confiscated, a good portion was supposed to be hidden away in various tax havens around the world. No one had yet identified Dr. Darkkon's mysterious accountant, who was believed to hold the key to the Darkkon Empire.

There was no mention of a son. No mention of a wife, or even a girlfriend.

Cadel examined the photographs of Phineas Darkkon. They showed a Yoda-like figure in his late seventies, squat and bald, with large ears, huge eyes, and a grayish complexion. Failed plastic surgery had left him with an almost nonexistent nose. Though he claimed to have stalled his own aging process with genetic manipulation and antioxidant flushes, Cadel saw no evidence of it.

He also saw no trace of himself in that strange-looking face.

Studying it carefully, Cadel turned various questions over in his mind. Why had there been no mention of Darkkon's family? If Cadel *was* a Darkkon (and why should Thaddeus lie?), then who had his mother been? When had she died? According to Cadel's calculations, he had been just under two years old at the time of Darkkon's imprisonment. Had his mother died before then? Was that why he had been sent to Australia—because one parent was dead and one was serving a life sentence? If so, where had the information on his birth certificate come from?

Cadel glanced around him. There weren't many people in the library, though all the computers were being used. No one was looking his way. The librarian had finished admonishing Linda and returned to her desk. Linda was scowling as she flipped viciously through a magazine about hairstyles.

Cadel slid his own magazine under the desk in front of him. Then, slowly and carefully, he tore out the article on Phineas Darkkon while pretending to read the book about GenoME that lay on top of his desk. Having folded the three-page article into a small, thick square, he tucked it into his pocket.

He did the same to the chapter about Phineas Darkkon in *Gene Crime*, and to the piece about synthogenes in one of the scientific journals. Then he got up, returned all his reading materials to their proper places, and left with Linda, who sighed with relief when they emerged into the sunlight.

During the next couple of days, Cadel pored over his stolen texts, in private. He couldn't leave them alone; he was unable to think about anything else. Yet he told no one about them. This was partly because Thaddeus had warned him against it, partly because he had no real friends, and partly because he wasn't sure that he wanted the world to know who his real father was. On the one hand, Phineas might have been a man of vision and genius, embittered by ill treatment. On the other hand, he might have been a loony. It was hard to tell from the media reports. They were so *very* incomplete.

"I couldn't find anything about my mother," he remarked when he was next in Thaddeus's office. This time he hadn't even approached the computer; he was sitting on the crimson couch.

Thaddeus sat facing him, legs crossed.

"No," Thaddeus replied. "It wasn't widely known that your father had a girlfriend. He tried to keep it a secret."

"Why?"

Thaddeus shrugged. "Less chance of anyone trying to get at him through your mother—or you. Of course the police found out. You were bundled off quick smart when they arrested him. I suppose they decided to hide you away in Australia so that Phineas would have a hard time trying to locate you." A soft laugh. "Although he did, of course. At least *I* did."

Cadel thought for a minute. "Are you a GenoME person?" he finally asked, whereupon Thaddeus winced.

"Cadel, please," he protested. "That garbage? Give me some credit."

"So where do you fit in? Are you his accountant?"

"I'm merely his right-hand man."

"Then why haven't you been arrested?"

"Because I've kept a low profile." While Thaddeus's foot flicked back and forth, the rest of him remained absolutely still. He didn't even blink as he watched Cadel. He was like a cat with a twitching tail. "One thing your father has learned, since his arrest, is that you don't draw attention to yourself. He's a brilliant man, Cadel, but that was his error. He knows better now."

"Does he?" Cadel was confused. It didn't seem to him that Phineas Darkkon had been all that smart. In some ways, yes—but not in others. The business with Doel the Disruptor . . . Cadel wasn't sure about that at all.

"Your father has certain ideas about the world, Cadel," Thaddeus remarked. Twitch, twitch, twitch went his foot. "Not many people share them, because not many people understand them. Not many people have made the mental leap. He had to find his own money to fund the research to support those ideas, and in doing so, he simply exploited the stupidity of others. You see, there are two types of people in this world, Cadel—"

"I know, I know," Cadel interrupted. "I read about it. Two types of people, like two types of DNA. But *I* wouldn't like to lose money in a soft-drink machine."

"Cadel, you wouldn't." Thaddeus spoke patiently. "If you ever set your mind to it, you'd never have to pay money into a vending machine ever again. You're the sort of person who would develop a means of getting the drink without paying the money. You have a supergenetic blueprint, Cadel—just like your father. The world is going to hell precisely because the junk DNA of stupid and talentless people has been swamping the potential of the human race. Think about it, Cadel. Think about what *you* have to put up with. It's as if you've been dragging invisible shackles around, isn't it? No one *wants* you to spread your wings. You're regarded as a problem, not a solution. Everywhere you turn, people want to rein you in. Stop you from doing what you want."

It was true. Cadel stared in astonishment.

"Have you heard about Galileo?" said Thaddeus. "Galileo was scorned and imprisoned because of his views, which were ahead of their time. One day, Cadel, your father will receive the recognition he deserves."

Cadel wondered. He wasn't completely convinced. But he *was* interested. After a long time, he said, "Do you know what I like about you? I like the way you talk to me. No one else talks to me the way you do. People treat me like . . . like . . ." Words failed him, briefly.

"Like an eight-year-old?" Thaddeus suggested, with a smile.

"Like I'm stupid," said Cadel. "Like I don't understand."

"Which isn't an error I'm likely to make."

"You're the only one who doesn't expect me to be stupid."

"As to that, I should point out two things," Thaddeus replied. "Firstly, most adults would find it impossible to admit that a child is smarter than they are. Secondly, your father is not among this group of people." Thaddeus narrowed his eyes. "He would very much like to speak to you, Cadel. If you have no objection."

Cadel had been swinging his legs. He froze. He stared, then swallowed. "On the phone, you mean?" he asked warily.

"I think not. Your father is under constant surveillance. He's had to find alternative methods of contacting me."

"How?"

"Via transmitter." A slow smile spread across the psychologist's face. "As a matter of fact, it's hidden in his arthritis bangle."

Cadel blinked.

"His first transmitter was in his wristwatch," Thaddeus continued, "but they took that away."

"It must be a pretty small transmitter."

"It's wired with DNA."

Cadel caught his breath.

"It's *what*?"

"You heard me." Thaddeus winked. "Someone was bound to master the technique sometime, and Dr. Darkkon has the obvious background."

"But . . . but . . ." Cadel's mind was working furiously. "But DNA is a bad conductor. Unless it's a substrate for metal plating, and that's so much work."

Thaddeus lifted a hand. "Don't ask me for details," he said firmly.

"Your father's the one who understands—your father and his nano-technology department."

"There's been no news." Cadel could hardly believe his ears. "Nothing. Not on the Internet or in the papers."

"Of course not. If no one knows it's even *possible* to hide a transmitter in an arthritis bangle, why would anyone think to look?" Thaddeus surveyed Cadel over the top of his clasped hands. "Well?" he drawled. "What do you say, Cadel? A fifteen-minute conversation during our next session together. How does that sound?"

"Fine," said Cadel, but his voice was flat. Experience had taught him to be cautious, and he still didn't know how he felt about his father. Only about Thaddeus.

He trusted Thaddeus, and admired him. If Thaddeus thought he should speak to Dr. Darkkon, then he would—no matter how nervous the prospect made him.

Besides, how else was he going to get a look at that DNA-wired transmitter?

FOUR

When Cadel turned up for his next appointment, he discovered a curious little screen mounted on Dr. Roth's desk. The screen was attached to a very small box of circuitry, which trailed an array of fine wires. Thaddeus directed Cadel to a chair in front of the screen and began to fiddle with connections and adjust frequencies. Cadel watched him with the motionless attention of a leopard waiting to pounce.

After about five minutes, a crackling noise issued from the plastic box. Thaddeus said, "Ah," and rubbed his hands together. The screen in front of Cadel filled with light.

A face appeared, then broke up again. There was a roar of static.

"Damn," muttered Thaddeus.

"Are there relay stations?" Cadel wanted to know. But before Thaddeus could answer, the shredded signal coalesced once again, and Cadel saw his father's face on the screen.

It was quite a shock.

"Good god," croaked a disembodied voice.

"Are you reading us?" Thaddeus demanded. "Dr. Darkkon?"

"I can see him," the fuzzy voice continued. "It's Cadel, isn't it?"

"That's right," said Thaddeus, nudging his client. "Say something, Cadel."

Cadel, however, was struck dumb. Reception wasn't perfect, and the color was poor; his father's face looked blue. It hung on the screen like a big blue balloon, bobbing and weaving with every breath that Dr. Darkkon took. Cadel saw first one eye, then another, each embedded in a nest of heavy creases. Dr. Darkkon had a frog's mouth and liver spots. His expression was hungry, his breathing loud.

"Cadel," he crooned. "Cadel. I can hardly believe it. You really are the image of your mother. Thad, can you believe it? He's the spitting image."

"Mmm," said Thaddeus.

"How are you, Cadel? Thad says you've been having a lot of fun lately." A sly grin. "Playing with trains and so forth."

Cadel swallowed. Then he nodded and licked his lips. He didn't know what to say. (This man was his *father*!)

"Mucking around with computers," Dr. Darkkon added. "You like computers, don't you?"

Cadel cleared his throat. "They . . . they won't let me use them," he stammered. "Not the way I want to."

"I know. I'm sorry."

"I don't even have one of my own anymore!"

Dr. Darkkon shook his head and clicked his tongue. "It's a shame," he murmured.

"Can *you* buy me one?" Cadel asked hoarsely, deciding not to beat around the bush. His father owed him a computer, after so many years of missed birthdays. It was the least he could do. "I've heard you have a lot of money."

"Well, I do, but—"

"Can you give me one with DNA wiring?"

"Cadel, it's not as simple as that," Dr. Darkkon said softly. His face lurched about on the screen. "I wish I could give you a computer, but if I did, the Piggotts would wonder where it came from."

"I could hide it. If it was small enough. If it had DNA wiring."

Dr. Darkkon laughed. Thaddeus said, "Too risky. Suppose they did find it? Word would get out. The computer companies would get interested. You'd have the world at your door, Cadel, and you don't want that."

"No, you certainly don't," Dr. Darkkon agreed. "If there's one thing I've learned, Cadel, it's that you must keep a low profile. You should never attract too much attention. Let Thaddeus guide you—he's always been inconspicuous."

"There's an art to it," Thaddeus conceded.

"But I want a computer!" Cadel protested. Tears sprang to his eyes. He had hoped that his father, by suddenly appearing, would be able to solve all his problems. "Why won't you give me one?"

"Because I don't need to," Dr. Darkkon replied. He didn't have a nice voice—not like Thaddeus. Dr. Darkkon's voice was high and scratchy and nasal, made worse by the distortions of the transmitter. "Someone with your brains, my boy, shouldn't have everything served up to him on a plate, even if it were possible. Think. Consider. Work your way through this. There isn't anything you can't get if you're smart enough." With a flourish that sent colors bouncing wildly around the screen, he added, "Just look at me. They tried to take my son away, and they couldn't do it. I'm too clever to go without. Why should you be any different?"

"Because I'm not a grown-up," Cadel replied, in sullen tones. "Because I'm not a billionaire. Because I'm not in charge of an international business empire."

Dr. Darkkon chuckled. It sounded like water gurgling down a drain.

"Don't worry, my boy," he said, leering across the miles. "You'll be all of those things soon enough. I guarantee it."

And with that promise Cadel had to be satisfied. Dr. Darkkon steadfastly refused to give him a computer. What's more, though Cadel tried very hard, he was never able to obtain even the most humble laptop for more than a day and a half, because his withdrawn behavior always alerted the Piggotts or his nannies. It was as if they could *smell* the electrodes firing.

But he did achieve all kinds of other things, thanks to the encouragement he received from Thaddeus and Dr. Darkkon. They opened up new worlds for Cadel. After that first conversation, there were many others. Cadel, Thaddeus, and Dr. Darkkon discussed all manner of interesting things, from gambling to international smuggling laws. Cadel's various hobbies were thoroughly examined. His ambitions were applauded. Clever suggestions were made. In fact, it was thanks to Dr. Roth's advice that Cadel began to take an interest in Sydney's traffic flow—a far more complex, difficult system than the rail network, owing to its random and organic nature. Traffic jams in particular were a challenge to Cadel. He only gradually came to understand that a traffic jam is not the sum of the cars inside it. On the contrary, just as a human body can replace all its cells and remain a human body, so a traffic jam can have all its cars replaced by different cars, as some leave it and others join it, while remaining, in essence, the same traffic jam.

"Like my parents," Cadel remarked to Thaddeus, on one occasion. "You could replace them with two different people, and they'd still be my parents."

"Your *adoptive* parents," Thaddeus corrected.

"Whatever."

"Meaning they're never around?"

"Hardly ever."

"Just as well, don't you think?"

"I guess."

"If they were around more, they might notice how interested you've become in the traffic reports on the radio. Not to mention automotive engineering."

Cadel grunted. Though he was used to rattling around in the Piggotts' gigantic house, which had six bedrooms and five bathrooms and lay hidden at the end of a long, leafy driveway, he could never get over the feeling that he deserved more attention. Not necessarily from Mr. Piggott—who was just a corporate cog, uninterested in anything except asset securitization—but from Mrs. Piggott, who was *supposed* to be Cadel's mother. Sometimes he wondered why she had decided to adopt a child at all, before remembering that all her friends had children (loathsome children, Cadel had discovered). It was possible that Mrs. Piggott, being an interior decorator, had also wanted to try her hand at a nursery in her own house. She had certainly lavished a lot of care on Cadel's latest bedroom, covering the walls with storage boxes in shades of plum and mustard, designing a round "dart board" rug, and converting an old wooden dinghy into a wardrobe. She seemed more interested in Cadel's bedroom than she was in him.

Cadel, who didn't feel comfortable in the room, spent most of his time in the library, or in the little guesthouse on the south side of the pool. At least these spaces had sensible, adult color schemes and a calming arrangement of furniture. The colors in his bedroom made his eyes water, and all the PlaySkool soft cubes and sailing-boat bed linen set his teeth on edge. Cadel had never sailed a boat in his life. He never wanted to, either. It was as if his bedroom belonged to another boy.

Cadel's interests were more unusual.

Over the next year and a half, Cadel amused himself in various ways as he mastered Sydney's road network. Such mastery was hard-won for someone with no driver's license and only limited access to a modem. He made do by asking his current nanny to drive him around town every afternoon and weekend; by plundering the Road and Traffic Authority's information service; and by requesting several helicopter flights for his ninth-birthday present. These flights, needless to say, were always taken during the city's rush hour.

He also kept a calendar, marked with events such as football matches, parades, races, festivals, and school holidays. He paid particular attention to beach suburbs when the weather was hot, and tried to monitor roadworks on arterial routes. Busy points like the Harbor Bridge and tunnel were often his chosen destinations when they were most likely to be jammed up; stuck in a gridlock, his nanny would pound the steering wheel and give vent to explosive sighs, while Cadel studied the tunnel's electrical system or the bridge's signal array.

Meanwhile, his teachers had begun to notice a curious pattern in his behavior. He would suddenly become intensely interested in a particular subject—mathematics, say, or chemistry—which he would pursue in great depth for several weeks before dropping it in favor of another subject. His teachers would find themselves dodging questions about the table of elements or modular algorithms, and once again the issue of Cadel's promotion to high school would be raised at staff meetings. One teacher in particular was very impressed by Cadel; he had twice given the boy a lift home, and had been astonished at his knowledge of, and interest in, the car's engine. But there were disagreements about Cadel among the teaching staff. Though he had a sweet little face, his mode of speech was very odd. He would calmly advise a teacher on playground duty that she was "paying insufficient attention to nodes of activity in the northeast sector." He would station himself beside the playground equipment and carefully note down every accident or injury that took place on it, explaining that he was "interested in the energy flows." When asked to write a composition about a class visit to Taronga Zoo, he produced a ten-page essay on the movement of visitors around its many meandering pathways.

"He shouldn't be here," his class teacher declared. "Cadel just doesn't fit in. He never will."

"You think he should be transferred to a state school?" the principal responded. "A gifted-and-talented program?"

"I think he should be sent off to Harvard University. MIT. Somewhere like that."

"Somewhere far away," another teacher said and, upon receiving a quizzical look from the principal, added, "I don't like the way he hangs around the office at lunchtime."

"He's probably trying to grab a bit of time on someone's computer," the principal suggested. "Or he might not feel welcome in the playground. He doesn't have many friends, you know."

"He doesn't have *any* friends."

"It's a problem," the principal admitted. "But I prefer to regard problems as challenges. After all, it's not as if Cadel has ADD, or a personality disorder, or learning difficulties. Imagine how rewarding we'll find it, trying to unlock all his potentials."

"I don't know . . ." Cadel's class teacher shifted uncomfortably. "It's not so much his fads, or his questions, or even his manner. It's just that sometimes when he talks to me, it's as if he's studying some form of alien life." She shivered. "Have you seen *Village of the Damned*?"

"Oh, don't be ridiculous," the principal snapped, and the meeting moved on to other, safer topics.

Shortly afterward, school broke up for two weeks. On the first day of the new term, the teachers arrived back to discover that every pupil was absent—except Cadel. When the assembly bell rang, only Cadel appeared, a small figure standing in the middle of a vast stretch of gray concrete. The sleeves of his jacket fell over his pale hands. The hems of his trousers were puddling around his ankles.

The sight of him there roused his class teacher's suspicions. While the principal and deputy principal made frantic phone calls, she approached him across the asphalt, arms folded.

"What's happened, Cadel?"

He gazed up at her with innocent eyes.

"Nothing," he said.

"Where are the other kids?"

He looked around. "I don't know," he replied, and shrugged.

"Did you tell them something?"

"What do you mean?"

"Cadel, how come *you've* turned up when no one else has?"

Cadel put a finger to his chin, scanning the grounds with a blank expression.

"Because I don't have the flu?" he suggested.

Within an hour, the teacher discovered that a newsletter from the previous term had been tampered with. At the back, near the sports results, a notice had been inserted warning parents that the first day of the next term would be set aside for teacher training.

No one could ever work out how that notice had been slipped into the newsletter.

"It was on a disk I sent for printing," the principal fretted. "Could someone have messed with the disk?"

"Probably."

"But why? Because someone wanted an extra day's holiday?"

"Which rules out Cadel as a suspect. He came to school."

"Yes, he did. You don't find that suspicious?"

"I don't know. Do you?"

"I find it hard to see how anyone *else* could have pulled this thing off."

Despite the concerns of the teaching staff, it was never proven that Cadel had sabotaged the newsletter. Of course the principal invited Cadel into her office and pressed him for the truth. She flattered him, reassured him, and finally threatened him—all to no avail. Cadel knew better than to admit to anything. Thaddeus had warned him against it, over and over again.

So he simply sat there smugly, his feet in their expensive running shoes dangling a good five inches off the floor.

Finally, the principal had been forced to shelve her suspicions. Three weeks later, she told one of her staff to do the same thing when he accused Cadel of siphoning the gasoline out of the tank of his Nissan Pulsar.

"I filled it up yesterday morning. It was full. But I ran out on my way home. I was on the highway, near my turnoff—"

"Could there be a leak in your tank?" the principal suggested.

"No! I always check for leaks! Someone *stole* my gas!"

"I see." The principal frowned, drumming her fingers on the literacy reports. "And what makes you think it was Cadel?"

"Because I've been giving him lifts home! Because he borrowed my owner's manual!"

"Still . . ."

"I know it was him. I *know* it was. This morning he asked me if I was stuck in yesterday's traffic jam, like butter wouldn't melt in his mouth." The distressed teacher scowled at his boss. "After all these years, I think I know when a kid's been up to something. It's an *instinct*. Believe me—I know."

The principal sighed. She, too, had been caught in the previous afternoon's traffic jam, which had been of monstrous size. Almost three-quarters of the city's main roads had clogged up, for just over three hours. Footage on the evening news had shown impassable intersections, trapped commuters—even a car left abandoned in a two-mile gridlock.

It occurred to the principal that running out of gas on the Pacific Highway certainly could not have improved matters. But she didn't for one second connect Cadel with the chaos that had overtaken the city a few hours before.

Only Thaddeus knew who was really to blame.

"So," he declared when he next admitted Cadel into his office, "I hope you realize that *I* was caught in your god-awful mess, young man. I was stuck in my car for three hours on Tuesday night."

Cadel blinked sleepily, a smile twitching at the corners of his mouth. It was hard to conceal his own delight in what he'd done—the colossal feeling of satisfaction. But he tried.

"Oh," he said.

"I was told by a friendly policeman that the Harbor tunnel was closed because of a bomb scare."

"Really?"

"That's why I couldn't believe, at first, that you were responsible." As Cadel's smile faded, Thaddeus peered at him with hooded eyes. "A bomb scare? *Another* bomb scare? Cadel, have I told you what *modus operandi* means?"

Cadel stared, his expression somber.

"It means 'method of operating,'" Thaddeus continued. "It's Latin. Perhaps you haven't come across the term. It's a favorite way of establishing who might have done something. A *modus operandi*, Cadel, is like a signature. You might as well have spray-painted your name across the tunnel wall."

"That's not true," Cadel muttered.

"It is true. Suppose someone connects the traffic-jam bomb scare with the rail-delay bomb scare? Have you thought of that?"

Cadel's chin dropped, in a characteristic gesture.

"It worked before," he replied.

"And it won't work again. No more bomb scares, Cadel. They're clumsy. Unimaginative." Thaddeus surveyed the child in front of him. Cadel looked sulky; his bottom lip was sticking out in a way that made Thaddeus laugh. "Now, now," he said. "Don't be upset. The bomb scare might have been ill-advised, but the burst water main was good. The burst water main was *very* good." Thaddeus cocked his head. "How on earth did you manage it? Did you amend some kind of online sewage-system record? Tap into a radio communication frequency? Were you waiting for something like that to happen? How did you *know* it had happened—you were stuck at school, weren't you?"

Cadel, who had been pouting at the floor, glanced up. His scowl faded. His appearance couldn't have been more disarming.

"I don't know what you mean," he said.

But there was a naughty twinkle in his eye.

FIVE

A few weeks later, Cadel was examining the cistern in a school bathroom stall when he heard some boys talking.

The boys were huddled near the hand dryers. They were older than Cadel, who knew only one of them—Jarrod—by name. They were talking about the railway detonators that Jarrod had found in his uncle's shed.

"I exploded 'em," Jarrod declared proudly.

"How?" asked his friend.

"I hit 'em with a pipe."

"Cool."

"Are there any left?" another boy inquired.

"Nah."

"You should have kept one."

"Why?"

"Because I've never heard a detonator. Are they loud?"

"Course they're loud, you moron! They're *supposed* to be loud!"

Silence fell as one by one the four boys became aware of Cadel's presence. Having finished with the plumbing, he had drifted out of his toilet stall.

Jarrod scowled at him. "What are *you* staring at?" he said rudely. "Piss off."

"Piss off, you girl," his friend added.

Cadel looked from face to face. The contempt he saw on each of them made him reckless. He said, "You don't need railway detonators to make a big bang."

"Huh?" said Jarrod.

"You don't need railway detonators to make a big bang," Cadel repeated.

"What's that supposed to mean?"

"It means that you can make explosives out of anything." Cadel reeled off a list of bomb ingredients available in almost every storeroom, garage, laundry, or supply cupboard. Then, seeing how riveted his audience was, he explained how a mercury-switch detonation device could be constructed out of an ordinary thermometer. "Bags of potato chips can be highly flammable," he added, "especially in a small space. And you can build yourself a ten-minute fuse with a cigarette and a book of matches."

At that point the school bell summoned them back to class, and Cadel was forced to conclude his lecture. He was already beginning to wonder if he had made a mistake.

The next day, he knew he had: Word went round that Jarrod had blown off his left thumb trying to plant a bomb in a sports-equipment cupboard.

Jarrod wouldn't talk much about the incident. He admitted that he hated doing gymnastics, and never wanted to do it again. He did *not*, however, mention Cadel.

Nevertheless, Thaddeus wasn't fooled.

"So you've been blowing up your classmates?" he said to Cadel during their next session together.

"No. Of course not," Cadel replied.

"Oh, I understand that it was an *accident*." The psychologist's tone was sarcastic. "But really, Cadel—bombs again? What have I told you about bombs?"

From the transmitter screen, Dr. Darkkon added, "And as for that Jarrod character, what are you doing, putting your faith in some sixth-grade thug? Cadel, you can't trust people like that." By this time Dr. Darkkon's arthritis-bangle transmitter had been confiscated and he was using a pair of spectacles instead. Cadel's image was projected onto the lenses of these spectacles, and a transmitter embedded in their metal frame captured Dr. Darkkon's image for Cadel. Usually, Dr. Darkkon was able to remove his eyewear entirely and place it on a surface some distance away so that Cadel could have a better view of his father's face. When he was being closely monitored, however, Dr. Darkkon was forced to leave the glasses on, and Cadel caught a glimpse only of his father's right eye, greatly enlarged. "How could you have been so careless, Cadel?" Dr. Darkkon continued. "People of that sort can't be entrusted with *anything*. They're *bound* to screw up."

"You were right not to plant the device yourself," Thaddeus remarked from his crimson couch. "There's no need, when you can always delegate. The skill lies in choosing the correct tool."

"But I didn't choose anyone!" Cadel protested. "I didn't *ask* that boy to plant a bomb; he did it himself!"

"Naturally, we wouldn't expect you to admit it—," Dr. Darkkon began.

"But I *didn't*! *Honestly!*" Cadel was quite upset. "I'm telling the truth!"

There was a short silence. Then Thaddeus said, in his silkiest tones, "You'd like us to believe that you really did blurt out all your hard-won information about pipe bombs just to impress a few blockheads in sixth grade?"

Cadel flushed. He didn't know how to respond. Should he admit that he had enjoyed basking in the awestruck attention of Jamboree's toughest kids? It would make him look almost simpleminded—on the same level as stupid Jarrod and his dumb friends. At the same time, Cadel was alarmed that neither Thaddeus nor his father had believed him. And he was very confused. Should he have *known* that Jarrod would go off and make his own bomb? Was there something about Jarrod that should have warned him?

He was disappointed in himself for failing to anticipate the possibility. He felt that he had let his father down—his father *and* Thaddeus.

"Cadel," said Thaddeus, leaning forward and fixing him with an intent look, "if this whole episode was unplanned, as you say, then you have a lot to learn. Your father has told you, again and again, to *keep a low profile*. You won't do that by trying to impress people. You'll find it all too easy to impress most people, and then where will you be? Constantly watched. Admired. Pursued."

"It's bad enough that you're skipping years," Dr. Darkkon added. "I'd be happier if you were following a more normal educational pattern. You've already been identified as highly gifted. Now you'll be the subject of constant scrutiny."

"You have one advantage," Thaddeus went on, "and that's your face. People with pretty faces aren't expected to have brains."

"They stand out, though," Dr. Darkkon said gloomily. "They're noticed. They're watched."

"Perhaps," Thaddeus conceded. "So Cadel will have to learn to fade into the background. It really isn't hard. The right clothes, the right stance, the right attitude—"

"Like not boasting to morons," Dr. Darkkon interrupted.

"Like that, yes. *We* admire you, Cadel. You don't need the admiration of idiots like Jarrod."

Cadel stared at his lap, legs swinging. Occasionally—very occasionally—he still felt like a freak. It happened sometimes when he made a remark and a teacher stared at him as if he'd just sprouted another arm. Or when the other kids started giggling behind his back because he'd been staring at a handball game for fifteen minutes, trying to calculate velocities and outcomes. Or when Mrs. Piggott came home in a bad mood and blamed him for the fact that the thermostat in the hot-water system wasn't working. In these situations, Cadel always felt a powerful urge to tell everyone about his infamous traffic jam, or his brief penetration of the Pentagon security protocols.

Such a feeling, he knew, could be dangerous. He had to resist it with all his might.

"Should I have known that Jarrod was going to make his own bomb?" he asked, in a small voice. "Should I have expected that?"

Thaddeus blinked. Dr. Darkkon said, "It was in the cards, Cadel."

"There are certain personality types," Thaddeus remarked. "Self-destructive. Antisocial. I can tell you about them if you want. Though they can be useful, they're not reliable tools."

"But should I have *known* what Jarrod was going to do?" Cadel pressed. "Is there some way I could have known?"

After a long pause, Dr. Darkkon grimaced, and Thaddeus studied Cadel carefully.

"You had no idea?" Thaddeus said at last. "It never crossed your mind that you might be planting a seed in Jarrod's?"

Cadel shook his head. Thaddeus glanced at the transmitter screen, where Cadel's father was echoing his son's movement.

"Well, in that case, dear boy, you should focus your attention on human behavior," Thaddeus advised. "You'll never reach your true potential if you discount the importance of people and the way they think."

"Except that they *don't* think," Dr. Darkkon growled. "Most of 'em don't, anyway."

"Perhaps, but that doesn't mean they don't act." Thaddeus turned back to Cadel. "Being a bit of a behavioralist myself, I know there's a certain pattern to the chaos, if you look hard enough," he said. "So far, though, I haven't seen a 100 percent success rate when it comes to predicting people's actions."

"There isn't a formula? Or a program?" Cadel wanted to know.

"Not that I'm aware of," Thaddeus replied. "Nothing generic."

"There are programs that plot population expansion," Dr. Darkkon interjected. "Certain predictive formulas associated with actuarial work, and so forth. Sociological measurements."

"People are people," Thaddeus finished. "They tend to have fairly fixed personality patterns and routines—and there are usually danger signals that you can spot if someone's been traumatized, say—but on the whole, Cadel, even *I* can't forecast individual behavior. Not in a way that's scientifically admissible. I'm relying on instinct as much as anything else. Instinct and a very thorough knowledge of the person involved."

Cadel nodded, thinking hard. It occurred to him, suddenly, that there could be no system more complex than the system of human interaction. All the petty disagreements, the sudden friendships, the jealousies, the emotional outbursts that swirled around him at school— could they all somehow be codified? Could he find the key to the network of hopes, loyalties, and basic needs underpinning every community in the world?

He believed that he probably could, but not without a lot of work.

SIX

By the time Cadel was ten years old, the Jamboree teaching staff had had enough. They felt that Cadel was now beyond them: He was clearly bored with everything they threw at him. They decided that his interest in applied chemistry, his repeated attempts to sneak on to the school computers, even his slightly patronizing manner, would best be handled in an environment geared toward teenagers.

So Stuart and Lanna were left with the problem of where to send him. Stuart, who believed that Cadel needed more discipline, favored a boys' military academy with its own cadet training. Lanna was convinced that all-male environments were brutish and cruel, and that Cadel, with his girlish face and short stature, would be tormented in such a place.

Finally they compromised by enrolling Cadel in a nearby private school called Crampton.

Cadel had to pass an entrance exam before he was accepted into grade seven. He had to wear a straw hat whenever he donned his school uniform. During his first day at Crampton, he was assigned a counselor, who spent two hours with Cadel and the Piggotts, filling in forms that covered Cadel's goals, strengths, and faults, as well as his state of health and family history. Together, they also worked out his course program and timetable of lessons.

"We have some other escalated-learning students," the counselor informed Cadel. "They're not much older than you, and they're in eighth grade now. I'm sure you'll have a lot in common."

Cadel smiled and nodded. He had decided that if he was going to understand the way social systems worked, he would have to do more than study sociological and anthropological texts. He would have to make friends, and listen, and watch, and feign interest in the boring obsessions of normal teenagers. By doing so, he would also improve his chances of "fading into the background." A boy fascinated by DSL access multiplexers was bound to stand out. A boy who collected sports cards wouldn't.

So Cadel began to smile a lot. He studied the slang of his classmates, then copied it. He laughed at their jokes and admired their possessions. Mostly, however, he listened. He listened to complaints, gossip, and detailed descriptions of everything from holiday trips to new bikes. He listened to girls as well as boys. His placid smile and calculated distribution of sweets meant that he was tolerated, if not hugely popular; some of the boys still thought him a little weird—especially the more sensitive, intelligent boys. They didn't like the way he would sit in corners, his blank, blue gaze fixed on particular people for minutes at a time. Some of the girls thought he was cute, but kept this belief to themselves. Being at least two years younger than most of the kids in his year, Cadel was widely regarded as a baby. To have openly admired his long, dark eyelashes, or his dewy complexion, would have invited general scorn.

Cadel was treated like a baby by the teaching staff as well. He was still carefully watched whenever he went anywhere near a computer, with the result that he didn't often sit down in front of a computer screen. Instead, he concentrated on social networks. He noted down arrivals and departures. He observed the procedures for fire drills, cafeteria deliveries, and bus lines. Most importantly, he paid very close attention to his classmates. He learned that Paul hated Isaiah, that Chloe loved Brandon, that Sarah was jealous of Odette, that Jocelyn and Fabbio were inseparable. He watched—almost wistfully—as Erin and Rachael shared a chocolate-chip cookie, or as Jason kindly showed Fergal how to pitch a baseball. No one ever shared chocolate-chip cookies with Cadel. He was an outsider in grade seven, mostly because of his age. And few of the kids had parents as rich as Cadel's, so they expected him to be a source of chocolate-chip cookies.

There was one crew of rough boys who didn't like Cadel at all. They would jostle him in corridors and knock his peanut-butter sandwiches out of his hand. Cadel studied them with particular intensity. He picked out the lead bully, the comedian, the thinker, and the enforcer.

One of these boys was soon expelled; rumor had it that he'd been caught smoking marijuana. Another was laid up for two months with a broken leg, which had befallen him in the boys' bathroom—no one quite knew how. The third was made to repeat grade seven, and the fourth became a laughingstock for appearing at a baseball game in a T-shirt with the words GIRL POWER emblazoned on it. By the time he realized that he wasn't wearing his usual T-shirt, which was identical in size and color, the damage had been done.

Cadel watched this boy scurry back to the locker room, while all around him people fell down laughing. It was a gratifying moment that filled Cadel with a dizzy sense of achievement, and it soon led to more ambitious attempts.

Three months before Cadel's eleventh birthday, his French teacher left the classroom, briefly, to answer an urgent phone call. When she returned, she found the entire class in an uproar, with everyone fighting and shouting—except Cadel.

He sat in the midst of this chaos, quietly finishing the exercise she had set for all of them.

"It was weird," she said later, in the staff room. "It was just . . . I mean, I've never seen anything like it. They were all red in the face. Even Talitha Edwards was fighting. And Cadel was just sitting there, like butter wouldn't melt in his mouth."

"Cadel's always on the sidelines," a colleague pointed out.

"Yes, but he looked so *smug*."

"He always does."

"Yes, but . . ." The French teacher sighed suddenly. "Oh well, you're probably right. It was strange, though. It was . . ." She searched for the word. "It was *spooky*," she concluded.

It was also Cadel's first conscious attempt to manipulate a whole social system. His next effort was more complicated. It involved his encyclopedic knowledge of class timetables and cleaning schedules, his familiarity with every portion of the school fire drill, his awareness that a particular girl had to go to the bathroom at a particular time every day, and his close monitoring of one teacher, who always felt compelled to move his car whenever a more convenient parking spot became available behind the cafeteria. By using these pieces of information, and tampering with a deadlock, he engineered the disappearance of an eighth-grade boy. Then, when the alarm was finally raised, he mentioned having seen a strange man in the playground that morning.

It was only after the police had been alerted that the missing boy was found, locked in the "art cottage" bathroom. No one thought to blame Cadel for this incident. No one knew of his part in it except Thaddeus and Dr. Darkkon, who applauded his ingenuity.

"A harmless piece of mischief," said Thaddeus, "but very well executed. You've begun to grasp some psychological truths, Cadel. Well done. I'm impressed."

"So am I," Dr. Darkkon added, beaming. His teeth, magnified by the transmitter, looked like the rotting stumps of an old wharf; they were ragged and brownish, full of hairline cracks and black pits, and studded with greenish fragments that vaguely resembled lichen.

Cadel glanced from his father to Thaddeus and back again.

"Do I get a reward?" he asked.

Thaddeus removed his glasses and polished them carefully. From the screen on Thaddeus's desk, Dr. Darkkon growled, "A reward?"

"It's my birthday soon," Cadel pointed out. "My eleventh birthday."

The two men waited. To his surprise, Cadel found it hard to go on. But he did.

"The Piggotts are buying me a cell phone for my birthday," he explained. "One with a photo function. I was thinking that with DNA wiring, you could probably turn it into a computer."

There was a pause. With a little smile, Thaddeus put his glasses back on.

Dr. Darkkon screwed up his rubbery face. "*Who* could?" he said.

Cadel swallowed.

"Well, you could," he murmured. "We could switch phones. I could tell you what kind it is, and you could get another one and turn it into a computer for me. With a mobile capacity, of course," he added.

"Could I indeed?" Dr. Darkkon drawled. "And why should I do that?"

"Because I *need* one," Cadel said. He squeezed his hands into fists, then sat on them. "I've got an idea," he continued. "An idea for making some money. But I need a computer. One of my own."

"Go on," said Dr. Darkkon. He was clearly waiting to be convinced.

"I could be a child model, you know," Cadel announced, deciding to unveil his secret weapon. When he saw his father frown, he knew that his aim had been true. "I was at the shops on Saturday and a man came up," he said. "A photographer. He said he could get me work. He gave his card to Filomena." Filomena was Cadel's latest nanny. Cadel didn't add that the photographer had been surprised to learn Cadel's true age. ("I thought you must be eight or nine," he had said.) That part of the conversation had been a bit humiliating. In fact, the *whole* conversation had been a bit humiliating because Cadel didn't much like his own looks. Given the choice, he would have preferred a few more muscles and a square jaw. There could be no doubt, however, that the meeting in the mall had provided him with some great ammunition. "Lanna likes the idea, but Stuart doesn't. They've been arguing about it." Out of the corner of his eye, Cadel saw Dr. Roth's smile widen. "I could make lots of money," Cadel finished. "Lots and lots. Enough to buy my own computer."

"Which the Piggotts would confiscate," Dr. Darkkon snapped.

"Not if I paid Filomena to say that it was *her* computer. I'd have enough money for that, too."

"Cadel, you're not going to be a child model," Dr. Darkkon declared. "You know what I've said about keeping a low profile. How can you keep a low profile if your face is plastered all over television ads for fruit chews?"

"But—"

"I'll make you a computer phone," Dr. Darkkon said abruptly. "I'll do it if you tell me how."

Cadel's bubbling excitement suddenly went off the boil.

"Pardon?" he bleated.

"Tell me how, and I'll do it." Dr. Darkkon squinted into the transmitter. "You're the one who made the suggestion. You'll have a screen the size of a postage stamp, and precious few keys—it'll be a third generation, I suppose?"

"Probably."

"Even so, there'll be a bloody great DSP cluttering up its innards, DNA wiring or no DNA wiring. You'll have your work cut out. We all will. Not that it can't be done. We're heading that way as it is, what with texting and calendar functions and multiplayer gaming and video-conferencing—in fact, I seem to recall reading somewhere—"

"I know," Cadel interrupted. He was feeling very low because he had just realized how long it would take him to design such a piece of technology—if he could do it at all. "Will you . . . will you help me?" he stammered. "If I need to ask questions?"

Dr. Darkkon smiled. (It wasn't a pretty sight.)

"Of course I will," he said. "You can have all the help you need."

"Thanks."

"And when we put this thing together, you can have the patent on anything new you come up with. That means you'll get most of the money when we launch it on to the market—though we won't attach your name to your Swiss bank account, of course."

"Oh, but—"

"Relax, son. We won't go public unless someone else is catching up fast." Another ferocious grin. "It'll be like this transmitter, won't it? Our little secret. For the time being."

"Okay."

"Now it's down to you," Dr. Darkkon finished, settling back, so that his image careered wildly around the screen. "We'll have to see how long it takes you to come up with something workable."

In the end, it took just over eight months. By then, Cadel had been promoted to ninth grade and had begun to worry a few of the more intelligent teachers on the Crampton staff. The trouble was, they couldn't quite work out exactly why he worried them. Perhaps it was his obvious isolation. Perhaps it was his placid blue gaze. Or perhaps it was his tendency to be hanging around on the sidelines during those peculiar events that seemed to overtake the school more and more often, as Cadel moved quickly up the educational ladder.

First there was the brawl that occurred among a baseball team waiting to bat. (Cadel was on that team, hovering at the edge of the fight.) Then there was the teacher who slapped another teacher in full view of several students—including Cadel. Then there was the sprinkler system in one of the science labs that suddenly turned itself on and doused the whole lab with a strange, red, strong-smelling, jamlike substance. (Cadel wasn't anywhere in the vicinity, but he had used the classroom.) There was the teacher who was found passed out in the school vegetable garden, drunk, wearing only his jockey shorts. (He couldn't remember what had happened.) There was the case of the disappearing gym mats, the mysterious sighting of a "green pig" in the cafeteria, and stories of a haunted art cupboard. Finally, there was the incident of the teacherless morning.

This occurred after Cadel had been promoted to grade ten (having waltzed through his ninth-grade syllabus in record time). One Monday morning, the students of Crampton turned up at school to discover that none of their teachers was present. So the kids milled around for a while—some went home; some stayed. At last the vice principal appeared, at about half past ten, and from then on, the staff trickled in until three-quarters of them were at their posts. The rest telephoned with various excuses, mostly to do with being ill, though one had to wait for a plumber to mend a burst pipe and one didn't telephone at all until the next day: He had been lost on a weekend hiking trip.

The teachers who *did* make it had all been held up by a peculiar combination of traffic problems, rail delays, stopped watches, and the wide-ranging failure of telephone company wake-up calls. They were completely flummoxed.

There was one teacher, though—a math teacher named Mrs. Brezeck—who felt that Cadel might have done something to her fancy new digital watch. The watch possessed certain functions that she never used, and Cadel had been advising her on their finer points the Friday before Monday's fiasco. She had spent half an hour on Sunday reprogramming international times and dates, according to Cadel's specific instructions.

Could she have accidentally programmed the watch to "reboot" during the night, and lose a few hours?

The answer, of course, was that she had—and that there had been nothing accidental about it. But Cadel wouldn't confirm her suspicions. He simply gazed at her, looking puzzled. He could do that very well. And she went away unsatisfied, with a niggling sense of unease.

From that day on, she watched Cadel more closely. There was something about him that she didn't quite trust.

As for Cadel, these amusing little experiments boosted his self-confidence whenever his cell-phone research hit a snag. He had a lot of electronic theory to master before he could present his father with a blueprint for his computer phone. He had to plunge into the murky world of DRAM, SRAM, ROM, and EPROM, of bootstrap loaders and chip sets, of transistors and capacitors. He also had to read up on nanobiometrics, using information fed to him by Dr. Darkkon. He loved nanobiometrics. He loved learning about alkanethiols, ATPase nanoturbines, and ion channel switch biosensors. It was a fascinating new world. But welding the two specialties together wasn't easy.

He was forced to appeal to his father for help, not once, but many times. Though he hated to do it, he didn't have a choice. Not if he was going to have a computer phone by the time his twelfth birthday rolled around.

His circuitry plans, when he finished them, had to be transmitted to Dr. Darkkon with Thaddeus's help. There followed three months of waiting, which Cadel found very hard to deal with. He spent a lot of it studying the plans for a new sports hall at Crampton. It occurred to him that if he did a bit of research on wind-loading, structural pressure points, and other aspects of architectural theory, he might be able to sabotage the new building—which was, after all, just a little system unto itself.

Finally, a week before his twelfth birthday, he arrived at Thaddeus's office to find a brightly wrapped package waiting for him.

He stared at it, then at Thaddeus.

"Is it . . . ?" he queried, breathlessly.

"Have a look," Thaddeus responded.

"Did *he* wrap it? Himself?"

"I wrapped it." Thaddeus's tone was dry. "You don't realize what it involved, getting this thing into the country, Cadel. It wasn't easy. It had to be smuggled."

"Does it work?"

"Of course it works," said Thaddeus. "Didn't you hear what I said? He wouldn't have gone to so much trouble if it didn't *work*."

Cadel picked up the little package and slowly pulled off its silver ribbon. He was holding his breath. When the machine inside the parcel was finally exposed, he saw that it looked just like his own cell phone. Right down to the scratch on the liquid crystal display.

"Wow," said Cadel reverently.

"Dr. Darkkon didn't send an instruction book," Thaddeus drawled. "I just hope you can remember what you told him."

Cadel looked up. There were tears in his eyes. As he blinked them away, he felt a light touch on his cheek.

"Happy birthday, Cadel," Thaddeus murmured. "Many happy returns."

It was thanks to Dr. Darkkon, and the marvelous computer phone, that Cadel finally met Kay-Lee McDougall.

SEVEN

Before Cadel turned thirteen, several important things happened.

First, he began to grow. His voice broke, and a few soft, dark hairs appeared above his mouth. Noticing this, Mrs. Piggott suddenly decided to redecorate his room. The sailing boats and nursery-school colors disappeared, to be replaced by muted shades of cream and gold and chocolate. A state-of-the-art desk was installed to match the new built-in bookshelves, concealed lighting, silk scatter cushions, and framed posters. Lanna had selected a poster of James Dean, another of Jimi Hendrix, and a third of a contemporary pop star whose name always escaped Cadel, but whose brooding intensity must have appealed to Mrs. Piggott. While Cadel didn't like the subjects of these posters any more than he had liked the sailing boats, he much preferred the new room to the old. It felt like a hotel room, but he didn't mind that, because it also had a serious look. And Cadel was a serious sort of person.

The second thing that happened was his promotion to grade eleven, despite the misgivings of every teacher at the school. Though bigger than he had been, he wasn't *that* big. Beside his new, older classmates he looked like a baby; the girls actually called him "baby," when they addressed him at all. For a while they treated him like a doll, or a mascot, and would ruffle his hair and coo over the size of his feet. But they quickly began to resent the way he topped every class.

Soon he was being ignored, much to the concern of his teachers. Despite their attempts to "integrate" him, with buddy schemes and age-specific sports programs and quiet talks with the library monitors, Cadel usually spent his lunchtimes reading.

"Though he's really no *worse* off than he was in seventh or ninth grade," his English teacher fretted. "I mean, he was a loner then. Things are no different now, I suppose."

"He'll be a loner all his life," another teacher pointed out. "It's just the way he is. You know his IQ's off the chart, don't you? I mean, really off the chart."

"He's certainly left *me* behind," Cadel's math teacher remarked. "I just let him do what he wants. He's been looking into quantum computers—I've been sending his work off to my old math professor at the university. Personally, I can't make head nor tail of it. Can you, Anna?"

Mrs. Brezeck shrugged. She never commented on Cadel. She just watched him and kept her thoughts to herself. When he was moved up to twelfth grade, a couple of weeks before his thirteenth birthday, she welcomed him into her four-unit math group without enthusiasm. Already, she had begun to entertain suspicions about his role in the collapse of the new sports hall.

This collapse was another important event that occurred during Cadel's stint in eleventh grade. After nearly a year of construction, the dazzling new complex had been almost ready for its grand opening. It had contained two basketball courts, a small swimming pool, two changing rooms, a scattering of bathrooms, and a gym, as well as various cupboards, lockers, and electronic switchboards. Money had been poured into its rows of louvred windows, its dramatic roofline, its polished wooden fittings, its lavish trophy-display cabinet. Some of the staff had complained that the school principal, a former health-and-fitness teacher, was pursuing his dream at the expense of Crampton's library and computer science department. The librarian in particular was very bitter about what she called the "Taj Mahal." (Her library was squeezed into a double classroom near the boys' bathroom.) But work had proceeded, and three days before the grand-opening ceremony,

Crampton's principal had invited a group of municipal councilors to inspect the brand-new complex.

Together they had approached the building from the east, admiring the front door and the red-brick path sweeping up to it. From a second-story window in the science block, Cadel had watched his principal gesturing toward the sports hall's gleaming steel roof. One of the councilors had admired the choice of native shrubs planted on either side of the path. Then the principal had stepped up to the bank of glass doors at the front of the building, opened the middle one with a flourish, and . . .

Whoosh!

With a gigantic roar, the building's eastern end had collapsed. The principal and his guests had run for their lives as a huge cloud of dust enveloped half the school.

Everyone had rushed outside to have a look. The fire brigade had been called. It had all been very exciting.

Cadel, however, wasn't entirely pleased with the end result of his sabotage. Though he had planned it with immense care (not actually wanting to *kill* anyone), the collapse had been incomplete. The rear part of the sports hall had remained standing, though of course it was eventually demolished. Cadel would have preferred the full, comic effect of the entire structure tumbling down. It would have been funnier and more creatively satisfying.

Still, it wasn't a bad trick. Thaddeus certainly appreciated it. And because Cadel didn't much like sports, he neither felt nor displayed any concern at the destruction of the new complex. Mrs. Brezeck noticed this. She also noticed in his workbooks a number of diagrams and calculations that seemed to have some bearing on things like steel-girder construction, foundation laying, and load-bearing ratios.

She didn't really believe that Cadel could have sabotaged the building. This seemed impossible, however smart he might be. But she couldn't help fretting over what seemed to be a slightly sinister coincidence. She couldn't get it out of her mind. Especially since Cadel was strutting around with a more self-satisfied air than usual.

The last important event that occurred during Cadel's brief spell in eleventh grade was his creation of an online dating service called Partner Post. After spending two years observing the kids at school, reading the personal ads in newspapers, and studying soap operas, romance novels, and sociology textbooks, Cadel felt ready to try out his new idea. He had decided to start a service that claimed to link paying clients with other paying clients. The secret to success, he told Thaddeus, would be to make sure that every client found his or her perfect match.

"They'll have to fill in a really good assessment form," Cadel explained. "If it's good enough, it can tell me all I need to know. And I was thinking, maybe you could help me with the wording? If I paid you? I could pay you out of the profits."

Thaddeus smiled. In the six years that Cadel had known him, the psychologist's hair had become much grayer, and his face more lined. But his eyes were still as sharp as arrowheads as he blinked lazily up at Cadel from his crimson couch, which had grown rather shabby.

"So you've decided to make money from your study of human behavior, at long last," he murmured. "Very wise."

"Yes, that's just it," Cadel replied eagerly, his voice cracking on a high note. "I think this would be profitable, as well as educational." Thaddeus's sudden laugh made Cadel frown. "What?" he demanded. "What's so funny?"

"Nothing." The psychologist waved his hand. "Most of the time, Cadel, it's hard to remember that you're still a child. And then occasionally the way you talk reminds me. Yes, of course I'll help. If you think it's worthwhile. But the hard part, surely, will be kicking off? What happens if you start with five clients and none of them suits each other? Won't that be a problem?"

"Oh no," said Cadel dismissively. "That's my point. Because it's online, I can make up the partners. I can put them in Bulgaria or something."

Thaddeus's eyes narrowed. "I see," he said.

56

"I bet you half these people will be using an online service because they're ugly or old," Cadel continued. "Because they don't even *want* to meet people face-to-face. It'll be easy. I'll just have to make up characters. Characters who sound lovable and interesting—you know."

Thaddeus nodded. It suddenly occurred to Cadel that he knew almost nothing about Thaddeus. The psychologist had never mentioned a wife or children.

When Cadel tried to picture Thaddeus carrying a grandchild, he couldn't. He couldn't even imagine Thaddeus's house. Was it an old house? A modern one? Did it have a big garden around it and a gray-haired wife inside it? Why hadn't Cadel ever considered these questions before? Why had they never even crossed his mind?

Was it because he had simply taken Thaddeus for granted?

"Well, good luck," Thaddeus said. "It sounds interesting. But don't be disappointed if you fail to pull this off the first time round." Leaning forward, he fixed Cadel with a searching look. "People aren't motherboards," he said quietly. "They're not like chemicals—they don't always respond the same way when you mix them, no matter how precisely you might have measured and calculated. I can teach you about the Myers-Briggs Personality Test, and the Wechsler Adult Intelligence Scale, and the Global Assessment Function, but in the end, Cadel, there really isn't a formula for predicting people's behavior."

"Don't worry," Cadel replied, with a confidence that he could only afford to air in the privacy of Dr. Roth's consulting room. "If there isn't a formula now, there soon will be. I'm working on it. And this dating service will help me."

EIGHT

It was Dr. Darkkon's computer phone that allowed Cadel to develop Partner Post. Without the converted cell phone, Cadel never could have carried out his plans; he wouldn't have had enough time online. From the very start, he had to spend hours working on e-mail messages, organizing client information, and developing character charts. (Keeping records of the various people he created was especially important, because he had to be consistent. He couldn't afford to forget what color someone's eyes were supposed to be, or how many children they were supposed to have.)

Thanks to the computer phone, the Piggotts didn't get suspicious. Whenever they began to wonder what Cadel was doing and poked their heads into his room, they would find him lying on his bed, fiddling with his cell phone. That didn't seem to worry them. Apparently, they were delighted that Cadel even *had* any friends—especially friends who wanted to speak to him for hours at a time. As far as they were concerned, endless phone calls were a normal part of growing up. They congratulated each other, loudly and proudly, over the dinner table every night. Cadel, it seemed, was shedding his antisocial behavior. At last he was starting to blossom.

Maybe, said Lanna, he would actually bring some *girls* home soon. Like a normal teenager.

In fact, Cadel's off-line social life was almost nonexistent. Even online, he had separated himself from the society of his fellow hackers. There was a huge population of bright sparks out in cyberspace, and for a while Cadel had become involved in Internet associations like the Masters of Deception. He enjoyed the company of others who spent their spare time burrowing into heavily protected networks. He liked sharing thoughts on code-breaking modules, encryption programs, dynamic passwords, and electronic re-mailers. The trouble was that to some of these cyberspies, nothing was sacred. Because Cadel himself had whipped up some very challenging little firewalls featuring "asymmetrical ciphering" (to protect sensitive material like his Partner Post database) he became a target for some fellow hackers. They sent in sniffing programs to intercept his access code. They bombarded him with the contents of password dictionaries. They pestered him like mosquitoes until he became enraged.

From then on, his user name disappeared from newsgroups and bulletin boards frequented by the world's hackers. He simply didn't trust them enough to make friends, though he did keep an eye on the latest breakthroughs.

As for his face-to-face contacts, they were just as unsuccessful. He was only thirteen when he entered twelfth grade, around the beginning of first term. All the other kids in this grade were four or five years older than he was, and they thought him a joke. A freak. Their interests revolved around cars, clothes, sex, and (sometimes) exams, so Cadel didn't fit in at all. He wasn't old enough to drive. He was too small to wear most of the trendy clothes. And he'd never had sex, of course, though he was starting to think about it a good deal, simply because of Partner Post. There was a lot of sex talk on his secure sites— more than he'd ever anticipated—and he was reluctant to ask Thaddeus for help on *this* subject. Fortunately, the Piggotts kept a large stock of dirty magazines in their dressing room. And a few of the twelfth-grade boys talked about sex endlessly, obsessively.

So Cadel was able to piece together some convincing replies to his clients, many of whom, he thought indignantly, were quite disgusting. They didn't deserve to have real partners, in his opinion. They didn't deserve to have partners at *all*.

Cadel spent eight months in twelfth grade, and over this time the Partner Post client base grew from eight to sixty-eight. Only two of these clients were ever introduced to other clients; most of them were provided with fake partners, designed to meet their every need. Cadel even bought an old Photoshop program and pasted together fake "happy snaps" of his fictional clients. He enjoyed doing this. He also enjoyed the challenge of sparking someone's interest, and eventually managed to calculate a primitive kind of formula that allowed him to slot each applicant into one of ten different categories.

Thaddeus and Cadel had spent entire appointments thrashing out an assessment form that would define the personality of each client. "Sometimes," Thaddeus pointed out, "what they say they want in a partner isn't really what they need in a partner. You have to watch that. You have to watch for the red flags. The use of language—that's very important. There's always a subtext, Cadel, *always*. Never take *anyone* at face value. Everyone always has adjustments to make in this world."

"And what if they're lying?" Cadel queried. "What if they say they have a university degree, for example, and they really don't? How do I work out what they need if I don't know the truth about them? I can run online checks, but there might be gaps."

Thaddeus looked down his long nose at Cadel.

"You might as well ask the same thing about everyone you meet," he observed. "What have you been doing this last year? You've been researching Crampton. And how have you been doing it? By insinuating yourself into people's conversations. By watching and listening and judging. Isn't that so?"

"I guess . . ."

"Well, then." Thaddeus adjusted his spectacles. "Just continue to do what you've been doing, Cadel. Most people aren't good liars—not like you. They don't have the memory for it. They aren't comfortable with it. They overreach themselves. Don't worry," he added, turning back to the first draft of his personality-test questions. "They're bound to slip up before too long. And you're bound to notice when they do."

Cadel rubbed his nose. He said, in a small voice, "You think I'm a good liar?"

Thaddeus glanced at him. "Don't you?"

"I suppose so." Cadel had never really thought of it as *lying*. He had thought of it in terms of stalling, outwitting, omitting. He liked to regard himself as a heroic loner, battling mighty forces, not as a sneaky little outcast.

Thaddeus surveyed him with a detached, appraising expression.

"You have the face for it," he went on. "An innocent face. Not all of us are so fortunate. If you said that you'd never let food pass your lips, I'd almost believe it." Seeing Cadel's troubled look, he narrowed his eyes. "What I told you about never taking people at face value, Cadel, applies just as much to words. Words don't really have fixed definitions. You'll find that out as you grow older. The word *liar* isn't as straightforward as it sounds." Once again, he turned to his draft questions. "Now," he said, "we might throw in a few multiple-choice questions here. Just to relax 'em. What do you think?"

Much to Cadel's surprise, Partner Post attracted more male than female clients. This meant that he was forced to impersonate a lot of women, and he found it very difficult indeed. Women's magazines proved helpful, as did some of the novels he borrowed from the library. He also eavesdropped on the twelfth-grade girls, who talked ceaselessly about boys, movies, music, and clothes. He would copy down what they said, then use some of it in what he privately called his "smoochy" e-mails. Because he was so small and quiet, he was usually able to listen in without being noticed.

After a while, he even became quite attached to some of the twelfth-grade girls. He couldn't help it. Most of them were stupid, and a few were quite cruel, but two, at least, were bright, and nice, and pretty. Ayesha wanted to be a musician (she played the viola) and had long, smooth dark hair, a vivid, intense face, and an eccentric taste in clothes. Rhiannon was different; she was freckled and witty, with a bubbling laugh, generous curves, and a razor-sharp mind when it came to puns, insults, and one-liners. She was also very good at foreign languages, having mastered at least three.

Cadel admired both these girls. When he tried to talk to them, however, he didn't know what to say. Ayesha was often so distracted that she hardly registered his attempts to make conversation. She was always running off to rehearsals, or arguing with someone about Greenpeace, or scribbling frantically away in a notebook with a worn leather binding. Rhiannon was less busy, but she was always surrounded by a circle of laughing friends. She was hugely popular because she was so funny—and sometimes she was funny at other people's expense.

This became horribly clear to Cadel one day when he was in the library at lunchtime. It was a sunny day, and the windows were open; a soft breeze carried the sound of distant shouts and squeals from the playground into the dim corner where Cadel was sitting. Then, to his surprise, he heard Rhiannon's voice. He realized that she was perched on a bench just beneath the library window, talking to her friends Seth, Sally, and Caitlin. They were talking about a classic German film called *M*, and Rhiannon was impersonating an old movie actor called Peter Lorre. She was an excellent mimic, on top of everything else.

"But it was a silent film," Caitlin objected. "Peter Lorre didn't talk in that film."

"Jesus, didn't he?" Rhiannon retorted. "Then I guess it must have been the voices in my head. Come to think of it, they *were* telling me to 'kill, kill, kill.' Naturally, I assumed it was Peter Lorre."

"Peter Lorre went to Hollywood, you dong," Seth pointed out wearily, addressing himself to Caitlin. "He was in lots of films. That's why most of us know what he sounded like."

"Well, *I've* never seen him," said Caitlin. "What's he been in, anyway?"

"*Arsenic and Old Lace,*" Rhiannon replied promptly.

"Never heard of it."

"You've never heard of anything," Seth sighed.

"You know who he reminds me of? Peter Lorre?" Rhiannon suddenly remarked. "I was watching that film, and you know who I thought of? Cadel Piggott."

Cadel's heart skipped a beat as a burst of laughter greeted this comment.

"Cadel *Piggott*?" Sally exclaimed. "No."

"They don't look anything like each other," Caitlin declared.

"Except for the pop eyes," Seth mused. "And the pudgy hands. And the moon face."

"I'm not saying they *look* alike," said Rhiannon. "I'm saying they *act* alike. They sort of creep around like cockroaches—"

"You think Cadel Piggott's a *killer*?" Seth demanded in melodramatic tones.

"Who knows?" said Rhiannon. "I wouldn't put it past him. He's bound to be an underwear stealer."

"An underwear *sniffer*!" Seth yelped.

"Oh, for sure." Rhiannon laughed. "You can see the skid marks under his nose!"

Cadel got up and closed his book. He left the library. From that day on, his admiration for Rhiannon turned into acute dislike. He had overheard other twelfth-grade students joking about his personal life but had never considered Rhiannon capable of jumping on that bandwagon. It made him very bitter.

He became disillusioned with Ayesha shortly afterward. Rhiannon and Seth were an item, he knew, but Ayesha didn't appear to have a boyfriend. Although she enjoyed the company of Chris and Bruno, she didn't seem to be going out with either. Bruno was a handsome smartass who played in a band. Chris was a stringy-looking hippy with a gentle soul and no critical abilities to speak of. He played acoustic guitar.

In Cadel's opinion, Ayesha stood head and shoulders above both these boys. What's more, she scoffed at "traditional" attitudes toward mating and dating. So when plans were announced for the end-of-year formal, which was still several months away, it crossed his mind that this might be his opportunity to connect with Ayesha. If she had a problem with all the tired, conservative "pairing-up" that went on at a school dance, she might actually consider going to the formal with him. As a kind of statement.

"No thanks, Cadel," she said, when approached. "I don't think so."

"Are you going with someone else?"

"I haven't decided."

"Then, why not me?"

They were standing near a lilac bush, and there were tiny mauve petals sliding down Ayesha's hair. They looked so pretty—*she* looked so pretty—that Cadel had found the courage to speak out. "It would be a non-ageist decision, don't you think?" he pressed. "And we could do it in style."

"Style isn't my style," Ayesha pointed out.

"No. That's true." Cadel ticked a mental box. Of course, Ayesha wasn't a limousine sort of person. "All right, then. No limousine. But you have to admit I've got more up here"—he tapped his head—"than most of the kids at this school combined. So why won't you take a chance? Since you like to be different."

Ayesha gave an exasperated sigh. She shifted her books from one arm to the other and tucked a strand of black hair behind her ear.

"You see, that's exactly why I don't want to go with you," she said. "I mean, you're so damned smug. 'I'm rich, I'm smart, I'm pretty, I've got the lowdown on everyone.' You sit there looking superior—can't even be bothered talking to people—"

"But—"

"You might think you know everything about everything, Cadel, but you don't know a thing about yourself. If you weren't so snotty, I'd feel sorry for you, I really would. Coming up to me like you're doing me a favor . . ." She shook her head. "And if you really *are* gay, like everyone says, then it's even sadder. Be honest with yourself. Take a look at your-self. Don't be pathetic."

Cadel flushed. He was suddenly, overwhelmingly angry—so angry that he couldn't even speak. Ayesha must have seen the tears of rage that sprang to his eyes, because she seemed to relent, a little.

"I'm sorry," she said, "but I had to be honest. It's best to be honest. You've got a lot going for you, Cadel, if you'd just realize that you're not as wonderful as you think you are."

And she walked away. For once in his life, Cadel couldn't cope. He actually skipped half a day of school. Though it was only recess, he went straight home and lay down, his mind turning and churning. He told the housekeeper (he no longer had a nanny) that he was suffering from a stomach bug.

This was also his excuse the following day, when he presented his homeroom teacher with a note from Mrs. Piggott.

By that time he had formulated a satisfying revenge. The whole of twelfth grade would suffer—he promised himself that—but it would take a lot of hard work. Hard work and a cool head. He would have to calm down. He would have to control the terrible feelings of hurt and fury that kept bubbling up and clouding his vision. Only by focusing would he show all those junk kids exactly what they were worth.

During the remainder of the year, while his classmates grew pasty and tired from studying and revising, Cadel concentrated his energies on just two things: Partner Post, and the frayed emotions of his twelfth-grade enemies. He started to compile a database. In it, he organized every little fact that he knew about his classmates: their timetables, their past romances, their weak points, their ambitions. He noted the growing tensions in the air around him, as graduation slowly approached. Acne flared. Religious conversions became more frequent. A lot of couples split, made up, and split again.

Cadel was pleased to see the stress levels rising and did all he could to encourage the process. He started rumors. He blocked corridors, to direct certain people past certain conversations. He worked out who was betraying whom; who was taking drugs to ease jangled nerves; who was becoming overtired; who had just about decided to pack it all in and get a job at a beach resort. For hours every night he would sit and construct a mental image of all the links between the other sixty-three kids in twelfth grade.

He knew that the two weeks between their last day of term and the beginning of the exams would prove to be a challenge, because most of twelfth grade would then be out of his reach. He also knew that the twelfth-grade formal, on the evening of the last school day, would be his final chance to wrap things up. So he bought himself a pair of black trousers, a jacket, and a silk shirt. He paid his fee, which covered dinner and the cost of the venue. He endured the fussing of Mrs. Piggott, who insisted that he take a hired car to the event and who also presented him with a tie and a vest, both of which he took off in the car. Finally, he arrived at the hall where his classmates were celebrating the end of school—only to discover that his name wasn't on the list at the door.

"Well, I don't know," joked Bruno the smart-ass. "You look kinda small for a twelfth-grade person. What did you say your name was?"

"Oh, stop it," laughed his girlfriend—who wasn't Ayesha. "Don't be so mean."

"Yet another screwup," said the vice principal. "Sorry about that, Cadel. Don't worry, you can still go in. I know you've paid your money. Here. Don't forget your stamp."

The stamp was designed to discourage gate-crashers. Cadel held out his hand, received the stamp, and went in. The hall was dark and noisy. Colored lights flashed. There was a live band onstage. Food was laid out on tables near the walls: spring rolls, mini-quiches, marinated chicken wings. There wasn't supposed to be alcohol, but somehow it had been smuggled in.

As the music pounded and the dancers writhed, Cadel drifted from group to group. He sidled into the bathroom and out again. He saw pills, beer cans, and smoking butts being passed surreptitiously around shadowy corners. He even saw money change hands at one point, and he made a mental note of two particular names. Most people seemed to be getting high on something. Arguments broke out. One girl pushed another girl. Rhiannon started kissing Bruno. Caitlin staggered into the bathroom, retching, where she joined a large group of vomiting classmates.

Cadel watched.

For the most part, he was completely ignored. Only on three occasions was he addressed by anyone. The first time was when Sally and her friend, Jessica, stumbled over him. He was sitting on the floor with his back propped against a wall and his knees under his chin. Sally didn't see him there. She tripped on his black suede shoe and would have fallen if Jessica hadn't held her up.

"For Chris'sake!" she barked, peering through the dimness. "What the bloody hell are you doing down there?"

"It's Cadel," said Jessica, swaying slightly.

"Cadel?"

"Hello, Cadel."

"What the bloody hell are you doing down there?" Sally repeated. She sounded furious. "Get up! You're in the way!"

"Ah, don't be mean," Jessica protested.

"He's a bloody idiot."

"He's only a little kid."

"Are you *hiding*?" Sally demanded, and Jessica giggled.

"He's hiding from *you*," she said, then whispered something in Sally's ear. They both laughed and careened off into the throbbing crowd.

Cadel closed his eyes briefly. He was getting a headache. But when he opened them again, he caught a glimpse of Heather Parsons, who was almost certainly drunk, being hustled through a fire exit by someone who looked very much like Damian di Matteo. This sparked his interest. He rose, and pushed his way through knots of heaving bodies until he reached the fire exit. Then he shoved it open.

On the other side of the door lay a covered parking lot, poorly lit. Despite the lack of illumination, however, Cadel could make out two moving shapes. One was helping the other into a dark-colored van, which had white graffiti glowing on its flanks.

"Cadel?" said a voice.

Cadel whirled around. Behind him stood Mrs. Brezeck. She was quite small, even in high heels, and her eyes were almost level with his. Her glossy dark hair was pulled back in a bun, and the mole on her cheek cast a tiny shadow with every flash of the red strobe light behind her.

"What are you doing?" she asked.

"Not much," Cadel replied. "Just seeing where this goes."

"Well, you're not allowed outside once you're in. Weren't you told that?"

"No."

"Well, you're not. So come back, please."

Cadel obeyed without argument. As he retraced his steps, Mrs. Brezeck pulled the door shut behind him, firmly. Then, raising her voice against the blaring music, she said, "Having fun, are you?"

"Pardon?"

"I said, *are you having fun?*"

Cadel looked at her in surprise. "Sure," he rejoined.

"In your own particular way, I suppose."

Something about her voice made every nerve in Cadel's body leap to attention. He blinked, and held her gaze.

Masked by the dimness, her face told him nothing.

"In my own particular way," he echoed, slowly. "Yeah. I guess."

She nodded. "Well—I'd wish you luck in the exams, if there was any chance that you'd need it," she said, and abruptly walked away. Cadel was disconcerted. He wriggled back to his patch of floor, only to discover that it was occupied. Seth was lying there, looking vacant.

Cadel stepped over him.

About an hour later, Cadel was sitting on a chair beside one of the food tables, which was covered in crumbs, smears, and shattered remnants. In his hand he held a glass of lemonade and half a curry puff. His feet were planted firmly on the floor; it had been a long time since he had sat with dangling feet.

The crowd in front of him was thinning. A lot of people had left the dance floor, too drunk or sick or tired to stay upright. Through a moving screen of silhouettes he saw Ayesha's. She was draped all over Bruno.

The two of them approached the table beside him unsteadily, as if in search of something to eat. Ayesha was wearing a silk flower in her hair. Bruno's shirt was unbuttoned. They both looked disheveled.

"No more prawns," Ayesha groaned, scanning the finger-food wreckage. Then she caught sight of Cadel.

They gazed at each other for a moment, while Cadel slowly chewed his curry puff. His own shirt was still neatly buttoned. He wasn't even sweaty.

At last he swallowed, then said, "That guy beside you came with another girl, you know."

"Piss off," Ayesha replied, before dragging Bruno away.

Cadel didn't care, though. Because by then he had already begun talking to Kay-Lee McDougall.

NINE

Kay-Lee McDougall was a Partner Post client. She had filled in the assessment form, paid the joining fee, and sent Cadel a passport photograph. The photograph showed an ordinary-looking woman with long blond hair, finely plucked eyebrows, and a slightly squashed nose. Kay-Lee was twenty-five. She worked as a nurse in a hospital called Weatherwood House, in Sydney's western suburbs.

Studying the photograph, Cadel was surprised. Although Kay-Lee's face was pleasant enough, it didn't strike him as particularly unusual. Yet according to her assessment form, she was very intelligent indeed. Cadel and Thaddeus had included a set of questions designed to give a rough measurement of someone's IQ, and Kay-Lee's was exceptionally high. What's more, she gave her interests as number theory, cryptosystems, and detective novels.

"She says she likes guys who are 'a little bit crazy,'" Cadel told Thaddeus. "She says she doesn't care about looks, or age, but that she wants someone intelligent."

"I'm not surprised," said Thaddeus, frowning over Kay-Lee's assessment form. "Number theory? There wouldn't be many idiots interested in that."

"Except the ones still trying to square the circle," Cadel remarked. He was studying Thaddeus's face. "What is it?" he suddenly asked. "What's the matter? Don't you think she's telling the truth?"

Thaddeus didn't reply at once. He flicked through a few more pages, pulled at his nose, removed his glasses, rubbed his eyes.

Then he put his glasses back on.

"Up to a point," he replied at last.

"She's passed all those fail-safes—"

"I know. She has." Thaddeus picked up Kay-Lee's photograph and peered at it closely. "You can't see much from this, can you?" he murmured. "Nothing below the neck."

Cadel waited.

"I'm just getting a sense, here, that there's something about her body image." Thaddeus stabbed at the pages in front of him with a long, bony forefinger. "*Appears . . . appearance . . . looks . . . face . . . face up to . . .* so many loaded words."

Cadel was puzzled. "But she seems pretty stable," he pointed out. "I mean, there isn't a trace of any personality disorders."

"I'm not talking about personality disorders, Cadel. There's just a slight disjunction . . ." Thaddeus sighed. "I don't know. I suppose it's not unusual, for most women—body image is such an issue."

"Hang-ups, you mean? About the way they look?"

"Precisely."

This time it was Cadel's turn to pick up the photograph. "She looks all right to me."

"That's what I'm saying. She does. And yet I'm getting a whiff here of a really deep disturbance. I mean, consider her answers to questions forty-eight and fifty-four. That's a very strong response." Thaddeus removed the photograph from Cadel's hand and scanned it again. "I'd only be guessing, but I wonder if she's got burns or something? Some kind of deformity?"

Cadel blinked. "You think so?"

"It's possible. You said yourself, a lot of these people would be choosing an online dating service for a reason." At last Thaddeus laid the photograph back on his desk. "Just something to keep in mind, that's all."

Cadel nodded. He already knew that Kay-Lee's perfect match was going to be a lot more interesting than most: a seedy academic, about thirty-three or thirty-four, brilliant but unreliable, with a moderate drinking problem. Someone "a little bit crazy," in other words. Cadel settled on the name Eiran Dempster. He pasted together a blurry snapshot of someone with a scrubby jaw and lots of dark hair, sitting in a restaurant. A Canadian restaurant. Cadel decided to make Eiran a Canadian academic living in Toronto. That way the chances of a face-to-face meeting were very low. Of course, he had to do a bit of research, but he didn't mind that. Research was always interesting.

Eiran had a good position at his university but was busy throwing it away by turning up late for class, objecting to certain students (because they were "slow"), giving punishingly low marks, and drinking too much alcohol at lunchtime. He taught mathematics but hated teaching. Whenever he wasn't drunk, he wanted to spend all his time trying to discover the solution to an age-old mathematical problem: how to factor a number. Obviously, he was interested in number theory and cryptosystems.

Because he was so arrogant, however, he didn't think much of detective stories. He believed that most of them were inferior to what he could have written himself.

That was exactly what Cadel said, in Eiran's first e-mail to Kay-Lee. Kay-Lee agreed that most detective novels *were* clumsy, but not all of them. She asked Eiran if he had ever met Manindra Agrawal, the Indian mathematician who had produced the primality testing solution. (He was one of her heroes.) She challenged Eiran with a message written in a number code, which Cadel solved quite easily. He enjoyed doing it. *What's this,* he wrote, *playtime for preschoolers?* He threw back a message in another, equally famous code, which she deciphered. After drawing on his knowledge of six frequently used number codes, Cadel had to start looking up texts for further inspiration. He had a wonderful time. In the end, he and Kay-Lee devised their own code, using primality testing, the periodic table of the elements, and certain ideas that Cadel had picked up from the International Data Encryption Algorithm.

Why are you a nurse? he finally asked her, in code. *Why aren't you teaching math?*

Like you? Kay-Lee replied. *I thought you said it was pseudohell at your work, because at least in hell there would be some interesting people.*

You must be bored out of your brain.

You are *bored out of your brain. You told me so.*

And you're not?

The world is one big calculation, Eiran. How can I possibly get bored?

From there the conversation turned to the number pi, or the golden number, which is a marvelous ratio found throughout nature. Cadel and Kay-Lee talked about ratios, factoring, and even atomic structure, though Cadel had to rein himself in when the discussion strayed too close to nanotechnology. If he wasn't careful, he found himself being too *much* himself, when he was supposed to be Eiran Dempster. It was hard, though. It was hard not to get excited.

He couldn't help spending more time on Eiran than he devoted to any of his other fictional creations. Eiran, he felt, was his kind of guy.

And Kay-Lee was his kind of girl.

It wasn't just that she was clever. She had a peculiar kind of humor that charmed him. She called herself Il Primo, because the atomic number of K (potassium) was 19, and the atomic number of Li (lithium) was 3, and both were prime numbers. Eiran she called Stormer, because the atomic number of iron (or "Eiran") was 26, and 26 was one of the numbers in Carl Stormer's famous sequence. When Kay-Lee started talking about Stormer's numbers, Cadel had to look them up.

It's very elegant, Kay-Lee explained. *Let's say 26 is* n. *The largest prime factor of* n *squared plus one is at least 2*n. *Which makes 26 a Stormer number—its corresponding prime being 617.*

Right, said Cadel.

Or maybe I should just call you "hon," Kay-Lee went on. *Because 26 squared plus one is 677, and 67 is the atomic weight for holmium—Ho—and 7 is the atomic number for nitrogen—N. Hon. Short for "honey."*

Short for "honorable," Cadel corrected.

Well, I sure hope so.

Cadel began to suspect that Kay-Lee's mind was more finely tuned than his, at least in the field of mathematics. His mastery of systems was different from her mastery of numbers. For her, the world was a place of pure numbers, each of which had its own unique personality. She talked fondly of Napier's number, Apery's number, and Liouville's number, as if they were her friends. She regarded six, being a mathematically "perfect number," as rather stuck-up. Two, for her, was a calm and wise and beautiful number, because it was the only even prime. Zero was mysterious. Nine was elegant, because you could instantly tell whether any number was divisible by it. Ten and eleven were tricky, because they were binary versions of two and three. She saw numbers relating to each other, excluding each other, building things, reducing things. Cadel found that he had to work very, very hard to keep up with her—and convince her that he really was a teacher of number theory.

Even when they strayed to nonmathematical subjects, Kay-Lee had a funny way of expressing herself. As Cadel became more and more interested in her—as he asked her more and more questions about herself—she would retreat into language that was hard to translate, unless you were a mathematician. When asked where she lived, she remarked vaguely that she was a bit of a "Hamilton's quaternion." Only after consulting his texts did Cadel come across the following rule: *Hamilton's quaternions are not commutative.* This led him to conclude that Kay-Lee didn't commute, and that she lived either in or near her workplace. (She did, in fact; Cadel discovered her address by hacking into various databases.) When asked about her school years, Kay-Lee replied obscurely, *It was a ten eighty-eight, Stormer—work it out.* Cadel did work it out, in the end. He worked out that the Japanese name for ten to the power of eighty-eight was *muryoutaisuu*, which translated as "large amount of nothing." Clearly, Kay-Lee hadn't much enjoyed school—an understandable response, given her academic results. Cadel found her GPAs after a long online search of newspaper records

74

and was surprised at how average they were. Had she been like him? Too bored to concentrate?

She was more relaxed when they stayed off the subject of her life. She watched a lot of films, read a lot of books, and played a lot of games. She and Cadel both agreed that *The Name of the Rose* was an excellent detective story. Cadel was better at tactical games, like chess and Diplomacy, while Kay-Lee was better at number games, like Nim and Hackenbush. For this reason, Cadel stayed away from number games. Every time he lost to Kay-Lee, he worried that she was going to see through his disguise.

He didn't want that to happen. She fascinated him. And as the weeks rolled by, he often turned to her when he was feeling low. Like Thaddeus, she didn't make him feel like a freak. On the contrary, she praised him as being the one man she could really talk to, on all levels. She regularly communicated with mathematicians around the world, she said, but the minute they stopped discussing math, there seemed to be nothing else to talk about. With Eiran, it was different. *It's like we're part of the same equation,* she said. *It's like we're a perfect number.*

Cadel agreed. Eiran and Kay-Lee *were* a perfect number. But where did Cadel fit in? Increasingly, he wished that he could tell her who he really was. If he did, however, it would change everything. She wouldn't want to spend so much time chatting online to a thirteen-year-old boy. She was twenty-five and looking for a partner—a soul mate. It was odd, in fact, that she hadn't already suggested that they try to meet.

This often happened on the Partner Post sites. Cadel put a lot of effort into dodging invitations. Sometimes he simply had to cut off communications altogether; mostly he made sure that his fictional creations were living on the other side of the world from their perfect partners and were either too poor or too busy to travel. Eiran was obviously too poor. He lived in a squalid little studio apartment with a bathroom the size of a linen cupboard. Owing to his wild streak, he tended to squander most of his money on drinking binges and impulse buys—like presents for his girlfriends. Cadel had already sent Kay-Lee some lavish bouquets of flowers, several computer games, a book, a compact disc, and a little gold pi symbol on a chain, "with love from Eiran." This was far more than he had ever given any of his other clients, because of the effort involved. He'd been forced to seek help from some Canadian friends of Thaddeus's, lest an Australian postmark should make Kay-Lee suspicious.

Thaddeus didn't care much for this solution. He thought it overcomplicated. "If I were you, I'd bail out," he advised. "You've done it before. You're getting too involved."

Cadel said nothing. It was true, of course. He *was* getting too involved with Kay-Lee. And he was enjoying it too much to stop.

Thaddeus looked at him closely.

"I hope you know what you're doing, Cadel," he murmured. "Graduation exams are coming up, remember. You don't want any distractions."

Cadel snorted. "Exams?" he scoffed. "They'll be easy."

"I'm not talking about the academic side of things. I'm talking about your plans for those people who are *doing* exams." Thaddeus had heard all about Cadel's plot to avenge himself on the rest of twelfth grade. "You wouldn't want to fall behind in your preparations."

"I won't," Cadel declared. "I'm all set."

Thaddeus lifted an eyebrow.

"I am," Cadel insisted. "I can't do much more. From now on, it's just a matter of waiting."

"And studying."

Cadel made a dismissive gesture.

"I'll be fine," he assured Thaddeus. "You don't have to worry about me."

He was right. When the graduation exam results were finally posted, Cadel received a perfect score.

The results of every other twelfth-grade student at Crampton were utterly dreadful.

TEN

Mr. and Mrs. Piggott didn't worry much about Cadel anymore. Stuart had never been very interested in him, anyway, and Lanna was busier than ever, traveling all over the country to decorate other people's houses. Now that Cadel seemed to have a few friends, they left him to himself. Sometimes he wouldn't see either of them for days; his meals were cooked and his clothes washed by the housekeeper, Mrs. Ang.

Thaddeus insisted, however, that all three Piggotts join him to discuss Cadel's future, once his graduation exam results had been released. Obviously, it was important that Cadel's great gifts be properly nurtured and encouraged.

"He can't go overseas," Thaddeus observed. "He's too young for that. And besides, he needs to be cared for. Wherever he goes, whatever university he attends, he'll need extra attention, being the sort of person he is."

"I suppose so," said Lanna, vaguely. Once again they were sitting in Thaddeus's office. Nearly seven years had passed since their last family council on the same spot; in that time, Lanna had lost weight and Stuart had gained even more. Lanna's face was now skull-like, despite her bright orange lipstick and heavy eye makeup. Stuart looked permanently uncomfortable: red-faced, breathless, awkward. The crimson couch had long since been replaced by a maroon one, and the technology scattered around the room had changed a little.

Cadel had changed a lot. He had grown, though he would never be very tall. His curls had become quite dark. A few spots were popping up on his pale skin. He was beginning to fill out. His voice was stable. He was almost fourteen and looked it.

Only his hands and clothes seemed younger: his hands because he often chewed his fingernails down to the quick, and his clothes because Lanna now let him buy his own. Since Cadel had never been interested in clothes, he had kept buying the chunky cords, childish sneakers, and brightly trimmed parkas that Mrs. Piggott had always chosen for him.

"Cadel's very young to be going to college," Thaddeus remarked, glancing at Cadel's sneakers. "That's why we have to choose the right one. Universities can be extraordinarily cold and isolating places for any young person, and Cadel's been doing so well that I shouldn't like to put him at risk by thrusting him into a large and anonymous sort of campus where the support systems don't exist for a person of Cadel's unusual needs."

"You mean you think he should go to a small university?" Stuart asked. "Is that what you're saying?"

"Essentially. He has the pick of them all, of course, but—"

"It has to be in Sydney," Lanna interrupted. "He's too young for a residential college."

"Oh, I agree," said Thaddeus. "Again, it would be a very disruptive experience. And of course I'd like to continue our sessions."

"Why?" Stuart queried. His voice was harsh, his question blunt. "Cadel's doing all right. How long is he going to have to keep traipsing in here three days a week?"

Thaddeus pressed his fingertips together. Leaning forward, he replied smoothly, "As long as Cadel wants to come, he is welcome to come." Three heads turned, as the adults in the room all gazed at the child. "Do you *want* to continue our discussions, Cadel?" Thaddeus inquired. "Or do you think we have nothing else to explore?"

"I want to keep coming," said Cadel. Inwardly, he was alarmed that Stuart should even consider canceling his sessions with Thaddeus. Thaddeus was like a father—and Dr. Darkkon *was* Cadel's father. He couldn't imagine being cut off from either of them. "It makes me feel better," he said.

"Like a safety valve," agreed Thaddeus. He addressed Stuart once more: "Cadel *has* been doing very well, and will continue to do well as long as he has our sessions to fall back on. I hope you don't have any reason to doubt me on this?"

"Oh no," Lanna hastened to assure him. "Not at all. We're very grateful." And she gave her husband a poke in the ribs. "Don't be so silly, Stuart."

Cadel sighed. He felt hugely relieved. The prospect of losing Thaddeus was too awful to contemplate—especially now, when he had no idea what he should be doing with his life. Thaddeus, quite obviously, did. Cadel was willing to go along with any suggestions that Thaddeus might make. He had no alternative ambitions. In fact, he had never given the future much thought. All he wanted to do was to keep exercising his mind in a way that he found fulfilling.

"My recommendation is a place called the Axis Institute," the psychologist continued, pulling a thick brochure off his desk. "It's a very small and recent foundation, but tailor-made for your son, in my view. The focus is on the individual students, with courses carefully designed to suit them and with a great deal of structured counseling built in."

"It sounds like a loony bin" was Stuart's opinion, and his wife scowled at him.

"Stuart! Hush!"

"It's not a loony bin," Thaddeus assured Mr. Piggott patiently. "It's a tertiary college for bright young people who need extra emotional support. I thought you might at least like to inspect it. See what you think." He handed the brochure to Stuart. "There are some minor fees involved, but government funding helps allay most of the costs."

Cadel watched Thaddeus intently. He didn't know what this Axis Institute business was all about, but he had a feeling that Thaddeus was plotting something. Sure enough, Stuart suddenly exclaimed, "It says here you're the chancellor!"

"That's right," Thaddeus conceded.

"So you're trying to flog us a college that pays you?"

Thaddeus took a deep breath. "Of course, you're free to send Cadel anywhere you wish," he said. "My involvement with the Axis Institute came about solely because of my concern for young people of his type, whose circumstances are unusual, and whose potentials are enormous. Naturally, I wouldn't expect you to agree without inspecting the facility yourself. You'll find that while it's not yet well-known in the wider community, it *is* quite highly regarded by those government departments whose job it is to accredit and oversee such institutions. You can make all the inquiries you want."

Stuart grunted. He and his wife both looked at the brochure again. As they did, Thaddeus glanced toward Cadel, and his left eyelid flickered.

"I need hardly add"—the psychologist smiled—"that the institute must first meet with *your* approval, Cadel."

"Oh," said Cadel, "I'm sure it will. As long as they teach computers."

This remark had been deliberately designed to startle the Piggotts, who raised their heads in unison.

"Computers!" Lanna exclaimed.

"I thought we had an agreement," Stuart growled.

But Thaddeus held up his hands.

"Now let's all be calm, please." His voice caressed their ears. "This issue has to be resolved, sooner or later. I think the time has come, Stuart—Lanna—to give credit where credit's due. You've told me that Cadel's been doing very well. It's true—he has. And I think he's come to realize that what he did seven years ago was ill-advised. Isn't that so, Cadel?"

"Yes," Cadel replied.

"He's a lot older now, and he's not stupid," Thaddeus went on. "I think we have to accept that he's proven his ability to behave in a socially responsible manner, and that he ought to be permitted some free-dom with regard to computers. *Some* freedom." Surveying the doubt-ful expressions in front of him, Thaddeus tried to reassure Mr. and Mrs. Piggott. "The computer-science program at Axis is well super-vised," he observed, "and the course coordinator is brilliant. Dr. Vee. I know him quite well."

Lanna glanced at her watch. Then she glanced at her husband. Then she patted his knee and said, in a hesitant manner, "I don't see why we couldn't at least have a look. Stuart? What do you think?"

"I suppose so," muttered Mr. Piggott.

"If you'd like, I could show you around the institute myself," Thad-deus offered. "What would be a convenient time? I realize you're very busy—"

"Next weekend," Stuart interjected. "We can make it on Saturday."

"But my plane leaves at four!" Lanna cried.

"Then we'll start at one. After lunch," her husband snapped.

Thaddeus nodded. Heaving himself off the couch, he approached his desk and checked his diary.

Cadel, who was perched on Thaddeus's typing chair, had to move out of the way.

"Ye-e-es," said Thaddeus, flipping a page. "Yes, Saturday should be all right. At one, you say? Fine. No problem." He plucked a pen from the inside pocket of his tweedy jacket and scribbled something down. "Keep that brochure," he instructed Stuart. "It gives you the address. You can meet me out front—at the pedestrian gate. We're talking about the city campus, of course. You won't be interested in driving all the way to Yarramundi."

"Yarramundi?" Lanna echoed.

"The Yarramundi campus isn't very big," Thaddeus explained. "There's some agricultural research done out there, a bit of engineer-ing, nothing that Cadel's going to be interested in. Oh!" He pulled open one of his drawers and fished around inside. "Here's last year's course booklet for you, Cadel. Have a look. Even if you're thinking about a degree in computer science, you have the option to include a more varied range of subjects in your degree. A little bit of psychology, perhaps—media studies—the choice isn't bad for such a small institution."

Cadel accepted the handbook. It had a blue and gold cover. Flicking carelessly through it, he happened upon a photograph of Thaddeus. In the photograph, Thaddeus looked far more benevolent than he did in real life.

Thaddeus was a professor, Cadel noticed. He had a string of psychology degrees after his name.

"Thank you very much, Dr. Roth," Lanna declared, rising from the maroon couch. "You'll have to forgive us, but I have an appointment."

"Of course," Thaddeus replied blandly. "Good of you to come."

"Are you sure computer studies is the right way to go for Cadel?" Stuart inquired. "Seems a bit limiting for such a bright kid."

Thaddeus spread his hands and cocked his head.

"Rest assured, Stuart, that your son can do anything he sets his heart on. At the moment, his passion is computers. Later, perhaps, his tastes might evolve. But it's of no consequence—he's young enough to change his mind, don't you agree?"

Once more, Stuart grunted. He struggled to his feet, puffing and blowing, while Cadel quietly slipped the Axis handbook behind a pile of papers on Thaddeus's desk. He wanted a private word with Thaddeus. And this could only be done if he hurried back to retrieve something when his adoptive parents reached their car.

Five minutes after leaving the house, he abruptly returned. He found Thaddeus waiting for him, sitting on the typist's chair, the handbook in his lap.

"I didn't forget it," said Cadel.

"I know," Thaddeus replied.

The book was offered and accepted. Cadel asked, "What *is* this Axis place? You've never mentioned it before."

"It's a college. I told you."

"But—"

"It's funded by your father, Cadel. Pretty much for your sake."

"*My* sake?" Cadel blinked. "You don't mean—he created it just for *me*? To go to?"

"Not exactly." Thaddeus checked his watch. "I can't give you the details now—I haven't time. But rest assured it will suit you right down to the ground. It was tailor-made for you. *Tailor-made.*"

"Just so that I could get a degree in computer science?"

Thaddeus smiled. He rose from his chair, put his arm around Cadel's shoulders, and bent his mouth to the boy's ear. "Between you and me," he whispered, "we at the institute prefer to call it an *infiltration* degree."

Cadel pulled back, startled. He peered up into the psychologist's face.

Thaddeus was still smiling.

"If you check that handbook, Cadel, you'll find a little software chip inside," he said. "For your computer phone. It will give you a more thorough understanding of what the Axis Institute is all about."

"Okay."

"Just remember the golden rule," Thaddeus concluded. *"Never take anything at face value."*

On his way home, Cadel pondered this advice as Stuart swore at the traffic. Like his wife, Mr. Piggott had a meeting scheduled; he dropped Cadel at the house before whizzing off in a cloud of exhaust fumes. Cadel let himself in. Mrs. Ang had been and gone, so the wide, pale rooms were clean and silent. Cadel's rubber soles squeaked on polished wood floors and padded across expensive Persian rugs.

He kicked his shoes off when he finally flung himself onto his bed, creasing the handwoven cover in a way that would have enraged Mrs. Piggott.

Cadel had recently concealed a laptop computer in his hollowed-out world atlas. He had bought the computer with his Partner Post money and was able to use it quite often because Mr. and Mrs. Piggott were away more than ever. Thaddeus knew about the laptop, of course; yet he had given Cadel a tiny chip of software for the computer phone, which, despite all its marvelous features, was so small that it was harder to use than a normal computer.

Why had Thaddeus done this?

Cadel soon realized why. When he loaded the program, he discovered an alternative course handbook for the Axis Institute—and it wasn't the kind of thing you'd want falling into the hands of your parents. With growing astonishment Cadel discovered the *real* names of the institute's schools and departments. It seemed that the School of Deception offered not computer science, psychology, media studies, and accounting, but infiltration, manipulation, misinformation, and embezzlement. The School of Organic Distortion ran courses on contagion and mutation (both genetic and radiation-induced). The School of Destruction covered explosives, assassination (including poisoning), guerrilla skills, and something called Personal Growth.

When Cadel called up more information on the infiltration department, he was informed that infiltration—otherwise known as computer science—was only a unit in the first year of the Axis "World Domination" degree. As a School of Deception student, Cadel would have to attend certain compulsory courses as part of his first-year program. These courses would include Basic Lying (or "Coping Skills"), Pure Evil (or "Pragmatic Philosophy"), Case Studies I (or "Self-Discipline"), and Forgery (or "Cultural Appreciation"). He could then choose his electives—like infiltration, for example.

The philosophy of the Axis Institute, as determined by its founder, Dr. Phineas Darkkon, is one of transformation, Cadel learned from the "Overview" option. *His goal is to effect the transformation of individuals* and *society. Dr. Darkkon's purpose in founding the institute was to tap into the unrealized skills of those who have lost their way in a community of fossilized values and blunted minds. Axis is the seed of a new world order.*

Cadel leaped off his bed and telephoned Thaddeus.

"I'm afraid Dr. Roth is with a client," Wilfreda informed him in a singsong voice.

"Tell him it's urgent," Cadel insisted. "Tell him we *have* to talk."

"One moment, please."

Cadel was put on hold. Organ music played in his ear. Then he heard Thaddeus speaking.

"Hello?"

"Thaddeus?"

"I'm here."

"Is this *serious*?" Cadel exclaimed. "I mean, is this some kind of joke?"

A brief silence followed.

"If you're referring to the information I gave you," Thaddeus said at last, coldly, "of course it's not a joke."

"But . . ." Cadel didn't know how to express himself. "The Axis Institute . . ."

"Your father's pride and joy."

"Is it like a . . . a . . ." Still Cadel couldn't find the right words, and he sensed impatience on the other end of the line. "Like a *University of Evil*?" he finally squeaked. "Is that what you're saying?"

"I can't say anything at the moment. I'm with someone."

"But I don't understand. What's the point? I mean, *explosives*? I thought my father didn't like bombs!"

"All will be explained."

"I'm a hacker!" Cadel protested. "I don't poison people! I don't blow them up!"

"Of course not. You don't have to."

"But—"

"Listen." Thaddeus spoke firmly. "Listen to me. Remember what I said? About taking things at face value? That applies to words as much as anything else, do you remember?"

"Yes, but—"

"Calm down. Think about it. Think about what your father's told you. Think about his philosophy. And I'll speak to you again tomorrow, all right?"

Cadel hesitated.

"All right, dear boy?"

Cadel sighed. "I guess so," he muttered. "It just seems so weird."

"It won't," Thaddeus assured him. "Not when you understand. You have to free up your thinking a bit. That's all. Your mind-set's got too rigid, dealing with the sorts of people you have to deal with. Your father knows what he's doing. He's not a fool." There was a brief pause. "Trust me."

"You always told me not to trust anyone," Cadel retorted, and Thaddeus laughed his gentle laugh.

"You'll be fine. Just fine," he said. "Whatever happens, you'll always land on your feet." And he hung up.

Cadel sat for a while, staring out the window. He could see a hedge and part of a wall. After about fifteen minutes, he rose, pulled out his laptop, and wrote an e-mail to Kay-Lee McDougall.

In it, he talked of how Eiran had written approximately four thousand digits of pi on his bathroom wall, as something "interesting to look at while I'm taking a dump." He joked about trying to predict the pairing of his students using Fermat's two-square theorem. He discussed Kay-Lee's previous message about harmonic numbers, and her own relationship with music.

Then he wrote: *The word* harmonic *is a funny one, isn't it? Applied to numbers. Of course I realize it's derived from the Pythagorean tradition, but "harmonic" seems to imply that they're* good *numbers, in an odd sort of way.*

Do you ever think about bad and good, when you're thinking about numbers?

Kay-Lee replied the same evening, some time between five and six thirty. She wrote that, while of course pi was *the* transcendental number, she personally preferred the Euler-Mascheroni number y. She pointed out that Fermat's two-square theorem would only work if the students to whom Eiran referred wore boring clothes. (Ha-ha.) She talked about memorizing number sequences (like pi, for instance) by turning the digits into musical notes.

Finally, she said: *There are no "good" numbers. How could there be? Even when they don't compute, it's not their fault—it's yours. A number is a number, and they all have their different natures. Some are complex, some infinite, some coefficient, some rational. You can't judge them for being what they are.*

That's what I like about numbers, anyway. They're Beyond Good and Evil. You don't have to think *like that all the time.*

Of course, there's the order of the so-called Monster simple group, but he doesn't look so monstrous to me. Not even for a number that occurs naturally in an undeletable theorem. After all, he's not going to eat anyone. Not like infinitary calculus.

Speaking of which, has that student of yours—the one who never changes his jeans—submitted his calculations yet? Or has he come up with yet another fantastic excuse?

Cadel thought about this message for a long, long time.

ELEVEN

The Axis Institute was housed in an old seminary, where young men had once learned to be priests. Dr. Roth told Cadel this as they walked, with Lanna and Stuart, through the institute's large front gate. The gate was made of wrought iron. On either side of it stretched a high brick wall that looked much newer than the Gothic seminary's pointed windows, slate roof, and sooty, snarling gargoyles. Inside, the seminary was a curious mixture of old and new. The vaulted ceilings were high, the windows were of stained glass, the doors were thick and scarred and made of dark wood. But on the creaking floors lay industrial-strength gray carpet; there were notice boards all over the place, covered in leaflets about clubs and pubs and sports events; and every room and corridor was fitted with state-of-the-art security, extinguisher, and electrical systems, together with some kind of video surveillance network that Cadel spotted but couldn't quite understand.

He made no mention of this network to his adoptive parents. They were already suspicious about the Axis Institute.

"In this building," Thaddeus explained, "you'll find the library, the seminar rooms, the staff offices, and the microbiology labs. The residential wing is connected to it, and is where some of our students live. There's a separate block where you'll find the dining hall and the sports facilities. We call the dining hall our refectory," he added.

"I'd like to see that," said Lanna, who was getting restless. (She didn't want to miss her plane.)

"Well, perhaps we'll start there," Thaddeus politely offered. "It's a brand-new building." He ushered them through a couple of doors and out into the sunshine again. Across a bright green lawn lay a carefully planned parking lot, and beyond the lot lay "C" block. It looked exactly like a gigantic, balled-up piece of aluminum foil caught on the teeth of a monumental white comb.

"Very modern," said Stuart doubtfully.

"Extraordinary, isn't it?" Thaddeus beamed. "A brilliant piece of engineering." He headed off along a covered breezeway, narrowly avoiding a person who was scurrying toward the seminary building with his head down. Cadel could see nobody else except a gardener mowing the lawn.

"Not much action during the Christmas break," Thaddeus remarked. He pushed open a door that, though it may have looked like crumpled foil, seemed very heavy indeed—and was fitted with a remarkable series of locks, Cadel noticed. Immediately inside it was a security scanner ("An unhappy necessity, in these troubled times," Thaddeus lamented), past which they were forced to proceed one at a time. Beyond the scanner, Cadel was amazed to find himself on a walkway suspended above a large expanse of polished wood flooring. Someone below him was bouncing a basketball; this person wore a skin-tight, body-length black leotard with flames emblazoned on it. The noise of pounding feet echoed off the ceiling.

"Our basketball courts," Thaddeus observed. "Yoga classes are also held here, together with several martial arts courses—tae kwon do and so forth. The gymnasium is to your right, as you can see. We have some remarkable gymnasts. There's also an archery club, a shooting club, boxing—"

"What about football?" Stuart wanted to know. "Soccer? Rugby?"

"Unfortunately, our football teams have yet to materialize. This way, please."

Thaddeus walked on through a couple of glass doors and into a corridor. Cadel noticed several things about this corridor: It smelled of food, its carpet bore a large, circular burn-mark at about the halfway point, and it resounded with the distant noise of clanking crockery.

He saw why when they reached the door at its end and entered a spacious café, all tiles and Formica. The color scheme was chiefly black and red, with touches of white. Behind glass sat stainless-steel tubs full of steaming shepherd's pie, gray peas floating sluggishly in hot water, pale fillets of fish, battered objects in a gluey plum sauce. There was an array of limp sandwiches wrapped in cellophane, a selection of sticky muffins, and a case full of cold drinks.

The women behind the counter were forbidding, their faces set in a permanent expression of brooding discontent.

"Well!" said Mrs. Piggott brightly. Thaddeus fingered his chin.

"This is the dining hall section," he pointed out. "There's also a kitchen from which you can order more expensive food—the menu's right here." He plucked it from a box near the cash register. "Salads, you see. A noodle soup. Focaccia. The faculty tend to use the kitchen service. Ah." Someone had caught his eye. "Let me introduce you to a member of our staff."

It was now half past one, and the tables were mostly occupied. Cadel spotted a few clusters of people, but the majority of the diners were sitting alone. There was a huge, hulking figure with greasy dark hair and a face like a moldy potato; another pasty young man staring fixedly at a girl in camouflage colors; a bald youth swathed in an ankle-length blue cloak. Thaddeus ushered his guests over to a couple of people who looked fairly normal by comparison. "This is Carla, who teaches microbiology," he said, "and this is my friend Art, who runs a course on the finer things in life. You'll notice his rather splendid English wardrobe."

Carla was a small, neat, black-haired woman with bright red lipstick. She wore a white lab coat, and her expression was angry as she caught sight of Thaddeus—possibly because, with Thaddeus around, she could no longer scold the man who sat opposite her. This man, Art, was also small, but he appeared to be far more gentle and reasonable than Carla. He was quite old, with wispy gray hair and thick glasses. His teeth, when he smiled, were yellow and crooked. He wore a vest and a bow tie.

"Thaddeus," he murmured.

"This is Cadel," said Thaddeus. "He's considering Axis as an option for the coming year."

"Is he indeed?"

"And these are his parents, Stuart and Lanna."

Art rose to shake hands with Mr. and Mrs. Piggott, who were obviously reassured by this mild-looking, professorial man. Briskly, Carla also rose. She had left most of a chocolate croissant on her plate.

"Afternoon," she said to the Piggotts. "Have you considered my proposal, Thaddeus?"

"It's next on my list, Carla."

She sniffed, stuffing a cigarette packet into the pocket of her lab coat. Cadel felt Thaddeus recoil, then wondered if he had imagined it. Carla frowned at Art, adding, "Just don't forget. All right?"

"I won't forget," Art responded peaceably.

Carla turned. She marched off at a rapid pace, while Art and Thaddeus exchanged glances.

"Quite a strong personality," Thaddeus remarked to Stuart, by way of explanation. "Brilliant mind, though."

"You're not thinking of doing microbiology, are you, son?" Stuart inquired of Cadel, who shook his head.

"Cadel *might* like to consider accounting, however," Thaddeus observed. "As a secondary elective. If he does, he'll be taught by Brendan Graham, over there." Thaddeus pointed at a red-haired man in a white shirt and green tie, whose attention was fixed on a notebook in front of him. With one hand he was scribbling in the notebook, while with the other, he spooned some kind of pudding into his mouth.

"Brendan," said Thaddeus, "is a genius with numbers. An absolute genius. He has Asperger's syndrome, which is a mild form of autism, so he lives, eats, and breathes numbers. The whole world is a balance sheet, for him. We find him an excellent teacher, though quirky of course."

"Quirky?" Lanna repeated.

"Well, he often has trouble remembering names," Thaddeus confessed. "Especially students' names. So he tends to call everyone by a particular number."

"Really?" said Lanna. Intrigued, Cadel glanced up at Thaddeus.

"What's your number, then?" he asked.

Thaddeus looked down his long nose at Cadel.

"Oh, he remembers *my* name," Thaddeus replied calmly. "He always remembers *my* name. And speaking of names . . ." He suddenly reached out to catch the arm of a tall, blond woman who was clicking across the room in stiletto heels. "You may remember Tracey Lane, who worked for channel seven a few years back. She's on our staff now."

Cadel didn't remember Tracey—he was too young—but Lanna and Stuart did. Lanna gushed and Stuart mumbled as Cadel studied Tracey's makeup. It was even more heavily applied than Lanna's. Tracey's face was like a gleaming mask; it hardly moved, even when she was talking. Her carefully arranged hair looked as if it was held in place by a coating of lacquer.

Cadel had never seen such long fingernails in his life.

"Pleased to meet you," Tracey murmured, after being introduced to Cadel. She had a deep, breathy voice. "Welcome to the institute. I just *know* you'll be happy here." Though she smiled and said all the right things, it was rather like talking to a robot. Her wide green eyes were perfectly blank. "Are you enrolled in my elective?"

"Not this time, Tracey," Thaddeus replied. If Tracey was disappointed, she didn't show it. Instead, she remarked that she had to be getting on, that she hoped they would enjoy the rest of their visit, that it had been so nice to meet them, that they would have to excuse her . . .

"What a lovely person." Lanna sighed, watching Tracey clatter away. "I can't believe she's not on TV anymore."

"Neither can she," said Thaddeus, lifting one eyebrow a fraction.

"You'll have to do her course one day, Cadel."

Cadel grunted. He realized that, as far as Lanna was concerned, the Axis Institute was the right place to be. If Tracey was on staff, how could anyone fail to benefit? Lanna's doting expression said it all.

"Right," Thaddeus remarked. "Anyone want to purchase anything while we're here? No? Let's proceed, then."

They moved out of the refectory and back toward the seminary building. Thaddeus indicated the dormitory wing as they did so, but could see no reason to inspect it since Cadel wouldn't be using those particular facilities. Their next stop was the library, which was in the basement. Thaddeus decided to take an elevator. Positioned to the right of the seminary's main rear door, the elevators appeared to be constructed entirely of gray metal plates, bolted together. Inside each elevator was one glass indicator panel, and push buttons that looked like rivets in a ship's hull.

"Very modern," said Lanna, casting an appraising eye over the decor.

"They were only installed last year," Thaddeus rejoined, punching a button. The doors closed. After a short, smooth ride, they opened again.

Cadel stepped out into a vast space that smelled of books and hot computers.

He took a deep breath, closing his eyes for a moment. He felt instantly at home.

"We're very proud of our library," said Thaddeus with a sweeping gesture. "Below us are two more floors of stacks. Our catalog is fully online. We subscribe to just about every English-language publication there is, plus a great many foreign-language ones. We have our specialties, of course, but that doesn't mean we don't cover all the subject areas. That's the copying room," he remarked with a nod at the door they were passing. Beyond it, a man in overalls was tinkering with one of at least ten photocopiers. "We *do* have an occasional problem with vandalism," Thaddeus admitted, "though mostly our breakdowns are due to technical faults. We have some extremely advanced and complicated machines in there."

"Uh—I have to make a phone call," Stuart interposed. "Can I use my cell phone down here, or will I have to go upstairs again?"

"You don't have to use a cell phone at all," Thaddeus replied graciously. "Feel free to use one of *our* phones."

Gratified, Stuart took advantage of the offer. Lanna retired into the ladies' room. Thaddeus guided Cadel back to the elevators, promising to return in ten minutes. ("We'll just have a quick look at the stacks," Thaddeus explained.) As they stepped into one of the little steel boxes, he murmured, "It really is an excellent library. The genuine article. The stacks are a high-security area, by the way; certain people aren't allowed in. *You* will be, of course. It's a good place to do your research. Very quiet."

The elevator doors closed. Cadel watched the indicator panel. They descended one floor, two floors. Then the metal doors in front of them slid apart.

Cadel was suddenly propelled into a dimly lit aisle that threaded its way between rows and rows of metal bookshelves. There was a musty smell. It was utterly silent, except for the buzzing and clicking of a faulty fluorescent light.

"We have an interesting collection," Thaddeus continued quietly, leading Cadel off to the left. Their shoes slapped against a bare cement floor. "Some of it, as I said, isn't easily accessible. There's a code you'll need to break if you want to consult any of our more, shall we say, *controversial* texts. Some have to be kept at Yarramundi, in the armory."

All at once he froze and stopped talking. Cadel nearly collided with him. Listening hard, Cadel realized that the heavy silence was being disturbed by a faint, snuffling, shuffling noise.

"Hello?" said Thaddeus. His voice seemed very loud.

No one answered.

He advanced a few more steps, with careful deliberation, peering down a few of the shadowy aisles. Cadel stayed put. The ranks of silent, closed books unnerved him; they seemed to be protecting an ominous secret.

Then something tugged at the corner of Cadel's vision—something dark and swift, like a curtain flapping. He turned his head. The adjacent aisle was wrapped in darkness. But was there a movement—a faint movement—on the floor? A shadow unfolding against more shadows?

"Thaddeus!" he gasped.

"I'm coming," Thaddeus said. A few long strides brought him back to Cadel, who was now huddled against the wall beside the elevator.

"I thought I saw something," Cadel faltered, and Thaddeus frowned. "It wasn't a person. I don't think so, anyway. It was more like a—a—I don't know. Like a snake, or a crocodile . . ."

"If it was a crocodile, I'll have someone's guts for garters," Thaddeus announced crossly. "There's a rule about crocodiles. *And* snakes. And anything else that might be venomous or carnivorous."

Then he pressed the UP button, and an elevator arrived.

TWELVE

From the library, Thaddeus took Cadel and his adoptive parents up to the first floor. Here they went in search of Dr. Vee, the man described by Thaddeus as a "computer whiz." Proceeding down a long corridor, they passed a couple of scorch marks, some evidence of water damage, enough digital and laser-alarm locks to furnish the Pentagon, and many doors bearing the names of teaching staff. Thaddeus knocked at the door closest to the emergency exit, but there was no reply. The name-plate above the peephole was inscribed with the letter V; underneath it, someone had taped a cartoon that showed a packet of cornflakes standing with a suitcase in one hand and a ticket to Alpha Centauri in the other. The words UNIVERSAL CEREAL BUSPORT were written below this drawing.

Cadel laughed.

"Computer joke," he explained to Stuart.

Thaddeus sighed. "No one home," he said. Continuing the search, he led them up a step, around a corner, and through a stairwell, until he came to the entrance of what he called Hardware Heaven. A pair of swinging doors opened into a wide, white room full of computer equipment.

Cadel sucked in his breath. "Fantastic!" he exclaimed.

Two people were at work in the room, hunched over keyboards. One was the pasty youth from the canteen; he had brought a can of Coke back with him. The other was a fat man in a faded shirt. He had quite a lot of lank, gray hair flopping over his forehead; his face was mottled;

there was a sty in one of his little muddy-green eyes; and he smelled strongly of eucalyptus oil. Lined up on the desk in front of him were a box of aloe vera tissues, a bottle of nasal spray, a jar of Vicks VapoRub, and some pills in a plastic card.

He kept sniffing and blinking as Thaddeus introduced him to the Piggotts.

"This is Dr. Vee," Thaddeus informed them. "We're lucky to find him here—he does a lot of consulting work."

"Hello," said Lanna.

"Pleased to meet you," said Stuart.

Dr. Vee shook hands with them, giggling nervously. Then he turned to Cadel.

"Is this the one?" he asked.

"This is the one," said Thaddeus.

Another giggle. Mr. and Mrs. Piggott glanced at each other. Cadel didn't know what to make of this fat, unhealthy-looking man. He had fingers like sausages. Could he really be a computer whiz?

"So you're the baby hacker?" said Dr. Vee, blinking furiously at Cadel. "Thaddeus told me about you."

Cadel didn't know how to reply.

"I do a lot of firewall customization," Dr. Vee went on. "Bet you've never got through one of mine."

"That depends," Cadel retorted, "on which ones they are."

"Oh, I usually concentrate on port and protocol filters. I've done some neat little stateful inspection devices—viruses are my specialty."

"Oh," said Cadel.

"You weren't writing viruses, though, were you?"

"No," Cadel admitted, conscious of Mr. and Mrs. Piggott hovering at the edge of his vision. "Mostly I was doing application back doors, remote log-ins, tracking down personal keys, information gathering. No bombs or anything. No viruses."

"Right. Hmm." Dr. Vee coughed and reached for a tissue. "Interesting thing to study, viruses. That's where the money is. Stuff like denial-of-service attacks—they're all sewn up now. There's hardly a firewall that can't auto-apply blocking. But with viruses, it's a constant battle." Dr. Vee giggled again. "You should try to break the Axis firewall sometime. No one's ever done it. Our file-transfer protocols around here are like Fort Knox."

"Really?" said Cadel.

"Just warning you in advance." Dr. Vee blew his nose. "Take a tip from Richard over there. He tried to design a cookie-hopping application—spent months on it. Waste of time. Work down the drain. Now he's doing something useful, trying to write an encryption technology bug."

Cadel looked with interest at the pasty, chinless, flaxen-haired youth with the can of Coke. Then he focused his attention on Dr. Vee. Somewhere behind that heavy, moist, giggling facade, Cadel sensed, was an intellect of sly and formidable power. He was half repelled, half fascinated by it.

"I had a look at your course outline," he said. "I'm interested in hardware design, but you seem to be concentrating on software."

Dr. Vee blinked at him. "We're very flexible," he answered. "You can concentrate on whatever you like, as long as it's not the Axis firewall."

"You can *help* me with hardware design?"

Dr. Vee's face was suddenly serious. He regarded Cadel with narrowed eyes.

"Depends what you're interested in," he wheezed.

"Molecular electronics. DNA-directed assembly. That kind of thing."

Once more Dr. Vee giggled. "Nanoboy!" he crowed. "Oh, I'll be in on that! Big-time!"

"I'm also trying to develop a predictive software program," Cadel continued, "but it's tricky. Organizing the data—there's so much . . ."

"You need more flash memory?"

"Maybe."

"We'll take a look at it."

"Assuming Cadel decides in our favor," Thaddeus observed, and Dr. Vee shrugged. Abruptly, almost rudely, he twirled his chair back to face his computer monitor again. His big, fat fingers began to flutter with surprising delicacy over his keyboard. *Click, click, click.*

Thaddeus retreated, beckoning to the Piggotts.

"We might duck up to the labs," he said softly when they had exited through the swinging doors. "Then down to ground level, and that's the lot."

"Strange sort of bloke," Stuart remarked, glancing back at Hardware Heaven. "Can't say I took to him."

"Was he sick?" Lanna asked.

"Oh, he's always sick," Thaddeus rejoined, with a wave of his hand. "It's a permanent condition with him. Doesn't affect his work, though."

"I didn't think much of him," said Stuart. "What did you think, Cadel?"

"I think he must be pretty good," Cadel replied. And since no one else wanted to express an opinion, Thaddeus headed for the labs on the second floor. Here the Piggotts were allowed to peer through glass windows at rooms full of steel-topped benches and esoteric equipment. Cadel recognized an atomic-force microscope.

Very few people were about, and most of the rooms shown to Cadel were empty.

"A few graduate students," Thaddeus explained. He grimaced as they hit a very nasty smell, which was hovering around one of the closed doors marked with a HAZMAT (hazardous material) sign. Cadel had noticed a lot of closed doors. "Dear me," said Thaddeus. "*Someone's* been busy. I have to admit I don't come up here, as a rule—too many noisome odors."

"So what do they do here?" Lanna asked faintly, flapping her plane ticket in front of her face.

"Microbiology. Some biometrics. A little genetic research. Ah." Rounding a corner, Thaddeus spotted a tall, slim man in a lab coat, who was punching his pass code into a digital lock. "Just the person I was looking for. Terry! Come and introduce yourself! Terry is in charge here," Thaddeus revealed. "He's better placed than I am to explain what goes on."

Terry was quite young. He wore blue jeans under his lab coat, and his long, brown hair hung in a ponytail down his back. He had an olive complexion, and his teeth were very white; when he smiled, his eyes crinkled pleasantly at the corners. Lanna was obviously charmed by him, especially when he addressed her in a rough-edged baritone, and Stuart was pleased when Terry confessed that he had recently read about Stuart's firm in the papers.

Cadel decided that his adoptive parents must have missed the young scientist's hands. They were long and fine-boned, but covered in scratches, nicks, and Band-Aids. There was something dark under two of the fingernails, and a reddish smear on one thumb.

Terry's hands didn't seem to match the rest of him.

"Stuart and Lanna would like to know what goes on here," Thaddeus informed his colleague, who immediately launched into a rambling description of his department's activities, using lots of words like *erythrocytes* and *bacteriorhodopsin*. Naturally, Mr. and Mrs. Piggott were unable to follow him and so stood with glazed expressions, trying to be polite. Cadel couldn't follow Terry, either, but not because he couldn't understand the words being used. The words were perfectly clear to Cadel—they were just being put together in sequences that made no sense.

Catching the scientist's eye, Cadel saw him wink and realized what was happening. Terry didn't want Mr. and Mrs. Piggott to know what was *really* going on in the labs.

"Right," said Thaddeus, after Terry had finally finished. "So would you like to have a quick look at one of the lecture rooms before you leave? Stuart? Lanna?"

"Oh—uh—yes," said Mr. Piggott.

"Thank you *so* much," said his wife, addressing Terry, who flashed a big, white grin at her. Then he saluted Thaddeus, muttered a shy farewell, and loped off down the corridor, his ponytail swinging.

Lanna's gaze lingered on his receding back.

"Nice bloke," Stuart remarked absently, pulling a handkerchief from his front pocket. He used it to mop his sweaty brow. "One more stop, did you say?"

"One more," Thaddeus agreed. Again they all crowded into an elevator and were carried to the ground floor, where Thaddeus showed them a seminar room, a lecture room, and his own office. The seminar room was small and beige, with a stack of plastic chairs. The lecture room had been fitted out at least a hundred years before with rows of wooden benches, an elaborately carved lectern, and huge, dangling lights.

Thaddeus's office was very handsome. Through its Gothic window you could see a stretch of green lawn and a jacaranda tree. On either side of this refreshing view hung heavy velvet curtains. There was a Persian carpet on the floor, and a large, mahogany desk on top of it. Thaddeus sat behind the desk in a leather-upholstered wing chair, while the Piggotts faced him, each perched on a straight-backed chair of English oak. The carvings on these ancient pieces of furniture dug into their backs, making them shift and squirm.

"So." Thaddeus addressed Stuart and Lanna. "You've seen enough now?"

"Oh yes."

"Yes."

"What about you, Cadel?" Thaddeus's eyes were keen under drooping lids. He pressed his fingertips together. "Is there anything else you'd like to ask me?"

"No."

"Where's the money coming from?" Stuart demanded suddenly. "There's obviously a lot of it knocking around."

"We have some private benefactors," said Thaddeus. "They're listed here." He pushed a small pile of literature across his desk. "If you can't find what you want to know in here, you can always give me a call."

Stuart grunted and seized the proffered booklets. Lanna rose. She tapped her gold watch with one crimson fingernail.

"I'm so sorry, Doctor, but my flight leaves in eighty minutes."

"Of course. I understand."

"It was very interesting. Thank you."

"My pleasure."

"Maybe we can call Cadel a taxi? To take him home? Rather than dragging him all the way to the airport."

"An excellent idea," said Thaddeus, lifting the receiver of his telephone. A taxi was summoned. Later, after the Piggotts had left, Thaddeus took Cadel out to the gates of the Axis Institute, where they waited together for Cadel's taxi.

"What do you think?" Thaddeus inquired, laying a hand on Cadel's shoulder. "Can you make use of this place? Dr. Darkkon would like to think so. But it's entirely your choice."

Cadel craned his neck to look back at the towering seminary, with its bristling turrets.

"He's paying for *all* of it? Everything?"

"Everything," Thaddeus replied. "It's part of his plan to undermine the society of morons and procrastinators in which we're presently forced to live. If things go on as they are, Cadel, we're heading for disaster. The entire ecosystem is going to collapse, for one thing. We need a person in charge with a few brains. Someone who can make informed decisions and have them carried out by specially trained cadres of operatives." Thaddeus squeezed Cadel's shoulder. "So what about it?" he inquired. "Do you want to give it a try? You'll find it very invigorating, I guarantee you that. A really thorough preparation for life."

Cadel reflected on what he had seen. In front of him, a traffic jam was inching along; the hot air was laden with exhaust fumes, and horns honked irritably. On the other side of the road was a furniture warehouse, only partially painted, next to a dentist's office with a FOR SALE sign in the window.

Behind him, the stately old seminary building stood surrounded by closely cropped lawn. A sprinkler sprayed a glittering arc of water across a bed of glossy azaleas. It was very calm. Very quiet. It was like another world.

It *was* another world.

Cadel peered up at Thaddeus, whose gray hair was swept back from his forehead like a lion's mane.

He was waiting patiently.

"All right," said Cadel. "I'll give it a try."

"Excellent."

"As long as you explain it to me," Cadel went on. "I don't quite understand, you see, what everyone's supposed to be doing."

"All will be explained, Cadel." This time, Thaddeus patted Cadel's shoulder before releasing it. "All will be explained, I assure you."

THIRTEEN

At his next session with Thaddeus, Cadel found out more about the Axis Institute. Dr. Darkkon was only too pleased to answer all of his son's questions.

"Oh yes. Dr. Vee. We call him the Virus." Dr. Darkkon's spectacles had been confiscated by suspicious warders who had come to realize that he could see perfectly well without them, so he was now speaking into a toilet bowl. This piece of plumbing, which stood stark and gleaming in the corner of his cell, had been modified with a transmitter and a screen of thin plastic that floated on top of the water. Its only drawback lay in the fact that Dr. Darkkon now had to feign illness all the time. "The Virus is extremely talented," he croaked, and pretended to retch before continuing. "It's quite true—he *does* design customized firewalls. On his days off, he also creates methods for breaking through the same firewalls. That's the way he keeps himself in business."

"Then why does he teach at the institute?" Cadel queried.

"Because he can do whatever he likes," Dr. Darkkon explained, "without having thickheads continually snooping and interfering. He likes the challenge, too. He likes the sort of minds we attract. And of course we pay well. *Very* well."

Cadel pondered this. After a while, he said, "What about that Brendan guy? Why is he at the institute?"

"Because no one else will hire him," Dr. Darkkon revealed. "He puts people off, being autistic. People find him hard to deal with. Personally, I don't care *what* he says to the students. It's no skin off my nose."

"Brendan doesn't understand why he can't move numbers around at will," Thaddeus interjected. "For him, tax laws are simply obstacles to be surmounted. He has no comprehension of rules at all. Thinks they're illogical. He just wants to get on with things."

"And Art?" said Cadel. "What does he do?"

Dr. Darkkon coughed into the screen for a few seconds, his shoulders heaving. It wasn't a pretty sight.

"Art's our forgery lecturer," he advised Cadel. "Art's very good, but not good enough to feed his hunger for the finer things in life, which is why he makes extra money by doing a bit of teaching for Axis. Carla's our contagion expert. She has a difficult personality, and some of her habits worry people so much that she can't get a job anywhere else. She's interested in the breakdown of dead tissue—she likes to plaster her office with pictures of decomposing corpses. In many ways she's not entirely *stable* . . ."

"You'll hear about her vial," Thaddeus broke in. "She carries a vial around in her pocket. It's supposed to contain some sort of lethal microorganism that she's been tinkering with. She likes the feeling it gives her, having access to that kind of power."

"So don't push her against a wall, for god's sake," said Dr. Darkkon. "Terry is a professor of our School of Organic Distortion. He has the kind of tastes you can't indulge in a normal university environment."

"He's had some trouble with the RSPCA," Thaddeus added, and Cadel suddenly recalled the red smear on Terry's thumb.

"A lot of our staff are being blackmailed," Dr. Darkkon continued cheerfully. "Deakin's one of them—Barry Deakin. On campus, he calls himself Dr. Deal. There are a few little skeletons in *his* closet, so I've been able to force him to work for us. Plus, he likes all our young female students at the institute. You'll meet Barry—he'll be teaching you law."

"Law?" said Cadel.

"It's part of the introductory program. You can't get around the law unless you know what it is." Dr. Darkkon retched again, halfheartedly. "Who else? Adolf's being blackmailed, too—he teaches guerrilla tactics. People call him the Führer. The other School of Destruction staff tend to be aging mercenaries who don't want to go traveling all over the world to earn their living in swamps and deserts. Luther Lasco's one of them. He was a hired assassin. His specialty is poisoning. He's a professor of the school."

"You won't have much to do with him," Thaddeus told Cadel firmly.

"Or with Tracey Lane," said Dr. Darkkon. "She's a former television newsreader, but she got too old. Can't find another job for the same money we pay her. She teaches misinformation."

"Otherwise known as media studies," Thaddeus supplied.

"Who else will be teaching him, Thad? Max, of course."

"The Maestro. Yes."

"Max teaches pure evil. He's got his own reasons for working at the institute. Philosophical reasons." Dr. Darkkon grinned. "Seems like he's trying to rationalize all the questionable things he's done in his life."

"And Alias, of course, is looking for recognition," Thaddeus murmured, whereupon Dr. Darkkon laughed out loud. He quickly tried to disguise this laugh with a fit of fake coughing. "Alias is our teacher of disguise," he wheezed. "He's as slippery as an eel, but he does like to think his talents are appreciated."

"We're helping to hide him from the CIA," said Thaddeus.

"And that's about all, isn't it, Thad? No one else that Cadel will be dealing with?"

"The staff find Axis enriching," Thaddeus assured Cadel. "The students certainly keep them on their toes, and we believe in *very* strict discipline—as you'll discover. The faculty appreciates our discipline code. Naturally, they all have their own agendas, but nothing we can't deal with."

"Choose your tools," Dr. Darkkon stressed. "That's the secret, Cadel. *Choose your tools wisely.*"

Cadel nodded. He was a little overwhelmed, though he knew it wouldn't take him long to process all this information. Sure enough, he had soon composed in his mind a three-dimensional model of the institute's personnel structure. There were a lot of gaps, but he felt reasonably satisfied with it.

And when the first semester started, he was quickly able to fill many of the larger holes.

Mr. and Mrs. Piggott had agreed with Cadel's decision to enroll at the institute. Stuart wasn't entirely happy with what he had seen, but didn't care enough to make trouble. He conceded, in any case, that Cadel was young enough to make a few mistakes without suffering too much for it. So Cadel was enrolled. His fees were paid. And in early February, just three months before his fourteenth birthday, he arrived at the Axis Institute with a backpack slung over his shoulder, ready to begin his studies.

He had been told to report to lecture-room one for his introductory session. It was a drizzly day. Running through the front gate, shielding himself from the rain with his course handbook, he realized with a start that the institute's parking lot was three-quarters full; even on such a wet morning, there were people scurrying about like ants. Getting into the seminary building was quite a challenge, but Cadel was well prepared. He had all the necessary cards and keys and had been given detailed instructions about the correct sequence in which they should be used. The process could take up to three minutes, or even longer if you made a mistake.

Upon entering, Cadel encountered a loose crowd of people (most of them quite young) who were waiting to pass through the security scanner just inside the front door. A few were talking, but most slouched against the walls, silent and watchful. Cadel joined them. Patiently, he allowed his person and his luggage to be scanned for guns, explosives, and electronic listening devices. Then he headed for lecture-room one, which he had already inspected with Thaddeus. The door was closed. He tried the handle, without success.

Locked, he thought.

"Who are *you?*" a voice demanded.

Cadel turned. The young man standing beside him was of medium height, but well-muscled, with a thick neck and close-cut fair hair. His complexion was reddish, as if he had spent too much time in the sun. He had a burn scar on one hand.

"Who are *you?*" this person repeated, looming over Cadel in a threatening manner. "Get the hell out. You shouldn't be here."

"Yes I should," Cadel replied.

"Piss off, ankle-biter!"

"I'm enrolled," said Cadel, standing his ground. His gaze swept the faces of a converging crowd, but not one of them looked concerned. They were either bored, amused, or impatient. "My name is Cadel Darkkon, and I'm enrolled in the School of Deception."

A hush fell. All eyes turned toward him. At last a pale, slim, wild-eyed young man with lots of curly black hair and a straggling goatee broke the silence.

"Darkkon?" he said. "As in *Phineas* Darkkon?"

"That's right," Cadel rejoined. Thaddeus had enrolled him as Cadel Darkkon for his own protection. "Normally," Thaddeus had remarked, "the son of a university's founder would have a lot of trouble with the rest of the student body, but this won't happen in your case. Everyone's familiar with Dr. Darkkon's reputation."

Surrounded by these dead-eyed, gum-chewing, oddly dressed undergraduates, Cadel decided that Thaddeus had been right. He *did* need protection.

"Phineas Darkkon is my father," he added, to ensure that he was not misunderstood. The red-faced bully immediately edged away.

"You're kidding," said one of the two blond girls hovering near him. They were clearly identical twins: Both were tanned, pretty, and dressed in skimpy clothes, with their golden hair twisted up into matching ponytails. "You're kidding, right?"

"Nope."

"The guy who started this place? You're his *son?*"

"Yes."

Both girls rolled their eyes at each other. Then the one who hadn't yet spoken said, in a bright voice, "We're Gemini. I'm Jem, and this is Ni."

"Pleased to meet you, Cadel," said Ni.

"I guess you're really smart, huh? Like your dad. I guess that's why you're here so young."

They wriggled forward, all gleaming teeth and smooth brown skin. They smelled nice. Shyly, Cadel shook their manicured hands.

"Hi," he mumbled.

"You're cute," Jem trilled. "He's cute, isn't he, Ni?"

"He sure is." Ni ruffled Cadel's curls. "He's prettier than *you* are."

"Oh!" Jem gave her sister a playful slap. "You bitch!"

"It's nice to see we're not the only good-looking ones around here."

"What are you studying, sweetie?"

Jem was addressing Cadel. He was slightly confused; these two bouncy, beautiful girls, with their shiny lipstick and piercing voices, weren't what he had expected. Thaddeus had given him a quick description of every student in the first-year intake. Jemima and Niobe, Cadel recalled, were a pair of troublemakers with ESP potential. Since the age of nine, they had been robbing stores by means of a scam that they had refined and perfected. Just before closing time, they would choose a shop with only one attendant—preferably male. Jem would go in and plead to use the toilet. Ni, who was identically dressed, would then wait until the attendant wasn't looking, sneak into the shop, thank him for allowing her to empty her bladder, and depart again, very noisily. When the attendant had left and the shop was locked up, Jem (who had been hiding) would emerge and take what she wanted before rejoining her twin.

Mostly this method worked, though sometimes it didn't. The girls were caught several times without suffering any serious consequences because of their youth. Finally, Thaddeus, as a qualified psychologist specializing in troubled teenagers, was asked to review their case.

He found them fascinating, simply because they seemed to have mysterious powers of communication.

"It's the sort of instinct that can't be coincidental," Thaddeus had explained to Cadel. "I ran some tests. There was an extra level of EEG slow waves, and several other features, not all of them neurological. Your father and I thought that the twins might respond well to training."

Cadel had expected a pair of mystic-looking figures wearing Celtic symbols and hippy clothes. He had expected gypsy earrings and haunted eyes and whispering voices. He hadn't expected a couple of blond bombshells in tank tops.

"I'm studying computers," he said. "Computers and embezzlement."

"Oooooh," Jem crooned. "I knew he was clever. We're doing— what are we doing, Ni?"

"Channeling. A lot of channeling. Mind-power stuff."

"You mean you're pyrogenic?" the bully exclaimed, and his face turned an even deeper shade of red as the two girls turned their heads, in perfect unison, to look at him.

"Say what?" Jem drawled.

"*I'm* pyrogenic. I do channeling, too. I'm in your channeling class." The bully adopted a slight swagger. "You can call me the Bludgeon."

The twins glanced at each other, then burst into a fit of giggles.

"The *Bludger*?" Jem squeaked.

"The *Bludgeon*, not the Bludger. A force to be reckoned with." The bully sounded cross. "It's time to leave your old name behind. Your old self. This is a *metamorphosis*."

"You mean we afta change our names?" a worried voice suddenly piped up. It came from the transmission filter of a young man in a full-length, airtight suit attached to a tangle of breathing apparatus—a suit like those commonly worn by technicians dealing with hazardous materials. "*I* didn't change me name," he fretted, his voice muffled and distorted by the clear plastic mask he wore. "Were we supposed to?"

"No, we weren't," replied the pale, curly-haired young man. "My name is Abraham Coggins and it's *staying* Abraham Coggins. At least until I have a police record."

"Are you pyrogenic?" the Bludgeon inquired.

"No. I'm a microbiology student."

"Then butt out."

Cadel looked at Abraham Coggins with interest. According to Thaddeus, Abraham was a graduate of medicine who was paying money to attend the Axis Institute because he was obsessed with the idea of creating a race of vampires. He had a theory about how it might be done, and Terry had agreed to work with him.

"But—but do we really *want* vampires?" Cadel had stammered on being informed of this fact, whereupon Thaddeus had placed a comforting hand on his shoulder.

"We're not going to get vampires," he'd said. "It's all a mad dream. But the extra money will be useful. Most of our students are on scholarships—Dr. Darkkon pretty much pays their way. It's good to have a few fee-paying students to ease the load."

So that's Abraham Coggins, Cadel thought, *and if this bully here is pyrogenic, he must be Clive Slaughter.* Clive had been identified, by scouts of Dr. Darkkon, as someone with pyrogenic powers. He had the classic profile of an accidental arsonist, though he came from a comfortable family background. Dr. Darkkon wished to help him isolate and refine his powers, until he could be transformed into something resembling the superheroes in a Marvel comic. It was a long shot, Dr. Darkkon had said, but it was worth a try.

Cadel realized that if the bully was Clive, and the curly-haired guy was Abraham, then the youth in the protective suit must be Gazo Kovacs. Gazo was an interesting case. He had lived on the streets for most of his life, largely because he suffered from a unique condition. When stressed, he exuded an appalling stench—the kind that could fell a man at ten paces. Even at a greater distance, it could make people dizzy. For this reason he had been shunned and had led a very lonely life until discovered by Dr. Darkkon's agents. Cadel's father was interested in Gazo. He felt that Gazo might have a special, supergenetic power. He wanted to explore this possibility and had flown the friendless youth all the way from England for that purpose.

Gazo was boarding at the institute. He had to wear an airtight suit for the protection of other people. It was important that there should be no accidents at moments of high stress—during exams, for instance. Only when Gazo was alone, in his single-bed room, was he allowed to remove his suffocating outer garments and move about freely.

According to Thaddeus, Gazo regarded this restriction as a small price to pay for food, lodgings, and friendly encouragement.

"He's not very bright," Thaddeus had admitted to Cadel, "but he might be worth the money. We'll see."

Gazo, Clive, Abraham, Jemima, and Niobe. Cadel surveyed them all, committing their faces to memory, before turning his attention to the remaining students clustered around the door of lecture-room one. There were only two: a man and a woman. The woman was fat and middle-aged. She wore a black T-shirt over drab tracksuit pants. Her face was puffy and sullen beneath stray locks of fine, lank hair. This, Cadel decided, must be Doris Deauville, the only other woman in Cadel's year.

"A poisoner," Thaddeus had recounted. "Another fee-paying student. She's had a bit of success poisoning individuals in the past, and now she's interested in doing it on a wider scale. That's why she wants to study contagion, with Carla."

Cadel had frowned.

"Will I—will I have to talk to her much?" he'd queried, whereupon Thaddeus had shaken his head.

"I doubt it. She's a fairly solitary sort of person. Just make sure you don't eat anything she's baked." And he had laughed.

Looking at Doris, Cadel didn't feel like laughing. On the contrary, his heart sank. Gazo and the twins interested him. Abraham was someone he almost felt sorry for. Clive was obviously of no account. But Doris? There was something creepy about Doris. Perhaps it was the faintly damp smell that hung about her. Perhaps it was the dullness of her small, gray eyes, which were as expressionless as river pebbles.

Whatever it was, she repelled him.

The last of the year's intake—the person standing beside Doris— was a Japanese man who spoke hardly any English. Another fee-paying student, he was enrolled in the School of Destruction and would be boarding at the institute. His name was Kunio Sumita. He wore some kind of military uniform.

"All right, people!" Thaddeus's sharp tones sliced through the air like a knife, just as Clive was about to say something else about the need for a new name. *"Let's have a bit of quiet!* Thank you."

Thaddeus had emerged from his office, which was just down the hall. He was dressed in his usual baggy trousers and tweedy jacket, with spectacles perched on the end of his nose, but his lofty stature and piercing gaze managed to impress everyone. Even the twins shut up.

"Good morning," he said. "Most of you know me. For those who don't, I'm Professor Thaddeus Roth, and I pretty much fill the role of chancellor around here. Which is to say, I'm in charge." Students fell back as he headed for the door of lecture-room one. Upon reaching it, he removed a bunch of keys from his pocket and proceeded to use them, one by one, until every lock on the door had been released. Then he pushed open the door and stepped aside.

"In you go," he commanded, smiling to expose his long canine teeth. "Time to make a difference."

FOURTEEN

"As you already know," Thaddeus announced when everyone was seated inside the lecture room, "this institute was founded by Dr. Phineas Darkkon, five years ago, because he had a vision. He wanted to train an army of people with special skills and powers who could transform the world. Now, we all know that the world doesn't work. In fact, some of you are only too aware of this fact." Thaddeus glanced at Gazo for a moment, then at Cadel. "The power structures we see around us are entrenched," he continued, "and they are full of narrow-minded people with unremarkable genes. As a result, the human race is heading down a path that will almost certainly lead to its extinction, unless something is done pretty quickly. It is Dr. Darkkon's belief that if we harness and nurture mankind's more hidden talents, then we might save ourselves. In the process, we might also find ourselves with a two-tier society of genetically superior overlords and a genetically inferior underclass. If so, then it's the price we'll have to pay for survival. Let me just give you some statistics, in case you're in any doubt about the state of the world right now."

There was a pause as Thaddeus adjusted his glasses. Cadel, who had heard all this several times before, was more interested in the reaction of those around him. Gazo's face was hard to see through his mask, but his posture was attentive. Doris's expression was blank. Clive was frowning, and Abraham was doodling. Jem and Ni—the only students who were actually sitting together—fidgeted uncontrollably. They were using a pair of very silly pens, with multicolored spirals and tufts of feathers and bits that lit up when pressure was applied to the nibs.

All at once the door opened, and everyone—including Thaddeus—looked over to see who was coming in.

"Ah," said Thaddeus. He nodded at the newcomer, a short, sleek, plump man in a pin-striped suit, who wore a gold ring on the little finger of his left hand. "Max. Good. Come in."

"Thaddeus," Max replied. "Mind if I bring my boys?"

"Not at all."

Max swiveled and jerked his head. In response, two more men entered the room. They were very large. Though they were also dressed in suits, they would have looked more comfortable in leather jackets and studded belts. Both had huge hands, menacing glowers, and scars all over their shaven heads.

They positioned themselves behind the lectern, one on either side. Cadel decided that they must be bodyguards.

"Some of you," Thaddeus informed the class, "might have difficulty with these new concepts I've mentioned. Your minds will have been programmed in certain ways, and you may find it hard to reconfigure them. To help you, let me introduce a man we like to call the Maestro, who has made it his specialty to examine that loaded word *evil*. But before he does, I want to point out one thing. It's quite simple. You've heard it before: *No pain, no gain*." Thaddeus's gaze swept the room. "No pain, no gain," he repeated. "It's something we've learned throughout history. It's something we know in our gut. Read the Bible—Book of Revelations. Before the coming of Christ, we're supposed to be getting war, famine, disease, and death. Read Karl Marx. Before the new world order will come the revolution. There can be no gain without pain. So if you're having any niggling doubts, just remember that. You can't make an omelette without breaking eggs. Okay." He stepped down from the lectern, suddenly. "Over to you, Maestro."

Max inclined his head. He had large, dark, melancholy eyes and slicked-back hair. As Thaddeus seated himself on one of the wooden benches, Max began to address the class in a rather high voice that was stamped with a New Jersey accent.

"Tank you, Dr. Roth," he said, and put on a pair of reading glasses before removing a small stack of cards from his breast pocket. These he placed on the lectern in front of him, referring to them occasionally during his speech. "I won't beat around de bush, ladies and gents. Next time I see you, we'll have more time to concentrate on aspects of morality, but right now I wanna talk about an old saying, namely: Hell is udder people."

He paused for an instant. Niobe tittered. The two bodyguards shifted from foot to foot.

"If hell is udder people," the Maestro went on, "den so is evil. I'm convinced of dis fact. If you look up *evil* in any dictionary, you'll find it means everyting you'd expect it to mean: harmful, wrong, malicious— you name it. And of course it's a woid used by just about everyone when describing udder people. You never hear nobody call *himself* evil. Oh, no. Misguided, maybe. Mistaken. Lazy. Stoopid. Even cruel. But not evil. So what if you toss a cigarette butt out of a car window during a fire ban? It might make you careless, but it don't make you *evil*. So what if you kill a nest fulla ants? Does it make you evil? Society don't tink so. It don't call you evil if you kill a million fish wid an oil leak from a tanker. Greedy, but not evil. If you went and shot fifty horses in a stable, *den* maybe you'd be evil. Because society loves horses, and it couldn't care less about ants or krill."

The Maestro cleared his throat.

"*Evil* is just a woid," he declared, "used by society to condemn de actions of people it don't like. Evil is the opposite of what *society* calls good. Some people might call bullfights evil, but de Spanish don't. Some people call war evil, but you don't see it going outta fashion. De concept of evil is as flexible as a hunka clay. You can fashion it into practically any shape you want. So while some people might call dis institution evil, if dey ever found out about it"—he flashed a closed-mouth smile at Thaddeus, a smile that didn't reach his eyes—"let's not forget what de real problem is. People like dat are using de woid because dey're scared. Because Dr. Darkkon's ideas will rob 'em of any power. What dose people call evil is a respected philosophy of life known as survival of the fittest."

At this point, the door opened again. Alerted by a cool gust of air, as well as by the movement of heads and the creaking of seats, Max peered over his shoulder. In the doorway stood a middle-aged man with long, gray hair tied back in a ponytail. He had a seamed face, a casual slouch, and an earring in one ear. He wore very old clothes.

One of the bodyguards, Cadel noticed, had stuck his hand into his jacket. But he withdrew it when the Maestro frowned at him.

"Come in, Luther," said Thaddeus.

Luther closed the door. He slipped into a seat near Thaddeus, while the Maestro waited, watching him with mournful eyes that contained not one spark of animation or enthusiasm. Not until Luther was properly settled did the Maestro proceed.

"I want you to tink about dis woid, dis concept, *evil*," he said. "I want you to reflect on de idea of right and wrong. How much is *really* wrong? Is it *wrong* to lie, or cheat, or steal? Society says it is. But what if a lie does no harm? What if a cheater is a successful and benevolent businessman? What if a diamond-studded collar on some guy's dog is stolen by a starving street kid? My friends, it will be my job, over de next few months, to try and answer dese questions—or at least to get you to ask 'em."

Cadel, who had certainly never asked them, wondered why not. It was probably because of Thaddeus. Thaddeus had never left him any room for doubt. Thaddeus was the one who always asked—and answered—such questions for him. Thaddeus had always known what was right for Cadel.

As the Maestro wound up his speech, Cadel's attention wandered. He became interested in one of the bodyguards. Was he wearing false teeth?

"You need to free up your minds," Max finished. "You need to re-member your goals. And if you do, the woild will be a better place. At least in de long run." He dipped his chin, and looked out at his audi-ence over the top of his glasses. "We'll be reexamining dat loaded term *better*, too," he added, and Thaddeus chuckled.

"Thank you, Maestro," he said, rising. The two bodyguards stepped forward to join Max, who surrendered the lectern to Luther with an abrupt nod. Thaddeus lifted a hand as the Maestro made his way out, one bodyguard behind him, one in front. They seemed to cast a pall over the whole room. Only when they had vanished, and the door had banged shut, did the atmosphere lighten.

People began to move again, stretching and whispering. One of the twins giggled. Thaddeus faced the class.

"I hope that was clear enough," he said. "Anyone still in trouble can sort things out with the Maestro during the series of lectures he plans to give you. And now, to finish off, let me introduce Luther Lasco, pro-fessor of the School of Destruction. He's going to give you his first talk on the consequences that you might expect if you're stupid enough to blab about Axis. Professor?"

Luther acknowledged Thaddeus's words with a twitch of his lips. His face and body were oddly mismatched. While he had a shambling gait, and limbs that appeared almost jointless, and clothes that sagged and flopped, his face was as stiff and hard as flint. When he spoke, his voice was hoarse. His accent was difficult to place. Was it a New Zea-land accent? Cadel wondered. Canadian? Irish?

Luther didn't bother to mount the lectern. He simply stood up and swung around to confront the class, his hands buried deep in his pockets.

"This institution has been in existence for five years," he rasped. "It survives because its true purpose remains a secret. You were all given precise instructions about what you should say to anyone not involved with Axis. Should you fail to carry out those instructions, the penalties will be harsh. *Very* harsh. And if you think they don't apply to you, think again. They apply to *everybody*."

He spoke almost carelessly, as if reciting something that was a bit of a bore, and the effect was chilling. All movement in the room ceased.

"We've had people over the years who have thought they could get away with breaking the rules," Luther pointed out. "Over the next few weeks, I'm going to tell you about them, and about what happened to them. Case studies. My first case study involves a guy called Titus."

Cadel didn't really want to hear about Titus. While Luther described how Titus had been caught boasting about the institute to one of his former gang buddies—and had become a "missing person," as a consequence—Cadel watched the other people in the room. The twins were looking sulky. Abraham Coggins had sunk low into his seat, as if trying to make himself small. Kunio was nodding. The Bludgeon was chewing gum, very slowly, like a cow.

Thaddeus appeared to be examining his fingernails.

". . . because to make a problem go away, you have to be well organized," Luther continued. "Planning is the essence of all success. Without planning, you create more problems than you solve. Any questions?"

Cadel blinked. He could feel the surprise of those around him.

"Well?" said Luther, impatiently. "Are there any questions?"

Silence. People tried not to catch his eye.

"All right, then. Since you haven't got any questions for me, I've got one for you," Luther growled, folding his arms. "What happened to Titus? Can anyone tell me? *Anyone?*"

There was a pause. It was at least ten seconds before the Bludgeon raised his hand and replied.

"Uh—you made him disappear?"

"Wrong," snapped Luther, and the Bludgeon turned red.

"But you just told us!" he spluttered.

"Titus is alive and well and working on a South American container ship," Luther interposed. "We've got proof that he is. No one else has got proof that he *isn't*. You get my point? Hmm?"

His gaze traveled from face to face. One by one the class nodded, solemnly.

"Anything else you've heard, it's a rumor. No one can even prove that he was ever *here*. That's the way I work, and it's the way I expect *you* to work." Luther cracked an unexpected half smile, which broke up the planes of his jaw like a chisel. "There's a rule around here: *No killing on campus*," he said. "Well, that holds as long as you can't prove that it didn't happen. Sloppy assassinations cause us a lot of trouble. They're as bad as shooting your mouth off. Smart assassinations— they're called accidents. And we all know that accidents happen. It's a part of life."

There was a subtle shifting of bottoms on seats.

"But let me warn you," Luther added, his smile fading, his eyes narrowing. "We're not stupid. We've seen it all. So don't think you're going to pull it off, whatever it is, because you won't. You might fool the police, but you won't fool us. Not ever. You'll come to realize the truth of what I'm saying this semester, when I tell you what happened to the other punks who thought they were smarter than the faculty."

Without warning, he flung himself onto a bench. Cadel realized, with a start, that he had finished. Thaddeus stood up. He smiled benignly at his colleague.

"Thank you, Professor," he beamed. "Most illuminating. And may I add, ladies and gentlemen, on the subject of sloppy work, that while cheating and lying are encouraged at the institute, there is no place here for incompetent cheats or transparent lies. If we should *detect* anyone cheating or lying, or breaking into staff offices, there'll be hell to pay. Am I right, Luther?"

"Absolutely," Luther replied.

"And that's all I have to say at this time *except*"—Thaddeus raised his voice above the surge of chatter and shuffling of feet that greeted his dismissal—"*except* this. Quiet, please! Quiet! There's one more thing!"

The noise eased slightly. Thaddeus extended his hand, pointing at Cadel. "Can everyone see this lad over here?"

Everyone could, though Cadel shrank back in alarm. He didn't want to be singled out.

"This lad here is Cadel Darkkon," Thaddeus revealed. "He is Dr. Darkkon's son. Of course we don't want this fact to be generally known in the wider community, so if anyone tries to spread the news, you can guess what will happen." He wagged a finger at the class, almost playfully. "What's more, while you can compete as fiercely as you like *among yourselves,* Cadel is off-limits. Do I make myself clear?"

A few grunts were the only response.

"Do I make myself clear?"

His question was so sharp, so abrupt, that it was like a whiplash—like a slap in the face. It made everybody jump.

"Yes!" the students chorused.

"Very well, then. Off you go." It was startling how quickly Thaddeus could transform himself from a stone-faced dictator into a suave academic. Now he was smiling pleasantly, adjusting his glasses. "Good luck on your first day, and a word of advice from someone with experience." He waited until the whole class was looking at him. "The refectory's sweet-and-sour pork," he said, "is *poison.*"

And he laughed.

FIFTEEN

Cadel's next class was with Brendan Graham. It was held in Brendan's office, on the first floor of the seminary building, so Cadel didn't have to pass through any security scanners to get there.

Brendan's office enchanted Cadel. When he poked his head around the door, he was confronted by a room in which the walls were plastered with calculations. There were computer printouts of number sequences, handwritten algorithms on scrap paper, and pages torn from printed textbooks. Even the ceiling was covered with balance sheets.

Three people were sitting in the room. One was Brendan himself, recognizable because of his red hair and chalky, freckled face. Beside him sat a stiff, elderly man in a gray suit, and a plump, glossy woman who confused Cadel. Although she was very well groomed, with lots of shimmering makeup and flashy jewelry, her eyes had a lost, slightly fretful look, as if she were wandering around, ragged and starving, in a scene of utter devastation.

"Uh—hello," said Cadel. "I'm Cadel Darkkon."

No one said anything.

"I'm—I'm new?" he stammered. "I've got a class here?"

"Oh." Brendan frowned. "You're the addition."

"I guess so."

"Come in."

Cadel did as he was told. He was aware that, owing to the small size of the institute, many of its elective subjects were taught to composite classes made up of students from different years. Thaddeus had told him that he would be sharing his embezzlement class with one second-year undergraduate and one student in the final year of his degree.

"Douglas Prindle," Thaddeus had declared, "is an old accountant with lots of experience and nothing to show for it. He's very embittered. Nursing a grudge. Wants to enrich his remaining years and ruin a few clients in the process. Brendan seems to think he has a lot of potential. Phoebe Christos . . ." Thaddeus had shrugged. "Well, she's your standard bottomless pit. Banking background. Has to have her designer clothes and her fancy cosmetics and her trips to Paris. Brendan says if she can keep out of jail long enough to finish her degree, she'll be a handy little mole for us to have. Well placed in the banking system."

Cadel decided that the gray-suited man and the plump woman must be Douglas and Phoebe. They weren't introduced. Brendan simply waved Cadel into a spare seat and said, "Know much about accounting?"

"Uh—no. Not really," Cadel replied.

"Thaddeus says you're good with numbers. Top marks in mathematics."

"Well, I guess so."

"Accounting is different. In this class, we're not trying to find numbers. We're trying to hide them. We're trying to disguise them. Fake numbers. Hidden numbers. That's what it's all about." Brendan's rapid-fire voice was rather toneless. "Do you know anything about tax law?"

"No," Cadel admitted.

"Bank procedures?"

"A bit. Mostly credit cards."

"Then you'd better do some background reading." Brendan got up, went to a filing cabinet, and dragged a large book from the stack of publications that teetered on top of it. He poked around in the cabinet's bottom drawer and pulled out another book. Finally, he plucked a slimmer, smaller volume from the papers on his desk and added it to the pile. All the chosen books were photocopied, bound in ring binders, and covered with sheets of stiff, transparent plastic. Each bore a code as its title: *TL1:#1a-42*e, or *>4:base1-27*.

"Okay, that's most of what you need to know about tax law," Brendan declared, dropping the largest book into Cadel's arms. "Practical loopholes, basically. Things to remember. This is a procedural handbook that covers most financial institutions in Australia, though not in too much detail, of course." The second book joined the first. "And this is your basic accounting textbook, nothing fancy, though I've added an appendix on offshore instruments. You know—tax havens. Offshore instruments are *very* important." Brendan surrendered the smallest book, while Cadel felt his heart sink. The weight of his load was some indication of the work that lay ahead.

"There's no point staying," Brendan went on, dropping back into his chair, "unless you've got a grip on the stuff in these texts. Thaddeus says you're a genius, so you shouldn't have any trouble. Go away, read them, and come back. When's your next class with me?"

"Thursday," Cadel muttered.

"Come back on Thursday." Brendan didn't seem to think any further explanation was required. His tone was monotonous, his expression rather blank. Douglas and Phoebe rolled their eyes at each other when the word *genius* was mentioned, but Brendan seemed to regard it as an unremarkable term.

"If you've got any questions," he continued, "I'm usually here. Do you know anything about computers?"

"Lots," Cadel retorted.

"That'll help. It's mostly computers, these days, especially with foreign exchange and account processing. But we'll cover that a bit later." Having provided Cadel with all the information due him, Brendan appeared to forget that he even existed. As Cadel sat openmouthed, the red-haired lecturer resumed his interrupted conversation with Douglas. They had been talking about something called "abnormal items" before Cadel had interrupted them.

"So what you're saying is that you've got a $54 million write-off of future tax benefits on foreign losses," Brendan mused, restoring a stapled document to his lap and studying it closely, "which was recognized as an asset last year, is that right?"

"In a nutshell," said Douglas.

"But now you're not sure about the recovery."

"Right."

"I don't know. I agree it's got potential, but what's your documentation like?"

Cadel realized that he wasn't wanted. Phoebe was staring at him with raised eyebrows, as if wondering why he was still there.

Quietly, he got up and slipped from the room.

Cadel's next class was with the lawyer, Dr. Deal. But it was scheduled for eleven, and he had some reading to do before then. If it had been a sunny day, he would have taken his reading out to the lawn. Since it was wet, however, he went down to the library, where he took his load of embezzlement texts over to one of the tables. He sat down and began to leaf despondently through the book on basic accounting. As far as he could see, it looked fairly straightforward, but awfully dull. *Net interest income is simply the difference between interest income and interest expense,* he read.

"Hello," said a muffled voice.

Cadel looked up. He saw Gazo Kovacs standing in front of him.

"Hello," he replied.

"You're Cadel Darkkon."

"Yes."

"I'm Gazo Kovacs."

"I know."

Gazo dragged out a chair and sat down. He moved rather awkwardly, with a great rustling of man-made fibers. Through the transparent plastic of his headpiece, his face was thin and spotty, with big, pale, watery eyes.

"I'm super grateful to your dad," he said, his accent heavy with cockney vowels. "Your dad finks I've got potential." He pronounced the last word carefully, as if he wasn't very familiar with it. "He brought me all the way from England. He paid for the trip."

"I know," Cadel answered.

"Gave me a room upstairs, and I get all me food. But I afta work hard." Gazo leaned forward suddenly. "What's he like, your dad? I never met 'im."

"That's because he's in jail."

"I know. Dr. Roth told me. Have *you* met 'im?"

"I've spoken to him."

"What's he like?"

Cadel regarded the spaceman figure across the table. Thaddeus had been correct; Gazo clearly was *not* very bright. But even more strangely, he didn't seem very dangerous, either. Unless his dopey, puppylike demeanor was just an act.

"My dad's really smart," Cadel rejoined, cautiously.

"I know! He's the smartest guy in the whole world! That's why they put 'im in jail. So he wouldn't become president of the United Nations."

Astonished, Cadel stared at Gazo. "*What* did you say you were studying?" he asked.

"I'm studying to be a superhero. I've got powers, and your dad says I should learn to channel 'em."

"Yes, I know. The stench." Cadel waved this information aside. "But what else are you studying?"

"Um . . ." Gazo began to count the subjects off on his clumsy gloved hands. "Loopholes, forgery, disguise . . ."

All the core first-year subjects, in other words. Cadel wondered how Gazo was going to cope. It didn't seem likely that he would pass even the simplest subject. That stench of his, Cadel thought, must be pretty amazing.

"You're real smart, too," Gazo went on. "Just like your dad. How old are you?"

"Fourteen," Cadel lied.

"Wow! You must be a genius. I wish I was a genius." With a glance at Cadel's pile of books, Gazo added, "I can read, but I dunno if . . . what I mean is, it's gonna be hard for me."

"You'll be all right," said Cadel, though he didn't really mean it. He had learned to be supportive and reassuring at school, when he was researching social interaction. Being nice, he had discovered, usually paid off when you were collecting information and hunting down gossip. Now he often found himself being sympathetic automatically. Even when he didn't care at all.

Gazo responded with a grin so big that Cadel could see it through the foggy plastic panel.

"Thanks," said Gazo. "I hope I'll be all right. I don't want to let your dad down, not after what he's done for me."

Cadel grunted.

"So what do you finka the others?" Gazo continued. "The Bludgeon, and them? They're not too friendly, are they?"

Cadel peered at his companion in genuine disbelief. Surely the silly sod couldn't *really* be so clueless?

"They're not here to be friendly, Gazo," he pointed out. "If they wanted to be friendly, they would have gone somewhere else."

"I s'pose so." Gazo nodded solemnly. Then he perked up again. "But *we* can be friends, eh? I mean, you and me?"

Cadel blinked. He glanced around, but there was no one else in the library. He wondered what Thaddeus's advice might be. Was Gazo a tiresome, thick-skinned idiot who would prove impossible to shake off, or would he be a useful person to have on his side?

Cadel chose to take a chance.

"Okay," he murmured. "We can be friends."

Another big grin from Gazo. "I can look after you," he promised. "I'm a lot older than you are, and I've got this power. You ain't got no power, eh?"

"Only mind power," Cadel retorted.

"Then I can look after you, because you're so little. That's what I want to do, anyway, when I finish me course. Look after people. People like your dad, who want to make the world a better place."

"Really?" said Cadel.

"I won't afta wear this suit, when I learn to channel me power. I'll have a proper costume, like Spider-Man. Maybe somefink green. And I'd give meself a name, like that Bludgeon bloke did. Maybe Aromo? Or the Stench? What do you fink?"

Cadel said nothing. He didn't know what to say. He was beginning to feel sorry for Gazo, who seemed to be way out of his depth.

"Okay. Well, I s'pose I'd better let you study," Gazo said awkwardly. Then he laughed. "You look like you've got a lotta work to do. What's it for, anyway?"

"Embezzlement," Cadel replied.

"Oh. Right." Something about Gazo's voice made Cadel wonder if he even knew what *embezzlement* meant. "So will you be at Dr. Deal's class?"

"Yes."

"So I'll see you there, then?"

"Yes."

"Okay. Great. Well, bye!"

"Good-bye."

Cadel watched Gazo leave the library. Only when the elevator doors had closed did Cadel shift his blank, laserlike gaze, focusing it on the book in front of him. He sat quite still, reading with great concentration, until it was time to attend Dr. Deal's class. Then he packed the embezzlement texts into his backpack and dragged them up to the ground floor.

Here he found all the first-year students once again, milling about outside lecture-room one. It was like a replay of the nine-o'clock session, only this time Gazo waved at Cadel, and Gemini pounced on him, cooing.

"There he is," crooned Jem. "Hello, Cadel."

"Careful, Jem, you'll break him," said Niobe. "So Thaddeus says

128

you're off-limits, Cadel? What a *shame*. I guess that means you won't be coming to visit us in our room. Because you're off-limits."

"I guess we won't be allowed to sit with you in the dining hall, either." Jem sighed. "What a pity."

Cadel flushed and the twins squealed with laughter.

"Oh, he's so cute! Look at him!"

"I want to put him in my purse!"

"You can't, Ni, he's off-limits."

"Will you two shut up?" the Bludgeon suddenly growled. "Everyone knows why you're doing this. You're not fooling anybody."

"Did you hear something, Ni?" Jem trilled. "It was like a fart, or something."

"No, I didn't hear anything."

"You think you're going to suck up to Dr. Darkkon by drooling all over his kid," the Bludgeon snapped. "But it won't make any difference. It just makes you look stupid."

"Well, you're the expert when it comes to looking stupid," Jem sneered. "I mean, check out the *pants*, Ni."

"And the *hair*."

"Where'd you get that top, Bludger, did you make it yourself?"

"It's *Bludgeon*, you sluts."

"Who's bludging? Not me," said Ni.

"He's saying he bludged it off someone," said Jem.

"I did *not*!"

"Okay, okay!" A clear, calm voice cut through the argument. "Save it for your next court appearance. He*llo* there, am I seeing double? Who are you, ladies?"

A large, well-padded, affable-looking man had suddenly appeared in their midst. He was about forty, and balding, but he had a round, smooth, pleasant face with small features and laugh lines. He wore a very elegant dark suit. "They call me Dr. Deal," he said, taking Ni's hand in his own large, pink one. "You must be the twins I've heard so much about."

The sisters rolled their eyes at each other, smirking. Dr. Deal straightened. "So you prefer to keep silent in case you implicate yourselves? Very wise," he said. Then his roving gaze fastened on Cadel. "Ah," he murmured. "And *you* must be the boy genius. You don't look much like your father, Cadel. But your face will be your fortune, I would say. Now!" He whipped out a set of keys. "Let's get this show on the road, shall we? No, my dear," he added, turning to Doris with a dangerous gleam in his eye. "Don't even think about it."

Everyone looked at Doris, who seemed offended.

"What?" she whined, and Dr. Deal shook back his sleeve.

"This watch," he declared, displaying it to the class, "is a gold Rolex. It cost me ten thousand dollars six years ago. I've had it all this time and *no one* has managed to take it from me. I intend to keep it that way. Those of you who fancy yourselves as expert thieves, take heed— I've put away the best in the business."

He waited, but there was no reply. So he unlocked the door and pushed it open, allowing the entire class to enter lecture-room one before he did himself. While his students settled into their seats, he dumped his briefcase on the lectern and unbuttoned his jacket. Then he folded his arms and addressed them.

"Right," he said. "Let's get one thing clear. I'm not here to teach you law—I'm here to teach you loopholes. You're not here to become lawyers. You're here because you can't dodge the law unless you know what it is. You're also here because litigation, believe it or not, *can be your friend.* This semester, you're going to learn a bit of defensive law; I'll even give you a rundown on police procedures, and Terry will deliver a few lectures on the dangers of forensic science. Next semester, we'll tackle things like torts, and how you can sue your way to a fairly decent living, if you've got the skill and the nerve for it. But now I'm going to kick off with some really nice little case studies to show you how you can use the law to your advantage.

"Let's start with the 'Provocation' statute—"

Suddenly, the lights flickered. There was a muffled *boom*. And with a fierce little hiss, the sprinklers on the ceiling began to spray the whole room with water.

Cadel gasped. The water was very cold.

"Oh, for Chris'sake," Dr. Deal exclaimed in disgust. He grabbed his briefcase, trying to shield himself with it. "Come on, everyone, we'll do this in 'C' block."

"But—but what's going on?" Abraham Coggins stammered.

"Christ knows. Bomb, probably. Or some idiot pyrogenic." Dr. Deal seemed unconcerned.

"But—"

"Come *on*, will you? I paid three thousand dollars for this suit! I'm not about to stand here and let it get ruined!"

SIXTEEN

At lunchtime, Cadel found himself trooping off to the refectory with the rest of first year. He didn't have much choice; no one had provided him with a packed lunch. And because the refectory was almost full, he was forced to sit with his classmates, who reserved a table near the kitchen door.

Cadel was still damp in places, even after standing under the hand dryers in the bathroom for ten minutes. So he ordered a hot chocolate with his ham and cheese focaccia. The twins shared a salad sandwich. Abraham picked at a sausage roll, and Doris ate her way steadily through a meat pie, fries, and vegetables, followed by a large chocolate-chip muffin.

Gazo didn't stay to eat. He took a meal back to his bedroom, where he was allowed to take off his headpiece and breathing apparatus.

Clive was the last of their group to sit down, having spent some minutes, after collecting his plate of fries, in conversation with the gum-chewing, blank-faced woman behind the cash register.

"It was a pyro," he informed his classmates, when he joined them. "She self-combusted, up in the labs. That's why the sprinklers went off."

"Gross," said Ni, making a face, and Abraham remarked, "It wouldn't have been a bomb. They have regular bomb sweeps."

"Who says?" Clive queried aggressively. Abraham sighed.

"Didn't you read your handbook?" he said. "It tells you right at the front. In capital letters."

"Perhaps he can't read," said Jem. Clive stopped chewing and fixed her with a venomous look.

"You better watch your back, sweetheart," he hissed, spraying the table with fragments of chewed potato, "or you'll find a knife in it."

"Oh, yeah. Like you could smuggle a knife into this place," Jem taunted. "I don't *think* so, Bludger."

"I'm not the Bludgeon anymore."

"What?"

"*I'm not the Bludgeon anymore.* I'm calling myself the Scourge."

"The *Scourge?*" Jem echoed.

"Yuck!" cried her twin. "That's *disgusting.*"

Clive was taken aback. "What do you mean?" he spluttered. "There's nothing disgusting about it."

"The *scourge!*" Ni shrilled. "That's a disease!"

"It is not!"

"Is so! It's some horrible skin thing—isn't it? Jem? It's sores and things, isn't it? Lots of pus."

"It isn't," Clive protested. "It's a weapon."

"It's a whip," said Abraham, wearily. "It's another word for a whip. Also for an agent of punishment, or destruction."

"There! You see?" Clive was triumphant. "The Scourge. That's my new name."

"Well, *I* think it sounds revolting," said Jem. "It sounds like something you'd clean out of your nose."

"Like gunge," Ni agreed. "Or Scrooge. I think I'll call him Scrooge. You can tell he's mean. I bet he won't even give me one of his fries."

"Buy your own bloody fries," Clive growled, shielding his plate.

"And get fat? No thank you."

"What's your real name, anyway?" Abraham suddenly asked Clive. He had pushed aside his sausage roll; it was almost untouched. "Why can't you use your real name, for god's sake?"

Cadel blinked, before remembering that no one else in the class had access to the kind of background information available to himself and Thaddeus Roth.

Clive scowled at this point. "I'm not telling you my real name," he spat.

"Why not?" said Abraham. "What is it, Ivor Bigbum or something?"

The twins squealed with laughter. Clive turned red. He lunged for Abraham, who jerked back and fell off his chair. The twins nearly fell off their own chairs, they were laughing so hard.

"Shut your face!" Clive roared. "There's nothing wrong with my name! But I'm not stupid enough to use it, not professionally! Jesus, don't you know *anything*?" He glared around the table as Abraham staggered to his feet and picked up his chair. "Most of the staff here have an alias."

"One of the staff members *is* an Alias," Abraham muttered, but Clive ignored him.

"If you lot have any sense, you'll pick a new name," Clive went on. "Like me. The Scourge isn't just a name—it's a way of life. It sums up what I am."

"Which is?" Jem wanted to know, and Clive bared his teeth at her.

"Hell on wheels," he rejoined, brusquely.

"Hell On Wheels." She cocked her head, savoring the term. "H.O.W. How. Maybe I'll call you How. No—Howie."

"I'm the *Scourge*."

"Seriously, pet, I wouldn't use that one. It sounds too icky. It sounds like *scrounge*. Why don't you use something else?" Jem pulled at her bottom lip, concentrating fiercely. "What about . . . let's see . . ."

"Big Dog?" Ni suggested.

"No—the Terminator!" Jem cried.

"It's been *done*, stupid," her sister pointed out.

"The Decimator, then. What about the Decimator?"

They both giggled, but Clive seemed struck by the name. "The Decimator," he repeated, pensively. "The Decimator . . ."

"It's *you*!" Jem exclaimed. "It's so *you*, you big hunk!"

More giggling. Abraham cast his eyes to heaven. Kunio blinked, uncomprehending, and Doris munched away, looking glum.

Cadel cleared his throat.

"Um . . . ," he began, then hesitated. All eyes turned in his direction.

"What?" barked Clive.

"Well, I just thought you ought to know . . ." Cadel took a deep breath. "The proper definition of *decimate* is to kill one in ten. I don't know if that's what you're intending to do," he said, glancing at Clive.

There was a brief silence.

"Oh," said Clive. "Well, *that's* no good, then."

"You'll have to think of something else," Jem observed, and rose to depart. Her sister did likewise. Abraham, who had also finished, lurched to his feet and leaned across to clap Cadel on the shoulder. "Nice to know there's someone else here with brains," he said. Abraham didn't linger, though; in fact, within sixty seconds, Cadel was alone at the table, except for Doris, who sat at the far end slurping down a cup of tea.

She exuded an air of quiet menace. Not wishing to talk to her, Cadel soon got up and hurried away to attend his first infiltration class.

This class was the one that interested him the most. He was eager to talk to Dr. Vee again—eager to judge the depth and range of his teacher's expertise. It was really because of the Virus that he had decided to enroll at the Axis Institute. Embezzlement didn't interest him; he was only doing it to please Thaddeus. Forgery would be fun, and law would be useful, but since Cadel didn't particularly care for his fellow students, he wouldn't be enjoying either course as much as Thaddeus probably hoped. Clive and Gazo were frankly dumb. The twins were tricky. Doris was frightening. Naturally, Cadel understood that his father had plans for him—plans that for some reason required a stint at the Axis Institute. Well, that was all right. Cadel didn't mind, as long as he had his infiltration classes to keep him happy.

When he reached Hardware Heaven, however, he discovered that the Virus was not there.

"He comes and goes," explained one of the students who had already arrived. He was a sloppy-looking person, about eighteen or nineteen, with a long, bristly jaw, shaggy brown hair falling into his eyes, and grubby clothes that seemed to be in the process of sliding off him. He introduced himself as Sark, "like in Cutty," and the young man near him as Com. Com was pudgy and wore glasses. His black, shiny hair was cut in a straight line all around his head, just above ear level. He didn't look at Cadel or speak to him.

"Com's not really human," Sark explained. "I think he's forgotten how to talk. He relates best to computers, don't you, Com?"

No response.

"He spends most of his time here," Sark added, flicking a paper clip at the oblivious Com. It bounced off his shoulder.

"Um—have I got the right time?" Cadel queried. "I thought I had a class at two."

"Oh, we don't worry much about classes around this place." Sark was folded up in his wobbly typist's chair, his feet propped against the edge of his desktop. He wore grimy, ragged sneakers, one of them tied with a thin piece of cable. "When the Virus shows up, we generally discuss a few things. Otherwise we just plug away at our own stuff."

"But—"

"My personal goal is to create a superhacker," Sark went on. "A program that will do all my hacking *for* me."

Com clicked his tongue. For an instant, Cadel thought that the noise had come from Com's hardware.

"Shut up, Com," said Sark. "Nobody knows *what* Com's doing. He's lost the power to explain things in human terms."

"But what am I supposed to do?" Cadel demanded. "Just sit here, or what?"

Sark shrugged. His long limbs suddenly rearranged themselves as he dragged his feet off the desk. "You can have a look at your computer," he suggested.

"Which computer?"

"That one." Sark waved his hand. "Over there."

Cadel followed Sark's directions. He stopped in front of a rather elderly piece of equipment, which, Cadel knew, had very little to spare in the way of gigabytes.

"Oh," he said.

"You've got a network card in there, needless to say—most of Axis is linked up. Plus we have our own high-capacity backbone. An OC–48 line. Could be worse. Oh, and there's a supercomputer. In the back room. But you can only use it under supervision. And if you're wondering why it looks like a tank, the whole thing's shielded against Red Signal leaks, you know?" Sark seemed to be losing interest in Cadel; his attention was once more focused on his computer. "There's no sprinkler system in this room, either, by the way. Just halon gas outlets. And it's on a different switch, too. The Virus insisted, because there's so much combustion on this campus—it's like a goddamn blow furnace sometimes. That's why we didn't get soaked early on. In case you were wondering."

Cadel wasn't wondering. Not about the sprinklers, anyway. He *was* wondering why his computer didn't boot up when he turned it on.

After carefully checking the main socket, the power lead, and the keyboard cable, all of which seemed to be fine, he began to punch in a few basic commands. Then he became aware of a muted snicker.

It was coming from Sark. He could tell by the way Sark's hunched shoulders were quivering.

Cadel waited. He sat and stared at Sark's back until the older student glanced around—and caught Cadel's eye.

"Oh!" Sark seemed surprised by his classmate's steady regard, but recovered quickly. "Having problems?" he asked, with the utmost innocence.

"You know I am." Cadel got straight down to business. "So what's the deal?"

Sark seemed to debate something inside his head. Then he shrugged again.

"Second-class honors if you can start up," he explained. "It's one of the Virus's little tricks."

"Is it a test?"

"Don't ask me. Ask the Virus."

With a sigh, Cadel turned back to his computer. The power light was on. The key-lock switch was off. He sat thinking for a while, running through a checklist in his head. He tried a few more unsuccessful commands, pondered for a moment, and tried a few more. Then, with a grunt, he scrambled for the VGA cable.

By the time the Virus entered, some fifteen minutes later, Cadel's machine was humming quite nicely through a series of downloads.

"He did it," Sark announced in a flat voice. It hardly needed saying. The Virus, who was looking sweaty in a bright, short-sleeved shirt, peered over at Cadel.

"Oh," he said.

"It was the monitor," Cadel remarked.

"Yes."

"I checked the pinout—"

"Yes, yes." The Virus didn't seem interested. "Well done." Having reached his own desk, he began to remove various objects from his briefcase: the usual box of tissues, a packet of throat pastilles, a bottle of eyedrops, an ergonomic back pillow. "Sark, show the boy his computer, for god's sake," he added testily, and waddled off to refill the humidifier.

"When Doozy first tried, he had the whole box opened up," Sark informed Cadel, with a smirk. "Had the capacitor dismantled, and everything. Thought something was wrong with the switcher supply."

"Who's Doozy?" asked Cadel.

"He's a bloody idiot, that's who he is" was Sark's answer. "Here. This is yours. That other one—it's just a booby trap."

Cadel saw, with relief, that the new computer issued to him was of quite recent vintage, and well supplied with hard drive, RAM, and so forth. He was able to start it without difficulty. When the Virus reentered Hardware Heaven, Cadel put up his hand.

"Excuse me—uh—sir."

"Call me Vee," said the Virus. He threw himself behind his desk with a groan of relief. "What's the problem *now*?"

"Nothing." Cadel hastened to assure him. "I just wanted to know, am I allowed to install my own security?"

The Virus's fat face immediately screwed itself up into a grin. "What—you don't *trust* us?" He giggled.

"Well—"

"By all means, Cadel, do your worst. It won't make any difference. I'll still get in, if I want to."

"Yes, sir—I mean, Vee." Cadel had his doubts about *that*. "So I can download some programs? Right now? I brought them with me."

"Oh, you can do that later," the Virus rejoined. "When I'm not here. Right now, we should try to do something useful, for a change." He coughed, sniffed, then jabbed a fat finger in Com's direction. "Sark, will you reboot that boy? I don't think he's online."

"Hey! Wysiwyg!" Sark threw a stapler at Com, without eliciting any response. So he leaned over and yanked the plug from Com's main socket.

Com let out a strangled bellow, and the Virus clicked his fingers.

"I'm uploading here, Com, pay attention," he said. "You listening, Sark?"

"Yes."

"All right." The Virus blew his nose, mopped it, and continued. "You've both met Cadel. He's Dr. Darkkon's son. I've mentioned him. I've given you the protocol. Com? Are you processing this?"

Com nodded.

"Fine. Well, Cadel told me at our last meeting that he was interested in hardware—molecular electronics, to be exact." At the sound of Sark's muffled sigh, the Virus giggled. "So I thought, as base work, we might all dust off our synapses and have a fresh look at neural network models. Sark?" (Slyly.) "You got a problem with that?"

"No," Sark mumbled.

"All righty." The Virus fixed his twinkling eyes on Cadel. "I presume you agree with me, Cadel? That this is a good place to kick off?"

"Uh—yeah. Sure."

"Good. Because there's nothing like starting from scratch, I always say. If you can't wire your own neuron outputs, you can't call yourself a computer geek, in my opinion." The Virus bared his pointed teeth at Sark. "Sark's always had a lot of trouble with low-level digital integrated circuit design. You had a hard time getting past your first NAND gate, didn't you, Sark?"

Sark muttered something under his breath.

"Doesn't like to get his hands dirty," the Virus remarked to Cadel. "Believe it or not." He tittered, and Sark threw him a black look. "A lot of my boys here, they can't calculate to save their lives. Throw 'em a recursion equation and they run for cover. Sally was different." The Virus paused for an instant before continuing. "Sally was different, but she had other problems. *Personal* problems. Pity, really. *She* wasn't afraid of hard work."

"Look—are we going to do this or not?" Sark snapped, whereupon the Virus giggled yet again, wiping his eyes.

"Yes, yes, I hear you," he said, and drew from his pocket a tattered slip of paper, well folded, which he waved in Cadel's direction. "So. Cadel. You want to get us started on this?"

Obediently, Cadel rose and plucked the paper from the Virus's hand. Smoothing it out, he saw that it bore a single equation:

$$C_i \frac{du_i}{dt} = -\frac{u_i}{R_i} + \sum_{j=1}^{n} \frac{T_{ij}}{R_i} f_j(u_j) + \frac{I_i}{R_i}$$

"On the left, you've got an input current charging a capacitor C_i to a potential u_i," the Virus drawled. "On the right, $-u_i/R_i$ is a leakage current and I_i/R_i is an outside input. What else? Sum term is input currents from other neurons. Your $f_j(u_j)$ is the output of an amplifier. Your T_{ij}/R_i are conductances. Oh—and the numbers R_i aren't resistances, just scaling factors."

"Ri-i-ght," said Cadel, his mind working furiously. "So what do I do with this?"

"What you *do* is sit down and knock off a nice, simple layout of a basic electronic circuit for a neural network chip implementation, using that equation," the Virus continued, clearing his sinuses. "Nothing fancy. Just a sketch. Something we can *all* understand. In fact . . ." With a smile, the Virus surveyed his other two students. "In fact, why doesn't everyone give it a go?"

"Oh, but *Vee*," Sark protested, and Com sagged in his seat.

"No, no." The Virus raised his hand. "Fair's fair. This is good. It'll keep us on our toes. And if you don't like it, you know who to thank."

Another tiresome giggle. As Cadel shuffled back to his desk, he intercepted a poisonous glance from Sark and wondered if Thaddeus's message had found its way back to the Virus's students.

Did they know that Cadel was off-limits?

Cadel profoundly hoped so.

SEVENTEEN

"So how was it?" Dr. Darkkon wanted to know.

Cadel rubbed his eyes. He was very weary. After four hours in Hardware Heaven, he had rushed straight to Thaddeus's office for his usual appointment. The Piggotts had given him money for a cab.

"It was fine," he murmured. "The Virus was great."

"Ah yes." Dr. Darkkon nodded, so that his face disappeared from the screen for an instant. "Vee's a talented man. I thought you might find him interesting."

"Was he—did he have anything to do with my computer phone?" Cadel asked, and his father grinned.

"What do *you* think?"

"I'm not sure. Maybe—the early stages?"

"Maybe." Dr. Darkkon didn't seem eager to elaborate. He made a show of retching at the screen, which was floating in the bottom of his toilet bowl. His tongue looked like a blind, puffy, gray eel darting out of a hole. "What were the other students like?"

Cadel grimaced. Thaddeus leaned forward.

"Surely Vee's weren't disappointing?" he pressed. "I've heard some good things about them."

"Oh sure." Cadel shrugged. "*They* were all right."

"Some of the first-year intake is decidedly experimental," Thaddeus admitted. "Gazo Kovacs, the twins, Clive Slaughter—they're a gamble, I must confess."

"They're *dumb*," said Cadel, flatly.

"Well, yes. But that doesn't mean they won't be useful."

"We can't all be as clever as you, son," Dr. Darkkon wheezed. "I hope you found it stimulating, though?"

Cadel nodded. He *had* found it stimulating. Almost too stimulating. He was exhausted—and confused. The Axis Institute, though interesting, had also been . . . odd. Skewed. Off-kilter. Cadel sensed that he was failing to grasp it fully; it was like an alternative universe, constructed according to a different set of natural laws that he was unable to define.

"What's all that stuff in your bag?" Thaddeus asked.

"Embezzlement texts, mostly."

"What did you think of Brendan?"

"I don't know." Cadel tried to sort out his impressions. "We didn't talk much."

"What about Deal?"

"He was cross. Because of the sprinklers."

"Ah, yes." Thaddeus made a face. "It's hard. We'll have to fine-tune that emergency system."

"Uh, Dad?" said Cadel. He didn't know quite how to phrase his next question. "Do you—I mean, why do you think I should do embezzlement?"

Dr. Darkkon, who had been glancing over his shoulder, turned back to the screen and narrowed his pale froggy eyes.

"Why?" he echoed. "Why not? Do you have a problem with it, Cadel?"

"Oh no." Cadel retreated. "Not really."

"Because if you have a problem with it, then perhaps that's reason enough for you to be doing it. There's no gain to be had from an easy ride."

"Cadel," said Thaddeus. He waited until Cadel was looking at him before continuing. "Brendan isn't giving you any trouble, is he?"

Though the psychologist's tone was casual, Cadel's heart skipped a beat.

"Oh, no!" he exclaimed. "No, nothing like that!"

"Are you sure?"

"Yes!" Cadel had the feeling that if Thaddeus got the wrong idea about Brendan, Luther Lasco might soon be recounting another case study to his first-year class. Brendan didn't deserve anything so drastic. "I was just wondering why I'm doing embezzlement instead of—I don't know, explosives or something. That's all."

"Explosives are for grunts," said Thaddeus. "You know what your father thinks about bombs, Cadel."

"Money," Dr. Darkkon added, "is important. If you don't understand money, Cadel, you're at the mercy of your accountants. And they'll either rip you off or you'll have to hire *other* accountants to keep them honest. Believe me, I know what I'm talking about."

"Money can be very interesting," Thaddeus concluded, watching Cadel closely. "Some people find it the most fascinating thing in the world: the ebb and flow, the ups and downs. It's a system like any other."

"I suppose so," said Cadel.

"He's tired," Thaddeus informed Dr. Darkkon. "It's been a big day."

Dr. Darkkon agreed. It was time for the boy to go home, he said. "You'll be fine, Cadel. As soon as you get the hang of it, you'll be disemboweling banks and hijacking the International Monetary Fund like there was no tomorrow. You'll see."

Cadel smiled, in a halfhearted fashion. For once, he didn't think his father was right. But he nodded and changed the subject and was finally allowed to go home. Again, he used a taxi.

Upon reaching his bedroom, he immediately sat down in front of his computer.

Then realized that he didn't know what to say.

He was too tired to pretend that he was Eiran Dempster. In fact, Eiran was beginning to annoy him. The guy was useless—a lazy slob. Why did Kay-Lee like him so much? It occurred to Cadel that he was actually becoming jealous of Eiran, and he groaned.

What kind of idiot becomes jealous of one of his own fictional creations?

Hey Primo, he typed in code, then stopped. He wanted to ask advice without revealing too much. How could it be done? He thought a bit more before continuing. *Hard day at the office yesterday,* he wrote. *I'm whacked. That campus is a madhouse, I swear. Some of the students are so stupid I can't believe they're allowed through the gates. What do I do with a couple of blond bimbos who are all over me because they think it's good politics? I wouldn't trust them as far as I could spit, either—they make me nervous—so I can't exactly boot them up the ass. They might get their own back some other way. You're a young, good-looking blond, Primo—are there any tips you can give me?*

On the subject of tips, I'm wondering what you think about money. You know I'm not good with money. It doesn't interest me, for some reason. But I'm informed that I'd better get interested—fast—or I'll end up a tramp when I retire. What's your take on this? How come a guy who teaches number theory can't seem to budget his expenses? Or balance his checkbook? What is it that I'm missing here?

If there's some way that you can open up a door for me, and show me a whole, new, wonderful world of funds management, I'll be forever in your debt.

By the way, I've met a great new guy from the computer department. He's into designing hardware and software implementations of neural networks, and it's been fantastic talking to him. Have you ever applied things like Gaussian random variables to the calculation of how many fixed vectors a neural network might have? It's all to do with storing patterns so that they're stable, and establishing stability conditions for each bit on a chip. We spent several hours today proving that a pattern will be stable with probability 1 for a Hopfield network with sum-of-outer-product weights, if $n \rightarrow \infty$ and the number of patterns obeys the condition $m - 1 \leq \frac{n}{2lnr}$. Wish you'd been there.

Love from Stormer.

Having sent off this message, Cadel spent half an hour waiting impatiently for a reply. He wandered out to the kitchen and made himself a banana smoothie. He flicked glumly through his embezzlement texts. He checked his Partner Post mailbox, which was brimming with anxious e-mails that he didn't feel energetic enough to answer.

At last, after repeatedly checking, he received Kay-Lee's reply.

Darling Stormer, she wrote, *what the hell is a Hopfield network? Never heard of it—though I'm not surprised about the Gaussian random variables. Gauss pops up pretty much everywhere, anyway, and it's only to be expected that he makes an appearance in the field of neural networks, since he was a scientist as well as a mathematician. (Did you know that he and Weber designed an electric telegraph? Bet you didn't.) You'll have to give me a bit more information, though, if you want me to appreciate the beauty of your equation.*

As far as money goes, you're asking the wrong person. I wouldn't be working as a nurse if my share portfolio was behaving itself. However, I did once see a lovely piece of calculation in an annual report—something about a financial option called a perpetual floating rate note. It was a whole new take on transcendental numbers, as far as I could see. Very amusing.

But maybe we should both *put our minds to finding the fun in money—especially superannuation funds. Glancing through the prospectus in front of me, I can see that fees are calculated as a percentage of the amount invested, depending on the risk factors involved. I'm sure we could find some entertainment in running checks on this stuff.*

Darling Stormer, if you really want to get rich, let's get rich. I'm up for it. But remember that wealth always comes with strings attached. You think you've got problems with ruthless blond bimbos now? *Wait till you've got more money than you know what to do with! You won't be able to* move *for ruthless blond bimbos!*

I'm not ruthless, and I'm not a bimbo. I don't care how much money you have. If you were a septingentillionaire, I wouldn't love you any more than I do now.

Your own
Primo

P.S. I'm glad you've found a kindred spirit at work. I worry about you. If only there was an equation that would solve all your problems once and for all!

Reading this e-mail, Cadel wondered why it made him feel even worse than he had before. Because it contained so much genuine affection, which was being lavished on someone who didn't exist? He was sometimes overcome by a strange sense of discomfort (guilt, even?) when he considered Kay-Lee.

But that didn't stop him from talking to her. In fact, as soon as he'd finished reading her message, he launched into a full explanation of J. Hopfield's recipe for the synaptic matrix T.

With Kay-Lee, he could lose himself in a world of enjoyment that was utterly, refreshingly pure.

EIGHTEEN

The first semester at Axis was ten weeks long. By the end of the third week, Cadel had drawn several important conclusions.

To begin with, he had come to realize that embezzlement was never going to be his favorite subject. While his interest was sometimes sparked by things like corporate money-laundering trees, he couldn't always follow Brendan's way of thinking. Their minds seemed to work in different ways. What's more, Brendan's manner often disconcerted him. It was becoming clear to Cadel that Brendan didn't recognize him when they passed each other in the corridors—that Brendan didn't even acknowledge his separate existence, most of the time. To Brendan, Cadel appeared to be part of a subset, the different components of which were interchangeable. If Cadel had started calling himself Douglas, Brendan wouldn't have been surprised.

So while Cadel admired Brendan, he couldn't work up much enthusiasm for Brendan's subject. Hence his performance in Brendan's class. Though technically accomplished, it was less than inspired. He wasn't a very *creative* embezzler. He could follow models, and juggle uncleared funds, and competently disguise bad loans as good ones (on paper), but he never surprised Brendan with new ideas for siphoning off profits, or falsifying net interest income. Only with credit cards did he display any real flair—and that was mostly in the area of computer processing.

Oddly enough, despite the fact that he displayed even less natural flair in his forgery class, he enjoyed it far more than he enjoyed embezzlement. Never having devoted much time to building model airplanes or wiring up remote-control toy cars, Cadel's fine motor skills weren't very well developed. He didn't have the sort of coordination required by a really good forger, let alone the necessary eye for color and detail. He hadn't even liked studying art at school. Yet he threw himself into his forgery course with great enthusiasm, perhaps because, with forgery, he could see a *point* to it all. Drawing pictures of fruit in a bowl had always seemed a futile exercise, in his opinion. Why do it, when you could take a photograph? Reproducing a bank check, on the other hand, was a challenge. You had to get it right, or it wouldn't work. Cadel didn't always get it right. His fake university degrees and driver's licenses rarely passed inspection. But as his teacher pointed out, forgery wasn't *just* about ink on paper.

"It's about expertise," Art often said, "and expertise can be slow to acquire. It's not just about forgery; it's about knowing *what* to forge. A good forger has an interest in historic documents, for example. A good forger knows that the only money worth forging is antique. A good forger spends a lot of time, not just poring over encoded deposit slips or international drafts, but also looking at stamp catalogs and visiting museums."

Cadel took this advice very much to heart. Therefore, while some of his practical work needed improvement, his theoretical work was superb. He began to demonstrate a genuine understanding of the trade in rare documents, and the procedures for processing checks. (His embezzlement course proved most useful in the area of bank documentation.) When he finally received an A for a birth certificate, he couldn't bring himself to destroy it, as his teacher had recommended. Instead, he took it home and hid it in the lining of a winter jacket.

His first successful passport received the same treatment. As did many of the forged documents that came after it.

In the rest of his subjects, Cadel excelled. None of them—except infiltration—was especially demanding. The case-studies course required little more than dutiful attention. In Dr. Deal's class, there was a huge amount of rote learning, and Thaddeus's basic-lying unit consisted largely of role-playing scenarios and bluffing games, all of which Cadel won with ease. As Doris complained, he had the face for it.

"This isn't fair," she pointed out on one occasion. "He's got an advantage over the rest of us. He's really young. He looks innocent. Of *course* he's going to do better."

"Even if he's asked to impersonate an airline pilot?" Thaddeus raised an eyebrow. "We all have our strengths and weaknesses, Doris."

"I still don't think it's fair," Doris grumbled, and Thaddeus spread his hands.

"*Life* isn't fair, Doris. We wouldn't be here if it was, would we?"

His tone was slightly impatient because Doris often whined about things. In fact she was disliked by pretty much everyone at the Axis Institute, with the possible exception of Luther Lasco. The twins, who were in Doris's poisoning class, maintained that he was in love with Doris, because he treated her with such respect. But the twins, as Clive had repeatedly pointed out, were "full of crap." They couldn't be trusted. More than once they had given rashes to their fellow students by applying poisons to their stick-on fashion nails, then dragging those nails seductively across bare arms or necks. It was a trick they had learned in their poisoning class, so they didn't try it on Doris. Nor did they touch Cadel, after Thaddeus's warning. And Gazo, of course, was never out of his suit. Clive, Kunio, and Abraham were the twins' main targets. During the first three weeks of the semester, Abraham showed up twice with puffy red weals on his pale skin.

The twins also began to play around with knockout sprays in perfume bottles. They seemed to be throwing themselves into their poisoning studies with far too much enthusiasm. "Production, application, detection," they would chant, then collapse into giggles. It was hard to know what the joke might be. Cadel did wonder, sometimes, if they were actually reading each other's thoughts.

Increasingly, he tried to keep out of their way. He also avoided Doris. Clive was irritating, but he did provide Cadel with important information about the Yarramundi campus, which Cadel hadn't visited. Clive would talk about Adolf—"the Führer"—who taught guerrilla studies and was in charge of campus security. He would describe Adolf's private little regiment of security guards, which was used sometimes to help with military training. These fifteen or so mercenary types were known as "the Grunts." They tended to hang out at Yarramundi.

According to Gazo, Yarramundi was not a safe place to be.

"It's real weird," he told Cadel. "The security's worse than it is here. They have clampdowns all the time. Random checks, and stuff. They make us lie on the floor, and search us for concealed weapons. Sometimes they seal you off in a room for hours—I dunno why."

"Radiation leaks, perhaps?" Cadel suggested. "Radiation studies is located out there, isn't it?"

"I fink so. I never saw it. I don't do mutation." Gazo sighed and changed the subject. "What did you get on Dr. Deal's test?"

"An A," Cadel replied.

"I got a D. I didn't pass. What will happen if I fail the year? Do you know?"

"You won't fail the year," said Cadel. He didn't mean it, but had got into the habit of being polite to his fellow students. He'd discovered that it threw many of them off balance; they had forgotten how to deal with sympathy. Most were perpetually on the defensive because they never knew what to expect. They would turn up to class with broken bones from their guerrilla-training classes, or inflamed membranes from poison gas. Carla was famous for her screaming rages, and the Führer was always assaulting people. Hot-wired technology might give you an electric shock when you tried to make a telephone call; other common tricks included concealed razor blades and tainted food. Students ended up with radiation burns, mysterious rashes, breathing problems.

Little wonder that people soon became surly and aggressive. Doris had always been inclined to growl and glower as if mortally offended, but Cadel noticed the others growing less sociable, too. Even the twins stopped chattering to Clive and Abraham. They spent more and more time whispering to each other. Clive, who had once been a big-mouth, talked less and less about possible aliases. (Cosmos? Photonus? Magog?) Kunio's English hadn't improved, and as for Abraham Coggins—half the time, he was barely *able* to talk. His gums would be swollen, or his voice would be hoarse. In fact, he appeared to be disintegrating before their eyes.

While most of the students' injuries were the result of class work or practical jokes, or occasionally accidents, Abraham's were self-inflicted. Cadel knew this because Abraham would actually talk to him. Abraham loved to talk about his work, when he was physically capable of it, and Cadel was the only other student who impressed him as being clever enough to understand. So Cadel heard all about the microbiology labs, and Terry's experiments with gene-splicing, and how every few nights a whiskered figure in a baseball cap and blue overalls would quietly deliver to the seminary a load of stray cats and dogs for experimental purposes.

"I spend a lot of nights up there," Abraham once confessed. His eyes were ringed by dark bruises, and his voice was like the rasp of a crosscut saw. "It's a great setup. The atmosphere's perfect. I'd feel right at home if I was a vampire."

"I'm sure," said Cadel, politely. "And what are you actually working on so late into the night?"

"Oh, I'm looking at various blood disorders," Abraham replied. "Genetic blood disorders can be mimicked, you know. Either chemically or with radiation treatment. And it wouldn't be impossible to rewrite DNA sequences, not with the right kind of nanotechnology. You see, I'm really trying to create a *new* blood disorder." His tone became eager. He and Cadel had arrived early at their law class, and by now he was leaning over Cadel, who was pressed up against a wall. "With vampirism, you have what is essentially a metabolic problem and an allergic reaction. The allergic reaction is a skin condition similar to that experienced by people with albinism. The metabolic problem is related to hemoglobin levels and to digestive acids. All you have to do is identify the right *combination* of factors and then reproduce them genetically—"

"You're not trying to reproduce them on yourself, are you?" Cadel interrupted. It had suddenly occurred to him that Abraham was looking more and more like a vampire every day. "You've got very pale, did you know that? You don't seem well."

Abraham stiffened.

"It's a legitimate method," he rejoined. "Many great medical researchers have infected themselves."

"Yes, but haven't they usually died in the process?" It alarmed Cadel that Abraham was willing to turn himself into a vampire. Abraham had always struck him as a fairly intelligent bloke, and if a fairly intelligent bloke was capable of doing something so stupid—well, it confirmed all Dr. Darkkon's opinions about the state of the world. "I mean, isn't there some other way? Can't you try it out on rats first?"

"Human cells are different from rat cells."

"Yes, but—"

"You never heard of a vampire rat, did you?"

"No, I—"

"It's like Professor Roth said—no pain, no gain. That's what Axis is all about; surely you understand?"

Seeing the fanatical gleam in Abraham's eye, Cadel gave up. There was no point arguing. Abraham might be intelligent, but he was also obsessed. Very soon, Cadel was sure, he would be seen flitting around the institute's dormitories wearing a black cape and fake plastic fangs. Not that he would have looked out of place. On the contrary: At least two-thirds of the student body would have alarmed any security guard at a normal institution. There was one young man who seemed to have melted half his face off; one who scuttled from shadow to shadow like a crab; one who wore infrared goggles permanently clamped across his eyes; one who never removed his latex surgeon's gloves. There was a girl who ran everywhere, mouth open, lungs heaving, eyes bolting from her head, as if she were fleeing from a monster. There was a figure in a monk's cowl whose hands were always concealed in his or her sleeves, and who never lifted his or her head to reveal even a flash of expression. There was a hairy youth who walked around swinging a length of pipe, and another whose shoes were fitted with long, steely spikes on their toes.

Among these people, a vampire wouldn't have attracted much attention. Nevertheless, Cadel resolved to stay out of Abraham's way. This was more easily said than done because Abraham, like Gazo, would hunt Cadel down. Cadel was easy to talk to. There was nothing threatening about him. Thanks to his father's influence, he was safe from random attacks and could afford to be pleasant. At school, he had picked up a lot of interesting information by fading into the background and offering no kind of challenge. At the Axis Institute, people would confide in him because he looked harmless.

He didn't make much noise or take up much space. He wasn't enrolled in any of the more dangerous subjects. He was small, with a sweet smile and a disarming gaze. He seemed so insignificant that people underestimated him.

They didn't realize that, almost through force of habit, he was collecting information to feed into a special database.

They didn't realize that he was well on the way to designing his behavioral-prediction program.

NINETEEN

"I'm wondering if you're trying to start this from the wrong end," the Virus remarked on one occasion, after he had spent several minutes watching the computations unroll on Cadel's screen. "You're starting with populations and moving in. Why don't you start with the human brain and move out?"

Cadel sighed. "In other words, why don't I create a precise neurobiological map of the human brain?" he said.

"It can be replicated. Theoretically. You know that."

"Oh, right—*theoretically.*" Cadel pointed out that the number of neurons in the human brain, 10^{11}, was comparable to the number of galaxies in the observable universe. "It would be a bit of a *challenge*, don't you think?"

The Virus shrugged. "We have a supercomputer."

"Yeah, but does it really have the capacity?"

"It can calculate up to eight billion digits of pi."

"So? You're still talking about ten thousand postsynaptic potentials for each neuron. Every two milliseconds. It's big numbers, Vee. Especially when you're talking about probabilities."

"Oh, big numbers." The Virus waved his hand. "What's so scary about big numbers?"

Kay-Lee agreed. *If Georg Cantor wasn't afraid of big numbers, why should you be?* she teased Cadel. *We've been talking about the number of infinite numbers, and you're worried about $10,000 \times 10^{11}$? Get a grip on* *yourself!* Of course, she didn't know the true reason behind Eiran Dempster's sudden fretfulness about big numbers. Cadel hadn't mentioned neurobiological maps; he had simply been unburdening himself as much as he possibly could without arousing her suspicions. She came up with the idea that he was suffering from a peculiar form of mathematical vertigo. *I get it sometimes myself,* she assured him. *You hit the infinite, and you get dizzy. The best thing for it is to go outside and sit in the sun. Though I don't suppose you have much sun in Toronto.*

With the Virus on one side, keeping him on his toes, and Kay-Lee on the other, soothing his overheated brain, Cadel felt that he was finally realizing his true potential. It was stimulating, enriching, and surprising. He became utterly immersed in theory, to the point where he sometimes forgot to eat. The Piggotts often heard him singing as he got dressed in the morning.

The trouble was that, while his infiltration and forgery classes were making him very happy, other aspects of the institute weren't quite so pleasant.

Cadel was growing used to the odd explosion on campus, and the sudden sprays of water or gas that always followed. He was growing used to the strange cries that occasionally reached his ears, faint and muffled, as he waited for an elevator or crossed the front lawn. He didn't worry much when his classes were invaded by teams of Grunts with sniffer dogs or electronic-field detectors. While at first he was surprised to see an unexplained hole punched in a wall, or a dead dog on the grass, he soon began to take such things in his stride. He just tried to ignore them and concentrate on his studies.

Then Clive Slaughter combusted—and Cadel began to experience a faint sense of unease.

The accident took place at Yarramundi, so Cadel never saw any evidence of it. He simply heard about it the next day, from Gazo Kovacs. Gazo had taken to joining Cadel for lunch whenever possible; though Gazo himself couldn't eat in a public place like the refectory, he would sit and watch Cadel consume the institute's soggy fare.

"Poor Bludgeon," said Gazo. "He was a real mess. He only half combusted."

Cadel grimaced. "Don't tell me," he complained. "I'm eating."

"The Führer made us look," Gazo went on glumly. "He said we'd afta get used to it. I dunno why. *I* ain't gonna be killing nobody."

"What did they do with the corpse?" asked Cadel. "What about his parents? They must be kicking up a stink."

"They staged a car crash. The gas tank exploded. It musta looked like a accident."

Cadel grunted. Though he hadn't much liked Clive Slaughter, he felt queasy at the thought of what Clive must have gone through. So when Thaddeus organized a memorial service at the institute, Cadel attended, even though he realized that the event was designed solely to placate Clive's parents. No one else had ever been given a memorial service at the institute because no one else had ever had family who were interested enough to appreciate one. Most of the Axis students either hated their relatives or were alone in the world, like Gazo.

Gazo himself joined Cadel at the service, which took place outdoors. A plaque, engraved with Clive's name, was embedded in one of the seminary walls, and a little bush was planted underneath it. Gazo was impressed.

"I'd like me name put up when I die," he confided to Cadel. "Somefink nice like that."

For a week or so, Cadel noticed Clive's absence. There was a sense of something missing whenever he walked into his basic-lying and his forgery classes. Then, just as Cadel was growing used to the idea that Clive's space would never again be filled, something happened to Jemima.

One morning, she and her sister arrived late for their case-studies lesson. This wasn't unusual. The twins were often late and would creep in giggling, trying not to make any noise. This time, however, they banged the door open and marched in, heads held high. Jemima, Cadel noticed, was sporting a thick gauze bandage on one cheek.

Luther Lasco, who had been speaking, paused while they crossed the room.

"Ah," he said, when they had planted themselves defiantly in the front row, "now, here's a good illustration of what I've been talking about. You try to cheat, you pay for it. Isn't that right, Jemima?"

Jem stared at him stonily, refusing to comment. She and her sister barely moved for the next half hour. At last, when the class was dismissed, Cadel approached her in the corridor outside lecture-room one.

"What happened?" he asked. "Did Dr. Lasco do that?"

"None of your business!" snapped Jemima. Niobe took her arm and led her away protectively. Behind Cadel, Doris snorted.

"That'll teach her," Doris said.

Cadel generally tried to avoid talking with Doris. But Abraham was quick to seek an explanation.

"Do you know what happened?" he inquired. "Was it Dr. Lasco?"

"Sure was," said Doris. "He cut her."

"Why?"

"Because she was cheating." Doris's tone was placid. "I knew she was. She's such a fool."

"Cheating in her poisoning class?"

"That's right," said Doris, and shrugged. "She was warned."

"Still . . ." Abraham sounded hesitant. At last he walked away. Seeing the little smirk on Doris's face, Cadel also withdrew, thinking hard.

This injury, he decided, would have an excitatory potential. Some kind of action would almost certainly result, though the variables would be hard to calculate. He just didn't *know* enough about Gemini to plot a decent causation tree.

"Oi, Cadel!" Gazo was lumbering along, trying to catch up with him. "What do you fink? Bit scary."

"Mmm."

"Poor Jem. I feel sorry for her, even if she *can* be a bitch. Where are you going?"

"To Hardware Heaven."

"Oh." Gazo stopped. The Virus wouldn't let him into Hardware Heaven. "Well, I s'pose I'll see you later? At lunch?"

Cadel didn't reply. His head was too full of calculations. He made straight for his computer and spent the rest of the day wrestling with probability factors and external inputs. That evening, he couldn't help himself: He asked Kay-Lee if she thought it was possible to turn emotions into equations. *Perhaps,* she replied doubtfully, *if they were a form of* chemical *equation.* But chemistry, she added, wasn't her strong suit.

The next morning, when the twins turned up at their forgery class, both were sporting identical bandages on their right cheeks.

"We're twins," said Ni, when asked what had happened, and everyone was dumbfounded. Ni's message was clear. She had cut her own cheek so that, once again, it was almost impossible to distinguish her from her sister.

Even Doris was impressed.

"Talk about blood is thicker than water," she murmured. "Where would they stop?"

Cadel wondered the same thing. And he was sure that he could work it out, given enough information—especially since Niobe's sacrifice had hugely reduced the range of possibilities. In the two remaining weeks of the first semester, he struggled with his undeveloped program, lost in a mire of complicated mathematical and chemical equations. He also hovered around the twins as much as he could, trying to glean little nuggets of precious data. He had read their files, of course—Thaddeus had given those to him without a single protest—but the files weren't complete. He needed to know all kinds of things about Jem and Ni, like their comparative degrees of competitiveness, the composition of their combined self-image, what they liked to do in their spare time . . .

It didn't take him long to realize that their habits had suddenly changed. Though he had never before encountered them in the library, they now spent hours there, whispering together in the stacks. No longer did they giggle and flirt and expose their tummies in skimpy little tops. Now they dressed in leather and camouflage colors. Now they were wary of everything and everyone, including Cadel. Even *he* found it hard to monitor them, because they would edge away when he drew near.

Nevertheless, he didn't need round-the-clock video surveillance or even a predictive computer program to tell him what they were up to.

"I think they're going to plant a bomb," Cadel told Thaddeus. "I think they're mad at Dr. Lasco, and they want to blow him up."

"I'm not surprised," Thaddeus said dismissively. He was busy preparing for a transmission from Dr. Darkkon, tuning frequencies and plugging in cables. "Half the time, I feel like blowing Luther up myself."

"Oh. Right. Well . . ." Cadel didn't know how to continue. "I thought I'd better tell you, anyway."

"Thank you, Cadel, but you needn't worry." Thaddeus flashed him a smile. "The whole institute is wired for sound—and pictures. Besides, Luther Lasco can look after himself. And I can't say I'd put much faith in those dizzy blond extroverts. Pass me the pliers, would you?"

As it turned out, Thaddeus's lack of confidence in the twins' abilities was justified.

Just three days before the Easter vacation, Niobe blew two of her fingers off in a failed attempt to booby-trap Luther Lasco's car.

TWENTY

Cadel hadn't been looking forward to the holidays. He didn't have any friends to spend them with, and he wasn't sure what he was supposed to do with himself away from the institute. When he discovered that Sark and Com and the other infiltration students kept wandering into Hardware Heaven as if nothing had changed, he decided to follow their example. If *they* could spend their entire vacation tapping away at a computer keyboard, so could he.

The Virus wasn't around much, but that didn't matter: Cadel preferred to work on his own. If he was ever stumped by a particular equation, he could always ask Kay-Lee for help—and he frequently did. Sometimes, when he needed a break, he would work on his Partner Post correspondence. By now he was growing bored with Partner Post, and he wasn't devoting nearly as much time and effort to his e-mails. As a result, clients were beginning to drop off his list, disgusted that their perfect partners were forgetting their birthdays, not replying to their letters, and confusing them with other people.

Cadel didn't mind. He had saved up quite a lot of money, thanks to Partner Post. Much of it had been spent on fancy computer software, and the rest had been used to buy presents for Kay-Lee—until she stopped him.

No more, she'd instructed. *This is ridiculous. Anyone would think you were trying to prove something. I know how you feel, Stormer—just relax. I'm not going anywhere.*

At lunchtime, Cadel would buy his usual chicken roll or ham-and-cheese focaccia at the refectory, which remained open during the holidays. Here Gazo would wait for him like a faithful dog. It was clear that Gazo had almost no one else to talk to. Though he lived on campus, surrounded by students who also lived on campus, people avoided him, despite his protective suit.

"Them twins," Gazo complained one afternoon, "they look right through me, like I don't exist. Why do they afta be so snooty? They only got a C on their law exam."

"You mean they're still around?" Cadel was surprised. "I thought they must have gone away to the beach, or something. I haven't seen them. What do they do with themselves?"

"Shoplifting, mostly." Gazo leaned across the table, lowering his voice. "Did you hear what happened? Wiv them twins?"

Cadel, who had been peeling bits of alfalfa off his chicken roll, looked up. He studied Gazo's expression. "They're fighting," he said at last.

"Oh." Gazo slumped. "You heard."

"No." In fact, Cadel had calculated the probabilities. "What have *you* heard?"

"Only what's going round the dorms," said Gazo. "Jem decided she wouldn't blow her fingers off to match Niobe, even if Ni cut her own cheek for Jem's sake. So Ni's mad at her now. She's put some kind of poison in Jem's fingernail polish, because Jem's going round wiv her fingers all covered in Band-Aids. Weird, eh?"

Cadel grunted.

"They're not nice, them girls." Gazo glanced around the refectory, folding his arms. "They're not talking to each uvver no more."

Cadel wasn't surprised. Curiously enough, he wasn't too pleased, either. Although he had predicted this fight as a likely outcome, it was not one that he approved of. The thought of Jem and Ni slugging it out filled him with a deep sense of discomfort for some reason.

"They come and go," Gazo added, "but they don't do it togevver. I ain't seen 'em for a week. I ain't seen nobody much, except Kunio. Not from our year. What about you?"

"Not really," Cadel replied. In fact, he had seen Abraham only the night before. It had been late—about half past nine—when Cadel had looked up from his computer screen and realized that he would have to get home quickly or run the risk of alarming the Piggotts. (He didn't want to do that, in case they had second thoughts about the institute.) Hurriedly he had packed his bag, slung it over his shoulder, and scampered out of Hardware Heaven. He hadn't expected to find Abraham using the elevator.

Chalk white, his eyes concealed behind an enormous pair of wraparound sunglasses, Abraham had confessed that he preferred to work at night. He had even considered living in the dormitories so that he wouldn't have to brave the sunlight when classes began again.

"At least I'd be able to stay indoors," he'd said. "Out of the sunlight, you know? I hate sunlight. But it's cheaper to stay where I am now, since I'm living on my savings at present."

He had given Cadel a ride home in a little bomb of a Ford Cortina that smelled of chemicals and moldy carpet. During the trip, Abraham had talked nonstop about the dwindling sum in his bank account, the ghastly people he shared his house with, and the way his family kept sticking their noses into his business.

"They think I'm insane," he'd lamented. "They actually think I'm insane, when they wouldn't know one end of a chromosome from the other! It's ridiculous."

Cadel had looked out the window, clutching his backpack against his chest. The streetlights had flowed past. He had seen into people's houses, catching glimpses of families clearing tables and watching television. These glowing images always made him feel sad—he didn't know why.

"Why *do* you want to create vampires?" he'd suddenly asked.

"What do you mean?" Abraham had sounded astonished. "Why shouldn't I?"

Cadel had struggled to phrase his next question without causing offense. "The thing is—I can't quite see the point, really. Perhaps you could explain."

A long pause had followed. At last Abraham had said, in withering accents, "Well, if you don't know the answer to that already, Cadel, it makes me wonder what you're doing at the institute."

This remark had lingered in Cadel's head. He had pondered it that evening and again the next morning. Abraham was a little bit mad, of course, but was he also a little bit right? Was Cadel missing something really, really obvious? Were his occasional doubts shared by other students? Was the institute *really* his natural habitat?

Certainly Gazo wasn't entirely comfortable there. He didn't like the Yarramundi campus, or the way he would sometimes hear animals squealing at night. He complained about the students who set fire to trash cans and stuck razor blades into library books. He had even been forced to put rattraps in his dresser because of all the theft happening in the dorms.

But Gazo was an idiot. Surely, for that reason, his opinions didn't matter?

"I know Doris is visiting her granny," Gazo was saying, as the refectory slowly emptied. "She's lucky she's got one. I can't even get a job, wiv my suit on. It gets a bit boring."

"You should study," Cadel remarked, through a mouthful of chicken.

"I do study." Gazo sighed. "I study a lot. But I can't do it all the time. Not like you. Hey, what *are* you doing upstairs? Are you hacking into the CIA's computer system—stuff like that?"

"No," Cadel replied. In fact, he had recently decided that someone was hacking into *his* system. It hardly seemed possible that anything should have breached his firewalls, but he had started to notice one or two flickers of activity that worried him. They were very subtle, but they were unmistakably there.

His solution had been to build a special program, full of locks and traps, to lure the invader into an exposed position. This had worked, but only up to a point. The questing tentacles of code had, more than once, appeared in his system; but when he'd tried to trace them back to their source, they had broken up, dissolving into a meaningless soup. It was intensely frustrating. He did, however, have an idea for a virus that might stop the rot. If it was to *bond* with the invading code and prevent it from self-destructing, then perhaps he'd have a chance. But he would have to construct the virus on another system. A *discrete* system. Otherwise the mysterious hacker would know what he was up to. . . .

"Oh!" Gazo suddenly exclaimed. "Hello, Maestro."

Cadel jumped. He hadn't noticed Max's approach, despite the fact that the Maestro's bodyguards now numbered three. It was odd to see Max in the refectory. Normally, he didn't join his colleagues for lunch.

"Cadel," he said, surveying the two students from beneath weary eyelids. "What are you doing here?"

In response, Cadel lifted the remains of his chicken roll.

"You working? Studying?" Max wanted to know, and Cadel nodded. "Where?"

"Computer room."

"Private project, is it?"

"Sort of."

"Vee can't be around much."

Cadel shook his head. Gazo, who obviously couldn't bear to be left out, added: "Cadel's here all the time. He loves working here. Even during the holidays."

"Zat so?" Max studied Cadel's face, as if searching for something. Cadel kept his expression bland, though he was secretly annoyed. Why *shouldn't* he be working upstairs? What was Max's problem?

"Heard you talking about your old man," Max continued, removing a cigar from his pocket and lighting up. There were no nonsmoking areas at the institute. "Speak to 'im much?"

"Sometimes," Cadel rejoined, cagily.

"Keeping an eye on you, is he?"

"Yes."

Max nodded. Puffing at his cigar, he stared at Cadel for a moment longer. Then he jerked his head at his bodyguards, and they all went to buy cappuccinos—all four of them.

Cadel headed in the opposite direction, making his way to the door.

"Hey, Cadel." Gazo had followed him. "You didn't finish your roll."

"I wasn't hungry."

"They're a bit scary, aren't they? Them blokes." Gazo glanced back over his shoulder. "Do you fink they're in the Mafia? Abraham says they are."

"Gazo." Cadel stopped and turned. "Don't you have anything else to do?"

Gazo faltered. His whole body slumped.

"Not really," he mumbled. "I told you."

"Well, *I* have. I'm working. Why don't you go and—I don't know—watch TV? Go for a run?"

"I can't. Not in this. I can only run at night, when no one's around."

"Well, go and write to my dad, then," Cadel suggested. "Tell him how you're doing."

Gazo's face brightened behind its plastic shield.

"Yeah?" he said. "You fink I should?"

"Definitely."

"*Okay.*"

"Good," said Cadel, moving away. But Gazo's voice pursued him. "I dunno his address! Cadel!"

"Just give me the letter," Cadel called back. "I'll pass it on."

"Will you? Oh, great! You're a mate, Cadel, fanks a lot!"

Cadel went straight home to work on his virus. He worked away until two o'clock in the morning, undisturbed by the Piggotts. (Stuart was in New York at the time, and Lanna was in bed with a migraine.) The next day he also spent at home, working feverishly. The day after that he worked until three o'clock in the afternoon, before packing his bag and hurrying off to the institute. He couldn't wait another night. He wanted to test out his new program immediately.

When he arrived at Hardware Heaven, he found an envelope sitting on his keyboard. It was addressed to him. Inside were Gazo's letter to Dr. Darkkon and a covering note for Cadel.

Deer Cadel, it said. *This is my leter for your dad. I hope you get it. I hope your not sick. I dont know were you live or I coud visit you. I have to tell you importent news. Your freind Gazo.*

Cadel shook his head over this message. He wondered what the important news was. Something to do with theft in the dorms, no doubt. Cadel tucked the letters into his pocket and glanced over at Com. Com was always in Hardware Heaven, tapping away at his keyboard like a robot. He was more like a computer than a person; he never displayed the slightest interest in what anyone else was doing. That was why Cadel tended to ignore him.

Sark wasn't around; nor was Dr. Vee. Cadel had the room pretty much to himself and quickly took advantage of the fact. He set about tracing the source of the mysterious probes that were infiltrating his programs.

By eight o'clock that night, he had succeeded.

The culprit was Dr. Vee.

He wasn't entirely surprised. Infiltration, after all, was Dr. Vee's subject. What did surprise Cadel was the nature of the probe that Dr. Vee had created. For all intents and purposes, it was the superhacker program that Sark was attempting to design. Automatically, on a regular basis, it would do sweeps of the entire internal institute network, collecting huge amounts of information by keeping one step ahead of dynamic passwords. Using his own virus, Cadel was able to "ride" piggyback on Dr. Vee's probe as it wormed its way into countless files belonging to Luther Lasco, Maestro Max, Tracey Lane, Dr. Deal. He found Carla's various toxin recipes. He found a heated e-mail exchange between Adolf and Luther—something about security codes.

He discovered an invitation from Tracey Lane to Dr. Deal: *Meet me at Antonelli's, 10:45.* The private business of the institute's entire faculty was laid bare—except for that of Thaddeus Roth. Thaddeus didn't have much of a presence on the network.

"Well, well, well," Cadel murmured. His voice seemed very loud in the silence, but Com didn't even twitch an ear.

Then Cadel's cell phone rang.

"What on earth do you think you're doing?" Mrs. Piggott demanded, as soon as Cadel had uttered his name. "Do you realize what time it is?"

"Uh . . ." Cadel checked his watch. "Ten thirty?"

"Where are you?"

"At the institute. I told you. I had to do something—"

"Have you eaten?"

"Yes," Cadel replied. He didn't feel the need to explain that he had eaten only an old packet of pretzels that he had found in the bottom of his backpack.

"Well, I want you to come home, please. At once. You can call a cab, and I'll pay for it when you get home."

"Okay, but—"

"*NOW,* Cadel!"

There was no point arguing. It *was* very late. With a sigh, Cadel abandoned his detective work and packed up. He didn't bother saying good night to Com. He simply headed for the elevators and caught one down to the ground floor.

When its steel doors parted in front of him, he was surprised to see a black-clad figure waiting by the UP button. The figure was wearing a black turtleneck sweater, black pants, a black vest, black gloves, and a black balaclava. All the same, Cadel could tell it was one of the twins. They both had very distinctive eyes—and bosoms.

"Niobe?" he said. (Or was it Jemima?)

She brushed past him without a word. Was she unable to hear him, perhaps? Because of the balaclava? Cadel didn't like the look of that padded vest. It was covered with bulging pockets—the kind of pockets you could hide things in. Switchblades. Hand grenades. Things like that.

Of course, she wouldn't have been able to get a hand grenade past the security scanners; but still, there were other things you could use to create a big bang. Cadel knew that perfectly well.

"Are you all right?" he asked. The doors, however, were already closing. Cadel's view was blocked. His gaze shifted to the indicator panel above his head, where the elevator's destination would be displayed as a glowing yellow number.

First floor. Was she heading for the dormitories?

Cadel wondered if he should mention this sighting to anyone. In other parts of the world, you always notified the authorities if you saw someone wearing a black balaclava. At the institute, however, it wasn't *that* out of the ordinary. Many people wore balaclavas and bulletproof vests as fashion statements. Niobe wasn't necessarily on her way to blow her twin's head off.

With a sigh, Cadel decided that he'd better do something. Just in case. Once he had left the building, and before he called a cab, he would contact the emergency number supplied to each Axis student for occasions just like this. He would leave the building first, though. No use standing around like a moron, waiting to be blown up.

Though Cadel had not studied explosives, he knew enough to get well out of the way when there were people in black balaclavas around.

TWENTY-ONE

"A most unfortunate incident," Thaddeus remarked the following afternoon. "Difficult to handle, in all kinds of ways."

Cadel said nothing. The news wasn't good. Apparently, Niobe had been skulking around the campus in a black balaclava for a very good reason. She had been attempting to track down her twin, who had in turn been trying to steal some kind of deadly toxin from the microbiology labs.

Both had been caught—but not before Niobe had smashed a computer monitor over Jemima's head, fracturing her skull.

"Arrangements had to be made," Thaddeus confessed. "Jemima couldn't be found on the premises in that condition."

"Is she—is she all right?" asked Cadel, who had taken a seat on Thaddeus's maroon couch.

"Not at all. She's in a coma."

"Oh."

"Her sister has disappeared," Thaddeus continued. "It's very worrying. Luther's trying to track her down."

Staring out the window, Cadel said flatly, "Will she be all right?"

"Oh, I shouldn't think so." As Cadel turned to look at him, Thaddeus lifted an eyebrow. "Think about it, Cadel. She's effectively killed her other half. That's going to cripple her psychologically."

"No, I mean—will she be *all right*? You know. If Luther finds her." Cadel's urgent gaze had a curious effect on Thaddeus. For the first time ever, Cadel saw him glance sideways, as if trying to avoid Cadel's regard. He even scratched his nose.

"I believe we can trust Luther to do the right thing," he said smoothly. "I've left the matter to him. He'll weigh the risks and make a sound decision. He's not one to resort to drastic measures unless it's absolutely necessary. Remember, we have something to pin on Niobe now, if we choose. It's good leverage."

Cadel swallowed.

"The twins," Thaddeus added, "were my mistake. They were far more psychologically fragile than I anticipated. I'm afraid the blame rests squarely with me." His bright black eyes were like nail guns, pinning Cadel to his seat. "I can only hope this hasn't caused you to lose faith in my judgment."

"No," Cadel replied.

"They were particular friends of yours? The twins? I wasn't aware of it."

"No. They weren't."

Nevertheless, Cadel was troubled by their fate. Though he didn't want to think about it, unfortunate images kept popping into his mind. And when the new semester began a few days later, he found that he couldn't avoid talking about Gemini. Gazo, for one, kept worrying away at the subject like a child picking at a scab.

"They musta gone mad," he said gloomily. "I dunno why. Can you go mad handling poisons?"

"I'm not sure," Cadel muttered. They were standing by the door of lecture-room one, waiting for Alias. They had never seen Alias before but knew that he was supposed to be teaching them the art of disguise. Luther's case-studies lectures were now finished; Alias would be taking over his time slots.

Cadel wished that Alias would arrive and put a stop to all this discussion about the twins.

"Doris," said Gazo, "could you give yourself brain damage, mucking around wiv poisons?"

Doris smirked. "Those two *already* had brain damage," she retorted, adding, "Three down, five to go." Cadel didn't like the way she said this. It was almost as if she was taking credit for what had happened.

"I saw Ni that night," Abraham suddenly remarked. His voice was hoarse, and he was a dreadful color. Furthermore, his hair seemed to be falling out. Cadel could see white patches of scalp all over his head, showing through the thick, black curls. "She was sneaking around like a cat. At first I thought she was—well, somebody else." Abraham paused for a moment. "You get a few people sneaking around in the labs at night."

"Like who?" Gazo wanted to know. But Abraham simply made an impatient gesture. He had become very moody, Cadel thought. Even Terry had noted it in one of the daily computer reports that Cadel had logged into: *Subject demonstrating abrupt mood swings, hair loss, vision impairment, nausea.*

Whenever Cadel penetrated Terry's firewall, he did so reluctantly, with a sense of distaste. If he hadn't felt the need to build up a thorough database on the institute's faculty members, he wouldn't have bothered delving into Terry's secrets. They were all pretty revolting, and Cadel had a weak stomach.

"Should you be up?" he asked Abraham. "You don't look well."

Even Doris exhibited surprise at this remark. Abraham was obviously startled. No one openly expressed concern about other people's health at the institute. No one except Cadel, that is.

"I'm fine," said Abraham.

"Your lips are blue."

"I told you, I'm fine."

"I don't know why you want to be a vampire," said Doris, in her sneering, whining fashion. "Do you realize, if you become a vampire, you won't be able to eat any decent food anymore?"

"Yeah—and you won't be able to go out," added Gazo. "I mean, not even in a suit like mine. You'll be stuck inside all day."

It was Cadel who first noticed Luther walking down the corridor toward them. Surely, he thought, Luther wasn't heading *their* way? Was Alias sick, or delayed? Cadel's frown alerted his classmates, who turned to look, one by one. By the time Luther joined them, the little group had fallen silent.

Like Abraham, Luther was wearing sunglasses—together with fingerless gloves and a scarf wrapped around his neck. He coughed into his woolly fist before addressing them.

"Okay," he croaked. "Everybody inside."

"It's locked," Gazo pointed out.

"Oh. Yeah. Sorry."

Luther kept sniffing and wiping his nose as he slowly unlocked the door to lecture-room one. Nobody asked him what he was doing there. Most of those present had cause to be wary of Luther. Even Doris preferred not to speak before being spoken to.

They followed Luther into the room, which seemed very large for such a small class. Luther dragged a wooden chair from behind the door to a central spot in front of the lectern, and collapsed into it. He set down a paper carry-bag.

"Right," he rasped, when everyone was sitting quietly. "Let's talk about disguise."

Then he took off his glasses and grinned.

A murmur of shock rippled around the room. The man in the chair was not Luther. He didn't have Luther's eyes or smile. His teeth were better than Luther's. His face wasn't as narrow, or as rigid.

"Fooled ya!" he crowed. "Lesson one, my friends. I'm Alias. You don't need to know my *real* name."

Gazo laughed. When the others turned to look at him, he shrank back into his seat.

"What did I do, exactly?" Alias continued. "I put on a gray wig and a pair of shades, is all. That's right. No makeup, no prosthetics, no false teeth, no lifts in my shoes. Take a good look at me. I'm nowhere near Dr. Lasco's build. All I needed was the slouch and the shuffle—it was

a pushover. Why? Because you weren't expecting anything different."
He leaned back and linked his hands behind his head. "Now, I'm not
saying you can all do this," he added, his gaze traveling from Kunio to
Doris, before finally coming to rest on Cadel. "I've got the kind of
range you can only pull off when you're a bit on the average side. This
little guy here"—he winked at Cadel—"well, this little guy would
have his work cut out for him, trying to pull off a Luther Lasco. That
doesn't mean, however, that he can't be somebody else. Transformation
isn't as hard as you might think, if you've got the right attitude. Not to
mention a basic grounding from yours truly."

Gazo raised his hand. But before he could speak, Abraham suddenly toppled onto the floor.

He had fainted.

"I'll be looking at makeup, of course," Alias went on, just as if nothing had happened. "Makeup and wigs can do a lot for anyone. So can
clothes, obviously, and padding—"

"Er . . . Mr. Alias, sir?" Gazo's hand was still in the air. "Um, I fink
Abraham's sick."

"Don't interrupt, Mr. Kovacs."

"But shouldn't we take 'im to First Aid?"

"He'll be all right," said Alias dismissively, then began to talk about
the Alexander technique of posture awareness.

He was right, as it happened. Soon Abraham began to stir. After
about five minutes he sat up.

"Glad you could join us, Mr. Coggins," said Alias. "So what I'm
saying is this. Whether you're making yourself visible or invisible, the
thing about a disguise is that half the time you can hide behind just
one prominent feature. A big nose. An awful tie. Even a giant pimple.
People will be so busy noticing whatever it is that they won't pay much
attention to the rest of you."

Abraham managed to return to his seat, but only just. He looked
very ill. In fact, he looked so ill that he was distracting, and Alias finally
told him to get out. ("I don't want you throwing up in here, Mr. Cog-

gins.") Everyone watched in silence as Abraham shuffled out of the room—everyone except Cadel. He sat staring at the floor until he heard the sound of a door slam.

When the class finished, he and Gazo went to look for Abraham's car, which they found in the lot.

"So he's still on campus," Cadel observed.

"I don't fink he goes anywhere else much," said Gazo. "Not anymore. That car's here most of the time. Even at night."

They both stared at the beat-up old Ford. "Well, I have to go," Cadel said at last, abruptly. "I've got work to do."

"Could he be in First Aid? Should we have a look?"

"I told you. I'm busy."

"Have you got a class?"

"I'm busy!" Cadel snapped. In fact, he was planning to spend the rest of the afternoon in Hardware Heaven. All at once he couldn't cope with his classmates anymore. First the twins, now Abraham. He wanted to block them out of his mind. He wanted to concentrate on his *work*. (His work was the important thing.) "I'll see you later."

He started to walk away, heading back toward the seminary building. Gazo called after him, straining through his transmission filter.

"Cadel!" he cried. "Wait! Our homework for Alias—how we afta show up in disguise? For his next class?"

"What about it?"

"Well, do you know what your disguise will be?"

"No."

"What am *I* gonna do? How can I do anyfink in me bloody suit?"

"Wear a mustache," Cadel replied, before ducking through the seminary doors. Once he'd passed the scanners, he made his way up to Hardware Heaven—hurriedly, as a mouse might run to its hole. He wanted to hide. He wanted to escape. As long as he was in Hardware Heaven, he could forget about the rest of the institute, which was getting on his nerves.

But when he reached his computer and sat down, he discovered that the keyboard was speckled with drops of a thick, dark, tacky substance.

Looking up, he saw that it had leaked through the ceiling. From the labs on the next floor.

It was blood, of course. He recognized it instantly.

TWENTY-TWO

Cadel stood in the Piggotts' bathroom that night, looking at himself in the mirror.

His hair was plastered down with Vaseline and darkened with comb-through "party color." He had padded his waist with scarves and shoved gobs of Tack 'n' Stick behind his ears, to make them stick out more. He had even applied fake tan, having stolen a bottle from Mrs. Piggott's cosmetics drawer.

The more he did to himself, the more ridiculous he looked.

"This isn't a disguise," he muttered. "It's a carnival costume."

His assignment was simple: to come along to the Wednesday morning disguise class as somebody else. Alias intended to grade and comment on every student's effort. Cadel could just imagine what Alias would say about *this* attempt. "Pathetic," he would sneer. Or perhaps: "I'm in no mood for jokes, Mr. Darkkon."

With a sigh, Cadel removed the Tack 'n' Stick, which was hurting his ears. Slowly he unrolled the scarves and wiped off the tan. He didn't know what to do. Alias had talked a lot about posture, presence, and focal points, but Cadel couldn't see how any of it would work without expensive wigs and makeup and colored contact lenses. Not in *his* case, anyway. Even when his distinctive blue eyes were shielded by sunglasses and his hair was slicked back like an otter's pelt, he still looked like Cadel Piggott pretending to be cool.

"Cadel!" It was Mrs. Piggott. "Where are you?"

"I'm in here!" Cadel cried. The sunglasses belonged to Lanna. He took them off quickly, then stuck them in a drawer.

"What are you doing?" Lanna demanded.

"Uh—just having a shower!" Cadel knew that he would have to remove all the rubbish in his hair or face a barrage of questions. So he turned on the shower and began to pull off his clothes.

"Phone for you, Cadel!"

"Tell them I'll call back!"

The hot water pelted down, filling the room with steam. When Cadel stepped into the torrent, he watched the water that was swirling around his feet turn black with hair color. So much for his first attempt at disguise.

He racked his brain for a solution. "Keep it simple," Alias had said. "Don't go Hollywood on me. Like I told you—half the secret is *attitude.*"

Attitude. Confidence. But could a swagger in your step really add a few inches to your height?

He was still stumped when he emerged from the bathroom and approached Mrs. Piggott. She was sitting at the dining-room table with about five hundred fabric samples strewn all around her.

"Who called?" Cadel wanted to know.

"Hmmm?"

"Who was on the phone? You said someone called me."

"Oh." Lanna dragged her gaze from the swatch of silk in her hand. "Oh, yes. They didn't leave a number."

"Who was it, though?"

"They didn't leave a name."

"Did they say they'd call back?"

But Lanna's attention had wandered. She was staring at a price list and didn't bother to reply. Cadel trudged into his bedroom, where he banged out a message for Kay-Lee. *Sometimes I wish I looked different,* he wrote. *Do you ever wish that? Sometimes it's like my outside doesn't match my inside.* In Cadel's opinion, his outside had *never* matched his inside. If he had been tall and elderly like Thaddeus, he might have been getting the kind of respect that he deserved all these years. As it was, people took one look at him and dismissed him. They thought he was of no consequence.

It occurred to Cadel that, if he ever *did* learn to disguise himself, his life might improve dramatically.

"Cadel!"

He groaned. Lanna must have snapped out of her trancelike state.

"What?" he yelled.

"Come here, please!"

"Why?"

"I'm in my bathroom!"

Cadel winced. He knew what was coming. When he slouched into the Piggotts' bathroom, he found it still damp from his recent shower. He also found Lanna standing on the rumpled bath mat, her hands on her hips.

"Cadel," she said, "you know I don't mind your using this bathroom. I realize you like the Jacuzzi in here. But I've told you before to *clean up after yourself.* I don't want to find your dirty clothes on the floor, young man. I don't want to find the lid of the shampoo open."

"Sorry," Cadel muttered.

"And what's this?" Lanna pointed to a smear of fake tan that Cadel had missed. He hadn't wiped it off the marble counter. "What have you been doing?"

"Nothing."

"Is that my *foundation,* Cadel?"

"No." Cadel put on his innocent look. "What's foundation?"

The lines on Lanna's brow deepened. "Have you been using my makeup?" she pressed.

"No!" Cadel tried to sound insulted. "Makeup's for girls!"

And then the phone rang.

They heard it quite clearly, because there was a wall-mounted phone in every bathroom. Lanna only had to stretch out her arm to reach the one nearest them.

"Yes?" she said. "Oh yes. Hang on." She presented the cordless receiver to Cadel. "It's for you."

Cadel wondered who would be calling him on the household number. He had his own cell phone, after all.

"Hello?" he said with a wary glance at Mrs. Piggott.

No one answered. But he could hear breathing at the other end of the line.

"Hello," he repeated.

"I know it was you."

The voice was raspy. Cadel couldn't even tell if it was male or female. But he thought he heard a sob.

"Who is this?" he demanded.

"You bastard! How *could* you?"

There was a click, followed by the dial tone.

Cadel stared at the receiver.

"What's wrong?" Lanna asked.

"Oh, nothing."

"Who was it?"

Cadel shrugged.

"One of your friends?"

"I don't think so." Cadel was reviewing all the possibilities. He assumed that the call had had something to do with the Axis Institute, and he wondered uneasily if one of the crazier students had decided that he was responsible for a bad mark, or a successful piece of sabotage.

He hoped not.

"So you haven't been playing with my makeup? Cadel? Do you know how much cosmetics *cost*, by any chance?" Mrs. Piggott was saying. "If you've touched my lip gloss, there'll be hell to pay."

It couldn't have been a dissatisfied customer from Partner Post, Cadel decided. Not one of his clients even knew that he existed, thanks to the way he'd shuttled his messages through a series of re-mailers.

Could it have been some sort of test? Something that Luther had set up, or Maestro Max? Hmm.

"Cadel? Are you listening to me?"

"I didn't touch your stupid stuff!" he cried, suddenly irritated beyond endurance. "Why should I?"

"Because you can't keep your nose out of anything, that's why!" Lanna snapped. She had pulled the bottle of fake tan out of the cosmetics drawer. "Look at this! Look! It's almost empty!"

"Buy yourself a new one, then!" Cadel retorted. "I'll pay for it, just get off my back!"

"Cadel, what on earth—"

"I was trying to cover up my pimples, all right? Are you satisfied?"

As Cadel had expected, this excuse completely threw Mrs. Piggott. She seemed to deflate, like a balloon.

"Oh," she said faintly.

"Can I go now?"

"Yes, of course. But—there are creams, Cadel. Did you realize that? Special things you can get—"

"I know," he said, and made his escape. Lanna didn't follow him. She was good at nagging, but not so good at comforting. It embarrassed her.

He'd counted on that.

Upon reaching his bedroom, he checked his e-mail, to see if it contained any eerie or threatening messages. It didn't. So he spent the next few hours trying to trace the source of the mysterious call, hacking into phone company networks and databases.

When at last he came up with a name, it merely puzzled him.

Parsons. Matthew Eric Parsons. Who on earth was that? Nobody Cadel knew.

Unless he was somehow connected to that girl at Crampton—what was her name?—Heather Parsons? The location was certainly right.

If Heather Parsons was Cadel's nuisance caller, then she had to be calling about her graduation exams. She had failed these exams like everyone else in Cadel's year. Surely she couldn't have worked out that he was responsible? Possibly she was acting on instinct; there couldn't have been a proper *investigation*.

Still, it was a worry.

Fretting over this unforeseen development, Cadel checked his Partner Post e-mail. He found a note from Kay-Lee. *Dear Stormer,* she had written, *don't get me started on appearances. Just don't get me started. As far as I'm concerned, we'll be a lot better off when we've evolved into disembodied brains floating in tanks. Have you seen that movie,* The Man with Two Brains? *I'd like to be one of the brains in that movie. Bodies are just a waste of space. You have to feed them and clean them and take them to the dentist, and for what? So that they'll let you down, again and again.*

What I feel is this: Heaven, when we get there, will be Heavenly because we'll all have left our bodies behind. But you're not a girl, Stormer, so maybe you don't really understand what I'm talking about.

There was more. A lot more. But Cadel didn't read it until some time later, because as his eye alighted on the word *girl,* he was suddenly visited by the most brilliant idea.

Girls. Makeup. Lip gloss.

Of course!

TWENTY-THREE

"Cadel? Is that *you?*"

It was Abraham who first recognized Cadel. Having decided to disguise himself as a Buddhist monk, Abraham had shaved off what remained of his hair, got rid of his goatee, and somehow located a set of orange and purple robes. Cadel was very impressed by Abraham's effort. Kunio, too, had done a pretty good job. He wore a beard, a mustache, horn-rimmed spectacles, a dark suit, and a bowler hat; he carried a briefcase in his right hand and a rolled umbrella in his left. He looked like a business executive.

Poor Gazo, of course, hadn't been able to do much with his suit. Behind the fogged mask of his headpiece, his skin was a curious, unconvincing chestnut color. (Cadel suspected that he was trying to impersonate someone from India or Pakistan.) As for Doris, she was a pathetic sight. She had plastered her face with makeup, donned a corn-colored wig, and squeezed herself into some very tight, very revealing clothes. Anywhere else, her appearance would have been greeted by howls of laughter.

No one waiting by the door of lecture-room one, however, dared to comment on Doris's outfit. They were far too intimidated. Abraham was also rather ill. And Kunio, for his part, was so fascinated by Cadel's disguise that he didn't appear to notice Doris at all. He kept walking round and round Cadel like a tourist inspecting a famous statue.

Gazo, too, was impressed. "You look great, Cadel," he gasped. "Wow! You look *just* like a girl!"

"But would you have recognized me?" Cadel asked. "That's the important thing."

"I dunno." Gazo cocked his head to one side. "You look the same but not the same."

"Like your own twin sister," said Abraham hoarsely, and he began to cough. Doris snorted.

"He does *not* look like a girl," she sneered. "He's wearing great big hiking boots!"

"Yes, that's the whole point." Abraham shot Doris a weary, contemptuous look. His eyes were bloodshot. "He's not trying too hard. Teetering around on silly stiletto heels doesn't make a person more female."

Doris, who was teetering around on stiletto heels herself, flushed and scowled. Cadel tried to change the subject.

"You look good, Abraham," he said. "You had *me* convinced, for a moment."

Abraham grunted. Then Gazo said, "There's Alias. He's dressed up as Kunio."

Everyone turned to watch a figure in a military uniform stride briskly toward them. As it drew nearer, Cadel was astonished at the brilliance of the disguise that Alias had achieved. He looked *exactly* like Kunio, right down to the shape of his nose. It was astonishing.

Suddenly the advancing figure stopped and pointed. A babble of frantic Japanese filled the air.

"Wow," said Gazo, in reverent tones. "He even knows the lingo."

But as the bowler-hatted Kunio began to laugh, Cadel realized what was going on. The real Kunio had only just arrived. The other Kunio was, in fact, their instructor.

Behind the suit, glasses, wig, beard, mustache and makeup, he didn't really resemble Kunio much at all.

"Dear me," he said, with a big, toothy grin, "when are you people going to learn? Rule number one: Don't just ignore the foreign guy who can't speak the language and didn't understand what he was supposed to do today. Otherwise you might get caught out." He patted Kunio's gold-braided shoulder, confusing the Japanese student even more. "Okay, everyone, let me look at you. Properly."

Cadel didn't know if his disguise would pass inspection. He had applied some of Mrs. Piggott's makeup (lip gloss, mascara, and eye shadow), tied his curly hair up with a ribbon, bought an old Indian-cotton skirt and a pair of snap-on earrings from a thrift shop, and donned one of Mrs. Piggott's knitted jackets over an old black T-shirt. The bust concealed by this T-shirt had been achieved by stuffing a bra with sports socks.

As Abraham had said, Cadel now looked just like his own twin sister. But would such a transformation be good enough for Alias?

"Hmm," said Alias, stopping in front of Abraham. "Not bad. Not bad at all. I like to see a student getting serious about his assignments, Mr. Coggins: Shaving your head shows a lot of commitment. And a costume like this is like a uniform—people look at it, rather than at you. But remember, for that very reason, you're not going to slip in quietly when you're dressed as a Buddhist monk—not unless you're trying to crash the Dalai Lama's birthday party. Understand?"

Abraham nodded.

"Good. Okay. Now—Mr. Kovacs . . ." Alias confronted Gazo. "You're an unusual case, Mr. Kovacs, but you do have certain advantages. For instance, there's only about thirty square inches of your body that you have to worry about. My advice is: Listen and learn. Because today we'll be having a lesson on makeup." Moving sideways, Alias reached Doris. "Ye-e-es. You know, I like this one. A brave attempt. It would only work in a very small number of places, though. Might I recommend, Ms. Deauville, that you try something on the other end of the gender spectrum? You might find that you're highly successful when impersonating a *man*."

No one laughed at this. It wasn't meant to be a joke. Doris seemed bewildered but didn't ask for more details. So Alias moved on.

"Well, well," he said with a smile. "Mr. Darkkon. Or should I say

Miss Darkkon? That's a very elegant little disguise. Simple. Simplicity is important. You can't always be carrying around a briefcase full of false eyelashes and prosthetic ears." He waved his own briefcase to illustrate the point. "But since I *am* carrying around just such a briefcase, we might begin our lesson now—and we'll have to do that in the bathrooms. Staff facilities, of course. We'll try the men's, I think, under the circumstances." He winked at Cadel and offered his arm to Doris. "Need help in those heels, Ms. Deauville? I know I would."

For an employee of the Axis Institute, Alias was surprisingly polite. Even Doris was disarmed by his placid, friendly style. Like the other three students, she followed him obediently to the closest staff bathrooms, which were quite luxurious. The mirrors above the two vanity sinks were ringed with blazing lightbulbs, and there was a lot of polished granite scattered about.

One of the mirrors had been cracked, however (it looked like a bullet hole), so Alias set up in front of the other one. For the next hour, he demonstrated various tricks of the makeup artist's trade, transforming Abraham into an old man and Doris into a young one. He also distributed a shopping list of basic "must-have" cosmetics, lectured the class on what distinguishes a bad wig from a good one, and gave them each a set of fake fingernails. These were split, yellowish, and diseased-looking.

"You don't have to pay for them," he advised, in his strangely unmemorable voice. "I just want to see you make good use of them. Except you, Gazo, obviously."

Gazo, who had been looking worried, immediately brightened. When the class was dismissed, he took the opportunity to thank Alias. Cadel didn't bother to wait for him, but headed straight to the library, head down. He was embarrassed about his disguise. For this reason, he had donned it in one of the more obscure bathrooms, by the elevator on the upper floor of the stacks. As far as he knew, no one ever used this bathroom. Cadel had discovered it on his second trip to the stacks, when he had been looking for a special text on white-collar crime. He had managed to find the text, but on his way back to the elevator had heard a strange sound. His immediate reaction had been to dart through the nearest door, which had opened into a dingy men's bathroom.

Nothing had pursued him. After waiting a few minutes, he had risked returning to the elevator. Thereafter, Cadel had sometimes used this same bathroom as a hiding place when he couldn't cope with Gazo anymore, or as a spot where he could squeeze the odd pimple in private. It was the perfect place to peel off his twin sister, without any offensive questions being asked. He always felt pretty safe there because no one else ever seemed to be in it.

Until now.

He was stationed in front of a mirror, opening his backpack, when he heard the noise. A scuffling sound. Looking up, he scanned the reflection of the stall doors behind him, noting that they were all closed. There was a sizeable gap between the bottom of each door and the concrete floor beneath it, but the room was so poorly lit that Cadel couldn't spot any ankles or feet framed in these gaps.

"Hello?" he faltered.

No reply. Cadel, however, decided not to wait around. He slung his backpack over his shoulder and was on his way out when a stall door banged open behind him. Something large rushed across the room. Cadel screamed and grabbed at the door handle but was jerked back. Lifted. He kicked and clawed and was pushed to the ground. A heavy weight fell on him.

"Make one more sound," a voice rasped, "and I'll throttle you."

"Help!" Cadel cried. He hadn't meant to call out; it hadn't been a conscious decision. The punch that landed on his jaw took him completely by surprise.

It seemed to rattle every tooth in his head. He actually saw stars. When he recovered his vision, he was on his back, staring into the blotched, sweaty face of Dr. Deal.

"What you have to understand, my dear," Dr. Deal panted, "is that you can't just walk into the men's lavatories and expect to get away with it—"

"I'm not!" Cadel struggled to rise, and was slapped down again. *"Stop it!"* he screeched.

And Dr. Deal stopped. Abruptly, he reared back, his weight tumbling off Cadel, his expression changing. He went white.

"Cadel?" he gasped.

TWENTY-FOUR

Cadel and Dr. Deal stared at each other, both breathing heavily. Cadel put a hand to his throbbing cheek.

"Oh my god," said Dr. Deal. "Oh my god—are you all right? Are you hurt?"

"What were you *doing*?" Cadel was on the verge of tears but tried to blink them away. His voice shook. "Are you *crazy*?"

"No. I'm sorry. I didn't know it was you." Dr. Deal stretched out a hand, which Cadel knocked aside. "You looked like a girl!" the lawyer burst out. "How was I supposed to know . . . ? It was a mistake!"

Cadel scrambled to his feet. His knees were shaky; his lip was stinging. When he touched it, blood leaked onto his finger.

Dr. Deal began to pick up Cadel's scattered belongings, which he thrust into Cadel's backpack. "Ice," he said breathlessly. "I'll get you some ice."

"Go away," Cadel yelped. "Leave me alone."

"You don't want to swell up, Cadel. Christ!" Dr. Deal sounded scared. "It was an accident. You don't need to tell anyone. Here." Straightening, he reached into his jacket and pulled out a wallet. "Here. How much do you want? I've got—let's see—I've got six hundred and thirty-five dollars. Take it. It's yours."

Cadel narrowed his eyes at the wad of notes being thrust at him. Though still in shock, he was rapidly working out what must have happened. Dr. Deal had mistaken him for a girl. And so Dr. Deal had jumped on him.

No doubt the lawyer had jumped on a lot of girls. Cadel's father had mentioned Dr. Deal and female students in the same breath. Whether the lawyer simply liked to punch out girls, or whether he had other plans in mind for them, Cadel didn't know. He didn't *want* to know. He was disgusted—and furious. He was sure that one of his teeth was loose.

"Take it, Cadel, for god's sake!" Dr. Deal implored. "I tell you what—I'll give you a high distinction. You don't have to do another stroke of work for the rest of the year. I'll cover for you. I will. Just don't tell anyone."

Cadel regarded him somberly.

"Cadel, I'm *sorry!*" The lawyer was in tears now; Cadel wondered what it was that he had been threatened with, if he should ever lay a finger on Dr. Darkkon's son. Something pretty frightening, obviously.

Cadel turned to look at himself in the mirror. Blood was trickling down his chin. His cheek was red, turning purple.

"Here," said Dr. Deal, and ripped a paper towel from its dispenser. Cadel took it, wet it, and laid it on his lip.

Behind his own reflection he could see that of Dr. Deal, red and ruffled and bobbing about like a seagull on a choppy tide.

"Look," the lawyer continued, running his hands over his bald patch, "I'll draw up a contract. Free legal services for the rest of your life. Ironclad. We'll keep a copy in—"

"I'll think about it," Cadel interrupted. Whereupon the lawyer stopped moving.

"What?"

"I'll think about it." Cadel turned to face him. "I'll think about what I want."

Dr. Deal swallowed.

"And you won't tell?" he quavered.

"No."

It had occurred to Cadel that if his father was blackmailing Dr.

Deal, there was no reason why he himself shouldn't do the same thing. The trouble was, he couldn't decide what to ask for. His head was still spinning.

Dr. Deal hesitated. He looked slightly calmer.

"You should put some ice on that," he said.

"I'm going home."

"Fine. Good idea." Dr. Deal dabbed at his brow with a handkerchief. "I'll mark you present at class this afternoon, if you want me to. Do you need a lift?"

"I'll get a cab."

Cadel's skin crawled at the thought of entering Dr. Deal's car. Only a fool would do anything so stupid. For all Cadel knew, the lawyer intended to strangle him and dump his body rather than risk having Dr. Darkkon discover what had just happened.

"Don't do anything stupid," Cadel added, as he inched toward the door. "My dad has me under constant surveillance."

As far as Cadel knew, this was an empty threat, designed to throw Dr. Deal off balance. Only later, when he had escaped to another men's room and stripped off his disguise, did he begin to wonder: Could it be true? Could Dr. Darkkon actually be keeping an eye on him, using all the advanced technology at his disposal?

There was every chance, Cadel admitted to himself, that his computer phone had a location-tracking device embedded within it. Why not, after all? Dr. Darkkon had spent a great deal of time and money pursuing his son all the way to Australia. There was no reason why he should risk losing Cadel again, even for an hour. Not when the Axis Institute was probably crawling with fledgling kidnappers.

Cadel found the idea of being tracked a bit depressing. Sitting in a cab, nursing his sore cheek, he wondered if his father already knew about Dr. Deal's attack. What if that dingy men's room had been under video surveillance? Cadel hadn't noticed any cameras, but that didn't mean much. The level of technology available to Dr. Darkkon was such that he could have hidden a camera anywhere he wanted: in a hand dryer, a light fixture, a knothole.

Just in case he hadn't, however, Cadel ran through a list of possible excuses for skipping class. An upset stomach from the refectory food? An electric shock from a hot-wired doorknob? He definitely didn't want anyone to find out about the attack. For one thing, keeping a secret like that would allow him to blackmail Dr. Deal. For another, well, Cadel couldn't help feeling squeamish about what might happen should his father discover the truth. It was stupid—weak, even—but Cadel just didn't like the idea of assassination. Not even the assassination of Dr. Deal.

In the end, of course, Cadel didn't need an excuse for skipping class. If he hadn't been feeling so shaken—so muddleheaded and disinclined to think—he would have realized that the state of his face was all the excuse he needed. Despite all the ice that he applied to his bruises that afternoon, he walked into his five thirty appointment with Thaddeus looking badly knocked about.

Thaddeus rose. "What happened?" he said, his voice sharp. "Who did it?"

Cadel blinked.

"Oh, this?" he replied. "It was my fault."

"Who hit you?"

"No one."

"Don't be a fool!" snapped Thaddeus, and Cadel swallowed. Thaddeus was frightening when he wanted to be; his cold, chiseled face was enough to make anyone quail. Nonetheless, Cadel stood his ground.

"I was trying to break up a fight," he muttered.

"You *what*?"

"It was an accident. They weren't trying to hit me."

"Who wasn't?"

"It doesn't matter."

"It most certainly does."

"No. Really. I'm all right."

"Was it that Gazo creature? Your pet moron?"

"No!" Cadel was alarmed. While Gazo could be irritating, Cadel didn't want him smashed up in a faked car crash. Certainly not because Cadel had received a black eye. "It wasn't anyone in first year."

"Who, then?" Thaddeus demanded. "Why this misplaced sense of loyalty?"

"It's not that."

"No?" Thaddeus examined Cadel's head. He passed his fingers in front of Cadel's eyes, up and down, from side to side: "Can you see this? What about this? How many fingers? Three? And you didn't pass out at all? Good." Thaddeus looked very tall to Cadel—who, when he was finally released, sank onto the maroon couch. More and more, Cadel felt the need to hold back. Maybe this feeling had something to do with his earlier thoughts on surveillance. Maybe he just wanted to see what would happen.

He had never before concealed anything of importance from Thaddeus.

"It's a practical consideration," he said at last. Then he glanced up at the psychologist, who raised his eyebrows.

"Indeed?"

"Gratitude," Cadel went on slowly, "can be a great motivator." He took a deep breath. *"Choose your tools,"* he chanted. "Isn't that what Dad always says? I want to see how this pans out. I want to see if someone will work for me."

Thaddeus seemed to reflect for a moment, before dropping into the couch opposite Cadel. He sat with his hands pressed together.

"Gratitude," he drawled, "is a form of blackmail."

Cadel shrugged.

"Blackmail can backfire," Thaddeus went on.

"Not if you're careful."

"Careful people take out insurance policies," Thaddeus remarked, with a glint in his eye. "Drop a name in my ear, Cadel, and I can assure you that nothing will happen to its bearer *unless* something further happens to you. No one will ever know."

Cadel shook his head—whereupon Thaddeus smiled a chilling smile.

"Don't you trust me, Cadel? Don't you trust me to keep my temper?"

"It's not that." Cadel hesitated. He remembered what Thaddeus had always told him: *Never trust anyone.* "It's more . . . it's my dad. He might not be able to help himself. You know what I mean?"

There was a long pause. Finally Thaddeus said, "I take your point."

Cadel was surprised.

"He *is* very protective," Thaddeus conceded. "He also doesn't like it when people flout his rules."

"But it really was a mistake," Cadel insisted, sensing that he was beginning to convince Thaddeus. "They didn't do it deliberately. They were shattered."

"I should hope so."

"I can't let Dad see my face," Cadel went on. "Will you help me? Will you pretend you can't get a visual, or something?"

Thaddeus narrowed his eyes.

"You wouldn't be asking much, would you?" he said.

"*Please?* Please, Thaddeus, I can handle this myself. Really. How will I ever get a degree in world domination if I'm not allowed to handle something like this by myself?" Cadel marshalled his arguments. "This is my chance to start forming my own network! Recruiting my own people! I've got leverage now. Just like Dad did when he was starting the institute. Can't you give me a chance?"

Thaddeus stared at Cadel. Outside, a fir tree swayed in the wind, scraping itself against the gutters. There was no other sound for at least half a minute.

"I will," Thaddeus said at last, "if you give me a name. Just me. I shan't pass it on."

Cadel took a deep breath.

"I'll do that," he replied, "if I get worried."

Thaddeus smiled.

"Your father won't be pleased," he pointed out, "if he discovers that I knew about this assault and kept it from him. I need my own insurance, Cadel."

Almost without thinking, Cadel retorted, "He won't be pleased, either, if he learns that you promised not to tell him."

The words were barely out of his mouth before Cadel regretted them. His hands jumped up to his face, as if he was trying to grab the threat and force it back down his own throat. But the foolish remark had already escaped and was hanging in the air like a thundercloud.

Thaddeus's expression was hard to read.

"Well, well," he said. "Interesting."

"I—I—"

"It's all right, Cadel. Don't look so scared. You've no reason to be frightened of me."

"Can I please go home?" Cadel squeaked. "My head hurts."

"A headache?" Thaddeus cocked his own head, considering this proposal. "I suppose it's a reasonable excuse. We certainly don't want your father seeing you like this, do we? If he's to be kept in the dark."

Cadel gasped. "Are you—"

"Go home, dear boy. Rest up. Think of a reasonable explanation that might account for your bruises when you next speak to your father. Because they won't be disappearing in a hurry, I'll tell you that much."

Cadel was more bewildered than he was relieved. He had won so quickly. It didn't make sense. Why had Thaddeus suddenly capitulated? Would he *really* conceal the incident from Dr. Darkkon?

It hardly seemed possible.

"Th-thank you," Cadel murmured, peering at the psychologist's face. He thought he detected a trace of sly amusement but couldn't be sure.

He was on his way home in a taxi when it crossed his mind that Thaddeus might already know about Dr. Deal. The whole exchange in that office might have been a great big fake, designed to test Cadel somehow. The question was: Had he passed the test or failed it?

Cadel didn't know. He couldn't be sure of anything. There were so many possibilities, he couldn't even begin to catalog them.

Especially not when his head hurt.

TWENTY-FIVE

The next morning, Cadel slept in. His first class wasn't until eleven, so he could afford to take his time. By staying in bed until after nine, he also avoided Mrs. Piggott, who had left for work before eight thirty. Since she had also come home late the previous night, she hadn't yet seen Cadel's injuries.

Cadel was hoping that she never would.

He ate a mushy breakfast of oatmeal and yogurt, trying not to put too much pressure on the muscles around the left side of his jaw. Then he caught a cab to the institute, where he arrived just in time to see Carla being whisked into an ambulance. In the blazing sunlight, the ambulance looked very white against the vivid green lawn. Carla was lying on a stretcher, so heavily bundled up in layers of gauze and plastic that Cadel couldn't make out what was wrong with her. He could see only that she was connected to several suspended bags of liquid.

Quite a crowd had already gathered to watch, though Terry was trying to disperse it. Thaddeus was also there, talking to the ambulance officers. He caught sight of Cadel and nodded briefly before turning away.

At that moment, Carla's stretcher was heaved into the back of the ambulance. One of the ambulance officers jumped in with her. A couple of doors banged and the engine roared. Someone tapped Cadel's shoulder.

"What happened to *you?*" Gazo exclaimed.

For an instant, Cadel didn't understand what Gazo was talking about. He had forgotten his own injuries, which no longer pained him unless they were touched. Carla's plight had driven them straight out of his head. "Oh, nothing," he said, dismissing the subject with a wave of his hand. "What happened to Carla? Was it a booby trap?"

Gazo shrugged.

"Bound to be," remarked Douglas Prindle. The old accountant had appeared out of nowhere. He was regarding the scene in front of him with detached interest. "She's not exactly Miss Popular."

"Maybe it was an accident," said a pyrogenic student in red tights. "Maybe she got infected with one of her own bugs."

Cadel shuddered. Douglas said dryly, "Speaking of which, what happened to the famous vial? The one she's supposed to be carrying round with her all the time? I hope *that* didn't break when she fell."

"How do you know she fell?" Gazo queried. Whereupon the accountant threw him a contemptuous glance.

"Did she *look* as if she was standing up?" he replied, and turned on his heel.

The rest of the crowd began to melt away as the ambulance drove off. Thaddeus, heading for his car, called out, "*Cadel! Gazo!* Class is canceled! Tell the others!" He waved at them before disappearing around a corner.

Gazo and Cadel exchanged glances.

"I wonder if Doris already knows?" said Gazo. "She does a course wiv Carla."

"We should hang around outside the lecture room" was Cadel's opinion. "Catch them as they come."

"It's good this happened. I didn't do me lying assignment."

Gazo spoke without a trace of concern. Even Cadel couldn't dredge up much sympathy for Carla, whom he didn't really know. And when he informed Doris, Abraham, and Kunio of the latest developments, they were equally unmoved. Kunio probably failed to understand what Cadel was trying to tell him. Abraham looked too sick to care. Doris simply snorted, in her unpleasant way, and wanted to know about Cadel's bruises.

"Someone been beating you up?" she inquired with obvious satisfaction.

"No," said Cadel.

"Looks that way to me," Doris taunted, and Gazo frowned.

"Did someone *hit* you, Cadel?" he said.

"No. I told you."

"Whoever it was, they're sure going to pay." Once again, Doris sounded rather pleased. "Who was it?"

"No one!" snapped Cadel. And because he was tired of the whole subject, he marched off to Hardware Heaven, with Gazo clumping after him.

"Cadel? Are you all right?"

"I'm fine. I said so."

"What happened?"

"It was an accident. I was stupid."

"So you don't need help?"

"No." Cadel reached the elevator and stabbed at the UP button. The elevator door immediately opened. Cadel stepped inside.

"Well, tell me if you do," said Gazo. A steel panel slid shut, cutting off Cadel's view of his anxious face. As the elevator hummed up to the next floor, Cadel felt a twinge of guilt, which he strove to suppress. After all, it wasn't *his* fault that Gazo had a pathetic, puppylike nature.

When he reached Hardware Heaven, he found Sark and the chinless, pasty-faced Richard murmuring together beside the only window in the room. It was odd to hear them conversing (because no one talked much in Hardware Heaven) and even odder to see them out of their seats. Com, as always, was stationed at his keyboard.

"You missed all the fun," Sark told Cadel, by way of a greeting.

"No I didn't," Cadel replied, slinging his backpack onto his desk. "I saw the ambulance. Downstairs."

"That was no ambulance. That was the Grunts. Evacuation. They've closed off the whole top floor." Sark looked smug. "If you ask me, they're worried about the vial."

"It can't have been anything obvious," said Richard, arguing a point. "If there was an *obvious* threat, we'd all be in quarantine by now. They wouldn't have let Cadel up here."

"Maybe not," Sark conceded.

"Did you see anything?" Richard asked Cadel, who had turned on his computer. "Did you see any fluids leaking out of her, or anything?"

"No," said Cadel, after a pause. A few alarms had been tripped in his latest firewall, suggesting that someone was trying to hack into his data again. The Virus, no doubt. Cadel wondered what he was up to.

"Hoist by her own petard," Sark was saying. "I hope she enjoys whatever she's got."

"You don't *know* that," Richard objected. "For all you know, it could have been a heart attack."

"Oh, sure. A heart attack. Why would they close off the labs if it was a heart attack?"

"Because of the *vial*, stupid!"

"Would you two please keep it down?" Cadel requested. "Some of us are trying to work here."

Com suddenly made a creaking sound, as if to imply that he seconded the motion. Grumpily, Richard slouched back to his own computer. Sark folded his arms.

"What happened to *you*, genius?" he asked, studying Cadel's face.

"Nothing."

"I thought you were supposed to be off-limits?"

"It was an accident."

"Carla didn't beat you up, by any chance?"

"No." Cadel raised his eyes and fixed them on Sark, who suddenly blanched, as if the full impact of his own words had only just hit him. Had Carla been killed because she'd assaulted Cadel?

"It wasn't Carla," Cadel insisted, seeing the expression on Sark's face. "It wasn't anyone. I fell down." But Sark had sidled away, avoiding eye contact. Cadel had a feeling that from now on, Sark would be treating him with kid gloves.

He sighed and fixed his attention on the computer in front of him. After the incident with Dr. Deal, he had become more curious about all the institute staff. Nothing in Dr. Deal's computer records had alerted him to the risks that a young girl might run in being alone with Dr. Deal. So what else had Cadel missed? What secrets were the staff hiding? Cadel decided to piggyback on another sweep through their private data banks. This time he would do it properly. This time he would carefully consider every single piece of information that he found. He wouldn't just flip through it with one eye on the clock.

The material that he collected by this means took him hours to review. Despite concentrated scrutiny, however, he didn't find much that was new. Dr. Deal didn't have a lot to offer. His e-mails and spreadsheets, bank records and business calendar were all pretty dull. There were no payments to unnamed accounts, or threatening e-mails to young women. He didn't even appear to be involved in any of the feuds brewing between various other staff members.

Cadel already knew that most of the staff hated Brendan, whom they regarded as an insult. Someone who was autistic, they felt, shouldn't be receiving equal pay. There was also a lot of bad feeling about Tracey Lane; she was seen as a bit of an idiot, not to mention unreliable. Apparently, she had gone out with nearly every male working for Dr. Darkkon (including Maestro Max, Luther, Art, and, most recently, the Führer). At present she was seeing Terry *and* Dr. Deal: Her e-mails made that pretty obvious. Perhaps the relationship with Terry was one reason why Carla despised Tracey. "That ditz" was how Carla described the former newsreader in her private e-mails.

There was also a lot of tension on the Yarramundi campus. The Führer was always ordering expensive materials and seemed to require enormous budgets. Relations between Luther, who was head of the School of Destruction, and the Führer, who treated the Grunts as his own private army, weren't good. Part of the problem was that the Führer kept signaling yellow alerts. After carefully studying the Führer's security codes, Cadel had worked out that a yellow alert was far less serious than a red alert, but that it still involved all kinds of annoying lockdowns and authorizations. The Führer had once signaled a yellow "intruder" alert because Alias had turned up for class dressed as a pizza delivery boy. After that little misunderstanding, the Führer had tried to have Alias fired on the grounds that he was "too much of a security risk." Cadel wasn't surprised to see that Alias and the Führer hadn't got on since then.

So the Führer was at odds with Alias, Brendan Graham, Tracey Lane (the Führer's ex-girlfriend), Dr. Deal (the man Tracey had left the Führer for), and, of course, Luther Lasco. Luther, too, had a lot of enemies; Maestro Max was one of them. The cause of the problem seemed to be that Max had once refused to help Luther with his assassination course. Although Max had a lot of expertise in the area of assassination, he claimed that he was now "beyond all that." Luther wasn't the only one who disliked Max's attitude. It was argued by Carla and many other staff that while their own subjects were attracting fee-paying students, Max's "purist" course was of little value and shouldn't be as generously funded as their own. (Thaddeus, Cadel noticed, seemed to spend a great deal of time defending the way he'd divided up available funds between the pure and the applied sciences.) All in all, Max was a bit of a loner. In his letters and e-mails, he came across as isolated and paranoid. He disliked Carla, abhorred the Führer—whom he condemned as clumsy—and felt that Brendan was beneath his notice. Tracey he regarded with contempt, now that he was no longer involved with her. And he didn't trust the Virus at all. He had sent repeated warnings to Thaddeus about the security of software programs with someone like the Virus around. He was also, curiously enough, rather nervous about Cadel.

At first Cadel hadn't been able to understand why Max kept sending coded messages to Terry and Luther Lasco pointing out that he could find no official records of Cadel's birth. It had only gradually become obvious that Max was concocting a theory. He didn't trust Dr. Darkkon any more than he trusted the Virus, and was worried that Cadel might be some kind of spy.

Reading between the lines, Cadel had soon become convinced that Max was concerned about Dr. Darkkon's motive for founding the Axis Institute. Max refused to accept the explanation offered by Thaddeus Roth. He didn't believe that Dr. Darkkon was worried about the ultimate future of humankind. In Max's opinion, no one was ever *really* that selfless. No—the Maestro feared that Dr. Darkkon had created Axis to bring together all his possible rivals in crime. This, Max reasoned, would make them an easy target.

With the competition wiped out, Dr. Darkkon wouldn't have to share any of his global plunder.

It was a pretty far-fetched idea, though not totally stupid. Cadel had sometimes wondered about Dr. Darkkon's motives himself. He had one advantage over Max, however: He knew how important he was to his dad. If Dr. Darkkon had founded the institute simply so that Cadel could pit his skills against the best (or worst) in the business and thereby educate himself as to the workings of the criminal mind—well, it wouldn't have surprised Cadel. Not one little bit.

Scrolling through endless paranoid e-mails, Cadel began to feel sorry for Max. The Maestro, he decided, was slightly wrong in the head. So was Carla, to judge from her ranting messages. It didn't surprise Cadel that she had been mysteriously struck down. If she hadn't done it to herself, by accident, there were lots of other people who would surely have been happy to see her wheeled off on a stretcher.

Even Art had become the target of her fury. In one of her most recent e-mails, she had accused him of stealing her favorite earrings and replacing them with imitations so perfect that only she could tell the difference.

Crazy, thought Cadel, shaking his head. Really crazy.

He sat back and thought hard. The entire institute was riddled with fear, distrust, conflict. Everyone seemed to be fighting with somebody else—except perhaps Thaddeus. Art had even made a clumsy attempt to break into Brendan's computer files. (Cadel got quite excited when he stumbled on that little effort.) Brendan juggled a lot of bank accounts, owing to the nature of his job. He kept details of these accounts on his computer. Most of the accounts had been opened with fake names, and none contained much money. The money they *did* contain never remained in the same place for long. As a result, Brendan's security was very poor, and Art didn't have any trouble getting past it. But his forays into Brendan's database were so ill-disguised that there were bound to be problems one day, when Brendan finally realized what was going on.

It was an interesting task, trying to map out all the interconnecting feuds. Cadel had been doing it for a while, but only in a patchy, half-hearted way—not with the kind of unrelenting dedication that he now applied to the job. In fact, he spent most of the day piecing various feuds together in his head. But he was repeatedly interrupted: first by a brief power blackout (not unusual at the institute); then by the sudden appearance of Dr. Vee (who presented each of his students with an "exercise" that involved rescuing their data from a byte-munching virus); and then by Gazo Kovacs. Gazo slouched into the room around lunchtime, when Cadel was in the middle of Dr. Vee's exercise. Having just isolated a crucial anomaly, Cadel was in no mood to exchange campus gossip with Gazo; he didn't even reply to Gazo's first greeting.

Gazo, rebuffed, picked up a binary printout and stared at it, blankly, before putting it down again.

"Are you going to lunch?" he asked.

"No," replied Cadel.

"Have you eaten?"

"No."

"Me neither. I can't. They're searching me room. For Carla's vial. They're searching every room in the dormitory." He sighed. "So I can't get in."

"You're not supposed to be here, Gazo," Cadel pointed out, hardly aware of what he was saying. The computer screen held him mesmerized. "Dr. Vee doesn't like you here."

"I know." Gazo sounded glum, even through his voice-warping transmission filter. "Nobody wants me nowhere."

"Well, I'm in the middle of something. I can't help you."

"So the vial *has* been lost?" Sark suddenly inquired, raising his head. "I knew it."

"There might not even *be* a vial," Richard interjected. He had also become caught up in the conversation despite the fact that his computer memory was rapidly being consumed in front of his eyes. "It might be just a myth. Dr. Vee didn't seem worried."

"Dr. Vee *left*," Sark pointed out. "Or haven't you noticed?"

"And the sooner we stop this monster, the sooner *we* can leave," said Cadel. "Anyone had any luck? I think I have."

He fell into a technical discussion with the other infiltration students—a discussion so dense and difficult that Gazo soon drifted away. With his departure, only four people remained in Hardware Heaven: Com, Sark, Richard, and Cadel. By two o'clock that number had been reduced to two. In an unusual gesture of goodwill, the students of Dr. Vee had pooled their resources and defeated his virus after about only ninety minutes' work. Richard and Sark were too scared of Carla's deadly organism to compete with each other. They simply wanted to get out—fast.

Cadel wasn't worried. He had a feeling that if there was any real danger, Thaddeus would have ordered him home long ago. This hunch proved to be correct; when he attended Brendan's embezzlement class, he found that Douglas and Phoebe were both present. So after the class, he returned to Hardware Heaven, where he remained until late afternoon. Com also stayed. He was still there when Cadel left.

Cadel wondered, briefly, if he slept there every night, in front of his computer.

TWENTY-SIX

"What happened to your *face?*"

Mrs. Piggott was in the kitchen when Cadel arrived home. She was mixing herself some kind of alcoholic drink with the blender.

Cadel cursed his luck.

"Nothing," he said.

"*Nothing?* Don't give me that. You look like you've been hit by a truck!"

"I do not." Cadel was annoyed. It wasn't *that* bad. "I fell down."

"Why didn't you call me?"

Cadel shrugged. He was trying to get out of the kitchen. He wanted to talk to Kay-Lee.

"Oh god," said Mrs. Piggott, glancing at her watch, "I suppose I should take you to see a doctor but I've got a client waiting for me—I'm already late."

"I don't need to see a doctor," Cadel replied firmly. "It doesn't even hurt." It did, but he wasn't going to say as much. "I'm fine. It happened yesterday. Thaddeus had a look at it."

"Dr. Roth had a look at it?"

"Yes."

"I don't think he's a *medical* doctor, is he?"

"He said I was fine."

Fortunately, Lanna seemed to accept this. Perhaps she just wanted to because she was late for an appointment. After informing Cadel that he could order pizza for dinner—or maybe heat up a couple of boxes of Lean Cuisine—she whizzed off in a cloud of expensive perfume.

Cadel breathed a sigh of relief. He went to his computer and typed out a message to Kay-Lee. *Excitement at work today,* he wrote. *Unpopular teacher struck down by mysterious illness. There's probably a formula for that drifting around; in fact, newspaper headlines are often written to a "formula." "Unpopular Teacher Struck Down by Mystery Illness"—how would you reduce that headline to a nice, tidy equation?*

Nobody's much concerned about the sick teacher, probably because the staff all hate each other. It's interesting. I've been trying to get a handle on the politics of that place—in a spirit of scientific curiosity. I've got a feeling that it might be important.

He wrote and wrote—about computer glitches, and health-and-safety issues, and "a girl who was attacked in the library bathroom," wishing at the same time that he could write about defeating Dr. Vee's virus, and being jumped on by Dr. Deal, and having to cope with the threat of a deadly organism. Going to see Thaddeus three times a week was all very well, but on the days when he didn't, Cadel was often desperate to talk to someone. Someone with whom he could be completely honest, without worrying about the impact his honesty might have. Someone whom he could trust.

While he waited for Kay-Lee to reply, he ate a microwaved frozen pizza, a packet of chips, a cracker, a bowl of soggy cornflakes, and a chocolate bar, thinking about Dr. Deal. He had a class with Dr. Deal the very next day. Would it be safe to go? Probably. With so many witnesses around, Dr. Deal wouldn't try anything. Cadel didn't think he was going to try anything, anyway. After all, Dr. Deal wasn't called Dr. Deal for nothing. If possible, he liked to negotiate his way out of a problem; that was his specialty, in fact. He didn't think the lawyer would resort to violence.

Not against someone who wasn't a young girl.

Cadel wondered if Dr. Deal had ever attacked Gemini, and what the twins might have done if he had. He wondered what had actually happened to those girls. Nothing in Luther's online reports suggested that Niobe had been tracked down, but she could still be in danger. Cadel's heart sank at the thought of Luther Lasco. Luther was to blame for what had happened to Gemini. The scar he had left on Jem's cheek was the cause of the whole sorry mess in which the twins had become embroiled.

Oh well, Cadel told himself. *The twins weren't very bright, anyway.* Not like Kay-Lee.

After finishing his meal, Cadel expected to find Kay-Lee's reply waiting for him when he returned to his computer. But he found nothing. Disappointed, he reluctantly attacked his embezzlement homework, which kept him busy for another thirty minutes. By seven o'clock, however, Kay-Lee still hadn't replied.

Cadel waited up. He organized his data on the institute staff, wrote a few Partner Post e-mails, sorted out his finances, and finished an essay for Maestro Max. When Lanna arrived home, at eleven—alone, because Stuart was away—she told Cadel to turn off the lights and go to bed. So he was forced to wait in the dark until she had gone to sleep, before checking his e-mail for the last time.

Still nothing.

He didn't sleep very well. The next morning he sent another message to Kay-Lee, asking if she was all right. On the train to the institute he fretted about her. Could her computer be down? Could she be on holiday? She hadn't said anything about going away.

Then again, how much did he really know about her? Almost nothing.

Upon reaching the institute, Cadel went straight to Hardware Heaven. He checked his e-mail—still no luck. He poked around, looking for information on Kay-Lee that he hadn't already dug up from the various databases open to creative hackers. He knew her address, of course, and her date of birth. He knew her mother's name and her father's name, her GPAs, her nursing exam scores (they weren't so terrific, oddly enough), and how much she made on the job. He knew that she regularly shopped at a particular supermarket and sometimes bought her clothes in a city department store. He knew that she had a driver's license, one sister, two credit cards, and a subscription to a crafts magazine.

Cadel knew all these things, and they amounted to absolutely nothing. When he considered them (especially the crafts magazine), he felt as if he didn't know Kay-Lee at all. And though he tried very hard that day, he was unable to track down much more information. He did find out that she had lived in Drummoyne and worked briefly at a big teaching hospital before moving to the nurses' quarters at Weatherwood House. But what did these facts amount to?

Very little, in Cadel's opinion.

He kept checking his e-mail, with no success. And he had to drag himself away from his computer more than once; he had classes to attend, after all. The first was with Dr. Deal. It was in the morning and took place in lecture-room one. When Cadel trudged down there at ten o'clock, he wasn't concerned that he was about to confront the lawyer for the first time since their meeting in the men's room. Cadel was far more worried by his failure to receive any kind of response from Kay-Lee. It was distracting. It was *distressing*.

"Hi," said Gazo when Cadel arrived. So far, they were the only two who had turned up. "Did you hear about Doris?"

"Huh?" said Cadel.

"Did you hear about Doris?"

"No." Cadel wasn't particularly interested but tried to pretend that he was. "What about Doris?"

"They took her away." Gazo's tone was mournfully self-important. "Abraham told me."

"What?"

"He was in the labs, and she was in the labs doing some kind of Contagion project, and Luther came, and they took her away."

Cadel blinked. He tried to focus his mind.

"Who's 'they'?" he said sharply. "Luther and who else?"

"I dunno."

"What do you mean, 'they took her away'? Did they drag her away? Did she walk away? What?"

"I dunno."

"It was Adolf and Luther," a voice suddenly interjected. The voice belonged to Abraham. He had approached them noiselessly, padding down the corridor in enormous rubber-soled shoes. He was wearing dark glasses and a jacket lined with sheepskin—though it was quite a warm day for early May. His hair didn't seem to be growing back, and his white scalp gleamed.

"Oh. Hello," said Cadel.

"They cornered her in room 309," Abraham revealed in a tired voice. "There wasn't any fuss. They said they wanted to talk to her about anything she might have found on the floor of the labs. They were talking about the vial." Abraham swallowed. "I know, because they asked me about it, too. Last night. They talked to me for an *hour*." He wiped his fist across his shiny forehead and shivered, pulling the sheepskin jacket tightly around him. "They really gave me the third degree."

Cadel winced. "You mean . . . ?"

"Did they *hit* you?" Gazo demanded.

"No, no." Abraham hunched his shoulders irritably. "Nothing like that. They just went at me. On and on. Anyway, I knew that wasn't *really* why they wanted Doris."

Cadel frowned. "Oh?" he said.

"I was in 309 myself, when they found me last night, and they did it right there. Closed the door and got stuck in. They didn't make me go anywhere else. There's something fishy going on with Doris."

"But *you* were with her, weren't you?" Cadel pointed out. "I mean, perhaps they wanted a bit of privacy, don't you think?"

Abraham shook his head. "Nah."

"But—"

"They didn't know I was there," Abraham admitted. "I was . . . I was in the supply cabinet."

"The supply cabinet?"

Abraham scowled. "Sometimes the light gets too much for me, okay?" he snapped.

At that moment, Kunio joined them, with Dr. Deal following close behind. If the sight of Cadel affected the lawyer in any way—if his eyes flickered or his hands shook—Cadel didn't notice. He was too busy processing the image that had leaped into his mind, of Abraham cowering in a cupboard, shielding himself from the electric light.

Then Dr. Deal greeted them all, and the moment had passed. After unlocking the door to lecture-room one, he stepped back to let his class in. When Cadel glanced up, the lawyer wasn't looking in his direction.

Whether this averted gaze was deliberate or not, Cadel had no way of knowing.

When he and the lawyer finally did make direct eye contact, they did so without a change of expression. Dr. Deal was explaining the difference between battery and assault, when Abraham's nose started to bleed. The blood gushed out, soaking his handkerchief, his sleeve, and Cadel's supply of tissues (which Mrs. Piggott had insisted he keep in his bag, for emergencies). It was unnerving. After losing quantities of blood, Abraham was at last forced to excuse himself. He didn't really have a choice. He had run out of tissues and had turned a deathly color.

Dr. Deal, who had been speaking steadily through all the furtive nudging and dabbing, watched Abraham go, without pausing in his discourse on the *Butchard v. Barnett* case. He did, however, catch Cadel's eye. Cadel returned the look blandly, determined not to reveal anything.

". . . Assault is the *threat* of force to the person of another, while battery is the application of that force," Dr. Deal was saying. "These days, there's a lot of confusion between the terms, but let me put it this way: If I were to threaten to punch someone if they didn't shut up, and then

I punched them—well, that would be a case of assault *and* battery, punishable by law. Of course, I'd have been a bloody fool to do it."

Cadel dropped his gaze. Dr. Deal, he knew, was trying to apologize. Cadel hoped that nobody else in the class realized this, but one quick scan of the room left him satisfied. Now that Abraham was out of the picture, Cadel was the only student who had the ability to understand what was going on. Kunio was still floundering, defeated by his imperfect grasp of English. Gazo was too slow. Besides, they were both distracted by Abraham's retreat: the faltering steps, the trail of blood, the banging door.

Only three left, Cadel suddenly realized. Three out of the original eight in the class.

He swallowed and glanced at the clock over the door. It had been twenty-seven hours since Kay-Lee had sent her last message.

TWENTY-SEVEN

For the rest of the day, Cadel kept checking and rechecking his e-mail. Despite the odd interruption, he was able to stay at his keyboard, combing through staff databases, keeping an eye on his e-mail, and sending off the odd message to Kay-Lee, in the hope that he would finally get a reply.

He didn't.

At lunchtime, Gazo came looking for him. "I won't stay long," he assured Cadel, scanning the room nervously for Dr. Vee. "Just dropping off a sandwich."

Cadel watched in astonishment as Gazo placed on his desk a paper bag containing a chicken sandwich wrapped in greaseproof paper.

"You're bringing me *lunch*?" Cadel gasped, and Gazo shrugged, almost bashfully.

"I know you get caught up, and that," he said, obviously pleased at his own thoughtfulness. "I fought you mightn't eat, so I brought you somefink. It's not much," he added. "There's mayonnaise on it."

Cadel stared, dumbfounded. Was Gazo trying to suck up to Dr. Darkkon's son for selfish reasons? Or, even worse, did Cadel's appetite genuinely matter to him? Cadel feared the latter.

"Gazo," said Cadel, "are you sure you're cut out for this place?"

"What do you mean?" Gazo's tone became defensive. "It ain't no big deal. I didn't make that sandwich, I bought it."

"Well, thanks." Cadel was reluctant to become involved in a long discussion about friendly gestures and how they didn't belong in the

Axis Institute. Any further talk would simply encourage Gazo to hang around longer. "Thanks, Gazo."

"Did you hear about Carla? She died last night."

"I know." Cadel had been plugged into the electronic grapevine. "Poison."

"Really? Poison? Wow," said Gazo, his eyes widening behind his mask. "What kind of poison?"

"Look—uh—I think you'd better go," Cadel advised. "Before Dr. Vee gets back."

"Oh. Right."

"We can talk later," said Cadel, ignoring Gazo's obvious disappointment.

"Sure. No problem." Gazo nodded, then began to back out of the room. "Enjoy the sandwich!" he said, before disappearing.

Cadel didn't enjoy the sandwich. He didn't even sample it; he had gone off institute food. The Axis mailboxes were now full of reports on Carla's condition, which had finally been diagnosed: She had been poisoned with a fatal dose of thallium. Nothing could have been done to save her, since the effects of the poison can't be reversed once it has been in the stomach for more than half an hour. Gloomily, Cadel read through the e-mails that Luther Lasco was dispatching in all directions.

The thallium, Luther assured Thaddeus, had not come from his own stash. Like the rest of his poison supply, his own stock of thallium was completely secure. Had Carla read the early intervention training material distributed to every staff member, she would have known that symptoms like vomiting, diarrhea, and joint pain often mean more than a tummy bug. By the time she'd started to lose feeling in her toes and fingers, it had been too late.

I can't stress enough, Luther wrote to Terry, *the importance of early intervention in poisoning cases. At the Axis Institute, there is* no such thing *as a harmless tummy bug.* Thallium, he added, was tasteless and colorless, and in this case had probably been administered in the labs, since

Carla had been at work for more than three hours before being whisked away in the ambulance.

Luther advised Terry to have the labs thoroughly searched once again. Anything edible was to be removed and destroyed. The taps in the bathrooms had to be tested. Meanwhile, he said, he was "working the source" for further information.

Cadel wondered who, or what, this mysterious "source" might be. Just before leaving the institute, he found out. One last sweep through the network uncovered an encrypted message sent to Terry by Thaddeus. Cadel decoded it easily, to discover that Thaddeus wanted Terry's urgent assistance in disguising Carla's death as something "trouble-free." They had identified the culprit—Doris Deauville. They had identified the agent—thallium. Was there any way in which Carla's rapid decline could somehow be blamed on natural causes? Or would they have to resort to more drastic action? They couldn't afford to have the coroner order an autopsy, so the corpse might have to be disposed of.

Doris Deauville, thought Cadel, swallowing hard. He wasn't surprised. Though he did wonder why Doris, the expert poisoner, had used a poison that left traces of itself in the victim's body. Surely there were other, undetectable poisons? He remembered the twins talking about a certain substance—insulin, was it? Or something else?

Maybe Doris had simply lost her temper and used the first thing that came to hand. Whatever the reason, Cadel preferred not to think about it. He was far more concerned about Kay-Lee. On his way from the institute to Thaddeus's office, he decided that if he hadn't heard from Kay-Lee by eight o'clock that evening, he would call Weatherwood House. Just to make sure that she was all right. He didn't have to reveal who he really was. He could pretend to be collecting for a charity, or something.

When Cadel arrived for his usual appointment with Thaddeus, Wilfreda informed him "that the doctor had been delayed." She bared her blackened teeth at him and suggested that he wait in the upstairs office.

Then she asked Cadel if he would like something to eat. A cookie, per-haps? A drink?

"Yes, please," he replied. Wilfreda kept one jar of chocolate cookies under her desk, doling out the contents when she was in a good mood.

Cadel took two cookies and a glass of water before trudging up to the top floor. Nothing had changed on the staircase since his first visit. The same mottled engravings hung on the wall. The same shabby run-ner was pinned down by the same tarnished brass stair rods. The bath-room off the first landing had not been touched, save for the occasional scrub-down and change of toilet paper. It remained gloomy and old-fashioned, with its wooden toilet seat, dangling chain, and cream tiles.

But Thaddeus's room had changed. Thaddeus had installed two brand-new micro-suede couches the previous week, and hung new curtains at the windows. The carpet was now about three years old. And the technology, of course, was state-of-the-art.

Cadel sat down in front of the psychologist's computer. Munching on a cookie, he checked his own e-mail—and almost choked.

A message from Kay-Lee!

Weak with relief, he opened the file. There it was.

Get stuffed, it said. *This conversation is officially terminated.*

Cadel caught his breath. He couldn't believe his eyes. Get stuffed? What was that supposed to mean? *What are you talking about?* he wrote. *What's the matter?* Then he thought, *Why am I doing this?* And he picked up the phone.

He had memorized the Weatherwood House number. It rang three times before a woman's voice cut in, telling him that he had reached Weatherwood House and how could she help? He asked to speak to Kay-Lee McDougall.

"One moment, please," the voice trilled. There was a click, then "Greensleeves" began to play. After about two minutes, Cadel heard another click, followed by heavy breathing.

"Hello?" somebody panted. "This is Kay-Lee."

Cadel was suddenly speechless.

"Hello. *Hello?*"

"Kay-Lee," Cadel finally croaked.

"Speaking." She was beginning to sound impatient. Her voice was unexpectedly rough—she drawled her vowels.

"Kay-Lee, it's—it's . . ." For a moment, his mind went blank. "I'm a friend of Eiran's," he gasped, knowing that the pitch and rhythm of his own voice were a dead giveaway. He quite obviously wasn't a thirty-four-year-old alcoholic Canadian.

There was a long pause.

"Oh."

"Eiran wants to know what that message was all about," Cadel continued. "Why you sent it."

"Look—"

"He wants to know if you're all right. If something's wrong—"

"Look, forget it," said Kay-Lee. She sounded tired, and not particularly upset. "Just forget it, okay? Lay off."

"But—"

"Not interested. Okay? Sorry, but you've caused enough trouble." *Clunk.* She hung up.

For an instant, Cadel found it hard to breathe. That broken connection was like a punch in the belly. He thought he was going to be sick. It didn't make sense. It couldn't be true.

He was still sitting, motionless, at Thaddeus's desk when the psychologist walked in.

"Ah! Cadel. I'm *very* sorry, it's inexcusable to be so late, but I couldn't help it. Emergency at the institute. Well . . ." Thaddeus gave a short laugh. "I don't have to tell *you*, of all people. It was Doris, of course. We had our suspicions right from the start. Hmm." He had picked up some unopened mail from his desktop and was flipping through it. "How on earth do these people track me down?" he remarked, tossing a letter into his trash can. "Do you know I've dodged some of the world's leading intelligence agencies? But when it comes to charitable organizations and insurance companies—well, they always find me in the end." He looked up, and his gaze became intent as it focused on Cadel. "What's wrong with you?" he asked.

"What?" said Cadel stupidly.

"Are you feeling sick?"

"Uh—no."

"You're very pale."

"Am I?" Cadel glanced around vaguely, as if expecting a mirror to materialize. He knew that he was suffering from a mild case of shock. "I—I guess I didn't eat much today."

"Ah." Thaddeus nodded. "Stuck at your computer again, I suppose."

"Something like that."

"I'll send Wilfreda out to get you a bite." Because there was no intercom connecting the upper and lower floors of the house, Thaddeus strolled onto the landing to summon his secretary. He called to Cadel, "What do you want? Something hot? Fish-and-chips?"

Cadel couldn't think. He mentioned the first thing that popped into his head.

"Sausage roll?"

"Not very nutritious, Cadel."

"Pizza, then. Vegetarian."

As Thaddeus and Wilfreda discussed which restaurant she should call and how they would pay for the delivery, Cadel erased Kay-Lee's message from Thaddeus's computer. Although Thaddeus knew about Kay-Lee, he had never much approved of her. Cadel didn't want him to find out what she had done. It would be unbearable if Thaddeus turned around and said, "I told you so."

Cadel himself still couldn't believe what had happened.

"Your father wants to talk to you," Thaddeus announced when he reentered his office. "He has something important to say. I'm not sure what it is, but he was very insistent. We'll have a transmission download in exactly"—he checked his watch—"two minutes and thirty seconds. I've got it all set up, as you can see."

"Do you think . . . ?" Cadel hesitated, before plucking up his courage. "I mean, it can't wait, can it? Till next time?"

Thaddeus raised his eyebrows. He hardly needed to say no, because Cadel immediately backed down.

"No, of course it can't wait," he said. "Sorry. Not thinking. But can I go to the bathroom first?"

Thaddeus nodded, studying Cadel intently. Avoiding his gaze, Cadel hurried out the door and down the stairs. He shut himself in the bathroom. His stomach was churning, and he was afraid that he might be sick—or worse. But nothing happened.

Nerves, he decided. It must be nerves.

Mrs. Piggott often talked about her nerves. They caused her all sorts of problems, like headaches and stomach upsets. For the first time ever, Cadel found himself sympathizing with her.

Finally he washed his face and marched heavily back upstairs.

"Here he is," said Thaddeus, who was stationed in front of his most recent transmitter screen, which was larger and more advanced. Though Dr. Darkkon's transmitter was now concealed under a fake corn on his foot (a corn that he had to peel off when he wanted to speak to Cadel), advances in nanotechnology meant that Cadel saw more of his father than ever before: hands, shoulders, neck, even bits of his pudgy waist. Sometimes Cadel wondered if this was really an improvement.

"Cadel," said Dr. Darkkon, craning forward so that his bloodshot eyes became huge. "What happened to your face?"

Cadel opened his mouth. "Uh," he began, realizing that he hadn't thought up a good excuse. Fortunately, however, Thaddeus jumped in to save him.

"I'm afraid that's the result of faulty evacuation procedures," he said. "Cadel got pushed against a doorframe during a bomb scare."

"But—"

"I've got Luther on the case now, revising guidelines," Thaddeus assured Dr. Darkkon, who frowned.

"I should hope so," he said. "Are you all right, son?"

"Yes," Cadel replied.

"Sure it wasn't someone seizing the moment, taking advantage?"

"Yes."

"Well . . . as long as you're on the mend." Dr. Darkkon eyed Cadel's injuries for a moment before taking a deep breath. "Sit down, Cadel," he commanded. "There's something we have to talk about."

Obediently, Cadel sat. There was a burning sensation at the back of his eyes, but he tried to concentrate on what his father was saying. At least, whatever it was, it would take his mind off Kay-Lee. The cruelty! The *unfairness*!

No. He wouldn't think about that. Not now.

"Cadel, it's your birthday tomorrow," Dr. Darkkon declared. "You're going to be fourteen."

Oh yes, thought Cadel dully. I forgot about that.

"Have you decided what you want, son?"

There was only one thing Cadel wanted at that moment. And his father couldn't give it to him.

"Not really," he muttered.

"Well, there's no hurry," Dr. Darkkon continued. "When you've made your mind up, you can tell me. Meanwhile, I've got something to tell *you*. Something I swore to tell you when you turned fourteen. When you weren't a child anymore, in other words."

"But I am a child," Cadel pointed out, before he could stop himself. "Legally, I won't be an adult till I'm—"

"Yes, yes, I don't mean under *law*." Dr. Darkkon's tone was impatient. "I mean in the truest sense. You may not be an adult yet, but you're certainly not a child."

"The Romans didn't think so, anyway," Thaddeus interjected, and Dr. Darkkon flashed him an irritated look.

"Yes, well, that's neither here nor there," Dr. Darkkon said. "The point is, Cadel, I've something to tell you about your mother."

"My mother?" This was completely unexpected. Cadel struggled to concentrate. All at once, his heart contracted painfully. "You don't mean—she's not *alive*, is she?" he squawked.

"No. Oh no."

"Calm down, Cadel." Thaddeus put a firm hand on Cadel's shoulder. "It's nothing like that."

"She is dead, I'm afraid. There's no question about that." Dr. Darkkon's voice cracked, then grew hoarse. He cleared his throat. "But before she died, Cadel—well, you might have wondered about her. What she was like. Why I haven't shown you any pictures. That sort of thing."

Cadel realized, with growing astonishment, that he never *had* given much thought to his mother. Why was that? Because his mind had been fully engaged elsewhere? Because Thaddeus had almost never brought the subject up during their talks? Because both Thaddeus and Dr. Darkkon, on the rare occasions when they *did* mention his mother, spoke dismissively, as if she wasn't of any importance?

"The fact is, son, she left us before she passed away," Dr. Darkkon sighed. "She abandoned us both. She was taking drugs, and she got involved with the wrong sort of people, and—well, she disappeared. That's all I can tell you."

Cadel gasped. "You mean, you don't know what happened?" he squeaked.

Thaddeus, who hadn't let go of Cadel's shoulder, applied more pressure, and leaned down to address his bewildered client.

"What your father means," he said quietly, "is that Elspeth vanished, leaving behind all her possessions and what was left of her money. Her purse was found at the bottom of a cliff. No one's seen her since, except the people who killed her."

"But—but if no one's seen her," Cadel stammered, "then she could be alive! Couldn't she?"

"No, son." Dr. Darkkon spoke gravely. "She was killed. I never found her body, but I found the men who did it. At least, Thaddeus did. He took care of them, too."

"They disposed of the body," Thaddeus interposed. "They told me how, but I won't describe the method. It really doesn't matter."

"What *does* matter," Dr. Darkkon went on, "is that she betrayed us, Cadel. She walked off as if she didn't care. One day she just walked off, and that was that. I neither saw nor heard from her again. It was as if we'd never existed."

"But—"

"I was frantic." Dr. Darkkon stared off into space. "I never knew that she'd been living this other life. You had a nursemaid, so she didn't have to take you along with her." There was a pause as he brooded. Then he shook off his dark reflections and set his jaw. "Women do that, son. You can't trust 'em—not the best of 'em."

"Look at Doris," Thaddeus interrupted. "A natural-born poisoner. You couldn't trust her an inch."

"They just drop you and walk away," Dr. Darkkon insisted. "It happens all the time. I want you to know this, Cadel, in case you've ever wondered why I don't talk about your mother." He swallowed and blinked. "Frankly, it's far too painful," he finished.

Cadel simply stared at him, not knowing what to say. His mother. Kay-Lee. They'd done the same thing to him.

How couldn't he believe the worst about them both?

TWENTY-EIGHT

Mrs. Piggott decided to throw a party in Cadel's honor. It wasn't every day, she said, that a boy turned fourteen. Cadel couldn't argue with that, of course, but he was puzzled. It wasn't every day that a boy turned ten, eleven, twelve, or thirteen, either, and she hadn't organized any parties for *those* birthdays. His last birthday party had taken place when he was nine.

As soon as the guests began to arrive, however, he saw that the event had very little to do with him. His birthday had simply given Lanna an excuse to pay off countless friends for *their* invitations. Cadel knew almost none of the people who arrived for lunch the following day. The day after Kay-Lee dropped her bombshell.

Cadel had spent a bad night. He had slept very little, tossing and turning and finally getting up to pace the floor. He couldn't even turn to his computer for comfort, because his overwhelming impulse was to hammer at the keys with clenched fists. At one point he'd shed tears (silently, so as not to wake the Piggotts). When at last he had slept, Kay-Lee and his mother had become all tangled up in his dreams.

Upon waking, he discovered that his chaotic feelings had sorted themselves out a bit. He was now angry. Purely and simply furious. She hadn't given him a chance. Not one single chance. She had refused him even an *explanation*. That wasn't right. It wasn't the behavior of a decent human being.

He thought, *I'm going to get even with her.*

He shuffled out of bed and went to his bathroom. The face that stared back at him from the mirror was chalk white, except for the bruised bits, with gray smudges under his eyes making them look even bigger than usual.

"Oh my god," Lanna cried, when she first caught a glimpse of him. "Don't tell me you're *sick*!"

"No," said Cadel, heading for the fridge. It was nine o'clock and the kitchen was already in disarray, cluttered with unopened bottles of beer and wine, white cardboard boxes full of French pastries, packets of pretzels and water crackers, tubs of exotic dips.

"Don't touch that!" Lanna commanded as Cadel reached for one of the packets. "That's for later."

"How many people are coming?" asked Cadel, gazing at the rows of glistening wineglasses lined up on every available surface.

"Seventy-four."

"Seventy-four?" Cadel couldn't believe it. "I don't even *know* seventy-four people!"

"Don't be silly. You know lots of these people." Lanna was spooning low-fat yogurt into her mouth, one eye on the clock. "We're having the Mayles, the Van Hoorts—you know their two sons, Aidan and Kirby—"

Cadel groaned.

"And the Driscolls, you've met them—"

"No, I haven't."

"Yes, you have. Before they went to Hong Kong. And Dr. Roth's coming—"

"Thaddeus?"

"Oh *bugger*!" Mrs. Piggott slapped her forehead. "I forgot to call the florist!" Then the doorbell rang suddenly. "Stuart! *Stuart!*" she cried. "Will you *please* answer that?"

Cadel grabbed a granola bar and retreated before Lanna could ask *him* to open the front door. It wasn't until he was back in his room that he realized something: She hadn't wished him a happy birthday.

She had probably forgotten that it *was* his birthday.

He smiled grimly to himself. Then he sat down and turned on his computer, because today was the day. He was going to find out every tiny little thing that he could about Kay-Lee McDougall. And then . . . well, then he would see how it could be used. He already knew a great deal, of course. Thanks to the sloppy security on her computer, he had been able to fish around inside it the way most people would fish around inside someone's desk drawer. He had found and read through her conversations with various mathematicians around the world, with a friend called Ivy, and with a supplier of "assistive devices" for handicapped people. Weatherwood House being a kind of group home for disabled kids in wheelchairs, this last exchange had to be work-related. Strangely enough, there wasn't much else about work on Kay-Lee's hard drive. Cadel had picked up most of his knowledge about Weatherwood House from its information website.

The website included photographs of a large white building surrounded by trees, and other pictures of stick-thin kids trying to manipulate paintbrushes, or being supported in swimming pools, or simply draped in wheelchairs, grinning, with party hats on their heads and smiling adults clustered around them. Cadel scanned these photographs carefully but saw only one person who might have been Kay-Lee. It was hard to tell because she was in a swimming-pool picture, turning away from the camera and wearing a rubber cap. Nevertheless, he thought it was her.

The home had its own swimming pool, shuttle bus, kitchens, vegetable garden, trained physical therapists, and a "broad range of assistive technology." Cadel scrolled through the endless lists of goals, achievements, and useful links, looking for more information on the staff. There wasn't much. He did find out that Weatherwood House had staff "living on the premises" to allow for "maximum involvement and supervision."

That's Kay-Lee, he decided. She lives on the premises.

He had never paid much attention to the Weatherwood House website, and as he examined it more closely, he felt more and more left out. Kay-Lee had hardly ever mentioned her work. Yet here it was, in full color, and it didn't look like something you could easily ignore. A big house, stuffed to the brim with people and noise and color; parents coming and going; kids demanding attention; kids wetting themselves and spilling their drinks and needing comfort in the middle of the night. It looked all-consuming. Especially if you were living on the premises.

Cadel wasn't the least bit involved in this side of Kay-Lee's life. He was completely cut off from it—from something so big!

It suddenly occurred to him that he probably hadn't been as important to her as she was to him.

"Cadel!" It was Lanna, somewhere down the hall. *"Cadel!"*

"What?"

"Are you dressed?"

"Huh?"

"I want you dressed, please! I want to see what you'll be wearing!"

"Yeah, okay!" Cadel ignored her. He started to track down the Weatherwood House staff, using phone records as his jumping-off point. But he wasn't allowed to work in peace for very long.

"Cadel!" The door swung open. "What are you doing? You're still in your pajamas!"

Cadel glowered at Lanna like a small, cornered animal. But she refused to be intimidated.

"Get those off," she ordered. *"Now.* I want you in something decent. These will do. And these." She began to pluck various garments out of his wardrobe. *"Not* those disgusting shoes. I'm going to throw those away." She picked them up. "Your guests will be arriving in one hour, so I want you out of here and waiting by then. Understand?"

"My guests?" Cadel snorted.

"Don't you get smart," warned Stuart, who had suddenly appeared in the doorway. "If you give your mother any more lip, you can stay in here all day."

"I'd prefer to stay in here," muttered Cadel.

"*Without* the computer," Stuart added. Then there was a loud crash from the kitchen and his head jerked around. "For Chris'sake, what's that?"

"The caterers," said Lanna, despairingly. "Go and see what's happened, will you?" Frowning, she caught sight of Cadel's screen. "What are you doing? Some kind of project?"

With one swipe at a key, Cadel exited the site. He didn't want Lanna poking her nose into his private business. "Nothing," he said, and realized, with a sinking heart, that he wasn't going to be left in peace that day. After all, it was supposed to be his birthday party.

Sighing, Cadel stashed his computer back in its old hiding place, inside the hollowed-out atlas. Just to be on the safe side, he also implemented his fail-safe program, which was designed to keep his computer from booting up unless special codes were entered. Only he knew the codes, of course. Anyone else who tried to turn it on would be unable to do so. He would explain that the machine had broken down.

And that's exactly what he did say to the kids who turned up—at least, to those who actually noticed him. Despite the fact that it was his birthday, most of the guests ignored him entirely. Only one little girl, Leticia, even bothered with him, and she followed him around purely to annoy. She dogged his footsteps as he picked at the piles of chicken wings, pork dumplings, spring rolls, spiced cutlets, bread sticks, Thai salad, barbecued ribs, and vol-au-vents arrayed across the dining-room table.

"Yuck," she said, watching him deftly whip a spring roll off one plate. "What's that?"

"A spring roll."

"It looks disgusting."

"Good." Cadel stuffed it into his mouth. "More for me if you don't like them."

"Yuck! How can you eat that?"

"With my teeth."

"Eew! That one's *green*."

"Because it's made out of grape leaves."

"How can you eat *leaves*? Caterpillars eat leaves."

Cadel rolled his eyes.

"I'm hungry, and there's nothing to eat!" moaned Leticia. "Don't you have any sandwiches?"

"No," said Cadel, "but there's cheese." Leticia looked around suspiciously.

"What kind of cheese?" she queried, and pointed at a round of Camembert. "Not *that* kind. That's yucky. I won't eat that."

"Very wise," a smooth voice suddenly remarked. Glancing up, Cadel saw Thaddeus standing in the doorway. He wore a light jacket over a crisp shirt and was cradling a gift-wrapped parcel.

"You probably shouldn't eat anything you haven't pulled out of the ground yourself," Thaddeus went on gravely, addressing Leticia. "Processed foods are full of insect residue."

Leticia stared, openmouthed. "Huh?" she said.

"Little tiny bits of wings and legs and carapace," Thaddeus explained. "Stuff you can only see under a microscope. You can't keep it out of things like bread and meat and cereal. Most of us must eat the equivalent of—oh, at least two cockroaches a day."

"I do not!" Leticia protested, her eyes wide with horror. "I do not eat cockroaches!"

"Of course you do. We all do."

"I do not!"

"And spiders," Thaddeus continued with relish. He bared his long teeth in a wolfish smile. "And big, fat blowflies."

"Mummy!" Leticia cried, before bolting from the kitchen. Cadel and Thaddeus both listened to her clumsy tread and piercing cries, which slowly faded as she escaped into the garden.

"What a repulsive creature," Thaddeus finally observed, thrusting his present under Cadel's nose. "Happy birthday, dear boy. If you've already got it, I've kept the receipt—but I'm told that it's a must-have."

Cadel took the parcel with a shy smile. He was desperately relieved to see Thaddeus. Disoriented by his sleepless night, buffeted by the noise and the crowds and the unexpected blows he'd received, he felt safe in Thaddeus's company.

The psychologist's gift was a book: *Parallel Distributed Processing— Explorations in the Microstructure of Cognition, Volume 2.* Cadel examined it with pleasure.

"Thanks," he said.

"You haven't got it?" asked Thaddeus.

"Only volume one."

"Oh, good."

"It's the only decent present I've had today."

"Really? What did the Piggotts give you?"

"Nothing. Yet."

"Though they have pulled all the stops out for your party." Thaddeus jerked his head at the scene beyond the door: the tons of food, the vats of punch, the roaring mass of people. "I was actually forced to park in the next street."

"Oh yeah," Cadel replied, dryly. "Nothing's too good for the birthday boy."

"No wonder you're looking a little lost, if I may say so."

"I always get lost in this place," Cadel replied, and Thaddeus studied him closely. Before the psychologist could speak, however, someone else cut into their conversation.

"Your birthday, Cadel?" a harsh voice inquired.

Cadel turned around. He was astonished to see Mrs. Brezeck, his former mathematics teacher, standing about five feet away. She wore a long tan coat and a green scarf around her neck. She looked ruffled.

"Mrs. *Brezeck?*" Cadel exclaimed. "How did—gosh, they didn't tell me they invited *you.*"

"I wasn't invited," she said. "I just walked in."

"Oh." Cadel didn't know how to respond. It was odd, seeing her in such familiar surroundings—like seeing a ghost. She stepped forward suddenly, her purse clutched to her chest, her mouth set in a thin, straight line.

"I came here to say that I know what you did, Cadel." She almost hissed the words. "I've been following through. It all leads back to you, all of it."

Cadel blinked. Though he didn't feel strong enough to cope with this attack, he forced himself not to swallow or to glance aside. "What are you talking about?" he asked.

"You know *exactly* what I'm talking about," Mrs. Brezeck spat. "Just before the English exam, Angelique told Damian she was breaking up with him, and he ran his car into a tree. Couldn't take his exams. Angelique was so shattered that she failed hers. I've spoken to Angelique, and she said she gave Damian his marching orders because of a letter she received from Heather Parsons accusing Damian of taking advantage of her on the night of the formal. According to Heather, she wrote that letter because Jessica told *her* that Angelique had been calling Heather a slut—something that Jessica heard from *you*, Cadel."

Cadel stared blankly.

"Then there was Colm Cartwright. He somehow got a copy of several exam papers over the Internet before he had to do them. Funny, that, isn't it? When you consider that he can hardly manage a word-processing program. Naturally, they were fake papers. Naturally, he prepared for the wrong questions. I can't prove it yet, Cadel, but I know you were responsible for *that*, too!"

Cadel shook his head. "No, I wasn't."

"Don't *lie* to me!" Mrs. Brezeck yelped, and took another step forward, one forefinger raised. Before she could reach Cadel, however, Thaddeus's arm shot out, barring her way.

"I don't believe we've met," he said coolly, at which point she glared up at him like a snappy little terrier.

"Who are *you*?" she growled. "His father?"

"Just a family friend."

"Well, you should know, Mr. *Friend,* that this child is a *demon.* He's a *criminal.* He ought to be *locked up.*"

"Oh, what nonsense," Thaddeus drawled. "This little fellow here?"

But Mrs. Brezeck refused to be distracted any longer. She turned back to Cadel.

"I'm going to get you for this," she warned him, over Thaddeus's arm. "You've ruined the lives of dozens of great kids. I'm going to gather up my proof and I'm going to have you charged with being a public nuisance."

Cadel, who was beginning to lose his temper, stared at her with cold, hard eyes.

"Don't be ridiculous," he replied. "Nuisance laws are about the use and enjoyment of land, or property."

"Speaking of which," Thaddeus remarked, "isn't there something on the statute books about trespass? I believe you said you weren't invited?"

Mrs. Brezeck hesitated. Then she wagged her finger again.

"You think about it," she declared, thrusting her face as close to Cadel as she could. "Just think about it. Because if you don't come clean and give those kids another chance, then you'll pay for it, Cadel. I'll hunt you down in the end."

Abruptly, she turned on her heel. Thaddeus and Cadel both watched her walk out of the house, clumsily brushing past people who had glasses of beer in their hands.

"Don't worry," said Thaddeus, his gaze still on the teacher's back. "I'll take care of it."

"No." Cadel spoke firmly. "*I* will."

Out of the corner of his eye, he saw a flicker of pleasure tug at the corner of Thaddeus's mouth.

TWENTY-NINE

The party fizzled out at about six o'clock that night, by which time Thaddeus had departed. Never once had he left Cadel's side during the course of the afternoon. Though they hadn't been able to talk much (because of all the people), he did manage to reassure Cadel before he finally said good-bye.

"I'll put Adolf on it," he murmured into Cadel's ear. "Get him to send out a surveillance team to keep an eye on you."

"But—"

"Better safe than sorry, Cadel. You won't know it's here."

"But nothing's going to *happen*," Cadel protested. "It's only Mrs. Brezeck!"

"Now, Cadel." Thaddeus fixed him with a penetrating look. "What have I always told you?"

"'Never underestimate the enemy,'" Cadel quoted with a sigh. "But I really don't think—"

"Take it easy, Cadel." Thaddeus patted his back, straightening. "I'll talk to you soon."

Cadel was surprised at Thaddeus. He thought that the psychologist was overreacting wildly to any threat that Mrs. Brezeck might pose. Not that she *didn't* pose a threat. Cadel knew that she did; the woman was obsessed. But she wasn't about to hunt him down with a bow and arrow. She wasn't about to poison his food. What she *would* do, he feared, was take the whole matter to a lawyer. So, after returning to his bedroom, he dug out some of his law books.

Suppose Mrs. Brezeck did find proof? It was highly unlikely, but not, he feared, impossible. Though he had covered his tracks pretty well, he might have been a bit lazy, if only because he'd never expected that anyone would even *begin* to put two and two together. Even so, he wasn't sure that he could be charged with any civil or criminal offense. The common-law action of deceit, he knew, had to stem from purely economic loss; could the loss of missing out on a place in college be termed "economic"? As for the tort of injurious falsehood, that wouldn't apply here, surely? He had never directly told anyone a lie. Unless the planting of the fake exams could be classified as "false representation." But no one would be able to prove that he'd done any such thing—not with the kind of re-mailers he'd used.

It was all very confusing for Cadel, who had been given, in Dr. Deal's classes, only a quick, glancing overview of the law. He did wonder, for a moment, if he should consult Dr. Deal, but then dismissed the idea. No point giving the man any counter-ammunition. No, if he needed legal advice, he would ask Thaddeus. Thaddeus would find him a lawyer.

In the meantime, he would try to ensure that the whole business never reached the stage of hiring lawyers. His best bet would be to review all the steps he'd taken to bring down the twelfth grade, and to make sure he hadn't forgotten to plug any holes. He would also have to update and expand his old research on Mrs. Brezeck. If she had any shady secrets, Cadel would have to track them down and use them against her.

Oddly enough, he was pleased to be faced with such a mighty task, because it took his mind off Kay-Lee. Fishing around for electronic passwords was a good way of avoiding gloomy thoughts about Kay-Lee or his mother. While the Piggotts staggered off to bed, complaining loudly about being "worn out" because they'd had to supervise Mrs. Ang and the caterers, Cadel worked away at his computer. He worked until 2:00 A.M., then dropped, fully clothed, onto his handwoven bedspread.

The next day, he was woken at about eleven by the trilling of his cell phone. He nearly fell onto the floor trying to reach it.

"Hello?" he croaked.

"Cadel?"

"Thaddeus?"

"Oh dear. You were asleep."

"Um. Not really. I was just . . . I have to go to the bathroom."

"Before you do, Cadel, let me just say how much I admired the way you handled that incident yesterday. It showed great presence of mind."

"Huh?" It took Cadel a moment to remember the incident in question. "Oh. Right. Thanks," he said groggily.

"And don't worry—she won't be bothering you again."

"What?" Cadel suddenly jerked awake. "You haven't *done* anything? Thaddeus?"

"No, no." The psychologist spoke soothingly. "You told me you could handle it, Cadel, and I believe you. I just wanted to say that she won't be bursting in unexpectedly anymore. I've got a surveillance team posted, watching your back."

Cadel said nothing. He wasn't sure that this was entirely good news.

"So I'll see you on Monday," Thaddeus continued. "Same time, same place."

"Okay. Uh—thanks."

Click! Thaddeus had hung up. Cadel lay for a while, staring at the ceiling, his computer phone clasped in his hand. At last he rose. After a brief visit to the bathroom, he snatched a granola bar from the pantry and returned to his computer. He didn't bother to change. He didn't bother to shower, or to clean his teeth.

He wanted to immerse himself in an electronic world and forget that his body even existed.

Lanna was still sleeping, so he didn't have to worry about her. Clearly she was still recovering from the party and its stresses. Stuart was nowhere to be seen. (Off on another interstate trip, no doubt.) Cadel busied himself with various housekeeping tasks, which had to be completed before he could really settle down and foil Mrs. Brezeck. This didn't mean that he picked up all the Game Boys strewn on his floor or tidied the clothes in his closet; it meant that he checked his e-mail, switched re-mailers, fiddled with dynamic passwords, and generally cleared away a variety of small, annoying jobs, like Partner Post, for instance, so he could concentrate on more important things.

He had been on the verge of shutting down Partner Post even before Kay-Lee's devastating message. It had begun to bore him. Now, of course, he could hardly bear to download all the new stuff that had come in—all that whiny, sentimental, deluded garbage. He felt almost sick as he scrolled through what seemed like hectares of badly spelled, unoriginal pleas and promises. There was even a *new* applicant! Help! Cadel scanned the message that had been sent. *I've been led astray in my life . . . looking for the Right One . . . am caring person wanting to commit . . . green eyes, dark hair, 53 yrs old, 178.5 cm tall, 73 kg, birthday on the twelfth of January, divorced in '92, no one serious since then . . . need someone who can bring meaning to my existence . . . soul mate . . . looks not an issue . . . preferably a Cancer . . .*

He winced, then his gaze snagged on the name of the applicant: Jorge Heimstadt.

Jorge.

The name caused his heart to leap. Jorge was the villain in *The Name of the Rose.* Jorge had been passing himself off as a blind and helpless holy man, when in fact he'd been murdering people.

As for *The Name of the Rose,* it was the one detective story that Eiran Dempster liked. And that Kay-Lee McDougall also admired.

Surely this couldn't be a coincidence?

Cadel examined Jorge's message more carefully. It was written in plain English. There were no underlined words, no suspicious capitals, no odd spellings. Moreover, he couldn't see anything that remotely resembled the code he had devised with Kay-Lee. But as he reread each phrase, over and over, he sensed that he was missing something. Something obvious.

237

And then, at last, he spotted it. Two simple words.

Chemical affinity.

Jorge was talking about his need for a perfect match. *You could say I was looking for chemical affinity,* he had written. Suddenly, everything came together in Cadel's head. Chemical affinity. The periodic table of the elements. Atomic numbers.

Fifty-three years old. Fifty-three was the atomic number for iodine, whose symbol was "I." The next number was 178.5, which couldn't be an atomic number (because atomic numbers only go to 103) but *could* be an atomic weight. Cadel scrolled through the table in his head. Barium was 137.34, then came the lanthanides . . . then hafnium. Hf.

I. Hf.

Meaningless. Unless it meant "I have"?

He checked the next number. Seventy-three kilograms. That sounded more like an atomic number again—tantalum, to be exact.

I. Hf. Ta.

Birthday on the twelfth of January. What did that mean? Twelve was the atomic number for magnesium: Mg. *Divorced in '92* was easy, ninety-two being the atomic number for uranium (U). I. Hf. Ta. Mg. U. It didn't really make sense.

And then Cadel realized. The reference to January meant something as well. It wasn't just twelve—it was twelfth of the first, or 12.01. The atomic weight for carbon.

Number, weight, number, weight, number. I. Hf. Ta. C. U.

I have to see you.

It was as clear as day. Kay-Lee wanted to see him. She wanted to see him, but she couldn't tell him so. Not directly. Not even in the code they'd devised.

Why?

He jumped out of his seat and began to pace the floor, hardly knowing whether to dance for joy or wring his hands. What on *earth* was going on? Why this strange message? But perhaps it was incomplete. Perhaps there was more. Throwing himself at the computer again,

Cadel studied Jorge's e-mail with ferocious intensity. The only other numbers he could find were in the last paragraph: *I believe that life falls into* four *seasons, and I am, obviously, commencing my autumn years. But I don't believe that would make any difference, for kindred spirits. I believe the Beatles got it right—and even if I was* seventy-four, *or older, it wouldn't matter to the woman who saw past the exterior, to the core of my being. The True Self doesn't fade. Anyway, as Bismarck said, "Do not count the years, only the achievements." I believe I have a fathomless depth of love and experience to offer the one who digs deep enough.*

Four seasons. Four. The atomic number for beryllium. (Be.) Seventy-four was the atomic number for tungsten. (W.) Be W.

Bew?

No, no, no. There had to be something else. Be, W, something. He combed through the last few sentences. He sectioned them, dissected them, ran them through every possible test he could think of before it suddenly sprang out at him. Bismarck, Otto von. *Otto*—the Italian word for eight. Eight was the atomic number for oxygen, or "O."

Be W O.

No. That wasn't right. Be W . . . ox? Woxy?

Air? Not exactly scientific, but . . .

Be W Air. Beware.

It was a warning: *I have to see you. Beware.* Was Kay-Lee in some sort of danger? Was that why she had cut off all communications with him?

Clearly she was afraid that their main line of communication had been bugged. She was under the impression that someone had been *reading their e-mails.* Well, it might be possible. Cadel's own computer firewalls were almost impossible to breach, but the security on Kay-Lee's machine was hopeless—as he'd proven in the past. Perhaps the hacker had wormed into their exchange from her side? That was possible.

Curled up in his chair, furiously gnawing at his fingernails, Cadel considered his next move. He had to see Kay-Lee. To visit her, in other words—not to phone her, or to e-mail her, or anything else. The question was: How? He could catch a train to Weatherwood House easily enough, but could he just walk in the front door? Kay-Lee had told him to beware. It might be dangerous walking up to the front door. And besides . . .

Cadel glanced at the window. For all he knew, the Führer's surveillance team was sitting outside. It might follow him, and then what would happen? Maybe nothing. Maybe, if there was danger, it would be a good thing to have a few Grunts watching his back.

On the other hand, Kay-Lee McDougall was none of the Führer's business. Cadel had seen the Führer's data on other Axis staff members. He had seen the way Adolf collected background tidbits: police records, unpaid child support, outstanding warrants. The Führer seemed to regard this information as important to the security of the institute—in case he ever had to blackmail someone, perhaps. Like Cadel, he made a hobby of data collection. Unlike Cadel, however, he wasn't very good at it.

All the same, Cadel didn't want him finding out about Kay-Lee. As far as Cadel was concerned, Kay-Lee and the Axis Institute had to be kept as far apart as possible. Thaddeus, for example, wouldn't approve. Sending Kay-Lee presents had been bad enough. Going to *visit* her would be regarded as horribly unwise. *You're getting too involved,* Thaddeus had warned him a long time ago.

"That's your opinion," Cadel said aloud. Then he got up, dragged his backpack from under the bed, and stuffed it with items that he'd been hiding: his Indian-cotton skirt, his snap-on earrings, his bra, his hair ribbon. To these he added a plastic shopping bag from Sam's Boutique, a filmy chiffon blouse (filched from the laundry basket), and some of Lanna's makeup, which he was able to take from her bathroom quite easily. She didn't even stir when he slipped through her darkened bedroom; she was just a motionless lump under an embroidered silk duvet.

Having packed his bag, Cadel ordered a taxi, then walked boldly out the front door. He couldn't see anyone—no lurking cars or suspicious strangers lighting cigarettes—but that meant nothing. The Grunts might simply be very good at their job.

He hoped that they wouldn't be too good. If they were, he was in trouble.

The taxi arrived in about ten minutes. Cadel asked the driver to take him to the nearest mall. As they purred along leafy avenues and then swung out onto the highway, Cadel kept his eyes peeled for pursuing vehicles. One white Toyota stayed behind them for a suspiciously long time before turning off down a side street. There was also a motorbike that weaved in and out of the traffic like an Internet search engine spidering through the Web. But Cadel saw nothing that he could positively identify as a surveillance team.

At the mall, he headed straight for a computer store that he often frequented. It wasn't his favorite but it was the closest; it stocked a lot of telephone and entertainment equipment as well. Cadel spent about an hour poking around there, watching everyone who came in after he did. He was trying to lull any hovering surveillance teams into a false sense of security. Finally, he left the shop, ducking down a featureless corridor that led to a pair of restrooms. Two doors were placed side by side, one marked MALE, the other FEMALE.

With a quick glance around, Cadel entered the female bathroom.

It was the riskiest part of the whole plan. One protest could ruin everything. But he moved quickly, and the only person who saw him was a tiny girl, whose mother was peering into a mirror above the basins. The girl caught his eye and stared.

Cadel darted into a stall, slamming the door behind him.

In the unearthly fluorescent light, he struggled with buttons and zippers. Having forgotten to bring spare socks, he was forced to stuff his bra with toilet paper. His sneakers looked odd under the Indian-cotton skirt, but that couldn't be helped. (Alias had warned him about giveaway shoes, but that couldn't be helped, either.) Though he was able to tie his hair back inside the stall, he didn't attempt to put on any makeup. Not until he had a mirror to help him.

The little girl was gone by the time he emerged. Cadel plastered foundation over his bruises until they were barely visible. He then applied his lipstick carefully, with many surreptitious glances at the woman on the other side of the room, who was doing the same thing. He put kohl on his eyes, and a little blush on his cheeks. The mascara, however, defeated him. He decided that mascara wasn't necessary.

When he'd finished, he was pleased with the result. It was convincing. *He* was convincing. He shook out his Sam's Boutique bag and thrust everything into it that he wanted to take with him (discarded boys' clothes, makeup, backpack).

Then he walked through the exit door.

THIRTY

No one stared. No one stopped him. He might have been invisible, for all the notice he attracted.

With a dry mouth and a hammering heart, he wandered down to the street, pausing every so often to peer into the kind of shop windows that he usually ignored—windows full of lingerie, jewelry, scented soaps, floral cushions. He wasn't sure if anyone was following him. He thought not.

Once on the street, he turned left and headed for the station. The air was full of grit. He felt strangely exposed after the bright, enclosed world of the mall, but the eyes of the people he passed simply slid over him. His skirt swished around his ankles: a very peculiar sensation. He could taste lipstick.

When he reached the station, he bought a ticket from a machine. Every platform was crowded with people, but the train that he caught wasn't very full. Though he moved from carriage to carriage, no one seemed to be dogging his footsteps. After about forty minutes, when he finally reached his stop, he sat by the door until the last possible moment.

Only as it was sliding shut did he suddenly fling himself out onto the platform, nearly knocking down an elderly lady.

He would have apologized, if he'd trusted his voice. But he couldn't. So he brushed past her rudely and bounded up the stairs to the street, two at a time. He saw Chinese families, slouching skateboard riders, a woman with a baby in a stroller—nothing suspicious. Weatherwood House was a half-hour walk away, down a very long road. He had checked his street directory before coming; he knew exactly what to do.

It was overcast, though dry. The walk seemed endless. On and on he went, tripping sometimes on the badly maintained pavement, barely noticing the apartment blocks and brick-veneer houses that lined the road on each side. At one stage he thought he'd reached Weatherwood House, only to discover that he was looking at a nursing home. And Weatherwood House, when he finally got there, wasn't at all what he had expected. Somehow he hadn't pictured so many entrances and exits—so many signs: VISITOR PARKING, AMBULANCE ONLY, and KYLE MANLY WING. There were trees and a big white house, but the photograph on the website hadn't encompassed all the glass breezeways, parking lots, ramps, patios, and ugly additions.

He didn't dare hesitate, however. He had to look purposeful. Briskly, he crossed the front lawn and headed for the nearest entrance, which was the door to an enclosed verandah. The verandah contained all kinds of odd chairs, a wicker side table stacked with boxes of jigsaw puzzles, and an electric urn—but no people. From one end of this airy but slightly depressing space, a pair of double doors opened into a wide hallway. Here everything looked far less run-down. There was carpet on the floor and a plant in a pot. Bright pictures hung on the wall, interspersed with several bulletin boards. A faint smell of cooking lingered in the air.

"Can I help you?" a female voice inquired.

Cadel whirled around. He saw a compact, gray-haired woman in slacks and a short-sleeved blouse, carrying a pile of folded sheets. She was emerging from what appeared to be a storeroom or linen cupboard.

Her manner was anything but friendly.

"Uh . . ." Cadel was so nervous that his voice was a startled squeak. "Kay-Lee McDougall?"

"You want Kay-Lee?"

Cadel nodded, relieved that the woman didn't seem to find the pitch and tone of his request at all suspicious.

"Kay-Lee hasn't finished her shift," she said. "Are you sure you want to wait?"

Cadel nodded again.

"Well . . . perhaps you'd better come through here."

The woman led Cadel down the hallway, past lots of wide-open doors. Cadel saw an office, a bathroom, a floor strewn with toys. He had to dodge a wheelchair, which was being pushed by a young man in a pink T-shirt; the child in the wheelchair rolled his eyes at Cadel, his head juddering.

"In there," said the woman, and stopped. The hallway had widened into a large area that was in fact the vestibule of the old house. A polished staircase swept up to the second floor; it had some kind of stair lift attached to it. There was also an elevator, Cadel saw, and a row of upholstered seats near the massive front door.

"Just sit down and I'll tell her you've arrived," his companion instructed. "Who are you, anyway?"

She couldn't have been more blunt. Cadel was reluctant to advertise his presence, just in case the danger that Kay-Lee had warned him against lurked inside Weatherwood House. So he picked a fake name.

"Fe," he shrilled.

"Fee?"

Cadel nodded. Fe, of course, was the symbol for iron—Eiran. He hoped that Kay-Lee would understand.

"As in Fiona?" the woman pressed.

"Just Fe," he said firmly, hoping that his voice wasn't going to give him away. Perhaps if he pretended to have a cold? He coughed into his hand, wishing that he'd brought a handkerchief. Alias would have brought a handkerchief.

"Right," the woman sighed. She was clearly losing patience. "Just wait here, then."

And she left. Cadel was relieved. He sat down and picked up a brochure from the table next to him. It looked more interesting than all the dog-eared *Women's Weekly*s and torn picture books underneath it, because it was scattered with photographs of computer keyboards. Cadel soon realized, however, that these keyboards were of a kind utterly strange to him. There were keyboards with extra-large keys, with multicolored keys, with a feature ensuring that each key would only type one letter no matter how long you held it down. There were removable key guards, for people with a tendency to hit more than one key at a time. There were programmable membrane keyboards, with their own types of key guards.

Cadel was fascinated. He knew that keyboard shortcuts—or mouse keys—were usually employed by disabled people who couldn't use a normal mouse, but he hadn't been aware that special keyboards were being made. And special mice, too, by the look of things. He pored over descriptions of mice with extra-large roller balls, with joystick configurations, with drag locks, with different cursor speeds, with removable guards . . .

"Ahem," someone said.

Cadel jumped and glanced up.

He was face-to-face with Kay-Lee McDougall.

She looked exactly the same as her picture. There were no visible scars. Her sandy-colored hair was pulled back in a ponytail; she wore black mascara, a touch of lip gloss, and a plain white polo shirt over a knee-length skirt. Her arms were lightly dusted with freckles.

She looked tired.

"I'm Kay-Lee," she said. "Do I know you?"

Cadel stared. He was suddenly frightened—frightened and confused. It was as if he didn't know this woman. As if she was a stranger. She seemed so *old*.

What am I doing here? he wondered. *This is insane.*

"I—I—"

"What?"

"I've got a message," he said hoarsely. "From a *friend*."

He didn't want to spell everything out. Not in this public place. But Kay-Lee was disappointingly slow on the uptake.

"What friend?" she asked, sounding impatient. After glancing around quickly, Cadel fluttered his fingers, like someone using a keyboard.

Kay-Lee's head suddenly jerked back, as if she'd been slapped. Shock registered on her face.

"Christ," she said. "You mean—you don't mean—*Tom Carter?*"

Cadel frowned. Who was Tom Carter? "No," he said. "Eiran Dempster."

"Yeah, right." Kay-Lee had recovered somewhat. Her drawl was flat and nasal—almost sarcastic in tone. She folded her arms. "Alias Tom Carter."

"I don't know any Tom Carter," Cadel said impatiently. He wasn't bothering to disguise his voice, and Kay-Lee narrowed her eyes. She peered at him. Then she suddenly caught her breath and coughed.

"Christ," she exclaimed. "Christ, you're—you're not—"

"I'm a boy," Cadel said. "Don't talk so loud."

"You're *him*, aren't you? You're Tom Carter!"

"Look, will you stop?" Cadel grew more and more angry as it dawned on him that he didn't know this woman. He didn't feel any connection with her at all. "I told you, Tom Carter doesn't mean anything to me! My name is Cadel!"

"I don't believe it." Kay-Lee was shaking her head in amazement. "This is unbelievable. You really *are* thirteen."

This time it was Cadel's turn to be shocked. He changed color. He nearly choked.

"Who told you I was thirteen?" he demanded.

"The coppers."

"The *what?*"

"They came here," Kay-Lee revealed. "On Thursday. Barged right in, told me they had some information. About Partner Post." She spoke sharply. "Said it was all a big scam, run by some thirteen-year-old kid

247

named Tom Carter. Said he made up all the partners—wrote the stuff himself. Showed us printouts." She paused and waited. But Cadel was struck dumb. "Pretty smart thing to do," she continued. "Pretty low as well, I reckon."

Cadel put his hands to his head. "But—but this isn't right," he stammered. "I'm not Tom Carter. I'm Cadel Piggott."

"So you really did it? Shame on you."

"But they couldn't have found out! They *couldn't* have!" Cadel had been so cautious. And who was this Tom Carter person? "I was so careful! This doesn't make sense!"

"You're telling me," said his companion, watching him. There wasn't a spark of affection in her eyes. "Why did you do it? What for? How could a kid your age be so bloody *cruel*?"

Cadel flinched. The last word was like a whiplash. Frightened and disoriented, he gazed up at Kay-Lee in supplication. "I'm sorry," he mumbled. "I'm so sorry."

Kay-Lee stared at him for a moment, before looking away. When she spoke again, some of the steely quality had left her voice.

"Don't apologize to me," she said gruffly. "You didn't break *my* heart. It's someone else you should apologize to."

Cadel didn't understand. "Someone else?" he echoed, and Kay-Lee took a deep breath.

"I might as well tell you," she said. "You haven't been talking to me. I'm just a front. All this time, you've been talking to someone who was using my name. And my face."

Cadel blinked. He was already so overwhelmed, this new information didn't even affect his heart rate.

"I—I have?" he said, in dazed accents.

"That's why she couldn't stay mad at you. She was mad at first, obviously. But then she reckoned, well, she hadn't exactly been honest with *you*, either. So she wanted to warn you. That you were under investigation." Kay-Lee cocked her head, arms still folded. "Personally," she drawled, "I still don't think you deserve it. In my opinion, you're a parasite."

Cadel accepted this insult without comment. He was beginning to piece things together.

"You mean—this was all done for *my* sake? Jorge, and the hidden message? It was to warn *me*?"

"That's right."

"Because the police are after me?"

"At long last."

"But how can they be after me, when they're talking about Tom Carter? I'm not Tom Carter. I've never even used that name."

"I don't know and I don't care," Kay-Lee snapped. "All I'm worried about is Sonja."

"Sonja?"

"Sonja's the one you've been tricking all this time. That's why she deserves an apology. *In person*." Kay-Lee grabbed Cadel's arm and yanked him to his feet. "Come on," she ordered. "I'm taking you to visit Sonja."

Cadel didn't protest. He allowed himself to be hustled through another set of double doors and down another corridor. He hardly noticed where they were going. He was too appalled by this new state of affairs. The police! How had the police ever tracked him down? *Why* had they? Why bother with a silly little scam like Partner Post when there were international drug cartels to worry about? Was it something to do with his father? Were they trying to get at Dr. Darkkon through Cadel?

But no, that couldn't be right. The police had been talking about someone called Tom Carter. Could they have made a mistake and traced Cadel's messages back to a hapless nerd of that name? Or were they concealing Cadel's actual identity from Kay-Lee, for reasons that Cadel simply couldn't fathom?

It was all so strange. So very, very strange.

"Here," said Kay-Lee, and abruptly stopped. They were standing outside a closed door. Kay-Lee knocked at the door, and raised her voice. "It's Kay-Lee, Sonja! Can I come in?"

There was a long pause. Then a strangled noise, which Cadel couldn't decipher.

"Okay," said Kay-Lee, and pushed the door open.

She dragged Cadel into a large, sunlit room. A mobile of numeric symbols dangled from the ceiling, each symbol made of blown glass. As it moved in the draft caused by Kay-Lee's entrance, colored shards of light danced around the walls, which were covered in pages of printout, a photo of Stephen Hawking, a poster of a geometric eye-puzzle, a hologram of Albert Einstein, a giant numeral 2 executed in red paint, and a picture of the Count from *Sesame Street,* torn out of a coloring book. Beneath this dazzling array of images stood a bed, equipped with various poles and mounting arms. It was draped in a beautiful patchwork quilt, and Cadel suddenly remembered talking to Kay-Lee— Sonja, that is—about the geometric perfection of patchwork quilts. They had traded various formulae for the log-cabin, monkey-wrench, and courthouse-steps designs.

There was also a desk near the window, fitted with various adjustable shelves. A computer monitor was perched on one. The only thing Cadel could see that remotely resembled a keyboard was more like a small laptop, propped up on a mounting arm, which in turn was attached to a wheelchair.

In the wheelchair was a girl. She had dark hair, caught up in a barrette. She wore baggy jeans (from which her feet stuck out at a slightly uncomfortable angle) and a crumpled green blouse. The muscles in her neck were taut, as if she was straining to see something. Her arms were very thin, and her fingers almost clawlike. She had enormous, haunting brown eyes in a narrow face.

Her head jerked uncontrollably, and her mouth was open. Cadel could see her tongue writhing behind large, crooked teeth.

The wheelchair moved slightly, with an electronic buzz. He couldn't tell why.

"This is Sonja," Kay-Lee declared. "Sonja has cerebral palsy. Sonja, this—believe it or not—is Eiran Dempster.

"He's come to pay you a visit."

THIRTY-ONE

Cadel was speechless. He simply gaped like a fish.

Sonja also said nothing, though the muscles in her face worked convulsively.

It was Kay-Lee who finally broke the silence.

"Like they said, he's just a kid," she went on, closing the door behind her. "And he's not Tom Carter at all. He's Cadel Something-or-other."

"P-Piggott," Cadel supplied unsteadily. "Cadel Piggott." He couldn't believe his eyes. This, then, was the real Kay-Lee, the mysterious "Sonja." A disabled girl in a wheelchair, whose fingers were twisted into painful shapes, and whose head twitched as she craned to look at him.

"He must have taken you seriously," Kay-Lee remarked, addressing herself entirely to Sonja. "This getup is meant to be a disguise, I reckon. And let's just hope it's worked, or we're going to be in *big trouble* with the coppers, Son. They still think you're me, remember. I'm going to cop the flak here if anything goes wrong."

But Sonja was moving her arm. It lurched across to the device in front of her—a device that had DYNAVOX printed across its base—and began to skitter along the screen. For a moment, one rigid finger remained at rest in a particular spot; then it jerked onward. Eventually, the machine began to speak for her.

"*X-is-the-sum-of-unknown-quantities-y-over-one-x-minus-u-to-the-power-of-twenty-six,*" it said, in a toneless girl's voice—and Cadel knew, then. He knew that he really was talking to Eiran Dempster's perfect partner.

"I'm sorry," he mumbled. "I'm so sorry."

"You owe her," Kay-Lee pointed out. "Must be—what? Over a hundred dollars?"

"I'll pay you back," said Cadel, even as Sonja threw her head from side to side, making strained noises.

"Nyaa," she protested, and jabbed at her Dynavox.

"No," it said.

"I will, though. I—I . . ." Cadel didn't know what to say. Not with Kay-Lee there, listening. It was all so terrible. Sonja couldn't even talk. *She couldn't even talk.* Her mouth didn't move well enough—her face kept stiffening and bunching up. Her hands didn't always do what they were meant to do. She was fighting against herself all the time.

Cadel's eyes suddenly filled with tears.

"I'm sorry," he quavered, and he meant that he was sorry for everything. For everything that had ever happened to her. "I was stupid. I was so stupid."

"Oh, settle down," said Kay-Lee crossly, as the Dynavox began to respond to Sonja's agitated fumbling.

"Police-came-here—"

"I told him," Kay-Lee interrupted. "But they got the name wrong apparently."

"I don't know any Tom Carter," Cadel snuffled. "It doesn't make sense. My name is Cadel. Cadel Piggott."

"How-old-are-you?"

"Fourteen," Cadel admitted. "Yesterday." And Sonja began to laugh a slow, sawing, cawing laugh, her eyes searching for Kay-Lee.

"Sonja's only sixteen," Kay-Lee informed Cadel. "She was worried about the age difference, ha-ha."

"Between-me-and-Eiran," Sonja added, through the medium of the Dynavox. *"What-a-joke."*

"I'm sorry," Cadel repeated, in feeble tones.

"Only a kid would have the gall," said Kay-Lee. "They said you'd been ripping off hundreds of people."

"Oh no." Cadel shook his head. "Only sixty-eight."

"*Only* sixty-eight?"

"Interesting-number," said Sonja, through her Dynavox.

"But you were special," Cadel assured her. "You—I didn't—I wasn't friends with anyone else."

"Oh, sure," Kay-Lee drawled, and Cadel turned on her.

"I wasn't!" he cried. "You don't understand!"

"You can say that again."

"I *wanted* to tell you!" Cadel pleaded, addressing Sonja. "I did, truly! But I didn't know what to say. I didn't think you'd want to talk to me if you knew the truth."

"Got that right," Kay-Lee remarked, at which Sonja let out a bark of protest.

"Shut-up," said the Dynavox, and Kay-Lee apologized: "Sorry," she murmured.

"Butt-out."

"I will. Sorry. None of my business."

"Go-away."

"Can't, Son." Kay-Lee shook her head. "Can't risk it. We don't even know who he is, not really."

Cadel fumbled for his Axis security pass. On it were printed his name and address. "I'm Cadel," he insisted. "Truly. Look—see? 'Cadel Piggott.'"

"Then who's Tom Carter?"

"I don't know. Maybe they've made a mistake."

"I-bet-they-have," said Sonja. *"Small-one-was-weird."*

"Oh, god yeah." Kay-Lee snorted. "With the nose spray. What a creep. Giggled all the time."

It was as if a gear in Cadel's brain suddenly ground to a halt, then started up again.

"He *what*?" Cadel gasped. "He *giggled*?"

"All the time."

"What did he look like? Was he fat?"

"Oh, yeah," Kay-Lee drawled.

"Other-one-fatter," Sonja added.

"What color were his eyes?" said Cadel. "The giggling one?"

Sonja and Kay-Lee exchanged glances. There was a long pause, broken only by Sonja's noisy breathing. At last the Dynavox slowly ground out: *"Hard-to-say. All-screwed-up. Small."*

"He had a sty," Kay-Lee remarked, and Cadel sat down on the bed.

"Oh my god," he breathed.

"What? Do you know him?"

"What about his hair? What was that like?"

"Gray."

"Disgusting."

"Sort of floppy. Lank."

"He-smelled-of-eucalyptus."

The Virus, Cadel thought. It had to be the Virus. The sty. The giggling. The eucalyptus. Had to be.

But why? *Why?*

"What's-wrong?" said Sonja, through her Dynavox. Cadel, however, needed more information.

"What about the other guy?" he wanted to know. "You said he was fat?"

"Huge." Kay-Lee was watching Cadel carefully. "Enormous. Red in the face."

"No-hair."

No hair? That ruled out Maestro Max. Though Max wasn't all that fat, anyway. Just a little plump.

"He did most of the talking," Kay-Lee revealed. "What else, Son?"

"Pompous."

"Yeah, he was that all right."

"Lewis. Detective-Sergeant-Lewis."

"Old," said Kay-Lee. "Late fifties?"

"Big-mole-sticking-out-of-left-nostril," said Sonja, and Cadel blinked.

He stared at her, his mind balking.

The Virus, yes. That wasn't beyond the realms of possibility. He'd believe anything of Axis. But *Stuart Piggott?*

How could that be?

"You know them, don't you?" Kay-Lee inquired. "I can tell from your face."

"Did you see any identification?" Cadel asked her, ignoring the question. "Did they show you anything?"

"Sure did. Bloody everything."

"Photo-ID," said Sonja.

"Did they come in a car? Did you see it?"

Sonja's head rolled back and forth. Kay-Lee replied: "I did. Very flashy. Silver Commodore."

Stuart's car was a silver Commodore. Cadel felt suddenly as if he was going to be sick.

Dr. Vee and Stuart Piggott?

"What's going on?" Kay-Lee demanded. "Don't tell me they weren't real coppers. They had to be."

"I don't think so," Cadel whispered.

"You telling more of your porkies, little man?"

"Don't." The Dynavox voice was fairly flat, but Sonja was obviously disturbed. Her movements had become more erratic. *"He's-scared."*

"Why? What's wrong? Who were they, if they weren't coppers?"

"I think . . ." Cadel took a deep breath. "I think one was my—was the man who adopted me."

His two companions stared.

"Bull," Kay-Lee said at last.

"Are-you-an-orphan?"

"He's a liar, Son, remember? How can we believe anything he says?"

"I-was-fostered," Sonja continued, ignoring Kay-Lee. *"Didn't-take. Ended-up-here. Mother-insane. What-about-you?"*

Cadel looked at Sonja. The grin on her face had nothing to do with what she was feeling, he reminded himself. It was something over which she had no control.

"My mother's dead," he replied. "My father—my father's in jail."

"Chip off the old block," said Kay-Lee. "*You* should be in jail, mate."

But Cadel wasn't listening. He was trying to work out what had happened. If Dr. Vee had come with Stuart Piggott, to tell Sonja (alias Kay-Lee) that Eiran Dempster didn't exist—what did that mean? Surely they weren't *undercover* cops? It seemed unlikely, especially if they had given Kay-Lee a false name. Tom Carter. Why would they call Cadel "Tom Carter" if they were real policemen?

Dr. Vee and Stuart Piggott. It was a crazy combination. As far as Cadel was aware, they had met each other only once, during the Piggotts' tour of the Axis Institute. Yet they had been working together closely. Imitating policemen. Using false names. For what reason?

To warn Sonja?

Maybe Dr. Vee had tapped into Cadel's computer, found the Partner Post stuff, and gone to Stuart. Maybe Stuart had decided to put a stop to Partner Post before it *did* come to the attention of the police. But that didn't make sense. Stuart could simply have told Cadel to shut up shop—he didn't have to go to all the trouble of impersonating a policeman. Especially not when it was against the law. Stuart was a lawyer. Why would he want to break the law and risk his career?

Perhaps because he didn't have a career to risk. Perhaps because he wasn't a lawyer after all. It occurred to Cadel that Stuart didn't appear to have approached anyone else on the Partner Post client list. Most of them had been sending e-mails quite happily for days, as if nothing had happened. They would have reacted like Sonja if they'd been told. They would have taken their business elsewhere. And if Stuart's main purpose had been to shut down Partner Post, he would certainly have made a clean sweep of all the clients.

So why Kay-Lee—why Sonja, that is—and no one else?

257

Because Sonja's important, Cadel decided. Because Sonja is my friend. Because I confided in Sonja. Dr. Vee would know that if he'd hacked into my computer. What's more, Dr. Vee wouldn't have gone to Mr. Piggott with information about Cadel. Dr. Vee knew who Cadel's real father was. If Dr. Vee had been concerned, he would have gone to Thaddeus. With a message for Dr. Darkkon.

There were really only two possibilities. Either Stuart and Dr. Vee were working together as government agents, planted within Dr. Darkkon's organization to keep an eye on him, or they were both working for Dr. Darkkon. *Both* of them.

Whatever the case, Cadel's whole upbringing had been one big lie.

"Cadel. Hey!" Kay-Lee was shaking his arm. "Wake up! You can't stay here!"

"You-haven't-told-us-the-whole-story." Sonja had moved her wheel-chair around. Her intent brown gaze was fixed on Cadel. *"Is-Lewis-police-or-not?"*

"No," said Cadel, tugging at strands of his own loose hair. "I don't know what he is. He's been tricking me. All my life. His wife—god!" Cadel felt like pounding the wall. Could it all have been a *front*? Absolutely *everything*? If so, how on earth had he missed it? "I don't even know who they are! Either of them!"

"You're not making any sense," Kay-Lee said dryly.

"I know. It's hard to explain. My dad—my *real* dad . . ." He trailed off, but Sonja had missed nothing, despite her involuntary jerks and twitches.

"This-has-something-to-do-with-your-real-dad? The-one-in-jail?" she asked, and Cadel caught his breath.

He had remembered. The sequence of events: bang, bang, bang. On Wednesday, Dr. Deal had beaten him up. On Thursday, the two phoney policemen had visited Kay-Lee. On Friday, Sonja, masquerading as Kay-Lee, had given Cadel the old heave-ho.

Right afterward, Dr. Darkkon had started talking about Cadel's mother. *You can't trust 'em—not the best of 'em,* he had said. Really

258

drumming it in. *They just drop you and walk away.* As if trying to undermine Cadel's faith in his female friend, without mentioning any names.

Was it truly a coincidence?

"It can't be," Cadel said aloud. But if Dr. Darkkon had decided that Sonja (alias Kay-Lee) was dangerous, what better way to get rid of her than tell her the truth? She was bound to drop Cadel like a hot brick—just as his mother had done. Talking about Cadel's faithless mother was simply one way of driving the lesson home.

"God." Cadel started slamming his fists against his temples. "God, how did I miss it? How could I be so *stupid?*"

"Don't do that; you'll hurt yourself," Kay-Lee exclaimed, and Sonja said, *"What? Tell-me-what?"*

"It's my dad," Cadel croaked, in amazement. "It's got to be."

"What about your dad?"

"This is all him." Cadel looked from one to the other, from Sonja's tense face to Kay-Lee's puzzled scowl and back again. "It's hard to believe, but this is all his doing. I know it. I can feel it. He doesn't want me talking to you."

"Why-not?" Sonja questioned. She struggled with her Dynavox, but seemed to have trouble pointing. Kay-Lee, watching her uneasily, said, "It's nothing to do with you, Son. No one knows about you. The police talked to me."

"It's not you, Sonja." Cadel was thinking hard. Sonja had been his friend since his days at Crampton. But on Wednesday, for the first time ever, he had struck out on his own. He had kept something from Thaddeus: Dr. Deal's name.

And that had set off someone's inner alarm.

"It's me," he abruptly declared. "They think we're too close—I bet that's it. They think I'm getting too independent, so they want to separate us because they think you're a bad influence. They don't want me to have friends of my own. They're frightened."

"Who are?" asked Kay-Lee.

"My dad." Cadel was aware of a burning sensation inside his chest. He was almost gasping with rage. But such rage, he knew, was counterproductive. If you were too angry, you stopped thinking straight. You made mistakes. You were foolish.

Don't get mad, he told himself. Calm down. *Calm down.*

"Listen," he said, turning to Sonja, "if I sent you a couple of photos, could you tell me if you recognized the people in them?"

Sonja uttered a forced noise that was almost certainly a yes. As Cadel waited, she made one—two—three stabs at the Dynavox before finally connecting.

"By-e-mail?" she slowly inquired.

"No." Cadel shook his head. "No more e-mail. We can't use e-mail; they're plugged in somehow. I'll have to snail-mail the photos. I'll do it tomorrow. And then you can . . . you can . . ." What? They couldn't use their old code; someone had broken it. The Virus, probably.

"More-Jorge?"

"No. At least—no. I don't think so."

"I sent that last message," Kay-Lee pointed out. It was her first contribution for some time. "I went to an Internet café. Sonja was scared that they had her computer tapped somehow. She didn't want the police to know she was warning you."

"That's good," said Cadel absently. "That's really good. But we can't be too careful. Swear to god, I know what I'm talking about. That guy with the giggles? He's a computer genius. I bet you he's been monitoring us the whole time."

"Why?" Sonja queried.

"Because my dad probably put him up to it." Cadel couldn't imagine where to start. He gnawed frantically at his fingernails. "It's so hard to explain. My dad isn't normal. He's got plans for me. Everything has to be the way he wants it. He's got a whole network of people helping him on the outside."

"But—"

"I should never have come here." Now Cadel was beginning to

panic. "I might have been followed. The disguise might not have worked. Where am I going to say I've been? Suppose he broke the Jorge code? It wasn't too hard—"

"Hey. Calm down," Kay-Lee urged, with a degree of sympathy in her voice that Cadel found suspicious. "Just don't get upset, okay? There's nothing to worry about."

Cadel looked at her sharply. "I'm not a loony," he snapped. "I'm not paranoid."

"No, of course not."

"I'm not!"

"Show-me-the-photos," Sonja interjected. *"Then-I'll-know-for-sure."*

"Yes, but how can we talk?" said Cadel. "You can't send me mail— the Piggotts might spot it before I do. You can't call me at home—"

"Why not?"

"Because it's *dangerous.*" Cadel was getting annoyed with Kay-Lee. "He doesn't want me talking to Sonja—"

"Your dad, you mean?"

"Yes!" How many more times did he need to say it?

"Who-is-your-dad?" Sonja asked.

Cadel hesitated. The secret of Dr. Darkkon's identity was worth killing for. He didn't want to spread the risk around.

"I'd better not tell you," he said reluctantly. "The less you know, the better." Seeing the skeptical look on Kay-Lee's face, he struggled to control his temper. "Look," he added, "you're entitled to think I'm off my head. I know what this looks like. But if you recognize the people in the photos I send you, then you'll have to agree I'm not the only one who's acting crazy." An idea struck him. "Did they tell you where they were from? What station they were attached to? Because if they did, you should call up. I bet no one will have heard of them there."

Kay-Lee shot a sidelong glance at Sonja. "Well, maybe we will," she said.

"Meanwhile, how can we talk?" said Cadel. "Maybe I can call you. On a public phone."

"You're sure *our* line won't be tapped?" Kay-Lee asked with delicate sarcasm.

"I hope not." Cadel, in contrast, was quite serious. "God, you might be right. What if the phone's tapped? It might be. They might be afraid I'll try to contact you."

"Cadel—"

"And I'm probably being followed, too, so we can't meet. Unless I disguise myself. But I don't know if that'll work. I don't know if it *has* worked. God—" He was beginning to panic again. "What if they've bugged this place? What if they're listening now?"

"For Chris'sake!" Kay-Lee exploded. "What are they, the CIA? You're crazy. Just listen to yourself. You'll be saying you get messages over the TV next."

"No-bugs," Sonja interrupted. *"Not-here."* She paused, one arm bent back at a painful angle; she was beginning to sweat with the effort of communication. Helplessly, Cadel turned to Kay-Lee.

"They didn't come in here," Kay-Lee confirmed with obvious reluctance. "We were in the dining room when they came. But—"

"Wednesday-morning," Sonja went on. *"Post-photos-tomorrow-and-I'll-have-them-Wednesday. Library. Phone."*

Again, Cadel was lost. Again, he relied on Kay-Lee for an explanation.

"The local library," she sighed. "Sonja goes there every Wednesday morning, from nine to eleven."

"Call-there. They-know-me."

"Right. Okay." Cadel nodded. "And which library are we talking about?"

Sonja told him.

"Can I phone the desk?"

"Straight-through."

"Should I ask for anyone?"

"Beatrice."

Cadel committed all this to memory. He could easily find the number in the book. His only challenge now was to locate a public phone that he could use without arousing suspicion. Between nine and eleven on Wednesday morning.

He certainly couldn't use his cell phone. Or any of the Axis lines.

He realized that Kay-Lee and Sonja were both staring at him. Waiting.

"Okay—well—I'll call you," he faltered. "At the library. I'd probably better go now."

"I'll show you out," said Kay-Lee, and held the door open for him. But Cadel hesitated. He had to say something more. He had to make a connection—a real one. Gazing down at Sonja, who was writhing in her chair, he blurted out, "You're my best friend. The best I ever had."

Sonja didn't respond. She may have tried to; it was hard to say. Perhaps she was only lifting her hand in a gesture of farewell. Kay-Lee said gruffly, "You're tiring her out," and hustled him from the room.

She then marched him down a series of corridors, gripping his arm tightly.

"Has she always been like that?" Cadel asked, almost tripping over the hem of his cotton skirt.

"Since she was born," Kay-Lee replied. "There's no cure."

"It must be terrible."

"You've no idea."

"So—so she'll never be able to leave? Get her own flat, or anything?"

"They'll be shutting down this place soon," Kay-Lee replied, stopping to shove open a heavy glass door. "The trend is for smaller houses, with fewer people in them." She hesitated, looking down at Cadel with weary, bloodshot eyes. "I never knew about this Partner Post thing," she added. "It wasn't my idea. By the time I found out, you were her bloody lifeline. She's too young. Too vulnerable."

"I'm sorry," Cadel whispered.

"The Internet's been a godsend for disabled people," Kay-Lee continued, starting off again. They hurried past a series of closed doors.

"It's opened up the world for them. But it's exposed them to a lot of risks. And Sonja—well, she's too bloody smart for her own good."

Suddenly they were in the main entrance hall. Cadel recognized the black and white linoleum; the stained-glass fanlight; the keyboard brochure. Kay-Lee propelled him toward the EXIT sign.

"I'll take her to the library on Wednesday," Kay-Lee concluded. "But it would be better if you didn't ring. It might break her heart in the short term, but in the long term it would be better for her." She fixed Cadel with a wintry, forbidding glare. "I don't care how bright you are—or how pretty," she said. "You're still a mad bastard, and I want you out of her life."

"But—"

"Now piss off."

THIRTY-TWO

Cadel walked back to the station. When he reached it, he ducked into the restroom, changed his clothes, then caught a train to his local stop.

All the time, his mind was working furiously.

There were so many things to do; he found the prospect overwhelming. First off, he had to locate some photographs. That would be easy. Then he would have to post them—that would be harder. Then he would have to think of an excuse for trying to dodge the Führer's surveillance team—an almost impossible task. And then . . .

Then he would have to find out who he had really been living with for the past twelve years.

He felt as if he was standing on shaky ground—as if the support beneath his feet was about to collapse. Who were the Piggotts? Were they really agents of Dr. Darkkon? Had everything been an elaborate charade? Had the secrets he'd kept from them, the lies he'd told, been designed to trick *him* instead of the Piggotts? It didn't bear thinking of.

The alternative, of course, was that the Piggotts were government agents. Dr. Vee, too. Cadel decided that, if they were, it would be better. He would rather blame the government for his last twelve years than Dr. Darkkon. If he had to believe that Dr. Darkkon had chosen the Piggotts, out of all the people in the world, to take care of him— well, it was the ultimate betrayal.

Walking home from the station, Cadel tried to convince himself that the government-agent scenario made sense. Suppose an agency like Interpol had taken Cadel away from Dr. Darkkon, when he was a baby, then set him up with a family of government agents in the hope that Dr. Darkkon would eventually try to make contact and expose himself? Suppose they had installed Dr. Vee at the Axis Institute to monitor the activities of the staff there?

And suppose they had told Kay-Lee about Partner Post simply to protect her from Cadel's dad? If it was a secret operation, they *might* have used a false name for Cadel.

Cadel clung to this possibility. Contemplating any other was too horrible. But if the police or the government were worried about Kay-Lee, why hadn't they warned her about him a long time ago?

He couldn't be sure about anything yet. Not until Sonja had identified the two policemen.

When he arrived home, Cadel headed straight for the Piggotts' security system, which he neatly disabled. (He had been doing this on a regular basis since he was six, so no one was likely to think it out of the ordinary.) Having ensured that he was safe from prying eyes, he cut Dr. Vee's picture out of his Axis course handbook and removed a family snapshot from one of the photo albums. Then he sealed both in a pale gray envelope addressed to Kay-Lee. Finding a stamp wasn't hard. Stamps were kept in the spare-change bowl on top of the fridge. But getting to a mailbox—that would be difficult without arousing the suspicions of anyone stationed near the house with a pair of binoculars.

As he was pondering his options, Lanna arrived home. The sound of her raised voice made Cadel's blood run cold. He bolted into his room before she could catch him, wondering how long it would take her to discover that the security system wasn't working. A while, probably. She wasn't very clued in to things like that.

Or was she?

"Cadel!"

"I'm here!" He was proud of his voice, which didn't wobble one bit.

Clack, clack, clack. He could hear her approaching in her noisy high heels. The door creaked open and she poked her head into his room.

She didn't look any different. Somehow he had expected that there would be a change in her face.

"How was your day?" she asked. "What have you been doing?"

"Oh, computer stuff." He had never been very forthcoming with her, so his short response didn't come as a surprise.

"Well, I've got a dinner appointment this evening, but I'll be back by ten," she said, glancing at her watch. "What do you fancy to eat? I could make you some chops."

"Pizza, please."

"Oh, Cadel. You should eat something healthy once in a while."

"*Vegetarian* pizza, please," Cadel said firmly. He had had an idea.

"Well, all right." Mrs. Piggott sighed. "I don't have the energy to argue. You can take care of it yourself, I suppose?"

"I think I can probably manage," Cadel muttered. While Mrs. Piggott flitted around the house, ironing clothes and swigging white wine and looking for her fanciest shoes, Cadel sat at his computer, thinking. He couldn't be sure that it hadn't been invaded. He thought it unlikely, but he couldn't be absolutely sure. So how could he start chasing down the real Stuart Piggott without alerting whoever might be tracking his electronic movements? For all he knew, there might be people in a van outside, monitoring his computer's electromagnetic emissions with a sophisticated radio receiver: a Dynamic Science A-110b, for instance. The police were capable of that. Even the Virus might have managed it. And as for the Führer—well, *nothing* would be beyond the Führer.

If he was going to unmask the real Stuart Piggott, it might be best to start his search in Stuart's office.

"All right," Lanna declared, sticking her head into Cadel's room again. Her hair was slicked back, and she was wearing far too much makeup. "I'm going now, but I'll be back soon. Have you ordered the pizza?"

"I'm just going to."

"Have a salad as well, will you, Cadel? There's a bag of lettuce in the fridge."

Cadel waited until he heard the front door close and the noise of the car's engine fade. Then he waited a little longer, just in case Lanna had to return for a forgotten bottle of wine, or something. Finally, he got up and consulted the telephone directory, deliberately rejecting the Piggotts' usual pizza-delivery service for another one, chosen at random.

You couldn't be too careful—not in this house. He was aware of that, at long last.

The pizza arrived in thirty minutes. By that time Cadel was already in Stuart's office, rifling through desk drawers. There was nothing of importance in any of them—just cell phone brochures, hole punchers, Post-it notepads, electrical cords, ink cartridges, and unused fountain pens. The filing cabinets looked more promising, but there was a lot of very dull stuff to get through, including files full of phone bills, insurance documents, bank statements, and tradesmen's quotes. He was starting on his second drawer when he heard the doorbell ring, and he went to answer it.

A young guy in a leather jacket was standing there, unzipping a red-vinyl pizza bag. He looked tired.

"Oh, great," said Cadel. "Come in. I'll get the money."

It had to look natural. That was the thought uppermost in Cadel's brain: *It had to look natural from the outside.* By plunging back into the kitchen, Cadel managed to lure the pizza-delivery man into the house, where they were both safe from prying eyes. "Just put it down on the little table, will you?" he called, knowing that, to do so, the pizza-delivery man would have to cross the Piggotts' anteroom diagonally, thereby becoming invisible from the front door.

It was dead space, that particular location—ideal for Cadel's purposes.

"Here," he said, trapping his quarry in a corner as he counted out bills. "It's twenty-two for the pizza, right?"

"Yeah," came the weary reply.

"Okay. There you go." Cadel lowered his voice. "Listen," he added, gazing up into the scrubby, flat-eyed face that hovered above his own. "If I gave you another twenty, could you post a letter for me? After you've finished delivering the rest of your pizzas?"

The pizza-delivery man surveyed Cadel without expression.

"It's not a bomb, or anything," Cadel whispered, glancing over his shoulder. "It's a letter to my girlfriend. I'm not supposed to be seeing her. I'm grounded—"

"Yeah, whatever." The man didn't sound interested. He held out his hand, waiting.

Cadel was surprised.

"Oh, great. Thanks." He plucked the letter from his pocket, along with another twenty-dollar bill. "You don't mind?"

The man shrugged. "People ask me to get beer, cigarettes, you name it," he muttered. "It's no big deal."

Cadel was relieved. He paid over his money and tucked his letter into the vinyl pizza bag.

"Can you do it tonight?" he asked.

"No sweat," came the reply.

"There's a post office up at the shops. You can park right outside, at this hour—"

"I'm on it." The pizza-delivery man gave Cadel a mock salute, then headed for the door. "Enjoy your pizza."

Cadel didn't wait around to watch his receding back. It would have looked suspicious. He simply shut the door and retired to the kitchen with his pizza, hoping he had done the right thing. For all he knew, the letter might end up in a garbage bin somewhere. But he couldn't, at present, see that he'd had any alternative. The opportunity had arisen, and he'd taken advantage of it.

Now he would have to wait.

The pizza wasn't as good as the ones they usually ordered. Cadel ate about half of it, idly flicking through cable channels as he did so. Then he washed his hands thoroughly—it wouldn't do to get pizza grease all over Stuart's electricity bills—and returned to his unfinished task. The time, he noted, was half past seven. He still had an hour or two before Lanna came back.

Some of Stuart's filing-cabinet drawers were locked, but the locks were easy to pick. At the age of nine, Cadel had become briefly infatuated with locks; he had studied the locksmith's art with his usual avid concentration, even beginning (though not completing) a rather suspicious long-distance locksmith's course that operated out of a post-office-box address. While he had never finished his apprenticeship, he had certainly learned enough to open the drawers of Stuart's filing cabinet. What he found, however, was disappointing. In a file marked CADEL, he discovered his own school reports, immunization certificates, concerned letters from teachers, IQ test results, and so forth. There was also a set of documents relating to Cadel's adoption and a couple of lung X-rays taken during Cadel's most recent bouts of bronchitis.

Finally, there was his birth certificate. Cadel hadn't examined it for years—not since Thaddeus's entry into his life—and he saw now what he hadn't seen before. The document was an obvious fake. In his forgery class, Cadel had learned many things about the detection of forgeries. He had learned about carbon-dating techniques. He had learned about the way a scanning Auger microscope could be used to measure the migration of ions from ink to paper. In this case, however, he didn't need any fancy equipment to tell him that the birth certificate was a forgery. The ink didn't even have a proper shine to it. Cadel himself had done a better job forging a birth certificate for a fictitious young woman called Ariel Schaap. (It was now hidden in the lining of his winter jacket.)

A very clumsy attempt, he thought. Couldn't they have done better than this? And then he wondered who "they" might possibly be. His father's agents? The government's? Interpol's? Impossible to say—yet. He had to find more evidence. Apart from the CADEL file, Stuart's locked drawers contained only Microsoft handbooks, old tax returns, passports, and superannuation brochures. It was incredibly frustrating. There was nothing suspicious about it at all—except the very absence of anything personal. Possibly Stuart kept all his degree certificates at work, but what about letters of reference? College pennants? Postcards? Snapshots? School records? What about a marriage certificate? Cadel couldn't find a marriage certificate anywhere. Nor could he find any birth certificates for either of the Piggotts.

After a while he gave up and tried Lanna's studio. This room was as messy as Stuart's was neat. There were fabric samples everywhere, piled up on the drafting table, hanging out of drawers, dangling from hooks, spilling from in-boxes. Pages torn from magazines were pinned all over the walls, and stacks of brochures about bathroom fittings, floor coverings, window treatments, and kitchen appliances almost covered the floor. It was the sort of room that repels entry. Cadel had never advanced more than a few steps into it because he would have had to climb over half a dozen things to do so.

This time, however, he was determined. Very, very carefully, so as not to dislodge anything, he picked his way into the center of the room and stood contemplating it. Apart from the drafting table, it contained a desk, a couple of filing cabinets, and another cabinet with long, narrow drawers designed for blueprints, or something similar. All of these furnishings were bulging with stuff: Not one of the drawers would close properly. Cadel checked his watch (eight fifteen!) and wondered, with despair, where he was going to start. He wouldn't have to worry about leaving a mess. The room was so messy, more disarray wouldn't be noticed. But how was he going to sift through all this rubbish? How was he going to find anything of interest in all these piles of stupid decorating tips?

And then he noticed something.

The dust.

Everything was covered in a layer of dust. He couldn't touch a manila folder or a paint leaflet without leaving an obvious mark— something that wouldn't have been so peculiar if it wasn't for the fact that Lanna's appointment diary, on the desk, was also covered in dust. As was the blotter. And the telephone. And the button on her desk lamp.

It was as if no one had been in this room for weeks—even months. Yet Lanna had worked in it for some time only the day before. Or so she'd said.

Cadel sneezed. The dust was like a trap; he couldn't touch anything for fear of disturbing it. Clearly, Mrs. Ang hadn't even attempted to clean this room. (How could she, when it was barely possible to reach the desk?) Equally clearly, Lanna hadn't done anything with these fabric swatches and toilet brochures for a long, long time—if ever. Had Cadel not studiously avoided everything to do with the Piggotts and their tedious work, he would have noticed that something didn't add up.

He realized suddenly that he was gasping for breath, and turned on his heel. The Piggotts' bedroom was next door. It was enormous and had the impersonal, color-coordinated atmosphere of an expensive hotel room. There were about five hundred pillows piled on the bed, each a different shade of maroon or charcoal; the bed itself was elevated on its very own platform; there were recessed lights and a carved screen and a cashmere throw tossed carefully over a Louis IV chair upholstered in suede. The bedside cabinets supported nothing at all—not even a book or a glass of water.

Cadel knew, however, that the dressing room was as messy as Lanna's office. While she liked to have a clean, "uncluttered" bedroom, she couldn't achieve the effect without stuffing a lot of junk into her dressing room and bathroom. The bedside cabinets were also full up. Cadel went through them carefully with shaking hands. He had a funny feeling that he was getting closer to whatever it was he'd been searching for. He found tissues, empty lipsticks, medicines, a wheat pillow, an essential-oil burner, an eye mask, a suede brush, an English-French dictionary, an extension cord, a broken watch, and a camera battery. In the dressing room he looked through every bag, shoe, and pocket, but uncovered only a dirty handkerchief, a sticky tube of lip salve, and half a packet of mints. The scraps of paper scattered about were, for the most part, unrevealing: One was a screwed-up cinema ticket, one a brief shopping list, one a GRACE BROS label.

And then he spotted something on the floor of the wardrobe, tucked away in a corner: another slip of paper, squashed and soiled. Smoothing it out, Cadel saw that it was half a ripped credit-card receipt. He was about to throw it away when his gaze was caught by the card number.

Cadel knew all of the Piggotts' seven credit card numbers. And this, he realized, wasn't one of them.

THIRTY-THREE

"Cadel!"

Cadel jumped. Mrs. Piggott! It was only twenty past nine and she was home already!

He stuffed the receipt into his pocket and threw himself out of her room just in time. She caught him in the hallway.

"What have you done to the alarm system?" she demanded, hands on hips.

"Uh—"

"I've told you before, Cadel, that system is *out of bounds*!"

"Maybe it's broken." Cadel tried his trademark innocent look, but Lanna wasn't fooled.

"Get in there," she ordered, "and *put it back on*!"

"But—"

"Now!"

He did as he was told. There was no reason not to. He had found what he was looking for—a genuine clue.

Of course, it might be a red herring. As Cadel rerouted electronic signals in the stuffy little circuitry room, he considered the possibility that this discarded receipt belonged to someone else. But if that were the case, why did the Piggotts even have it? He couldn't help being suspicious.

So he would check that number. He would pursue it through the usual electronic routes, but not with his usual computer. He would have to employ another one, without arousing the suspicions of whoever was watching him.

Bit of a tall order, really.

In bed that night, Cadel racked his brain for a solution to the problem. It kept him too busy to think about anything else, and he fell asleep before he could resolve his dilemma. Then, at five thirty, he woke up shivering. His head ached and his stomach heaved. Something was wrong: He was sick, really sick. After staggering to the bathroom for an aspirin, he fell back into bed and didn't move again until Lanna checked on him at eight thirty.

"Cadel?" she said. "I'm going now."

He grunted.

"Cadel? Haven't you got any classes today?" Then she took a step nearer and caught her breath. "Oh my god," she exclaimed. "Are you sick? Cadel? Oh my god."

She put her hand on his forehead.

"Doesn't feel like a temperature," she fussed. "What's wrong, exactly?"

"My head hurts."

"Oh dear."

"My stomach, too. I feel sick."

"Oh lord. I've got a meeting . . ." She was beginning to sound shrill. "Are you *sure* you can't get up? Do you want to see a doctor?"

"No."

"Well . . . well . . ." Clearly, she didn't know what to do. "Well, how about I call Mrs. Ang, and she can come in early? I'll be back by lunchtime. Oh, trust Stuart to be away! He always is, in a crisis!"

Cadel buried his head in his pillow. He didn't want to listen to Mrs. Piggott complaining about her husband. (If he really *was* her husband.) After a while she left the room, returning a few minutes later with various sickroom accessories: a bucket, a box of tissues, a glass, a jug, a packet of pain-and-fever tablets. "Mrs. Ang's on her way," she informed Cadel. "When she arrives, I'll go. But I'll be back soon. It sounds like a migraine, Cadel."

Cadel said nothing. He retreated into a drowsy, muddled world that prevented him from thinking about anything except the pain in his head. After a while, his nausea drove him to the bathroom, where he threw up all over the floor. But by that time Mrs. Ang was around, so she cleaned up the mess without complaint.

Cadel only vomited once. He spent the rest of the day dozing and staring at the wall, with the occasional trip to the toilet or short period propped up against a pile of pillows with a thermometer under his tongue. He didn't do much thinking. He didn't feel up to it. His mind lay dormant until half past six, when the sound of a voice suddenly made every nerve in his body stand to attention.

"Cadel?" said the voice. "How are you feeling?"

It was Thaddeus Roth.

Cadel rolled over. He saw that Thaddeus was standing in the doorway of his bedroom, looking about ten feet tall. The psychologist carried a tin of hard candy and was dressed in a dark suit under a generous overcoat that swished and swirled around his ankles.

"Since you couldn't make it to your appointment, I thought I'd drop in on my way home," he remarked, entering the room. He sat down on Cadel's typist's chair, which creaked like a tree in the wind. "How are you feeling?"

"Okay. I mean, sick. But better. Than I was."

"Good," said Thaddeus, placing the tin on Cadel's desk. "These are for you. I always like to have them around, when I'm ill. Is it your chest again?"

"No, I—I don't think so." For perhaps the first time in his life, Cadel wasn't happy to see Thaddeus. A hot flush of guilt invaded his entire body, turning his face red. He didn't want to talk to Thaddeus. He was too confused. Too . . . frightened?

"Lanna says you don't have a fever," Thaddeus went on. "Just a headache, nausea, fatigue."

276

Cadel nodded, clutching the covers around him. His eyes actually *felt* huge as he stared at Thaddeus, who regarded him with a pensive expression, his own eyes dark and unreadable.

"What a shame," said Thaddeus. "You didn't eat something yesterday, perhaps? Something that might have disagreed with you?" His tone was tranquil, but Cadel knew exactly what he was getting at.

"No."

"It wouldn't be a hangover, Cadel? You didn't slip away to experiment with anything?"

Cadel blushed again.

"No," he repeated, then took a deep breath. "So the surveillance team lost me, did they?"

A brief pause. Thaddeus lifted an eyebrow.

"Yes," he drawled. "They did."

"I wanted to see if I could do it. Now that I've been studying disguise."

Cadel wondered if this explanation sounded as lame to Thaddeus as it did to him. Perhaps not. The psychologist was nodding sympathetically.

"Yes, of course," he murmured. "I wouldn't make a habit of it, though. Under the circumstances."

"I won't," Cadel promised, perfectly aware that this was the closest Thaddeus would get to a warning. "But you don't have to worry about Mrs. Brezeck. She won't do anything to me."

"She will if you don't do something to her first," Thaddeus replied. "Have you, Cadel? Done anything, I mean?"

Cadel shook his head. "Not yet," he faltered.

"Ah."

"But I will."

"Good."

"I've got an idea. I would have done it today, only—"

"You were sick. Of course. I understand." Thaddeus rose. "Well, I won't tire you out. You get a good night's sleep and perhaps you'll be up and about tomorrow."

Once again Cadel nodded. He was just beginning to relax when Thaddeus stopped at the door and turned back.

"Nothing's troubling you, Cadel?" he asked gently. "There's nothing on your mind?"

Cadel forced himself not to swallow.

"No," he squeaked. "What do you mean?"

"Oh, I just thought. Stress can sometimes manifest itself in physical symptoms: fatigue, headaches, that kind of thing." The dark gaze bored into Cadel. "No one's bothering you at the institute, for example?"

"No." *That* wasn't a lie, in any event. Cadel could speak calmly and firmly. "Not at all."

"You wouldn't be frightened of going there? After the incident last week? Because if you are, Cadel—"

"I'm not. Really. I'll be going tomorrow."

Cadel summoned up every bit of energy left within him and offered Thaddeus an earnest, wide-eyed expression that must have convinced the psychologist to some degree. After directing a long, searching look at Cadel, Thaddeus shrugged and glanced away.

"Well, that's a relief," he said. "I'd hate to think you were unhappy there, since I was the one who recommended the place. I'll tell a certain person that you're ill, of course. He'll be sorry to hear it."

"Yeah." Cadel spoke awkwardly. "Tell him—tell him I'll see him on Wednesday."

"I shall," Thaddeus replied. Then he smiled, lifted a hand, and withdrew.

At which point Cadel discovered that he was sweating.

He fell back onto his pillows, pulling his blankets over his head.

What if Thaddeus was right? What if he wasn't really sick? What if he was simply stressed, and the headache was his brain's way of trying to wriggle out of a nasty situation? He felt the tears rising, and pressed his hands against his eyelids to hold them back. He was so tired. So confused. And Kay-Lee—Sonja, rather—what was he going to do about *her*? How could he go on if they weren't able to e-mail each other?

I don't want this to be happening, he thought desperately.

But it was.

THIRTY-FOUR

Cadel had only one class on Tuesday—his forgery class—which was scheduled for ten o'clock. Despite feeling rather sluggish when he woke up, he was well enough to go. He wanted to go. He had things to do, information to track down. So he tucked a packet of aspirins into his backpack (along with his old school hat, blazer, and tie), and caught his usual train to the institute.

He didn't know if he was being followed. He didn't really care. As he sat in the swaying car, he occupied himself with the question of how he was going to make contact with Sonja the next day. The question of finding a computer no longer troubled him. He had solved that problem in the early hours of the morning.

"Cadel! Where have you *been*?" exclaimed Gazo, when they met in front of seminar-room four. "You had me worried!"

"I was sick," said Cadel. He looked around. There was no one else in sight.

"Good job you came," Gazo went on, jigging from padded foot to padded foot as if he needed to empty his bladder. "Abraham wants to see you. He's in the hospital. Royal Prince Alfred."

"Huh?"

"He rang me at the dorm. From the hospital. He's real sick. He didn't know your number."

"He wants to see *me*?"

"Yeah."

"Why?"

"Dunno."

Cadel found it hard to concentrate on this particular piece of news. He had to force himself to stop thinking about Sonja and the Piggotts.

"That's not all," Gazo continued, with an air of importance. "Did you hear about Kunio?"

"Kunio?"

"He killed himself."

Cadel stared.

"Committed hara-kiri. Or whatever it's called," Gazo explained. "Happened on the weekend."

"Why?" asked Cadel dully. So much had been thrown at him recently that he found it difficult to absorb this latest shock. "I mean, why did he do it?"

"Dunno." Gazo didn't seem to know anything much.

Cadel surveyed the corridor again. It was empty. "So we're the last ones in the class," he said. "Is that right?"

"Yeah." Gazo paused, studying Cadel with obvious concern. "*You're* feeling all right, aren't you? I mean, you're not *really* sick."

"No. I'm fine."

"You always look so pale, it's hard to tell."

Then Art arrived and the lesson began. It was an interesting one, about forging seventeenth- and eighteenth-century documents. Art showed them how to burn a piece of eighteenth-century leather to extract its tannic acid for ink that would date correctly. He lectured them on the characteristics of antique paper, explaining that blank sheets could be torn from the ends of old books. He demonstrated how a certain fungus could be chemically applied to this paper to create the yellow stains found on aged documents. Finally, he placed a forged document in a glass chamber and charged the air inside it with an electric spark. This spark generated ozone, which bleached and oxidized the new ink, making it appear old.

He also encouraged them to practice their copperplate.

"All this kind of thing is pointless unless you can reproduce the handwriting correctly," he declared. "And even then, you won't convince anyone unless you get the spelling and syntax right. I once saw a forgery of a nineteenth-century letter in which the forger had used the word *scatty*. That word wasn't invented until 1911."

He made no comment about the reduced size of his class.

For homework, different kinds of handwriting were given to Cadel and Gazo to copy with different kinds of nibs. The two were then dismissed. Gazo followed Cadel out into the sunshine.

"When are you going to visit Abraham?" Gazo inquired. "He said it was urgent."

Cadel sighed. "I don't know. I've got a lot to do."

"When's your next class?"

"Uh—tomorrow."

"Tomorrow?" Gazo seemed surprised. "Then why don't you go today?"

Exasperated, Cadel turned on his companion. "Why don't *you*?" he snapped, and Gazo slumped.

"I would, if I was allowed. I'd afta take off me suit. They don't like it when I wear this suit off campus—not unless I'm in a car."

"Oh. Right." Cadel was abashed. He had forgotten about the suit. It no longer looked strange to him. "Sorry."

There was a brief silence. Cadel didn't feel energetic enough to send Gazo packing. He was suddenly overcome by a desire to sit in the sun with his eyes shut.

"We could take Abraham's car," Gazo finally suggested, in hesitant tones. When Cadel gazed at him in surprise, he added: "It's still here. In the lot. He got sick in the labs and called an ambulance. A *real* ambulance. So his car's still here."

Cadel thought about this.

"Terry mustn't have been pleased," he observed. "About the ambulance."

Gazo shrugged. Cadel checked the time. Ten past eleven. It would be three hours before he could be sure that all the teachers were out of a certain Crampton staff room. And until then . . . ?

Until then, he had nowhere to go except Hardware Heaven.

"Do you have the keys?" he asked Gazo. "The keys to the car?"

Gazo grinned. It was the first grin that Cadel had seen behind that plastic mask for a long time.

"What do you fink I've been doing at Yarramundi since I started?" Gazo said. "You fink I can't hot-wire a car by now?"

"Oh. Right," said Cadel. "Sorry."

"I can drive one, too," Gazo added. "Trouble is—I mean, I dunno if I can drive wiv a helmet on. And if I take it off, well, it's a big risk. For you."

Cadel considered this. He had no idea how bad Gazo's stench was, but it had to be pretty dangerous or Dr. Darkkon wouldn't have been interested in him.

"You're right," Cadel conceded. "It would be a risk. Maybe I'll skip it for now."

"But you should still go." Gazo's tone became suddenly urgent. "He's *real* sick, Cadel. Know what I mean? If you don't go now, you might not get the chance."

"Really?"

"Really," said Gazo in a solemn voice. "Bleeding from every pore, I 'eard."

Cadel shuddered. He didn't relish the prospect of seeing *that*.

"He wants to talk to you. No one else. Just you," Gazo pointed out. "Maybe he's got a will or somefink."

"Oh hell," Cadel groaned. "I suppose I'd better. It might be important." (To him, as well as to Abraham.) "I guess I'll call a cab. Do you want me to tell him anything? From you?"

"Just that I woulda come if . . . well, you know."

"I know."

"He don't like me, anyway," Gazo concluded, with his usual air of resignation. Cadel left him there, standing alone in the sunshine. On reflection it was better not to risk Gazo's driving. Cadel was positive that Gazo didn't have a license, let alone a firm grasp of the Australian road rules. And Abraham might not appreciate anyone hot-wiring his car.

Because it wasn't rush hour, Cadel's trip to the hospital took only about twenty minutes. When he arrived, however, he spent a good deal of time trying to locate Abraham Coggins. First he went to the wrong desk. Then he waited in the wrong line. Then he went to the wrong department, where he had to wait some more, until a busy nurse's aide had checked a computer. (He could have done it twice as fast himself, but smothered his impatience.) At last he was directed to the Intensive Care Unit, where he was questioned vigorously by one of its staff.

After that he was forced to wait another half hour for a doctor, who came and sat down opposite him with a clipboard and wanted to know why he had come.

"I'm a friend of Abraham's," Cadel replied, trying not to lose his temper. "He wanted me to come."

"He made a phone call," the doctor said. "Was that to you?"

"To my friend." Cadel paused for an instant, before deciding that "friend" wasn't a bad way of describing Gazo. "My friend told me."

"You're the first visitor Abraham's had. He's very sick. Did you know that?"

"Well—yeah. He's here, isn't he?"

"How old are you, Cadel?"

"Fourteen."

"Your parents didn't come with you?"

"They're at work."

"Do they know you're not at school?"

"Yes," Cadel replied, with candid, wide-eyed confidence. "They definitely know I'm not at school."

"Well . . . all right." Obviously disarmed by Cadel's innocent manner, the doctor moved on to another topic. "As I told you, Abraham is very sick. And we don't really know what's wrong with him. He has a lot of nasty symptoms, but nothing that adds up to a recognizable syndrome. We're still running tests. Can you help us at all?"

Cadel stared, with the air of someone who might at any moment stick a thumb in his mouth. Then he shook his head slowly.

"No," he said.

"Have you known him very long?"

"No."

"Do you know why he wanted you to come?"

Again, Cadel shook his head by way of reply.

"His housemates have informed us that he's a medical student, doing some sort of research. Is that right?"

"I think so." Cadel didn't want to be too definite.

"Do you know if he's been researching any kind of toxic micro-organism? Anything like that?"

"No. I mean—I don't know. He doesn't talk about that stuff."

The doctor sighed and scribbled something down.

"All right," he said. "We're trying to get hold of his supervisor at the moment, though we're not having much luck. Meanwhile, I have to warn you, we're not even sure if he's contagious, so he's in an isolation unit. Which means that you might find it hard to talk."

"Oh."

"You can see him, but he's behind glass. Only authorized personnel are allowed in there."

It occurred to Cadel that Abraham must be causing quite a stir in the medical community. Thaddeus didn't like it when Axis students attracted that kind of attention. It was possible that the Führer might be called in to sort things out.

Cadel realized that he should have checked the institute network before visiting Abraham.

"Is there some kind of intercom?" he inquired.

"Pardon me?"

"Some kind of intercom. Like an internal phone system, or something. That Abraham and I could use."

285

"Oh." The doctor looked faintly surprised. "Well—um—I suppose we could arrange something. Though he's not very well, Cadel. I doubt he'll be able to talk. He hasn't been able to talk to *us*."

The doctor was wrong, however. Abraham could talk. But he would only risk doing so after Cadel had been left alone outside the isolation unit, with strict instructions that he wasn't to stir from the spot in which he had been placed. All he could do was lean against the window, staring through it at a figure on a high white bed.

The figure lay very still, hooked up to at least three humming machines, as well as two suspended plastic bags. He didn't look well. His face was a very peculiar color: sort of bluish, with dark gray patches, and puffier than usual. He was still as bald as an egg.

Cadel watched the doctor place a gentle hand on Abraham's shoulder, while a masked nurse hovered in the background. There was no response. The doctor studied two of the machines closely, exchanged a few quiet words with the nurse, then left the room, stethoscope swinging. On his way out the door, he stopped beside Cadel. "If he does wake up while you're here, we might see if you can get him to talk," the doctor said. "We really need to know what this disease might be, and he might have some idea, since he's a medical student."

Cadel nodded. For the next ten minutes, he stood with his nose pressed against the glass as the masked nurse busied herself around Abraham's bed, changing plastic bags, scribbling on his chart, adjusting his position. Finally, she, too, left the room.

"I'll be back in a few minutes," she told Cadel, her voice muffled by her mask. "Don't go in there. All right?"

"All right."

"Good boy."

She bustled down the corridor, pulling off her latex gloves, her rubber soles slapping crisply against the linoleum. At last she turned a corner and disappeared.

Almost immediately, one of Abraham's eyes flicked open. The

whites were blood-colored. Slowly, painfully, he turned his head. Then he crooked one bony finger, beckoning to Cadel.

Cadel looked around. There were some white-clad figures in the distance, but they weren't paying him any attention.

He turned back to the window.

I can't, he mouthed, shaking his head. *They won't let me.*

Abraham beckoned again—more urgently this time. Cadel decided to go in. If he didn't, the whole trip would have been a waste of time. Besides, what could the doctors actually do to him? Have him arrested?

After casting another quick glance up and down the corridor, he sidled into Abraham's glass box.

"I'm not allowed in here," he said, wrinkling his nose at the smell of disinfectant. "So you'd better make it fast."

"Cadel?"

"I'm here. What is it?"

"Cadel . . ." Abraham was hoarse. His mouth flapped vaguely. Frowning, Cadel wondered if he was feverish.

"This is Terry's fault," Abraham suddenly rasped. "He's got the vial. Did you know that? I saw him pick it up, that day in the labs. When Carla collapsed. I told the Führer when he questioned me. I had to." The weak voice suddenly cracked. "It wasn't my fault! I had to!"

"Shh—"

"So now this is Terry's revenge. He's made me sick, I know it. He emptied the vial into my coffee."

"Abraham, you were sick before." Cadel glanced behind him, through the glass, but saw no medical staff approaching. "Don't you remember?"

Abraham, however, didn't seem to hear.

"I might die!" he croaked, a thin trickle of blood running from his nose, down the side of his jaw. "I might die if Terry doesn't help me. That's why I want you to go to my house. My room. There's a key in there: the key to a post-office box. I want you to hide that key, then tell

Terry this: If he doesn't bring me the cure, I'll tell everyone what's written on the paper in that post-office box. I'll tell the Führer! I'll tell Dr. Roth." A feeble cough. "Or you will, if I . . . if I . . ." The breathless ranting trailed away.

"Well, all right," said Cadel. It sounded crazy to him, but he had to humor the poor fellow. Upsetting a sick man wouldn't help anyone. "I guess I could do that, as long as you don't expect me to talk to Terry myself. I mean, I could leave a letter. A computer printout."

"The key's taped to the inside back cover of my *Principles of Internal Medicine*," Abraham went on, as if he hadn't heard Cadel. "There's a spare key to the house on top of the fuse box. You've got to go *now*. Quickly. Before it's too late."

"Abraham—"

"The post-office box is number twenty-three at—oh god—at Strathfield. Twenty-three." The trickle of blood was now more like a stream, pooling darkly on the white sheets. "You're the only one I can trust. The only one. You asked me how I was feeling . . ."

"Abraham, I don't know where you live," Cadel said nervously. He wondered if he should summon a nurse. The sight of all that blood was making him queasy. Alarmed. "Abraham? *Where do you live?*"

But Abraham wouldn't listen. He was muttering about his work; Cadel had to save his work from being destroyed by the evil and envious Terry. His files, all his notes—they had to be rescued.

Cadel slipped out of the room. He went over to the nurses' station, where Abraham's nurse was labeling something.

"Excuse me," he said, "but Abraham's bleeding."

The nurse looked up.

"What?" she said.

"He's bleeding. From his nose."

She bolted. One second she was there, the next she was gone. When Cadel turned, Abraham's door was swinging; the nurse was already inside.

Cadel left her to it. While equipment beeped and voices were raised,

288

he quietly scanned the area for a familiar face. (There weren't any, that he could see.) Then he made his way out of the hospital.

From the taxi stand beside the main entrance, he caught a cab to his local mall. There he once again made use of the restrooms near his second-favorite computer shop. Having locked himself in a stall, he donned his old school tie and his old school blazer, which looked quite convincing over a new white shirt and pair of gray pants. He also slicked his hair down with gluey soap from the soap dispenser, then jammed the school hat firmly over it. Finally, he went to a pharmacy and bought himself a pair of off-the-rack reading glasses. By pushing them way down his nose, he found that he could see over the tops of these glasses well enough to avoid bumping into poles, or giving himself a headache. And they were a very effective disguise. From a distance, with his slicked-back hair, he didn't look too much like himself.

Not that he was trying to dodge any experts. All he had to do was fool a few schoolteachers. Nothing very challenging.

All the same, he was nervous.

Time constraints meant that he was forced to catch another cab, to Crampton. He arrived with five minutes to spare, and had to lurk behind a bus shelter while a distant siren blared, announcing the start of the second-to-last period. Cadel waited. He gave the students another five minutes to swap classrooms. Then he emerged from behind the bus shelter and sauntered over to a side gate, reminding himself that it wouldn't do to look furtive.

He had to convince any onlookers that he had a clear conscience— that he was arriving back at school after a dentist's appointment, perhaps. With a note in his pocket. With a bag full of textbooks and a class to go to.

Cadel wasn't familiar with the latest Crampton timetable. He did know, however, that the next-to-last period on the third Tuesday of the month was traditionally reserved, at Crampton, for a meeting between English staff and library staff. (Something to do with Book Week activities and literacy programs.) Since this meeting always took place in the library, the English department's staff room would almost certainly be deserted.

And the computers within it would almost certainly be free.

Cadel moved briskly along the familiar paths and beneath the familiar brick archways. As he passed a high bank of windows, he heard a teacher's raised voice cutting through the babble of a noisy class. *"We'll have a bit of quiet, please!"* (Mr. Ricci, by the sound of it.) Nothing seemed to have changed except the notices pinned up around the place. As he neared the staff room, he ticked off various landmarks along the way: the twelfth-grade lockers, the broken fountain, the dirt track trodden into the grass between the drinking fountain and the assembly hall.

When he reached the staff room, he stopped to tie his shoe. A quick glance around convinced him that no one was in sight. The door to the staff room was locked, of course, but that didn't matter. He had brought with him the keys that he had so painstakingly copied while still a student at the school. They were labeled in code.

The English staff-room key still fit the English staff-room lock.

Once he was inside, he was careful to lock the door behind him. Then he headed straight for Ms. Barry's computer. He had chosen it partly because it had an Internet hookup, and partly because, owing to the L-shaped layout of the room, it was invisible from the door. If someone *did* pop in unexpectedly, he would have more time to hide.

Time. Time was the problem. He had half an hour at the most, and half an hour wasn't long. Not if you were trying to infiltrate a credit-card database.

Cadel set the alarm on his watch before booting up.

The credit-card receipt that he had retrieved from the Piggotts' wardrobe had given him a card type and a card number. With these, and with his precious collection of bank passwords, access keys, and code-breaking modules, he was able to track down the accompanying name and transaction record. The name was unfamiliar to him: James

Herbert Guisnel. The transaction record, however, contained one valuable nugget of information among a load of dross.

James Herbert Guisnel was paying off his credit card with transfers from another account: a savings account. And when Cadel pried his way through the firewalls protecting *that* account (rather clumsily, because he didn't have much time), one decoded entry jumped out at him.

James Guisnel was receiving large and regular credits from an account that Cadel recognized. During his rare forays into Thaddeus Roth's database, Cadel had spotted the same company account being used by Thaddeus for business-related expenses. It was a disbursement account.

Cadel would have followed this trail still further if his alarm hadn't gone off. As it was, he was obliged to shut down the computer as quickly as possible. Even as he made for the door, he heard the warning blast of a siren heralding the end of another period. Kids immediately came bursting out of every classroom like water out of a breached tank. They poured into the corridors, slapping against walls and swirling around lockers. Cadel, who was caught up in the flood, forced himself not to hurry. He kept his head down, trying not to catch anybody's eye.

For the most part, he was successful. But just as he emerged onto the front lawn, someone's head suddenly snapped around.

"Cadel?" said a boy's voice. "Cadel *Piggott?*"

At that point, Cadel stopped walking and started running.

He ran all the way home.

THIRTY-FIVE

So now he knew. Thaddeus was paying big money to a certain James Guisnel, whose credit-card receipt had been lying on the floor of the Piggotts' wardrobe. It couldn't be a coincidence: Stuart Piggott must be James Guisnel. And Stuart almost certainly worked for Dr. Darkkon.

When Cadel arrived home, Mrs. Ang was there, mopping the kitchen floor. If she was surprised to see him in his old school uniform, with his hair slicked back, she didn't show it. She simply stared at him with her black, impenetrable gaze.

No doubt she, too, was employed by Dr. Darkkon. To spy on Cadel. Just like everyone else in that house.

Cadel went straight to his bathroom. Automatically, he stripped off his clothes and hopped into the shower. But as he started to lather his sticky head with shampoo, he began to shake. He felt sick again. Sick to his stomach. He had to prop himself up against the tiled wall.

He didn't know if he was genuinely ill or in a state of shock. The shock of knowing that his whole life was a lie. That his own father had handed him over to a couple of people who didn't give a damn about him. Who were only looking after him because it was part of their job description. Who were probably away so much because they had *real* lives to live—not this pathetic, empty, feeble excuse for a life. To his fury, Cadel found himself crying. Angry tears mingled with streaming hot water as he fought to contain his hiccuping sobs. He dropped his head, trying to smother the noise in case there were hidden cameras installed in the room. In case Dr. Darkkon wasn't allowing him any privacy at all—not even in the shower.

They had played him for a fool. They had planned it out, from the very beginning. He doubted now that the authorities had even heard of his existence. Or maybe they had, but not to the point where they were keeping an eye on him. No—the whole story of his being stolen away and hidden, like a smuggled prince, was probably Dr. Darkkon's. His goal for Cadel must have included some kind of siege mentality, to go with a carefully cultivated distrust of everyone in the world except Dr. Darkkon himself. Oh, and Thaddeus Roth. It wouldn't do to forget Thaddeus.

Even as he sniffed and gulped, Cadel was reviewing his situation. At last he could see it clearly, from every angle. Dr. Darkkon had made good and sure that the Piggotts were bad parents. After all, he couldn't have wanted Cadel to bond with them. For the same reason, he had arranged it that not a single pleasant person had ever been invited to the Piggotts' house. He had encouraged Cadel's efforts to divide and conquer his classmates at school, condemning the stupidity of some while scoffing at the pastimes of others. Cadel's isolating intelligence, his obscure interests and awkward manner, had further cut him off from the rest of the world—until Sonja arrived on the scene. *That* must have been a nasty surprise. How frightened of Sonja Dr. Darkkon must have been! No doubt he had been monitoring every e-mail exchange with great concern, comforted only by the fact that the whole friendship, being founded on a lie, was as fragile as a spider's web.

Then, after Dr. Deal's assault on Cadel, Phineas must have decided that enough was enough. Cadel was becoming too independent, holding back information, arguing with Thaddeus. Sonja (or Kay-Lee, as she called herself) would have to go. It didn't matter that she was Cadel's only friend. It didn't matter that he needed her. What mattered was that Cadel had to remain his father's puppet so that Dr. Darkkon could take his revenge on society. Cadel Darkkon, after all, meant "Battle Lord."

Cadel was to be his father's heir in everything.

Fighting back the urge to scream, Cadel beat the wall with an open palm. He felt utterly used and shamefully stupid. How could he have been so blind? But then, the foundations had been laid when he was so very, very young. He had been taught to despise the Piggotts in order that he might come to love and trust his father. His father *and* Thaddeus Roth. They were the only support he'd had—until Sonja.

Once again, hysteria bubbled to the surface. Once again, he fought it off. He had to. He knew now that he could not afford to put a foot wrong. For every unusual activity he must have an excuse. There was a good chance that the entire house was under surveillance, inside and out, twenty-four hours a day. Perhaps it had always been so.

For twelve years he had lived in a cage. A trap. His whole life was a prison, carefully designed to stop him from even *wanting* to get out.

But Sonja had breached the prison walls, just a little. And at last he knew what he had been missing all these years. He realized that there were people out there—people living in the world that Dr. Darkkon hated—who were just as intelligent and interesting as Cadel was. Who deserved respect. Who had the sense to respect *him*, but demanded nothing in exchange for their admiration. Sonja didn't expect anything from Cadel. She didn't want him to change. Dr. Darkkon, on the other hand, wanted Cadel to be—well, to be a clone. A clone of Dr. Darkkon.

It occurred to Cadel that his father had been poisoning his mind for years. He and Thaddeus had been feeding Cadel tales of a hostile and narrow-minded society—tales that probably weren't true. Oh, there were idiots and bullies around, of course there were. But there were Sonjas as well. There had to be. Mathematically, it didn't make sense that she should be unique.

And if there was more than one Sonja in the world, Cadel thought, then why should the world go to hell if Dr. Darkkon failed to seize control of it? He realized, suddenly, that the human race might very well survive without Dr. Darkkon's guidance. And that the Axis Institute was therefore unnecessary.

Cadel turned off the shower and dried himself. He was no longer crying; his red eyes could be blamed on the shampoo. He tried not to display any emotion as he got dressed. With a blank expression he combed his hair, retreated into his bedroom, and shut the door. Even here he wasn't safe. There could be hidden cameras. Listening devices. He didn't want to be paranoid, but he couldn't afford to make a mistake.

So he curled up under his bedspread, shut his eyes, and firmly swallowed the lump in his throat.

He couldn't bear to think about the betrayal. The manipulation. It was too painful—it made him gasp. So he forced his mind down other paths, trying to ignore the waves of hurt and fury that kept welling up, disturbing the logical progression of his thoughts.

What did he want to do? He wanted to escape. Why did he want to escape? It was his only option, really. If he didn't, and he continued to communicate with Sonja, he would be putting her life at risk; there was no doubt about that. If, on the other hand, he *stopped* communicating with Sonja—well, he might just as well kill himself. He *would* be killing himself. He wouldn't survive. Little by little, he would fade away to nothing. A dry husk. An empty puppet.

A soulless clone.

His father was mad. Why hadn't he ever seen that before? Perhaps at the beginning, when he was very young—but then Thaddeus had convinced him that all was well. Even more than Dr. Darkkon, Thaddeus had guided Cadel's every step. Thaddeus was so clever, so cool, so—so *kind*. No one else had ever been as kind to Cadel. Certainly not the Piggotts.

Even now, Cadel's feelings for Thaddeus were complicated. He hated his father with a pure and simple hatred (god—oh god—he felt like smashing that froggy face in), but Thaddeus, Cadel realized, was neither mad nor obsessed. Just what did Thaddeus want from life? Cadel had never before asked himself that question. Nor could he provide an answer. Thaddeus's motives were a mystery. Thaddeus was . . . unreadable. Secretive.

Unnerving.

Though Cadel had always liked and admired Thaddeus, he had never ceased to regard the psychologist with a touch of fear. Thaddeus would make a formidable foe. And Cadel also knew that Thaddeus wouldn't stop—ever—until he tracked Cadel down. It wouldn't be hard, not for Thaddeus. He knew Cadel so well. Cadel had confided in him, trusted him, believed in him. . . .

Suddenly, Cadel leaped up, driven to his feet by the force of his own feelings. With clenched fists, he moved about distractedly from wall to wall, bouncing off them like a ball in a pinball machine. The sheer *scale* of the deception—the *perfidy* of it! Oh, but he had to calm down. He had to focus on the task at hand. He had to work out what was the best thing to do.

He sat down again and doggedly, desperately, reviewed his options. He knew that if he was going to disappear, he would have to do it properly. Half measures would not be good enough. He would have to find himself another home, another identity—perhaps even another country. Of course, if he made contact with the police, then the police would do it all for him—but Cadel was wary of the police. To begin with, he wasn't sure that the police could outwit Thaddeus Roth. For another, he didn't know if Dr. Darkkon might have employees working within the police force.

Moreover, once the police were involved, there would be no turning back. He would have declared himself Dr. Darkkon's enemy for all time. And as Dr. Darkkon's enemy, he would also be Thaddeus Roth's enemy.

That was something he very much wanted to avoid.

Cadel considered his cache of forged documents. Many of them were made out in the name of someone called Ariel Schaap—an eighteen-year-old girl he'd created for his course work. Suppose Ariel became the girl in the Indian-cotton skirt? She already had a birth certificate, and even a series of bank accounts. (Fake bank accounts were fundamental to his embezzlement course.) He could easily whip up a passport to match, using his own photograph. Ariel had become his "John Citizen"; her existence was something he had been working on almost as a hobby. Though perhaps, deep down, he had known that he would need her sometime. Perhaps he had known that she was his ticket out of this cage.

Except, of course, that she wasn't. Not while Art and Brendan and Alias were around. All of them had marked his Ariel assignments. All of them knew about Ariel. Alias had actually *seen* her, dressed up in her Indian-cotton skirt. If Cadel was going to escape (and he would have to do it soon, or somehow—he was sure—Thaddeus would begin to read his mind), then he would have to arrange that those three Axis staff were out of the picture. Those three and Dr. Deal, who had also seen Cadel in his Ariel disguise. And perhaps even Luther Lasco? Cadel didn't want Luther called in to "deal" with him.

Yes, Luther was a problem as well.

Cadel tried to work out if there was a flaw in his reasoning. It really didn't seem so. Students were supposed to destroy the documents that they produced for Art's course, so he had been very careful with the ones he'd kept. Unless cameras had been installed inside his wardrobe—a very remote possibility, in Cadel's opinion—then no one would have seen him transferring Ariel's documents from the pocket of one garment into the lining of another. What's more, if Alias had told Thaddeus about the Ariel disguise, then the Führer's surveillance team wouldn't have lost Cadel in the mall. It was clear, Cadel thought, that Thaddeus wasn't keeping a very close eye on his course work—just on his results. Just on what would please Dr. Darkkon, no doubt. Because did either of those two *really* care about Cadel? Of course not. Cadel was just another tool—another means to an end—another step in the program. . . .

This time the rage and misery seemed to blast through Cadel's head with such strength that they propelled him off the bed, across the room. They scattered all his well-organized arguments and interfered with his breathing. At last, unable to stand the confusion, he slammed his head against the wall: once, twice, three times.

The shock of the impact helped him, oddly enough. He recovered a little. His hands stopped shaking, and he was able to catch his breath.

Yes, he had been abused. Yes, it was unbearable. But he had to move on. He *would* move on. He would remove those five institute staff from the picture and create a new life for himself.

Of course, he wouldn't be able to focus his attention solely on his own teachers; not if he wanted to avoid all blame. Someone, probably Thaddeus, would put two and two together. No, he would have to involve other staff. Other staff from the other campus. Staff who had nothing to do with him.

Cadel returned to his bed and lay on it. Slowly he allowed his tangled emotions to settle at the back of his mind, like sediment at the bottom of a pool, as he concentrated on the problem he had set himself. His brain began to turn over, smoothly and efficiently. Synapses began to fire. Patterns began to emerge. He knew that his half-completed predictive program would have been very helpful, but he didn't know who might have been monitoring his databases. So he was forced to rely on the complex programs in his own head.

Even committing an equation to paper was out of the question. He couldn't let anyone see what was going on. It was *vital* that he keep his plans secret, especially from Thaddeus Roth.

Cadel lay thinking until dinnertime. Mrs. Ang was the one who called him to the table, informing him as she did so that she was going now but that Mrs. Piggott would be back soon. Cadel therefore ate alone in the big dining room, forcing himself to swallow a few mouthfuls of the casserole that Mrs. Ang had heated up in the microwave. He wasn't the least bit hungry. Afterward, he stared at the television for a while, his mind working busily as the pictures unfolded before his blank gaze. He couldn't go to bed—not yet. It would have seemed odd. Unusual. He couldn't afford to relax his guard for a moment.

Finally, at nine o'clock, he retired for the night. It was a great relief to lie in bed again, though even here he had to be careful. For all he knew, there were infrared cameras planted in the air-conditioning vent above him. Therefore, although he would have liked to thrash about, pace the room, and perhaps go outside to stare at the stars, he could not. For most of the night, he lay with his eyes shut, thinking and thinking.

Only when the dawn light filtered into his room did he drop into a restless slumber. For by then, at last, the new construction in his head was complete.

THIRTY-SIX

Mrs. Piggott woke him at eight.

"Cadel! Pet! How are you feeling?" she crooned, entering his room without knocking first. "I'm going now, but I'll be here tonight. And Dad will be home, too, thank goodness. We can all have dinner together!"

Cadel grunted. Blearily, he realized that he could think of nothing worse.

"Are you okay? Yes? Then you'd better get up, honey, or you'll be late for your first class. Come on, now. Up, up, up!"

Cadel's first class was at ten. He had a busy day ahead of him. Pure evil would be followed by disguise, infiltration, and Dr. Deal's law class, which was at four. He probably wouldn't make the Maestro's session; he had other things to do. Poor Gazo would have to face Maestro Max alone.

He felt sorry for Gazo, but it couldn't be helped.

After skipping breakfast, Cadel began to look on the Internet for Abraham's address, careless of anyone who might be monitoring his activities. When he found it, he scribbled it down, threw on his clothes, and ran to catch a train.

It was his normal train, but it didn't take him to the institute. Instead, he alighted before he reached his usual stop, emerging into a soiled, gritty area of inner-city streets and dark little row houses. Toiling up and down hills, past murky corner shops and dressmaking businesses, and little parks smeared with dog poo, Cadel kept glancing back, trying to work out if anyone was following him. It was impossible to tell. There were quite a few odd-looking people walking around, any one of whom could have been a Grunt.

At last he found the dingy row house where Abraham lived. The handkerchief-sized front yard had been paved over, though there was one dark-leaved tree, which grew out of the cement and threw gloomy shadows over the building's facade. Since it was now 9:45, Cadel was hoping that all its other occupants (there were three, if he remembered correctly) would be out at work.

As promised, the key was sitting on top of the fuse box by the entrance. In fact, there were two keys: one opened the iron-barred gate that protected the front door, and one opened the door itself. Cadel was careful to lock both behind him, conscious of the house's smell even before he noticed its layout. The smell was a moldy one—moldy and septic, like the smell of bad drains. From the front entrance, a long, dark hallway led past two open doors, to a flight of stairs. Behind the stairs was a larger, lighter room, but before Cadel could explore it, a voice rang out from somewhere down the back of the house.

"Who's that?"

Cadel's heart missed a beat. *Damn*, he thought.

"Uh—my name's Cadel Piggott."

"What?"

"I'm a friend of Abraham Coggins."

Padding footsteps heralded the approach of a young woman who appeared suddenly at the top of the stairs. She was dressed in a short black skirt and a neat white blouse, but her feet were bare. Gazing down at Cadel, she said, "How the hell did you get in?"

"Abraham told me where the key was," Cadel replied. "He asked me to get some things."

"Abraham's in the hospital."

"I know. I saw him yesterday—"

"You're just a kid!"

Cadel didn't know what to say to that. He waited as the young woman descended the stairs, doing up the buttons of her sleeve. It occurred to Cadel that, had he waited a few more minutes, this occupant too would have been hurrying off to work.

Bad timing.

"Abe shouldn't be telling all and sundry about our spare key," she complained, stopping in front of Cadel. "What did he want, anyway?"

"Uh—some of his clothes. One of his books." As Cadel racked his brain for a likely list of requirements, he blinked his big blue eyes and sucked in his mouth.

It worked.

"Well, *I* can't help. I'm late already," the young woman snapped, brushing past Cadel and turning toward the kitchen. "Do you know where his room is? Upstairs, right down the back. Don't go into any of the others. And if we're robbed, we'll know who to blame. What's your name again?"

"Cadel Piggott."

She grunted and disappeared. Finding himself alone, Cadel mounted the stairs. He noticed that the plaster on the walls was cracking and that the light at the top of the stairs was a naked bulb hanging on a wire.

When he passed the bathroom, he realized that it was the source of the smell: Its ceiling was covered with mold.

Yuck, thought Cadel, *what a place to live.*

Abraham's door was shut but not locked. When Cadel pushed it open, something fell off the hook that was nailed onto its back: a belt, Cadel saw. The room contained one double bed, one bookcase, and one clothes rack—there wasn't room for much else, except a few stacks of plastic storage boxes full of paper. A limp curtain hung over the window, so Cadel turned on the light.

Almost immediately a cockroach skittered across one wall, disappearing behind the bed.

Cadel gritted his teeth. He went straight to the bookcase, which he scanned with a practiced eye. *Principles of Internal Medicine* was a large volume sitting in the middle of the bottom shelf. When Cadel pulled it out, the dust he dislodged made him sneeze.

He was half afraid that Abraham had been feverish, so he didn't necessarily expect to find the key. But it was there, taped to the inside back cover as Abraham had promised. Cadel removed the key and replaced the book. Then he looked around the room for the sorts of things that Abraham might need in the hospital, finally choosing a grubby old bathrobe, a little address book full of phone numbers, a couple of pairs of underpants (from a plastic bag hanging on the clothes rack), and a bottle of pills. He didn't know what the pills were for; he just pushed them into his backpack with the rest of the stuff.

"Can I use your phone?" he loudly asked Abraham's housemate, as he descended the stairs. He knew that she was still around, because he hadn't heard any doors shut. "I'll pay for it. It's just a local call."

"It's in here," came the reply. Cadel followed her voice into the living room, where she was standing in front of the mirror that hung over the mantelpiece, pinning up her hair. The room made Cadel's skin crawl. Its shaggy carpet looked like the coat of an old and filthy dog. Its white sofas were stained and sagging. Only the TV and sound equipment were in good condition.

"Did you find what you wanted?" the young woman asked, twisting and turning in front of the mirror. She was now wearing shoes.

"Oh, yes, thanks," said Cadel, offering her his backpack. "I got the bathrobe, and the address book, and the underpants—"

"Ugh," she interrupted. "Don't tell me. I don't want to know." Then, because she was obviously satisfied with her hair, she turned to Cadel with an outstretched hand. "So?" she went on. "Where's the money?"

Cadel blinked. Then he realized what she was talking about.

"Oh! For the phone, you mean? Here." He dug into the front pocket of his trousers, drawing out a few coins. "I promise, it's only local. I don't have a cell phone."

"You can call whoever you want," the young woman interrupted. "I won't have to worry about the phone bill. I'm leaving this dump next week—it's impossible living here." On her way out, she picked up her handbag and addressed him over her shoulder. "Lock up when you leave, all right? And don't even *try* to get into my room. It's padlocked."

As if a padlock could keep me *out,* Cadel thought. But he said nothing—just waited until the front door slammed. Once again, it seemed, his innocent appearance had worked in his favor.

Or perhaps she was *hoping* that he would steal something from her fellow occupants? She certainly didn't seem to like them very much.

Cadel picked up the sticky beige receiver of the telephone and punched in the number of Sonja's local library, which he now knew by heart. After two rings, the call was answered by a female voice. Cadel asked for Beatrice.

"Speaking," said the voice.

"Oh." Cadel took a deep breath. "Look, I'm sorry to bother you," he said, "but I need to talk to Sonja. The girl in the wheelchair? She should be there now."

"Sonja Pirovic?"

"Uh—yes. She told me she'd be there."

"Hang on."

Canned music intervened, and Cadel breathed a sigh of relief. The first hurdle was cleared. As the minutes dragged by, however, he began to grow nervous. What was going on? Wasn't Sonja at the library? Had something happened to her?

At last there was a click, and then someone spoke.

"Hello? Is that Cadel?"

It was Kay-Lee.

"Where's Sonja?" Cadel exclaimed. "Isn't she there?"

"She's here."

"I have to talk to her!"

"It's awkward, Cadel. She's right here, but that Dynavox—"

"Did she get the photos? Did she see them?"

"Yes."

"And?" Cadel couldn't keep the urgency out of his tone. "Well? Were they the same guys?"

A pause. At last Kay-Lee said, "Yes. They were."

"I told you! Didn't I tell you?"

"Hang on." There was a brief interval during which Cadel heard the muffled noise of stilted conversation. Finally, Kay-Lee addressed him again. "Sonja wants to know if that was you in the photo with the bald guy? You wearing boys' clothes?"

"Yes, of course, but—"

"She says you ought to be an actor. She says you look like a movie star in that photograph."

"Well, thanks." Cadel was somewhat taken aback. "But that's not important. Right now I have to talk to her. Will you let me talk to her, please?"

"You know we're at the borrower's desk, here—"

"Yes, I know! But I have to talk to her! You don't understand! It's *important*."

Kay-Lee sighed.

"I'll have to hold the receiver up to her ear," she said, "so make it quick."

"I'll try." Cadel suddenly thought of something. "And don't pretend!" he warned. "Don't pretend, because I'm going to ask her something that only she would know!"

"Oh, for god's sake," Kay-Lee growled. "Don't get your knickers in a knot—she's not going to *let* me pretend, you idiot. She'd run me over if I did. All *right*, Sonja, it's okay. He wants to talk to you."

Suddenly there was silence. Only it wasn't really silence. Listening hard, Cadel realized that he could catch the faint sound of someone's hoarse breathing.

"Sonja?" he said—and she made a noise. It was a wordless noise, but it was unmistakable.

"Listen," he continued, "I'm going to tell you something. You can't tell anyone else. It's my father—my real father. The one in jail. His name is Dr. Phineas Darkkon, and after we're finished, you can go and look him up on the Internet. But not on your own computer. On the library computer—Kay-Lee can help you. Because if you do some research on Dr. Darkkon, you'll realize why I'm acting the way I am. Sonja?"

"It's me," said Kay-Lee, suddenly. "She wants me to tell you something." Another long pause, full of distorted voices. "She says she knows who the man is," Kay-Lee finally announced. "And now I'm putting you back on."

Again, the rasp of heavy breathing.

"Okay." Cadel himself was breathless. He sat down on one of the filthy white couches. "So you know who he is. Well, that's who I'm trying to dodge, Sonja. That's who sent those two agents posing as policemen. Those two men are the man who adopted me and the man who's teaching me about computers. They're in Dr. Darkkon's pay. You probably think I'm mad, but it's the truth. And he'll get you, Sonja, if he ever finds out we're still talking. That's why I have to . . . to get away. To find myself a hiding place. If I do that, maybe we can talk again. I'll be *free* then."

His heart lifted at the thought. Free! He couldn't picture it—though he *could* imagine the feeling it would give him. Then Kay-Lee said, "Sonja wants to know how she can help. Even though she shouldn't be—ow! Sonja!"

"Let me talk to her again." Cadel waited until he could hear Sonja snuffling away at the other end of the line. "Sonja? Listen. There's one thing I do need. One thing that you'll do much better than me. I need a conundrum. A mathematical conundrum. Something—something like the formula for pi, or a factoring puzzle. Something really, really clever, that will keep a brilliant mind fully engaged and distracted. Maybe something that one of your mathematician friends has been working on. But nothing widely known. Nothing that's been doing the rounds. Do you know what I mean?"

A pause. "Yes," Kay-Lee said. "She's—hang on. She's saying *yes*."

"Put her back on."

"I hope she didn't just agree to do anything stupid, Cadel."

"It's a math problem, all right? A math question! Now *put her back on!*"

Kay-Lee obeyed. Cadel continued. "I need it fast," he said. "As fast as you can get it to me. And you can't e-mail it. You can't post it. Oh! Wait a minute—you *can* post it." Cadel had remembered Abraham's post-office box. He gave the details to Sonja. "My father doesn't know I have access to that address," he explained. "If I check it in a few days, I can always say . . . well, that I was doing it for someone else." For Abraham, perhaps. "And if everything works out, I might be able to e-mail you sometime. Soon." He found that he had suddenly run out of things to say. He had given her his instructions. Now all he had left was a strange, tired, weepy feeling. "Is—is there anything you want to tell me?" he croaked. "I wish we could talk properly. I wish we were on our computers."

A clunk. A long break. After a lot of confusing noise, Kay-Lee addressed him again. "She wants to know"—Kay-Lee sighed—"if she can keep the photo. The photo with you in it."

"Oh," said Cadel. He couldn't help feeling pleased, even though it was an alarming request. "The thing is, I don't know if that's a good idea. You really ought to destroy it. Just in case."

More conversation: Kay-Lee's murmurs and Sonja's honks.

"She says she'll hide it," Kay-Lee finally informed him. "She says it's her payment. For whatever you've asked her to do—and I sure hope it won't get her into any trouble, my friend, because—what? Hang on." Murmur, murmur. "We've got to go, Cadel. We're hogging the line here."

"Oh, wait!" Cadel cried. "Tell Sonja—tell her . . ." Tell her what? "Tell her I'll be in touch. I will. Tell her everything's different now. I'll never do anything like Partner Post ever again."

"Yeah, right," said Kay-Lee, then hung up.

———

Cadel had planned to go to Strathfield next to check Abraham's post-office box. But that was now out of the question. He couldn't go there yet—not until Sonja had sent her conundrum. If he went anywhere near Strathfield post office, Thaddeus would hear of it, and the box might be plundered. He couldn't risk having Thaddeus find any sort of communication from Sonja.

So he headed straight back to the institute. On the way, he reviewed his situation—something he was doing more and more. The trip to Abraham's house could be fully explained. Abraham had told him to fetch various possessions from the house and deliver them to the hospital. A trip to Strathfield post office could also be explained, if the occasion arose. And the trip to his old school? Well, that would fall under the heading "Mrs. Brezeck." Thaddeus wanted Cadel to do something about her. Cadel would claim that the school trip was part of his cunning plan to sabotage Mrs. Brezeck's attack on him.

Of course, having the excuse prepared was one thing. Presenting it to Thaddeus was another. While Thaddeus had often praised Cadel for being a good liar, Cadel dreaded lying to the psychologist. He had a feeling that Thaddeus would see right through him.

This was one reason why he had to get away. Quickly.

It was ten thirty when Cadel arrived at the institute. After letting himself through the front gates, he saw that everything was very quiet. Not a single figure was flitting across the rolling green lawn, or traversing the parking lot. The high walls surrounding the complex seemed to shut out every strident noise from the city that lay beyond them. "C" block's steel roof shone like a flame in the sunlight, so brightly that it hurt Cadel's eyes. The seminary building, in contrast, seemed to absorb the light, its gray slate and brown stone providing a grave and dignified backdrop to one shimmering spray of water that arched across the lawn, jetting up from a concealed sprinkler head.

To the untrained eye, it was a serene and reassuring sight. But Cadel's eye wasn't untrained. He saw the blinking electronic security lights embedded in the black steel fence posts that ringed the lawn. He saw the shrouded windows on the top floor of the seminary building. He saw the elaborate configuration of antennae attached to its turrets, and the black smudge beside one door, and the scowling faces of the gargoyles. He saw the glint of Clive Slaughter's memorial plaque, and the black van parked near the breezeway.

Cadel lowered himself onto one of the concrete seats placed on either side of the front path. From there, he had a perfect view of the whole campus. He watched as a small figure scurried from "C" block to the seminary building, its shoulders hunched. Once again, Cadel's trained eye took note of a significant detail: The figure was dragging its right leg.

Yet another "accident" among the institute's rapidly diminishing student body, no doubt.

Cadel took a deep breath. This, he thought, is what I'm up against. This and the Yarramundi campus. I'll have to research that campus— perhaps even visit it.

Meanwhile, there was an entire teaching staff to master.

Hugging his backpack, Cadel gazed across the flawless stretch of green. There was a knot of apprehension in his stomach. He felt very small and isolated. He also felt as if the shadowy windows of the seminary building were staring back at him with a grim, hard-edged glare.

So he got up and went to join Gazo in Maestro Max's class.

THIRTY-SEVEN

Cadel missed half of the Maestro's class but behaved himself very well the rest of the day. He listened patiently to everything Max said about genetic time frames, and how the concept of eons reduced the idea of good and evil to a mere nothing. He concentrated hard on the photographs presented to him by Alias, who wanted him to identify the same person in ten different disguises. (He managed eight.) He even earned Dr. Deal's guarded approval by rattling off a quick but thorough description of the forensic applications of X-ray diffractometry, ICP spectrometry, and infrared spectroscopy.

"Very good, Mr. Darkkon," the lawyer drawled, eyeing Cadel in a quizzical manner.

"We've covered some of this stuff in Art's class," Cadel explained. "Soft X-rays, gas chromatography . . ."

"Just because it's covered doesn't necessarily mean it's absorbed. I'm impressed," said Dr. Deal. "Of course, forensic matters aren't the primary focus of this course. I'll be even more impressed if you can give me, at our next meeting, a one-thousand-word description of what constitutes 'reasonable apprehension' in the context of an assault charge, using at least three demonstrative cases. That goes for you, too, Mr. Kovacs."

"Uh . . ." Gazo cleared his throat. "Right—um . . ."

"It's all written down," Dr. Deal said smoothly, handing out his usual buff-colored homework envelopes. Though never sealed, these envelopes were always used. Dr. Deal seemed reluctant to expose any document to public scrutiny. Something to do with the legal mind, Cadel thought. "I'll accept efforts up to fifteen hundred words," the lawyer continued, "but nothing longer. Thank you, gentlemen."

Glumly, Gazo accepted the envelope. He wasn't coping well with the reduced size of the first-year class. It left him very exposed, especially when Cadel was the only other student. The contrast between them was too stark. While Cadel was able to answer every question thrown at him, Gazo could barely manage to keep up.

"I'm gonna fail," he'd said gloomily earlier that day, after he and Cadel had been dismissed from Alias's lesson. "I can't do nuffink right. I even missed the *shoes*."

"They were easy to miss," said Cadel, whose mind was on more important matters. "I think I'll have lunch now. What about you?"

Gazo didn't seem to hear.

"Yeah, but what'll happen if I do fail?" he fretted. "Will they send me back to England? Will they give me a job here? A cleaning job?"

"I don't know."

"Cadel." Gazo put a sheathed hand on Cadel's shoulder. "Wait. I wanna ask you somefink."

Surprised, Cadel turned his blue gaze on his companion. He saw Gazo glance around fearfully. Although they were standing outside, halfway between "C" block and the seminary building, Cadel understood his friend's caution. At the Axis Institute, every blade of grass could be wired for sound.

"You don't fink I'll get the chop?" Gazo inquired, as quietly as he could in his sound-absorbing headdress. "They wouldn't . . . you know . . . *do* somefink? Just because I failed me courses?"

Cadel blinked. The possibility had never crossed his mind. Nothing, however, would have surprised him about the institute.

"Why?" he said cautiously. "Have you heard anyone say anything?"

"No." Gazo sighed. "It just worries me. Well, you know."

"I know," said Cadel, with complete understanding. He thought for a moment, his brow furrowed. Then he shook his head. "I can't remember my father ever implying that good grades were a matter of life or death. Not once. Thaddeus, either." Again, he looked up at Gazo. "I wouldn't put it past them, though," he confessed.

Gazo hissed through his teeth. "What am I gonna do?" he muttered, his hands tucked beneath his armpits. "I dunno what to do. If I run away, they'll find me for sure."

Cadel suddenly felt a profound sympathy for Gazo. And when he squeezed his friend's insulated arm, he wasn't surprised by the startled look he received. It was the first time that he had ever touched Gazo.

"Hang in there," he advised. Unable to explain himself further, he tried to inject as much meaning as possible into his voice and expression. "Just hang in there, and it'll work itself out."

Then he turned—before Gazo could reply—and went off to buy himself some lunch. Already he was regretting his friendly gesture. From a distance, it would have looked suspicious. Who else at the institute would deliberately touch someone else's arm unless searching for a concealed weapon? At the institute, people kept themselves to themselves. It was safer that way.

Cadel didn't linger long in the refectory. He was afraid that Gazo might corner him there. So he bought a soft drink and a ham sandwich, then took them up to Hardware Heaven, where he was surprised to find himself utterly alone. Even Com was absent. Cadel couldn't believe his luck.

The timing was perfect.

His first job was to scan the Axis network. It had been some time since he'd last piggybacked on Dr. Vee's regular sweep, and he needed to know the latest—particularly on Terry, Luther, Art, and Alias. He was aware, now, that Terry had the vial. He was also aware that Luther and Adolf knew this; Abraham had confessed to telling them. As a result, Cadel discovered, Adolf had recently placed a "code red" status on Terry, as well as on Terry's current girlfriend, Tracey Lane. A code-red status meant that you were followed everywhere, your phones were bugged, your mail was X-rayed, and your possessions were searched. Clumsily, sometimes. Cadel found several e-mails discussing a meeting that was to be held on Friday afternoon, involving Tracey, Luther, Adolf, and Thaddeus. The subject of the meeting was to be Tracey's complaints about Adolf's "intrusive behavior." Her office, she'd told Thaddeus, had been "trashed" by the Führer's Grunts. She therefore wanted to make an official complaint.

Cadel committed the details of this meeting to memory. Friday, three o'clock, at the Yarramundi campus. It might be important. He wondered what Luther was making of Terry's code-red status. It must be awkward, because the two men had become involved in some kind of secret experiment. Cadel realized this as he sifted through their e-mails and found the cryptic, encoded little messages that they were sending to each other. These notes were all about "poetic justice" and blood counts and tissue proteins. There was even mentioned a "perp," whatever that meant.

Could the experiment have something to do with Carla's vial? Cadel tried to calculate the probability factors but didn't have enough data. If the vial was the subject of this mysterious experiment, it could certainly explain why Luther didn't seem to be putting any pressure on Terry to surrender the deadly thing. In fact, he had even warned Terry, in a private e-mail, to "watch his back." Luther, in other words, was undermining the Führer's efforts.

And this was the kind of tasty detail that Cadel could use.

He thought for a while. Then, after adjusting his calculations slightly to take into account various recent developments, Cadel switched off his computer, turning his attention to Sark's instead. It was by far the easiest prospect in Hardware Heaven because Sark was sloppy. Though he was blessed by the odd flash of brilliance, Sark's boredom with the drudgery of daily housekeeping routines and security procedures meant that he often hung on to the same passwords for far too long, and he was always leaving his encryption keys lying around. As a result,

Cadel managed to bypass his firewalls without too much trouble. It took about ten minutes, during which time Cadel kept one eye firmly on the door. Though he only wanted to type a letter using Sark's word-processing function, the security measures employed in Hardware Heaven meant that this was far more easily said than done. Especially since he wanted to delete all trace of the letter from Sark's data banks.

At last, however, the job was finished. Cadel carefully wiped down Sark's desk and keyboard. There was every chance that he might have been filmed (the institute being what it was), but at least the hard copy in his pocket had left no electronic echo on Sark's hard drive. It would be impossible to prove what he had actually been *doing* on Sark's computer. And raiding the programs of fellow students was a common practice at the institute.

Having completed this final task, Cadel drained the last few mouthfuls from his can of pop, heaved his backpack onto his shoulder, and caught an elevator up to the labs. His heart was beating too rapidly; he was thankful that the institute didn't monitor physical changes in its students, or he would have been identified as a possible arsonist. There was too much sweat on his hands.

He wiped them as he stepped out of the elevator, immediately aware of an unmistakable smell from the labs, a smell that hinted at disinfectant, ozone, harsh chemicals, and blood. Cadel swallowed.

All around him, the hallways and glassed-in rooms looked deserted. He could see no one and hear nothing, except the hum of the air-conditioning system. Because he had no intention of searching the labs themselves (even if he could get into them), he headed for Terry's office.

Before he could reach it, however, Terry suddenly banged through the door from the fire stairs. He was carrying a box under one arm and held a marking pen between his teeth.

"Cadel," he said, after removing the marking pen. "What are you doing up here?"

Terry's white coat was smudged and splattered with stains: brown stains, red stains, black and green stains. Cadel tried not to look at them. Instead, he concentrated on Terry's face, which was the nicest thing about him, all clear eyes and white teeth and laugh lines and chiseled cheekbones.

"Abraham wants his stuff," Cadel replied. "I went to see him yesterday, and he told me he wants his notes and things. His work."

Terry blinked. He stared at Cadel for a moment, wearing an odd expression. Then he said, "Just let me put this down," and staggered toward his office.

As soon as he arrived at the door, his box hit the carpet with a thump. He fumbled through his pockets, produced a set of keys, and spent the next half a minute punching buttons and swiping cards. At last the door clicked open.

"Come in," he said, nudging his box over the threshold with one foot. Reluctantly, Cadel followed him in.

But the office, as far as Cadel could see, held nothing particularly sinister. It was just an ordinary office, full of filing cabinets. The only sour note was struck by a dead plant in one corner. It was a brown, shriveled fragment in a block of parched soil.

"So you saw Abraham yesterday, did you?" Terry asked. "Visited him at the hospital?"

"Yes."

"I see." Terry cast around, apparently looking for a place to put his box. Then he turned back to Cadel. "The thing is, Cadel, Abraham died this morning. They got hold of me about an hour ago. It's very awkward, I can tell you. They're talking about the coroner's court, because they don't know what killed him. Thaddeus is throwing a fit."

Cadel dropped his gaze to the floor. He took a deep breath, then let it out slowly.

Abraham, dead!

But the news wasn't entirely unexpected.

Cadel didn't quite know how he felt. Sick? Sorry? Sad? Scared? When you thought about it, Abraham had been a pathetic figure, chasing his unattainable dream.

All the same, he was fully responsible for his own unhappy fate.

"Was Abraham a friend of yours?" Terry went on, studying Cadel curiously. "I didn't know."

"He—he must have liked me," Cadel replied, not knowing how to answer. His mind was working furiously. Would Abraham's death require a change of plans? No, probably not. No, he would stick to his original scheme. Terry had the vial. Terry could therefore be rattled. And if Luther was involved, too, then Terry was bound to contact him. "If he hadn't liked me, he wouldn't have asked me to collect all his stuff."

"Well, feel free," said Terry. "You might as well clear it all out. *I* certainly don't want it."

Cadel frowned. "You don't?"

"Course not. Load of rubbish. Sorry to say it, but he was a mad bugger. Completely mad." Terry surveyed his office again, hands on hips. He seemed to be losing interest in Cadel. "There isn't much here, as far as I know, because poor old Abe was paranoid. Used to drag most of his notes and things home with him. But what there is, you'll find in his desk. It's in 311. Hang on—I'll punch the code in for you."

"But—I mean, if he's dead, he won't need his stuff, will he?"

Terry shrugged. "If it stays here, it'll get thrown away. Up to you."

"Well . . . there's not much point. I don't think I'll bother," said Cadel, and took a deep breath. *Now,* he thought. "Abraham gave me something for you. He said it was his last will and testament. I don't know if it really is. He told me not to read it." Cadel produced the folded printout from his pocket, concentrating fiercely on his hands. If they shook, it would be fatal. "He wasn't very well, so . . . I don't know." Cadel hesitated, willing himself to adopt a wry tone. "It might not make much sense."

Terry sighed. He took the paper but didn't open it up.

"Right, right," he said. "Thanks, Cadel." Once again, his attention was focused elsewhere. "I'll look at it later."

"Do you know when the funeral is?"

"What?"

"Do you know when the funeral is?"

It took Terry a moment to process this question. Once he had, he shook his head.

"Sorry. No idea."

Cadel nodded, then took his leave quickly. All of a sudden his pulse was jumping. He was dizzy with terror. His heart felt as if it was in his throat, and sweat was breaking out all over his body. Plunging into the bathroom near the elevators, he shut himself in a stall, where he sat on the toilet seat and took deep, calming breaths.

He had done it. He had taken the first step—removed the first brick. Somehow, though, this was different from anything he had ever done before. The sports hall, the rail system, his fellow twelfth-grade students—none of these targets had been the least bit frightening.

Never before had he been so close to losing his nerve.

"Don't be a fool," he told himself, blinking back tears. "Don't be a *sissy.*" He had been shaken by the news of Abraham's death—that was his problem. He couldn't stand the thought of all that *waste.* The precious notes, trashed. The feverish brain, snuffed out. It was so pathetic. Poor Abraham. Poor, pitiful Abraham.

Cadel swallowed fiercely. This was no good, he told himself. He had to stay sharp. If he stayed sharp and didn't let his emotions get the better of him, then this audacious plan might just succeed.

With an enormous effort, he pulled himself together. Washing his face helped, as did one of Thaddeus's hard candies, which he had tucked into his backpack. He glanced at himself in the mirror. *Not bad,* he thought. A bit pale, but not bad.

He squared his shoulders and marched back out the bathroom door—only to find Terry, waiting for the elevator.

Cadel couldn't help flinching as the lecturer swung around.

"Cadel!" Terry exclaimed. "Did you read that thing?"

Cadel decided to play dumb.

"What thing?" he asked, bringing his most ingenuous look into play.

"You know what thing!" Terry snapped.

"Oh, you mean that—"

"The thing you gave me! The letter! Are you sure you didn't read it?"

"No." Cadel's tone was hurt. "He told me not to. Why, was it stupid? I'm sorry, but he was sick. It's not my fault if—"

"He was blaming me for *making* him sick," Terry interrupted. "Did he tell you that? Hmmm?"

"He—"

"Because it's not true. It had nothing to do with me."

"I know."

"The crazy fool was losing his mind."

"Yes." Cadel nodded sagely. "I said he was. But you don't have to worry—everyone knows he was doing it to himself."

Terry stared at Cadel intently for a moment, studying his artless face. Then he seemed to dismiss any suspicions that he might have had, turning abruptly to jab at the DOWN button. "Come on," he growled. "Where is this stupid thing?" Overcome with impatience, he abruptly headed for the fire stairs.

Cadel waited. He moved to the window, from which he had a clear view of Terry's sleek red convertible. After about five minutes, Terry emerged from the seminary building and hurried toward the parking lot. He was holding his cell phone to his ear.

His *phone*!

Cadel couldn't help cursing aloud. Why was the stupid moron using a *cell*? Didn't he realize how insecure a cell phone could be? Cadel's heart sank as he realized how incomplete his data was. He had calculated that Terry would use his normal e-mail route to alert Luther. Obviously, his calculations had been wrong. Were his IQ specifications at fault, or had he underestimated the panic factor?

Perhaps Terry was simply calling Tracey. Canceling a lunch, or something. But his gesture of frustration, when he apparently failed to connect with the person he'd called, seemed a little too violent for that.

Cadel watched him kick the front tire of his car, take a deep breath, and regain control of himself. Then he spoke into the cell, but only briefly. (Leaving a message, Cadel decided.) Even as the cell phone snapped shut, Terry was climbing behind the wheel of his convertible. The driver's door slammed so loudly that even Cadel could hear it from his lofty position; as its engine roared to life, the zippy vehicle shot out of its parking spot, did a three-point turn, and careened off into the distance.

Cadel waited. Sure enough, another car—small and gray—pulled away from a nearby curb and began to follow the convertible. The question was: To where? There was a high probability that Terry had gone to rifle through Abraham's bedroom. He would have had the address, after all. But Cadel wasn't taking anything for granted. Not after his phone mistake.

He scurried back down to Hardware Heaven. Here he would be able to monitor Terry's movements, tracking the regular reports filed by the two Grunts who were dogging his footsteps. Adolf had installed a rather elegant little system, which involved routing coded telephone text messages through to a continually operating program on his computer, via a modem. Cadel liked this system very much. He liked it because it gave him full access to every surveillance report received by the Führer, including those that concerned his own movements. From the surveillance reports, Cadel learned that he himself had been followed to the hospital. To Abraham's house. To his old school. The latest report was brief, but informative. *Subject Ib02 at A.I. seminary building. (Bastards*, thought Cadel, *why don't you leave me alone?)*

Checking the other reports, he saw that the Grunts in the gray car were entering their latest update. *Subject Ir31—en route. In pursuit. Stand by.*

Obviously, it was too soon for a destination.

Then Cadel had an idea. He abandoned his computer and picked up Dr. Vee's phone, dialing Luther's number. *You have reached extension 3812,* Luther's recorded voice informed him. *Please leave a message after the tone.* There followed three beeps, signaling three messages.

Could one of them have been left by Terry?

It took Cadel just ten minutes to chase down Luther's message-access code. Chasing down these codes was a hobby of his. He had used his skill to good effect when sabotaging the exam efforts of his fellow twelfth-grade students at Crampton. Having identified Luther's code, Cadel listened to the three recorded messages.

Sure enough, the third had been left by Terry. *Luther, where are you? We've got a problem. Someone found out about our project. He's not in the picture now, but there might be others. Call me.* Click.

Cadel, who had been holding his breath, released it in a great sigh. *Thank god,* he thought. But how to copy it, from this distance? Before it was erased? Through a modem, onto a disk drive?

Though it was a complicated little piece of engineering, it wasn't beyond him. The trouble was, it would have to be done on his own computer, after which every trace of the operation would have to be utterly erased. He couldn't risk using Sark's computer. He wouldn't have time. It was only fifteen minutes until the scheduled start of his next session with Dr. Vee, and someone might walk in at any moment.

Fortunately, there was a stack of blank compact discs in the stationery cupboard, available to everyone who spent time in Hardware Heaven. You simply had to open the cupboard door with your personal access code. Cadel, of course, didn't use his own; he used Sark's. Then he sat down and copied Terry's message to the disk he'd chosen.

He was just finishing up when Sark slouched into the room, looking disgruntled.

"Where's Com?" Cadel asked, and received a shrug in reply. "Is he sick?"

"How should I know?"

"Where were you? Where is everyone?"

"What are you, my mother?" Sark flung himself into his chair and turned on his machine.

Cadel held his breath. He had done his best to wipe out all traces of recent activity, but things like a warm monitor were impossible to disguise.

"For Chris'sake," Sark spluttered.

"What?" said Cadel, his heart contracting.

"This bloody DN server hasn't crashed! I must have missed one of the goddamn machines, goddammit!"

Cadel breathed a quiet sigh of relief. Then Dr. Vee waddled through the door and announced that it was time to "extrapolate, gentlemen."

For the time being, Cadel knew, he would have to abandon his spy work.

THIRTY-EIGHT

From his infiltration class, Cadel went straight to Dr. Deal's, where he informed Gazo that Abraham was dead. (Gazo didn't say much. What, after all, was there to say?) They parted at five, after collecting their buff-colored envelopes. Gazo wandered off to the dormitories in his increasingly hapless way, while Cadel jumped into a cab. His usual session with Thaddeus was scheduled for half-past five. It wouldn't do to run late. He had to appear as keen as he always had been, despite his true feelings.

When he arrived at the psychologist's office, he was allowed to go straight up. Thaddeus was waiting at his desk, reading a newspaper.

"Ah, Cadel," he said. "You're here. I take it this means you're feeling better?"

Cadel nodded.

"No more nausea? No headaches?"

"No."

"So it must have been some kind of twenty-four-hour bug, then?"

"I guess."

"Good, good." Thaddeus rose and stretched. The way he did this made Cadel think of a panther. "I suppose you wouldn't have been running around so much if you hadn't been feeling better," Thaddeus added, with a glint in his eye. Cadel met the challenge head-on.

"Oh, you mean the hospital and that," he said.

"The hospital. Your old school. Number sixteen Waterloo Street . . ."

"I had to go see Abraham," Cadel insisted, allowing a touch of impatience to enter his voice. "He asked me to go and pick up his stuff. Said I was the only one he trusted."

"Ah. Yes. Abraham. What a pity."

"And now I've got his stuff, and I don't know what to do with it." Cadel grimaced. (*Don't overact*, he thought. *Keep it natural.*) "Underpants and things."

"Underpants? Dear me."

"What should I do with it?" Cadel gazed up at Thaddeus in a guileless fashion. "Should I take it back to his house, or what?"

"My dear boy," Thaddeus replied, his expression unreadable. "Why should you feel it necessary to ask?"

Cadel blinked.

"You mean—"

"I mean that if there's any reason not to throw it in the nearest trash can, I should like to hear what that reason might be." In the pause that followed, Cadel flushed. Thaddeus seemed to register this. "It amazes me that you went to visit that pathetic creature in the first place," he continued. "Were you hoping to gain anything from it? Anything specific?"

"I—I don't know." Cadel thought back. Why *had* he been moved to answer Abraham's summons? Because Gazo had asked him to? Because he was searching for a way out? Because it seemed like the *right thing to do?* None of these reasons, he knew perfectly well, would be acceptable to Thaddeus. "I suppose I thought it might be interesting," he said. "In case he had something useful to say."

"And did he?"

"Not really," Cadel lied.

"So it was a complete waste of time."

Cadel scratched his arm.

"Instilling loyalty is all very well, Cadel," Thaddeus went on, propping himself against the desk, "but only if the subject is worth the effort. I have to tell you, your father is not pleased. Abraham should never have called that ambulance. He should never have gone to the hospital. Now there's talk of bringing the coroner in, and *you*, Cadel, have been identified as Abraham's friend. You gave your name to the medical staff. How could you have been so stupid?"

Cadel swallowed.

"Perhaps you're still not quite well," Thaddeus suggested slowly, his gaze locked on Cadel's face. "You seem to be behaving in a very heedless manner—one might almost say an *impulsive* manner. That isn't like you."

"Sorry," Cadel murmured, and Thaddeus shrugged.

"It's done now," Thaddeus said. "We must simply make sure that you don't become further involved in Abraham's mess. You say you collected some of his possessions?"

"Oh, yes. Right here. His address book and his bathrobe—"

"Give them to me. I'll have someone return them. I don't want you approaching that house, or that hospital, again."

Obediently, Cadel surrendered everything in his backpack that had belonged to Abraham. He did so without disturbing the precious computer disk concealed in one of its pockets.

In a way, he was glad that he had blundered around and upset his father. If Thaddeus and Dr. Darkkon were fretting about his public involvement in Abraham's death, they were less likely to be interested in other aspects of Cadel's recent conduct.

"God help us," Thaddeus remarked, as he gingerly plucked the crumpled robe and grayish underpants from Cadel's grasp. Screwing up his nose, he transferred them to one of his in-boxes. "What on earth possessed you, Cadel? You could have *caught* something, lugging these things around." With a shudder, he carried the in-box to a remote corner of the room. "By the way," he said, "there's a transmission scheduled in three minutes. You'll have to face the music, I'm afraid—your father's not at all happy." Seeing Cadel's expression, Thaddeus suddenly smiled. "Don't look like that, dear boy, he's not going to eat you. Just sit tight and take it like a man. Everything he says will be for your own good—you can't go galumphing around the world like an ordinary person, dropping your name here, there, and everywhere. It's not the sort of mistake you should be making at your age."

Cadel stared at the floor. He had been overwhelmed by a sudden, fierce rush of hatred, and was doing his best to hide it. His eyelids drooped. He pressed his lips together.

When Dr. Darkkon finally addressed him, from a jail cell thousands of miles away, Cadel was able to absorb each harsh word impassively. Dr. Darkkon was disappointed. More than that—he was disgusted. What had Cadel been thinking of? Not much, by the look of it. There were two categories of people in the world: enemies and tools. Abraham hadn't even had the makings of a useful tool. And yet Cadel had missed half of the Maestro's class, just for the purpose of picking up that wretched maniac's old clothes! Like a valet!

"That isn't what you're here for, son," Dr. Darkkon growled. "Do something like that and your only reward will be a whole mess of trouble. Do you understand?"

"Yes, sir."

"It's *you* I'm worried about, Cadel. I don't want to see you cast adrift again, lost in a world of morons. It could happen, if they find out who you are. What you're capable of. They might put you in a reform school—a juvenile detention center. With all the little drug addicts and antisocial personalities. Isn't that right, Thaddeus?"

Thaddeus inclined his head. Cadel said nothing. He was so filled with cold disdain that he couldn't risk uttering a word. Having recognized this cascade of lies for exactly what it was—an exercise in manipulation—he was finding it hard to control the rush of color to his cheeks. He could only pray that Thaddeus, if he saw it, would identify this color as a blush of shame.

"Some people are just a waste of space," Dr. Darkkon was saying. "On a microbiological level, they'd be viruses. Parasites. They can't support themselves, so they feed off the time and energy of those who should be focusing on more important and worthwhile things. They want this, they want that, yet they're inherently useless. More useless than a paralyzed athlete."

Cadel suddenly thought of Sonja, in her wheelchair. The image was so strong that tears rose in his eyes.

Thaddeus saw them and leaned forward to press Cadel's shoulder.

"You won't make the same mistake again, will you, Cadel?" he said, before addressing Dr. Darkkon. "He's not been well, remember. He's not been himself."

You can say that again, Cadel thought. But he remained silent, folding up his mouth and fixing his wet, stricken gaze on the transmission screen.

As always, this trick was effective. Dr. Darkkon couldn't help softening.

"Well, we'll drop the subject now," he said, with an indulgent grin. "Dammit, boy, I wish I had your face. I wouldn't be in here if I did. Just one word of advice, though. Don't think a hangdog look is always going to solve any problems you might have got yourself in. Because it won't. And remember—just because you *look* friendly doesn't mean you have to *be* friendly. Understand?"

"Oh yes," said Cadel.

He thought, *I understand, all right. You just watch me.*

THIRTY-NINE

That evening, Cadel decided to listen to some music.

Long ago, Mrs. Piggott had given him his own stereo system, which was kept in his bedroom. "I don't want you hogging ours all the time," she had said. In fact, Cadel only used this system about once a week, because he wasn't a music addict. He didn't follow the pop charts, or borrow the Piggotts' CDs, or record late-night music programs. Unlike most other kids, his preference was for complex vocal harmonies or pieces played by large orchestras (which were systems of an unusual kind). As a result, his small collection of CDs was dominated by classical and choral music, though it included the odd flamenco guitar and rap recording.

Cadel found rap very soothing to listen to, if the rhymes were perfect. It had the same effect on him as the sight of a beautifully wired circuit board, or the smoothly functioning mechanism of a watch. It didn't matter to him *what* was being said, as long as the words clicked together in a pleasing way.

When Cadel arrived home, he pulled all his compact discs out of their cases, dumped them on his bedroom floor, and sat listening to one of them with his eyes closed and an enormous pair of headphones clamped over his ears. Although this ruse gave him time to think without making anyone suspicious, its main purpose was to allow him to switch CDs. In the confusion that he had created, he was able to insert his CD recording of Terry's phone message secretly into a rap compilation CD case.

Then he slipped the compilation case into his backpack, along with one more CD, just to make things look convincing.

After all, lending people CDs wasn't an unusual activity for a fourteen-year-old.

He didn't eat much that night. Nor did he get much sleep. His mind, like a computer, would simply not turn itself off; it kept grinding through various calculations while he tossed and turned, and missed Sonja. He was used to exchanging e-mails with Sonja when he was upset or disturbed. Now he had no one to talk to. He certainly couldn't talk to Thaddeus.

His only other friend in the world was probably Gazo. He felt that Gazo could be trusted, because he, like Cadel, was all alone. The trouble was that Gazo had a pretty low IQ. Though trustworthy, he perhaps wasn't entirely reliable.

Still, he was better than nothing. *Choose your tools.* If Cadel had had a choice, he might have looked elsewhere. But he didn't have a choice. Besides, poor Gazo—Cadel felt sorry for him. It was impossible not to. If Gazo wanted to drop out of the institute, why shouldn't he?

There had to be something that Cadel could do for Gazo. If Gazo, in turn, would do something for him.

The next morning, Cadel headed for the institute as early as possible, arriving at 9:15. He went straight to Hardware Heaven, where he found Com and Richard toiling over their machines. He didn't bother to greet them.

He just sat down and hitched a ride on Dr. Vee's spy sweep.

There had been only a few changes overnight, and those had mostly occurred because of activity on Adolf's computer. Surveillance reports told Cadel that Terry's trip, the previous day, had been to Abraham's house. It appeared that Terry had found the spare key (after a short search) and had let himself in. An hour later he had emerged again and driven to the hospital—looking for Abraham's "important information," no doubt. Cadel thought of Abraham's post-office-box key, which was sitting snugly in his own wallet. He wondered if Abraham might have left the box number and location carelessly scrawled somewhere. He hoped not. It was easy enough to get into a post-office box, even without a key. If Terry should find the box in question and pry it open, he might stumble upon a letter from Sonja. That would be very bad indeed.

But according to the surveillance reports, Terry had gone nowhere near Strathfield post office the previous day. Instead, he had returned from the hospital to the institute, where he had stayed until one in the morning. Then he had spent the rest of the night at Tracey Lane's house. According to the surveillance team, he was still there. So was Tracey.

Tracey herself had recently been promoted to "double-code-red" status. This was because she had been looking for love outside the institute. Despite the fact that she was seeing both Terry *and* Dr. Deal, the Führer's report to Luther described how a pair of Grunts, sent to tail Tracey, had seen her kissing another lawyer in his car. *Owing to this gentleman's well-known crusade against prominent underworld figures, we should be treating her activities with the utmost seriousness*, Adolf had written. *I would suggest placing the entire institute under yellow alert until we get to the bottom of what looks to be some sort of conspiracy.* Apparently annoyed by Luther's careless response *(Tracey Lane is notorious, we all know that—she would kiss a prize ferret if she felt it would help her career)*, the Führer had notified Thaddeus. In a security-coded e-mail, he had informed Thaddeus that he entertained grave concerns about the safety of the institute. Certain members of the staff seemed to be conspiring together, he warned, but Luther Lasco had refused to authorize a yellow alert. Adolf therefore wanted to discuss his concerns with Thaddeus in private.

Cadel knew Thaddeus. He knew the way Thaddeus talked and wrote. He could tell from Thaddeus's reply that the psychologist was weary of Adolf's paranoia. Nevertheless, it was impossible to ignore

Adolf entirely. What if the Führer was right for once? So Thaddeus had agreed to meet him at two o'clock on Friday, an hour before his scheduled meeting with Luther, Adolf, and Tracey Lane.

We'll use the armory, wrote Thaddeus, *if that's private enough for you.*

Bingo! Suddenly Cadel had a mental vision of pieces falling into place, like the mechanism of a complicated lock when the key is inserted. He saw Adolf's empty office, Gazo's class schedule, the CD, the buff-colored envelope in Gazo's gloved hand, Abraham's car . . . a perfect plan, knitting itself together.

He felt quite breathless, and tried to slow his breathing. In the hushed atmosphere of Hardware Heaven, noisy breathing would certainly have been noticed.

If only he could have got up and paced the floor!

As it was, he had to fix his eyes on his computer screen and think without moving. Staring at a computer screen didn't look suspicious. Even Com used to slip into a trance now and then, as if hypnotized by the glowing pixels in front of him. Cadel stared so hard at his own screen that he could almost *see* the three-dimensional structure of his plan erecting itself on its luminous surface . . .

"Oi!" said Richard sharply. "Shut up, will you?"

Cadel blinked. He turned his head.

"What?"

"Stop making that noise!" Richard snapped. Then, seeing Cadel's puzzled look, he added, "You were drumming your fingers! Drives me mad, that!"

"Oh," said Cadel. "Sorry."

"Don't you have anything better to do with 'em?"

"I do, as a matter of fact," said Cadel. He focused on the spy sweep again, jumping off when it hit Max's database. The Maestro, he had discovered, was a man obsessed with his own money—a man who liked to know exactly how his investments were doing all the time. For this reason, he had been unable to resist computer banking. Of course, he had made a brave attempt to protect his account details. Most people would have found them utterly inaccessible behind a wall of passwords and access keys. But thanks to the Führer's background files—and his own excursions on the Net—Cadel knew Max rather well by now. He had been able to isolate the Maestro's passwords without too much trouble.

He copied the account details to Brendan's exposed database. There, he knew, Art was bound to find them because Art made a habit of poking around in Brendan's system, as Cadel had already discovered.

It was a mean trick, in some ways. Though Art and Brendan weren't exactly the nicest people in the world, they had never done anything to Cadel. They didn't really deserve to have Maestro Max thrown at them.

Cadel felt bad, but there was nothing else he could do. He simply had no choice.

Cadel's Thursday schedule was undemanding. He had one basic-lying class, one infiltration class, and one embezzlement class to attend. For the rest of the day, he was free to pursue his own interests.

The trouble was, his own interests preoccupied him so much that he found it hard to tear his thoughts away from them.

Thaddeus noticed this. He could hardly fail to, since there were now only two students in his first-year class. During his lecture on polygraph lie detectors, he paused once to address Cadel, who was staring out the window. "Something in the parking lot that I should know about, Mr. Darkkon?" he inquired.

Cadel knew better than to apologize. Thaddeus would have regarded this as a very feeble response, especially in a basic-lying class. Instead, he replied, with an innocent look, "I'm just a bit concerned, Dr. Roth. Two men have been sitting in a car out there ever since we arrived. You don't think they're undercover cops or anything?"

Cadel knew full well that these two men were Grunts assigned to tail either himself or Terry. Perhaps Thaddeus knew that he knew it; Cadel couldn't be sure. He could only fold up his mouth, pucker his brow, and wait to see if Thaddeus found him convincing.

The psychologist narrowed his eyes. He glanced out the window, registered the two Grunts, then turned back to Cadel, poker-faced.

"I wouldn't worry about *them*, Mr. Darkkon," he said mildly. "You concentrate on what's happening in here and I'll worry about what's happening outside. It's my job."

Cadel did his best to obey. But during Brendan's class, he was again distracted. He couldn't be sure about Brendan—not until he received Sonja's mathematical mind-bender. Unless Brendan was occupied with a really challenging puzzle, he might notice that his database had been tampered with. This, above all, was what Cadel feared. So he was jumpy and inattentive, less interested in foreign currency loans than he was in Brendan's computer. Even Brendan, who rarely noticed anything about his students, noticed this. "What's happened to your head?" he asked, fixing Cadel with his vacant, pale-blue gaze. "Isn't it working?"

Fortunately, the homework he gave to Cadel was an incomplete money-laundering chart: something that Cadel could finish without much effort. He took it back to Hardware Heaven and tackled it there. For the rest of the day he kept his eye on the Axis network. (Terry, he noticed, had been promoted to double-code-red status. There was no indication that Art had infiltrated Brendan's computer again. The reports on Cadel remained terse and uninteresting.) He also researched Yarramundi's complicated security system, which protected dangerous areas like the armory, the magazine, and the "fission lab." Access to these "code-one" areas was restricted.

Fortunately, security in the rest of the complex was far less strict.

Cadel couldn't afford to store all this information on his hard drive—or even on a disk. He had to commit it to memory and hope that it would stay there. Sometimes he wished that his mind was more like a computer. It was so easy to access a computer's memory.

At five o'clock he packed up and departed, leaving Com in charge of Hardware Heaven. On his way out, he chanced upon a strange figure in blue tights, who appeared to be glued to the ceiling. As Cadel stopped and stared, the figure slowly extended one arm, clamped his hand against a light fixture, and dragged himself forward. It was like watching a fly on a wall.

Cadel wondered if he should risk passing underneath.

"Go on!" the figure snapped irritably. Cadel obeyed. He had just reached the front entrance when he heard an exclamation, then an almighty *thud*.

Turning, he saw that the human fly had hit the floor.

"Are you okay?" he asked.

"Piss off," came the reply.

"But—"

"Piss off."

Cadel shrugged and withdrew. It did no good at all, offering to help people at the Axis Institute. Everyone thought you were simply pulling a scam.

He caught a train back home, where he ate a whole packet of corn chips in front of his computer. There was nothing much he could do just yet, except wait. Outside, the Grunts were probably circling his house, their eyes peeled. Inside, the refrigerator hummed and the clocks ticked. Cadel skimmed through his Partner Post files. He did some research into Mrs. Brezeck's background, just to be convincing. He looked for Abraham's name, dipping into a coroner's database, but found nothing.

At seven o'clock, he heard the doorbell ring.

The Piggotts weren't around. No doubt they were with their *real* families. Cautiously, Cadel shuffled to the front door and peered through the peephole. In the glow of the porch light, he could see a young woman waiting on the doorstep. There was a badge pinned to her jacket lapel, but Cadel couldn't read it.

No one else appeared to be with her. In fact, she looked a little scared.

Cadel fastened the security chain and opened the door a fraction. He saw the young woman start, then relax visibly when she caught sight of Cadel's face. She had frizzy brown hair and freckles.

"Hello," she said. "I'm sorry to bother you, but I'm collecting for the Cerebral Palsy Center." She jangled her tin, which had a printed label pasted on it. "Would you like to contribute? Donations over two dollars are tax deductible."

Cadel hesitated. Beyond the figure on the doorstep, somewhere in the thickening darkness, the surveillance team was lurking. He couldn't see it, of course. He couldn't see anything except the faint shine of glossy camellia leaves, and the pool of light cast by a nearby garden lamp, and—

Hang on, he thought.

The Cerebral Palsy Center?

"The Cerebral Palsy Center supports people with cerebral palsy and their families in the community," the young woman continued, with a pleading smile. There was something strained about the way she kept her eyes fixed on Cadel. The name on her badge was EMMA. "I can give you a receipt. We *always* give receipts. I have my receipt book."

"Wait," said Cadel. He fished around for his wallet, which was well supplied with cash. As he did so, he saw a wash of color mount across Emma's freckled cheeks.

His own heartbeat began to speed up.

"Here," he said, thrusting a fifty-dollar bill at her. "And give me a receipt," he added.

"Yes, of course."

"It's for my parents. You can put their names down—Lanna and Stuart Piggott." While the young woman fumbled with a large and un-wieldy receipt book, Cadel was trying to think up an explanation that would satisfy Thaddeus. The Piggotts never donated anything to charities. They even turned the Salvation Army away from their door during the Red Shield Appeal. So Cadel intended to "wave the receipt under their noses," just to "irritate them." That, at least, was what he proposed to tell Thaddeus. "Fifty dollars!" he would say. "It practically gave them a heart attack! And I made 'em pay me back, too."

Emma suddenly extended her hand. "Your receipt," she said, with a fixed smile. "Thank you *very* much. We really appreciate it."

Cadel took the receipt, crumpling it in his palm. He knew that he couldn't linger. So he stepped back inside, closing the door firmly behind him. He dared not even check the peephole again, because such curiosity would look suspicious to anyone who might be monitoring his movements. His only option was to stuff the receipt into his pocket and appear to forget its very existence.

Even though he was desperate—*desperate*—to look at it.

Returning to his computer, he made a pretense of surfing the Net to satisfy any cameras that might be trained on him. His fingers moved automatically, while his mind was elsewhere. What on earth did Sonja think she was doing? The Cerebral Palsy Center? Couldn't she see how *risky* that was? Suppose news of this little incident got back to Thaddeus somehow? It would certainly get back to the Führer. He had probably told his Grunts to keep a close eye on innocent-looking door-to-door pollsters and charity collectors, who could so easily be assassins in disguise. And what about that girl—Emma? Was she a nurse? A friend? Had Sonja told her the whole story? He certainly hoped not. The fewer people who knew about him the better.

And how had Sonja tracked him down, anyway? The Piggotts' telephone number was unlisted. Had she used the Internet? It seemed unlikely. Her expertise was with numbers, not computers.

Cadel realized that he was sweating like someone who had run a marathon. Then it occurred to him that a shower might be useful. It might be exactly the cover he needed.

Needless to say, he choreographed the whole activity very carefully in his head before he even left his seat. The secret was to make it all look natural: dropping his jeans, checking the pockets, finding a few candy wrappers and the Cerebral Palsy Center receipt, casting a puzzled glance over the same receipt (front and back) . . . It had to be done swiftly, casually, efficiently. Just in case.

And he had to keep moving. If he didn't, any cameras focused in his direction might get a firm lock on the receipt itself. Cadel didn't want anyone reading it. Not if it happened to be what he thought it was. And he couldn't disable the security system because it might look odd right after Emma's visit. Someone was bound to wonder about that.

Taking a deep breath, he rose from his chair. He plucked a pair of underpants and a pair of clean socks from his chest of drawers. He went into his bathroom, turned on the shower, and began to undress.

When the moment came, he found out everything he needed to know. There, on the back of the receipt, was scrawled a long and complicated series of algorithms. There was no accompanying explanation—there didn't have to be. Cadel knew what he was looking at. Or rather, he knew where it came from. He didn't know *exactly* what it was, because he didn't have time to untangle the knots of numbers.

He had to lay aside the precious document in case he was being watched. He had to tuck it into his wallet, with an obvious lack of interest, and leave it there for the rest of the evening. Perhaps tomorrow, on the train . . .

Cadel had never been forced to exert such self-control. It actually gave him a headache. Unable to think about anything else, he slumped in front of the widescreen TV until the Piggotts arrived home, together, at about eleven o'clock. They appeared to be slightly drunk. Stuart was noisier than usual, and Lanna was tripping in her stiletto heels. Upon catching sight of Cadel, they immediately packed him off to bed. Then they kept him awake for another hour by knocking over wineglasses and laughing loudly.

Cadel was almost tempted to tell them that they should go back to their real families. But he didn't. He simply lay in bed, wondering what he should do about Abraham's post-office box. Now that he had

Sonja's brainteaser, there would be no risk of exposing her if he went to Strathfield post office. And he wanted to confirm, once and for all, what Terry and Luther's secret experiment was all about. Abraham had already told Cadel that Terry possessed the vial—could that be what they were experimenting with?

Cadel's eyes widened as this explanation popped into his head. It occurred to him that if Terry and Luther were experimenting with the vial's contents, then they must be experimenting *on* something. Or somebody. Poetic justice . . . poetic justice . . .

Could they be experimenting on Doris Deauville?

It would make sense. Doris had disappeared around the same time as the vial had. Everyone assumed that Luther had "taken care" of her. But what if he hadn't done it through the usual channels? What if he had hidden her away in Terry's lab, to use as a subject?

Cadel swallowed. It was a dreadful thought. Not only that, it wasn't something that Thaddeus would approve of. Experimenting on stray dogs was one thing; experimenting on people was dangerous. There were rules governing the disposal of troublesome students. Cadel had seen them on the Axis network. The important thing was always to get the bodies off campus. The institute must never, ever be implicated.

No, Thaddeus wouldn't like this at all. As Abraham would have known.

Cadel wondered if Abraham might have stumbled on Doris in the labs. It was likely. In fact, the odds were pretty high. But he needed proof. He needed to check Abraham's post-office box.

The only thing that worried him was Thaddeus. Thaddeus would find out that Cadel had visited the post office, and what then? Thaddeus hadn't liked it when Cadel ran around doing things for Abraham—who was dead now, in any case. What kind of excuse would it be if Cadel told Thaddeus that he had been collecting Abraham's precious "work"?

No, he wouldn't mention Abraham. He would say . . . he would say . . .

Ah!

If asked, he would say that the post-office box belonged to Mrs. Brezeck.

It was a far-fetched explanation, which could be disproved quite easily. But that didn't matter.

According to Cadel's calculations, there was an 82.3 percent chance that he would be gone before anyone thought to check it out.

FORTY

The next morning, Cadel set his alarm for six thirty. He had to get up early because he wanted to be in Strathfield by nine. After taking great delight in banging around the kitchen (until, from the Piggotts' bedroom, a shrill wail begged him to *please* be quiet), he headed for the station and wriggled into the crush of a commuter train. It was packed so tightly that Cadel doubted very much if the surveillance team could have got on, too. Still, he wasn't concerned if it had. He'd prepared an excuse. He wasn't trying to be furtive. When the crowds piled out at Central Station, he didn't try to lose himself in them. On the contrary, he hung back. Already half suffocated from a trip spent wedged under somebody's armpit, he needed a little air.

It was no joke braving the rush hour when you were smaller than everyone else.

The train from Central to Strathfield was almost empty. For that reason, Cadel was able to spread out a bit and even glance at Sonja's brainteaser. Of course, he had to be careful. It wouldn't do to study the crumpled document with too much interest. But he pretended to go through his pockets, examining every candy wrapper, expired train ticket, and used handkerchief before checking his wallet. The train tickets and candy wrappers were tossed on the floor. The used handkerchief was returned to his pocket. The Cerebral Palsy Center receipt was smoothed out and placed between the pages of his embezzlement homework, which he reviewed with unseeing eyes as the train clattered along. Revising his homework was a natural thing to do. And leaving a loose piece of paper tucked into it was natural as well, if you looked absentminded enough.

Cadel didn't know if the little Asian lady sharing his carriage was employed by Adolf. He thought perhaps not. The only other occupant—a fat, elderly man who was snoozing away in a corner seat—didn't look like a Grunt, either.

But Cadel wasn't taking any chances.

At Strathfield, he found the post office without difficulty. A quick scan of the premises told Cadel that there were no awkwardly placed security cameras scattered around. He was able to open box number twenty-three, extract two sheets of paper from inside it, and read through them without running the slightest risk of sharing his discovery with someone else. After all, any nearby Grunts could hardly sidle up and peer over his shoulder.

Abraham's secret did concern Doris. In a signed statement, Abraham declared that he had overheard Terry and Luther whispering together about how Doris's corpse might be disposed of when they had "completed their experiment." On another occasion, Abraham had seen Terry slipping into a supply cupboard and locking it behind him. Terry had not emerged again for another forty minutes.

When he did so, Abraham wrote, *I heard a woman groaning.*

Cadel shut his eyes for a moment. *I heard a woman groaning.* He felt sick just thinking about it. He didn't *want* to think about it. But he had to. He had to keep reading. *Having also seen Terry filch Carla's vial,* he read, *I am convinced that he is using its contents to infect Doris Deauville. This is a dangerous and foolhardy act.*

By now, Cadel thought, *she might be dead.* And he rammed the statement into his pocket, wondering what to do. Should the document be kept or destroyed?

He pondered this question all the way to the institute, where he was just in time for Dr. Deal's class. He decided, as he walked into lecture-room one, that he would destroy the statement. Flush it down a toilet, perhaps. A *public* toilet.

"Ah. Mr. Darkkon," Dr. Deal remarked. "So you've decided to join us? Excellent. Two's company, as they say, but I prefer a crowd."

Cadel knew better than to sit beside Gazo. It would have looked too friendly. Instead, he found himself a spot down in front, where he spent the next hour fielding every question that Dr. Deal threw at them both. Cadel even answered the questions specifically directed at Gazo, who would not, he knew, be able to answer them.

"There's no need to show off, Mr. Darkkon," Dr. Deal finally said. "We all realize that you're a genius, you don't have to rub our noses in it."

Cadel was pleased. He preferred it that Dr. Deal should have thought him vain rather than kind, since kindness was regarded with such suspicion and hostility at the Axis Institute.

Gazo, however, didn't make the same mistake as Dr. Deal. Though dim-witted in some ways, he was always on the alert for compassionate gestures.

"You're a mate, Cadel," he said, after they had been dismissed. "You really saved me arse today."

Cadel said nothing. They were skirting the parking lot, but they still weren't safe. Cadel knew of only one place where they could talk frankly.

"Abraham's car's still here," he observed, stopping in his tracks. Gazo did the same.

They both stared at Abraham's beat-up old Ford Cortina.

"I wonder who'll get it now?" said Gazo. It was exactly what Cadel had hoped he would say.

"Maybe it'll be finders keepers," Cadel replied, and gazed up at his friend. "What do you think?" he asked. "Do you think you can get in?"

Gazo's eyes widened behind his plastic face-screen. He glanced at the car, then back at Cadel.

"I bet you could drive it away and no one would notice," Cadel continued. "Could you? Drive it away?"

"Well, yeah, but—"

341

"No one's going to give a damn. You realize that, don't you? Who's going to care?" As Gazo hesitated, Cadel added, "Except Abraham's family."

"Abraham's family," Gazo mumbled. "He really hated 'em."

"Yeah. He did."

Gazo looked around. There was no one in sight, though that didn't mean much. Several banks of seminary windows overlooked the parking lot.

"It's no big deal," said Cadel, scanning the windows for signs of life. "What's to stop you? The owner's dead, isn't he?"

Gazo didn't need any more encouragement. He waddled over to Abraham's car, removed a long steel implement from his bag, and had the driver's door lock disabled in a matter of seconds.

Despite himself, Cadel was impressed.

"Wow," he said. "You really *can* do that!"

"Hop in," Gazo urged, his nervous gaze skipping from car to car, from window to window. "No point hanging about."

Thanks to his suit, Gazo was barely able to fold himself into the front seat of Abraham's little car. But he managed it somehow and unlocked the passenger door for Cadel. Then he began to fiddle around with the steering column.

But Cadel stopped him.

"Wait," said Cadel, placing a hand on Gazo's wrist. "Wait. Just listen."

Gazo froze, looking surprised. Cadel released him, and began to poke around in the glove box. He wanted to look like a scavenger, not like a conspirator.

The glove box, he noticed, was full of CDs—most of them featuring organ music.

"I'll make this quick," he said. "You want to get out of here, don't you?"

"Huh?"

"I know you do, Gazo. You're failing. You're scared stiff. Isn't that right? Don't worry, this car won't be bugged. Not yet."

Speechless, Gazo stared at Cadel, who began to lose patience.

"Look," he snapped, "do you want my help or not? Because I can help you, if you help me. We can *both* get out."

"You?" Gazo gasped. "But—"

"I hate this place. I hate it. My dad wants me here, but he's crazy. I swear. He's off his head. And Thaddeus—well, Thaddeus does everything my dad tells him to do."

Gazo winced. Cadel, who knew how big a risk he was taking, reminded himself that if Gazo should ever repeat this conversation to Thaddeus, there was always one excuse that might sound convincing. "It was a trick," Cadel would say. "Of course I don't hate my dad. But I had to make Gazo trust me."

"Listen," he now declared. "If I can get away, then I can help you. With money and things. Identification papers. But I need you to do something first. Without telling anyone. Will you?" Dragging a CD case out of the glove box, Cadel waved it under Gazo's nose. "We don't belong here," he said, taking the opportunity to focus his laserlike gaze on Gazo's face mask. "You know we don't belong here, this is a madhouse. And we're not mad. *Please*, Gazo. We don't have much time."

"All—all right," Gazo stammered. "But what do you want me to do?"

"It's very simple." Cadel explained quickly what would happen. That afternoon, when Gazo was at Yarramundi, Cadel would infiltrate the Yarramundi security system via Adolf's computer. For exactly ten minutes, he would disable the program that controlled the surveillance cameras near Adolf's office. "Your first class isn't until three, is it?" he asked.

"Yeah, but—"

"And you usually get a lift with someone?"

"Yeah, but—"

"Gazo, listen. You can take this car."

"This *car*?"

"You have to. You have to get there early. By 2:15. You can do it, if you've got your own car. Between 2:15 and 2:25, I'll disable the cameras. That's when I want you to slip Dr. Deal's homework envelope under the door of Adolf's office. The envelope he just gave you then."

Gazo gaped.

"It won't have your prints on it, Gazo, because you always wear gloves," Cadel explained. "The only prints on it will be Dr. Deal's. No one will be able to connect you with it."

"But—"

"You just have to take the homework out and put something else in." Folding himself double, Cadel pretended to be searching under the seat. In fact, he was removing from his bag the rap-compilation CD case. After wiping it with a tissue, he carefully handed the case to Gazo, without allowing his skin to touch it again. "Here," he said. "Stick this in the envelope. Not the case—just the disc. Have you got a watch?"

"It's in my bag. But—"

"Go now," Cadel instructed. "Enjoy yourself. Drive around a bit. Just make sure you're inside Yarramundi by two. Then slip this CD, in Dr. Deal's envelope, *under Adolf's office door.* There won't be anyone behind the door, I guarantee it. The Führer will be in a meeting."

"And that's all I have to do?"

"That's all you have to do."

"Well—it sounds okay," Gazo conceded. "But the car—"

"This is the Axis Institute, Gazo. For god's sake, you'll probably earn extra marks for stealing Abraham's car."

Gazo blinked. Then he smiled.

"You're right," he chuckled. "Hey, I might even pass if I do this!"

"I hope not," said Cadel seriously. "If you pass, it'll mean that you're like the rest of them. And you're not. You're better than they are. You're like me—you're a fully evolved human being." He took the rest of Abraham's CDs from the glove box and stuffed them into his

344

bag, just to lull the suspicions of anyone who might be watching. Breaking into a car was all right as long as it was done to steal something. Breaking into a car so that you could talk with a friend—*that* was questionable.

"All right," Cadel said, his fingers clamped around the door handle. "You got all that?"

"Yeah."

"You know what to do?"

Gazo nodded.

"Good luck, then." Cadel pushed open his door. "I'll see you later."

As he walked away from the parking lot, he didn't look back to watch Gazo drive off.

He couldn't afford to.

FORTY-ONE

Cadel's next stop was Hardware Heaven. Here he pretended to be correcting his embezzlement homework. In fact, he was copying Sonja's algorithms to the back of his money-laundering exercise. To do this effectively, he had to hunch over the document, shielding it from wall-mounted security cameras and even from his own computer screen. (Because who could tell what kind of monitoring devices were installed around the institute?)

He was sweating by the time he'd finished.

The homework went back into his bag. Then he hitched a ride on Dr. Vee's spy sweep and hopped off at Brendan's database. Sure enough, Art had been poking around in Brendan's financial files, so clumsily that he had left electronic fingerprints all over the place. Upon checking Art's computer, Cadel saw that Art had made copies of the Maestro's account details.

He wondered how long it would take Art to steal the money that was in these accounts. Not long, probably. Not when he could easily forge a driver's license or a passport bearing his own photo alongside Max's name. Cadel was quite sure that Art *would* steal the money, because there was a lot of it—several million dollars. And why sift through Brendan's financial files unless you were planning to steal something? According to Cadel's calculations, Art wouldn't be able to resist several million dollars. He had once spent three years in jail because he hadn't been able to resist three hundred thousand.

The trouble was that stealing from Brendan would be a good deal safer than stealing from Max. Cadel realized this. He had taken it into account when drawing up his plans. Art wouldn't steal a cent from Max unless he was fully prepared to duck out of sight once the money was his. Ducking out of sight wouldn't be a problem for Art: No doubt he had plenty of false identification papers to fall back on. Cadel was counting on the fact that Art would disappear before Max found out what he'd done. And if he *was* discovered—well, that would be another way of removing a name from Cadel's list. It wasn't Cadel's preferred way, but it would have the same result.

In either case, Art would no longer be around to talk about Cadel's Ariel disguise.

Moreover, if Max did catch Art, then Cadel's name wouldn't even be mentioned. Brendan would cop all the blame. (He was an embezzler by trade, wasn't he?) Again, this wasn't a possibility that Cadel much liked. He didn't *want* to see Brendan's head blown off. But he had made certain other plans, involving Alias and Dr. Deal, which would ensure that Brendan was given some warning. Some warning and a chance to disappear.

He couldn't warn Brendan himself. He couldn't risk it. Writing out the brainteaser had been dangerous enough. Anything more and he would look too involved.

"I've got to do it," he muttered to himself. "I can't help it. I've got no choice."

Having satisfied himself that everything was going to plan, Cadel shut down his computer and went to give Brendan his homework. Sooner or later Brendan would mark that homework. And when he did, he would see Sonja's brainteaser, written out in Cadel's hand. There was nothing that Brendan liked so much as a mathematical puzzle. With any luck, this one would distract Brendan from his computer files until after Art had stolen Max's money.

Then it would just be a matter of ensuring that Brendan was warned before Max found out.

After dropping his homework off at Brendan's office, Cadel went to buy some lunch. He was worried about Gazo. There was nothing terribly complicated about sliding an envelope under Adolf's door, but if anyone could mess up such a simple exercise, Gazo certainly could. Standing at the refectory counter, Cadel checked his watch. Eleven forty-five: two and a half hours to go. He wasn't concerned about the Yarramundi security system. It would be easy to disable. And if anyone ever tracked down the cause of the glitch, it would be traced to Dr. Vee's spy sweep. No one would start investigating Cadel—at least, not until he was long gone.

No, his only worry was Gazo.

Cadel took his lemonade and his chicken roll back to Hardware Heaven. Here he scanned the Axis network for security alerts involving Gazo, the Ford Cortina, or anything else that might have an impact on his plan. He found nothing. There was very little activity on the network. The Grunts reported that Tracey Lane was heading for Yarramundi. Terry was at work upstairs. Luther was taking a class.

Dr. Vee strolled into the room at about one, by which time Com, Sark, and Richard were also present. Dr. Vee challenged them all to download the password-management files of a certain university's computer network. He asked them to bombard the management files with as many possible passwords as they could, as quickly as they could. Dr. Vee was interested in how fast they could be. "If you find the right password," he said, "there's some cutting-edge software being tested on that network, and you'll have first dibs. But I'm giving top marks for top speed. You can use your password dictionaries or whatever else you fancy. I want to see how far you've got. Just go, go, *go*."

Com won, in the end. Cadel might have done better if he hadn't been watching the clock. The countdown to 2:15 was distracting him. When Dr. Vee finally left, at five past two, Cadel breathed a huge sigh of relief.

Ten minutes wasn't much, but it was enough.

Yarramundi's Banksia Wing cameras went down at two fifteen precisely. Cadel put a block on the fail-safe as well, but couldn't do much about the backup alarm, which was attached to a separate, closed-loop system. This alarm began to sound at 2:18 in the control room, where the Grunt on duty spent about five minutes trying to find out what had happened, doggedly working through the correct procedures, which Cadel had memorized. (Cadel, who was plugged into Yarramundi's security system, registered every query and reroute.) Having failed to correct the problem, the Grunt called Adolf's office. Cadel had anticipated this step, because it was laid out clearly in the procedures. He also knew that the call wouldn't be answered, because Adolf was in the armory with Thaddeus. The Grunt then called Luther, at 2:23, and this call *was* answered. At 2:24, the connection was broken as Luther hung up.

Luther's office was just around the corner from Adolf's. It was possible that Luther marched straight around this corner and passed Adolf's door—an activity that would have taken him as little as thirty seconds. Cadel prayed that Gazo hadn't lingered in the corridor until 2:25. If he had, there was a slight chance that Luther might have seen him. Not that it would matter now, of course, because Luther would have other things on his mind. But later?

Cadel quickly brought the camera network back online. He knew that by the time Luther reached the control room, everything would be restored to its normal state. With any luck, there wouldn't even be an investigation. Luther might simply blame the Grunt for spilling coffee over the circuitry panel, or something equally stupid. The systems-failure report might simply record the incident, and conclude with the words: *Failure undiagnosed. Functions normal. Recommend systems upgrade.*

Cadel very much hoped so.

He would have liked to shut down his computer and go for a walk, but he couldn't. He had to stay and monitor the Axis network for any alerts that might crop up, owing to his minor act of sabotage. Only at three o'clock did he feel safe enough to leave his computer and wander off to his embezzlement class, which he didn't dare miss. For one thing,

Thaddeus didn't like it when he missed embezzlement. For another, Cadel wanted to know if Brendan had looked at his homework yet.

When he arrived, however, Brendan's door was shut. And Douglas Prindle was waiting outside.

"No answer," he informed Cadel, in his dry, croaking voice.

"Oh."

They both gazed down the corridor, first to the right, then to the left. There was no one about. Douglas glanced at his watch.

"Phoebe, too," said Cadel.

"Phoebe's always late. Brendan never is."

"I suppose so."

"He'd better turn up soon," Douglas rasped, more to himself than to Cadel. "I can't hang around all day—I told the boss I was going to my cardio checkup."

Suddenly the elevator chimed, and they both turned to look. When the metal doors slid open, Phoebe stepped out. She was as plump and glossy as a Chinese pheasant in black and gold and purple. Her feet were wedged into glamorous high-heeled shoes.

"What's up?" she inquired, clicking toward them. "Isn't he here yet?"

"Apparently not," Douglas replied.

"Have you tried?"

"I knocked."

Phoebe made an impatient noise. She went straight up to Brendan's door and turned the knob. Much to everyone's surprise, it yielded to her pressure.

"Hello?" she said, pushing the door open. "Oh! Mr. Graham?"

Cadel stood on tiptoe to peer over her shoulder. He saw that Brendan was inside his office after all, sitting at the desk, staring at the wall. He didn't respond to Phoebe's voice.

"*Mr. Graham,*" she repeated, more loudly. "It's three o'clock. We're all here."

Still no reaction.

Phoebe turned to look at Douglas, her dark eyes wide and frightened.

"You don't think he's . . . he's . . . ," she stammered but was unable to finish the sentence. Douglas pushed past her. He approached Brendan and touched him lightly on the shoulder. "Brendan?" he said. "Hello?"

"Is he breathing?" Phoebe squawked.

"Of course he's breathing!" Douglas sounded cross. This time he grabbed Brendan's arm and gave it a shake. *"Brendan! Snap out of it!"*

"Maybe he's had a stroke," Phoebe suggested, as Douglas waved a hand in front of Brendan's glazed blue eyes. When they didn't blink, he frowned and stepped back suddenly.

"This is no good," he muttered. "Something's wrong."

"We should get someone," said Phoebe. "We should call an ambulance."

"Don't be a fool." Douglas walked back into the corridor. "This has nothing to do with us—it's staff business. We'll just knock on a few doors. You start that side, I'll start this side."

He completely ignored Cadel, who wasn't important now that Phoebe had arrived. As she and Douglas began to pound on neighboring doors, Cadel moved into Brendan's office. Cautiously, fearfully, he advanced toward the desk. Brendan didn't twitch a muscle. He seemed utterly absorbed in some private meditation, blind and deaf to the outside world.

In front of him lay Sonja's brainteaser.

"Brendan?" said Cadel, in a small voice. "Can you hear me?"

No reply. Cadel reached for his homework. He had a horrible feeling that it might have something to do with Brendan's condition, and he didn't want anyone else to find it. But he couldn't remove it without lifting Brendan's hands, one by one. They were limp and cold and heavy.

Staring into Brendan's eyes, he could see his own reflection—and nothing else.

Cadel broke into a sweat. He stuffed his homework into his bag and headed for the door. On the threshold he almost collided with Art, who had been summoned by Phoebe. "Just let me have a look," Art was saying. "Oh! Hello, Cadel."

"He's sick," Cadel mumbled. "There's something wrong with him."

"Let me have a look," Art said again.

It didn't take him long to reach a decision. Something definitely *was* wrong. Brendan appeared to be in a kind of cataleptic state. Having made this diagnosis, Art ordered Phoebe to fetch Thaddeus. But Thaddeus was at Yarramundi. So Art called Thaddeus there and was told to wait. Thaddeus would head back immediately. In the meantime, no one was to touch anything.

"It might be some kind of poison," Art revealed, after speaking to Thaddeus. "Terry's supposed to take a look. Would someone go and get him, please?"

"I will," said Douglas.

"All right." Art waved a hand at Cadel and Phoebe. "You two can leave. There'll be no class today. If you're needed, you'll be informed."

Cadel swallowed. "But—"

"There's nothing you can do here, Cadel," Art assured him. "You're not a doctor, are you?"

"No, but—"

"Then off you go."

There was no point arguing—it might have looked suspicious. So Cadel trudged away, acutely conscious of the folded sheet of paper in his pocket. Was Sonja's brainteaser really the cause of this whole frightening incident? Or was it a coincidence that Brendan had plunged into a trance while marking Cadel's homework?

Cadel had a horrible feeling that he had miscalculated. Badly.

FORTY-TWO

Cadel couldn't stay at the institute for much longer: He had his usual session with Thaddeus at half past five. So at 4:40 he left, catching a train to the psychologist's office. On the way, he disposed of Abraham's letter and Sonja's brainteaser. He tore them up into very small pieces and flushed them down a railway-station toilet.

When he reached his destination, he discovered that Thaddeus was late.

"The doctor's been delayed," Wilfreda informed him. "You're to go up and wait—he won't be much longer."

Cadel grunted. He knew perfectly well why Thaddeus had been delayed, and he didn't want to think about it. Nevertheless, he had to. Upon reaching the psychologist's office, he sat himself down in front of the computer. Thaddeus's e-mail files weren't hard to penetrate; Cadel soon found an encrypted one from the Führer, which he decoded immediately.

URGENT!! it read. *New evidence regarding conspiracy discussed! Please contact me at earliest opportunity! Double-red status on Deal, Terry, Luther. Please authorize campus-wide yellow alert URGENTLY. Will explain.*

A double-red status on Dr. Deal undoubtedly meant that the Führer had not only listened to Cadel's recording of Terry's phone message to Luther, but had scanned the envelope in which it had been delivered. Fingerprints had been found and had matched Dr. Deal's prints, which were kept on the Führer's computer files. These files contained the prints of every person who had anything to do with the Axis Institute.

They were required for safety reasons.

Please authorize campus-wide yellow alert. Clearly, the meeting between Thaddeus and Adolf hadn't resulted in anything concrete. Perhaps Thaddeus had told Adolf that he would "think about" the request for a yellow alert. Cadel wondered how thinly the Führer was willing to stretch his little army of Grunts. With Luther, Terry, Tracey, and Dr. Deal all being followed, there wouldn't be many Grunts left to man Yarramundi. Or to keep an eye on Cadel, for that matter.

Unless Thaddeus had access to another troop of surveillance specialists? That Cadel didn't know about?

"Cadel."

It was Thaddeus. Like a cat, he had mounted the stairs and entered the room without making a sound. Cadel jumped.

"Well, well. What are *you* up to?" Thaddeus drawled. "Sneaking into my e-mails, again?" He clicked his tongue. "How many times do I have to tell you, Cadel?"

Cadel had often used Thaddeus's computer but had never jumped like a frightened rabbit before. He decided to brazen it out. "It's not my fault," he whined. "You have such obvious passwords."

"Get off," said Thaddeus, lightly slapping Cadel's hand. He clearly wasn't concerned. But when Cadel asked him how Brendan was, he frowned and looked suddenly tired.

"I don't know," he said. "It's like some sort of catatonia. Terry thinks it might be epilepsy, but I have my doubts. You look at Brendan . . ." Thaddeus sighed and shook his head. "He seems to be completely focused on something. It's bizarre. He hardly even responds to a steel ruler across the knuckles."

Cadel winced.

"Terry shot him full of drugs, and all he did was start shaking," Thaddeus continued. "We'll have to get a doctor in—someone we can trust. To do all the blood tests and so forth. Terry's ruled out the more common poisons. At the moment, Brendan's under observation in the labs, but I'm convinced it's more psychological than physical. A 'locked-in' syndrome. Something autistic, perhaps?" He shook his head. "I'm not having much luck with my staff lately. First Carla, now Brendan. I only hope the two incidents aren't connected."

Cadel cleared his throat.

"I don't see how they can be. Doris poisoned Carla, and Doris has been gone for ages."

"Mmmmph."

All at once the phone rang. Thaddeus's dark brows came together; he picked up the receiver impatiently.

"What is it?" he snapped. "I told you not to put through calls when—who? Oh, for god's sake. Urgent my ass. Yes, yes, put him through." Thaddeus rolled his eyes at Cadel. "I'm sorry about this, dear boy—it's Adolf on a rampage." He proceeded to address the telephone receiver. "Yes? What? No, I haven't checked my e-mail, I've been dealing with a medical emergency." There followed a long pause as Thaddeus listened to the yammering voice at the other end of the line. "I see," he said at last, thoughtfully. "Well, I have to admit, that *is* interesting. Right. Right. Yes, but if the prints are only on the envelope, how can you be sure . . . ? Yes, I know Tracey was there. Yes, I realize she's involved with Barry, and she *could* have left the envelope, but she's involved with Terry, too, so why should she be snitching on him? Oh, you think so? That's a very romantic explanation, Adolf; I didn't know you had it in you. Love triangle, eh? Barry and Tracey against Terry?" Thaddeus winked at Cadel as he continued to talk to the Führer.

"Yes, well, I do see your point, though you have to understand that Axis staff aren't *ordinary people*," he continued. "You can't expect them to behave themselves all the time. What? Oh, I see. So the cameras went off, did they? That is odd. Yes, you might want to follow that up, though it could have been a coincidence. You think so? Really? Well, I don't know, Adolf, it's a bit far-fetched. Vee and Barry can't stand each other, you do realize that, don't you? They wouldn't be caught *dead* in the same conspiracy. Especially when it has something to do with Tracey's love life. What?" Thaddeus rolled his eyes again. "No, I realize that. Of course. Yes, all right, that's a good idea. You do that. And you might look into this business with Brendan while you're at it . . . Hmmm? You haven't heard? Really? Well, then, I suggest you talk to Terry about it. See where you think it might fit into this big picture of yours. Then talk to me afterward—I'm rather busy right now."

Clunk! Thaddeus hung up. Cadel, who knew exactly what this phone call had been about, tried to look curious. All the while, he was thinking hard. So Adolf believed that Tracey had delivered the envelope. That was good. Adolf knew, of course, that Tracey was involved with Dr. Deal. He must have decided that Dr. Deal was jealous of Terry, who was also Tracey's boyfriend. Therefore, in Adolf's opinion, Dr. Deal must have recorded the suspicious communication between Terry and Luther. He must also have asked Tracey to drop it off. But why should Tracey want to betray Terry? Cadel couldn't imagine what Adolf's explanation for *that* might be, though it didn't really matter. What mattered was that no one suspected Gazo.

Unfortunately, Adolf did suspect Dr. Vee. He seemed to be suggesting that Dr. Vee had disabled the cameras. So why hadn't he promoted Dr. Vee to double-red status? Because the Virus might find out that he was under suspicion? Perhaps. Even Adolf had to realize that if the Virus had disabled the cameras, he might be plugged into Adolf's security files as well.

It was a shame about the Virus, but Cadel wasn't too worried. If there was one person who could look after himself, it was Dr. Vee. The trouble was, if Adolf started to investigate the Virus and discovered the spy sweep, then Dr. Vee would almost certainly try to find out who had been infiltrating his computer program. And then?

I'll have to be gone before then, thought Cadel.

"Cadel?" said Thaddeus. "Earth to Cadel!"

"Oh!" Cadel blinked. "Sorry. I was just thinking . . ."

"We've missed the scheduled hookup time for your father's transmission," Thaddeus observed, checking his watch. "I don't know if he'll still be there, but we can try. They're timing him with a stopwatch these days."

"Thaddeus?"

"Yes?" The psychologist was already lifting up one corner of the carpet to expose the hatch that concealed all his cables, amplifier components, and other vital equipment. "Can you help me with this, please, Cadel? Or we're going to miss our transmission window."

"Do you think Brendan's going to be all right?" Cadel asked, rising and joining the psychologist. "I mean, does Terry know if he's going to snap out of it?"

Thaddeus paused. He looked at Cadel quizzically, a smile touching one corner of his mouth.

"Your concern for Brendan is really touching," he drawled. "I know how much you must have regretted missing your embezzlement class today."

"I—"

"Tell me, Cadel." The black eyes narrowed, though the smile remained. "*You* didn't have anything to do with Brendan's little problem, did you?"

The attack was too sudden. Though Cadel cried, "No!" there must have been a false note somewhere in his reply. The amused expression disappeared from Thaddeus's face. In the silence that followed, Cadel frantically reviewed his options. Could he? Should he?

"I didn't—I mean, how could I?" he said faintly. "I don't know anything about poisons. Or contagion. It's not my field—you know that."

Thaddeus waited.

"I don't know what happened to him," Cadel insisted. "Honestly. I mean, I can't be sure. It's too weird . . ."

357

Thaddeus blinked slowly, almost lazily, and Cadel felt his defenses giving way. It didn't matter, though. Not really. Not if his confession was incomplete.

"Brendan was marking my homework," Cadel admitted. "I saw it in front of him—"

"Your *homework?*"

"I took it away. I'm sorry. I thought—I didn't want—I was afraid it might be the reason for what happened." Cadel didn't have to fake the anxiety in his tone. He began to move his hands about, not knowing what to do with them. "It probably didn't," he continued. "I was probably being stupid, but I . . . I didn't want to get involved."

"Very admirable," said Thaddeus dryly. "And may I ask what the homework was?"

"A money-laundering tree."

"Ah." Though the psychologist's expression didn't change, Cadel sensed an easing of some hidden tension. "Well," said Thaddeus, "your misgivings are understandable, but I wouldn't worry. I don't believe that a money-laundering tree, no matter how complex, could lead to an electrical short circuit of the brain. Where is this tree, anyway?"

"I—I destroyed it."

"Ah."

"In case . . . well, you know."

"In case it implicated you?"

"In case it had the same effect on anyone else," Cadel replied, before realizing that this was an ill-judged remark. Why should he care what happened to anyone else? He was a student of the Axis Institute.

"A wise precaution," Thaddeus said slowly. "Perhaps, though, you should have considered its possible uses. If your homework was really that deadly, why not test it out on that Brezeck woman? Putting *her* in a catatonic state would save you an awful lot of trouble."

There was a hint of reproach in this last observation. Cadel wondered if Thaddeus was referring, in a roundabout way, to the fact that Mrs. Brezeck still hadn't been "dealt with."

"I'm getting there," Cadel assured him. "I know what I'm doing. I've got access to her mail."

"Good."

"It's the homework. It gets in my way. If I didn't have so much homework . . ."

"Yes, of course. The homework." Although Thaddeus nodded sympathetically, there was a glint in his eye. "Never mind, Cadel. If that money-laundering tree is anything to go by, you won't be given homework for much longer. No one will *dare* give it to you, for fear of what it will do to them."

"Oh." Cadel was confused. Was Thaddeus joking, or . . . ? "But you just said it probably wasn't my fault. That we couldn't be certain—"

"Cadel, Cadel." Thaddeus squeezed his shoulder. "What are you fretting about? I'd be pleased as punch if you *had* blown Brendan's mind—even more pleased if you had done it on purpose. Why all this soul-searching and double-talk? Surely your conscience isn't troubling you? Or were you afraid that I'd be disappointed?"

"Well, yes," said Cadel. "You hate it when I miss embezzlement."

"Oh come, now, give me some credit. You think I can't find another embezzler to take Brendan's place? I could find ten of 'em in a week. Don't trouble yourself with my concerns. You concentrate on your own."

"But—"

"Come on, Cadel. We've more important things to do. Your father might be waiting."

Silently, Cadel began to help Thaddeus erect the transmitter. He was feeling distinctly odd: a bit sweaty, a bit shaky, a bit light-headed. He felt the way he had several years before, when a motorbike had almost knocked him down.

It occurred to him that he'd just had another narrow escape.

FORTY-THREE

That night in bed, Cadel lay thinking about Sonja and her mysterious conundrum. It was hard to believe that the wretched thing had crippled Brendan's powers of reason. After all, it hadn't had the same effect on Sonja. And Sonja was rather like Brendan. Both were obsessed with math. Both had certain weaknesses, though Sonja's was a weakness of the body rather than the mind. Both were to some degree cut off from the world. Why would Brendan have crumbled when Sonja hadn't?

Perhaps because Brendan's strange condition had nothing to do with any brainteaser?

Cadel wished that he could talk to Sonja about it, but he couldn't. He didn't dare. He couldn't risk even thanking her until he had made his escape and they were both beyond the reach of Thaddeus Roth and his minions. Cadel could not be sure how long that would be. A week, perhaps? Certainly no longer. If Thaddeus hadn't uncovered his plan by then, the Virus would have.

The next morning, Cadel headed straight for the Axis Institute. He reached Hardware Heaven at around eight o'clock, only to find Dr. Vee installed there. The Virus was in a grumpy mood; he had a streaming cold and a touch of asthma, and didn't even look up when Cadel entered.

Cadel wondered, with a sinking heart, how long he would have to wait. He couldn't check the network while Dr. Vee was around. Yet he had to, as soon as possible. There was no telling what might have happened since the previous afternoon.

"What's this?" he asked, upon reaching his computer. There was a sealed envelope propped against the keyboard.

Sealed envelopes could be dangerous things at the Axis Institute. Cadel didn't even want to touch this one before he found out where it had come from.

"Vee?" he said. "Do you know what this letter is?"

The Virus made an impatient noise. He rubbed his red, bleary eyes and said, "The spaceman left it."

"Gazo?"

"He was in here this morning. Now shut up, for god's sake, my head's killing me."

Obediently, Cadel fell silent. He opened the envelope and found a sheet of blue cardboard tucked inside, with the word *done* written on it.

Cadel replaced the card quickly and stuffed the envelope into his pocket. He realized that he should have told Gazo not to communicate with him. Not like this, anyway. It had been a stupid oversight. Sloppy planning.

He collapsed onto his chair with a sigh.

Though anxious to read the Führer's latest surveillance reports, he couldn't go near them until the Virus had left. All he could do was check the state of Max's bank accounts—something that didn't require direct access to the Maestro's own files but which could be done through the bank instead. To Cadel's astonishment, all the accounts were empty: Art had drained them dry. Cadel couldn't believe it. A single day and the money was gone! That was faster than he had ever expected.

He wondered if Max had been alerted yet. Almost certainly, to judge from his past behavior: Max tended to check on his money every six hours or so.

Cadel was working his way toward confirming this when a voice said, "Ah! You *are* here."

It was Dr. Deal. He stood in the doorway, dressed with his usual flair but looking somewhat flustered, all the same.

He was staring straight at Cadel.

361

"Who—me?" said Cadel.

"I want a word with you."

"Now?"

"Come here."

Reluctantly, Cadel rose. He glanced at Dr. Vee: Would the Virus raise an alarm if Cadel didn't return within half an hour? But Cadel need not have worried. Though Dr. Deal drew him out of Hardware Heaven, they went no farther than the elevators before stopping to talk.

"Have you told anyone?" Dr. Deal murmured.

"About—"

"The incident," Dr. Deal hissed. "*You* know! In the men's room!"

"Oh." Cadel shook his head. "No."

"Are you sure?"

"Yes."

Breathing heavily, Dr. Deal squeezed Cadel's shoulder.

"I'm not angry, Cadel. I just want to know. If you have, it would explain something."

"What?"

"Never you mind. Just tell me the *truth*."

"I did," Cadel insisted, wriggling out of the lawyer's grip. "I've been keeping you in reserve, in case I need something."

"So you haven't told Thaddeus?"

"No."

"Or Luther Lasco?"

"No." Cadel realized, suddenly, that he was being unwise. "But I've written it all down," he said. "In case anything ever happens to me."

If Dr. Deal heard this last remark, it didn't seem to register. He stared hard at Cadel, then stared through him, as if thinking about something else.

"In that case, what the hell is going on?" he muttered. The question wasn't addressed to Cadel. Dr. Deal suddenly turned on his heel to face the elevators, and punched the DOWN button. He was looking more flustered than ever.

"What's wrong?" Cadel asked, with all the innocence that he could muster. In fact, he knew what was wrong. Dr. Deal had probably realized that he was being followed, or that his house had been searched. Something, at any rate, had alarmed him.

"Dr. Deal?" he said, having received no reply. "What's happened?"

"Nothing," the lawyer snapped, just as a chiming noise announced the arrival of one of the elevators. Cadel watched Dr. Deal step into it. When the doors had closed, Cadel raised his eyes to the illuminated panel above them.

Dr. Deal was getting out on the ground floor.

Cadel rushed down the fire stairs in pursuit. He wanted to see where the lawyer was going, and couldn't rely on surveillance reports. Not yet. Not while Dr. Vee was still in Hardware Heaven.

Upon reaching the ground floor, he was very careful. Through a window in the door that separated the fire stairs from the foyer, he scanned the elevators and their surroundings before he dared even to show his face. There was no one in sight. But when Cadel pushed open the door, he immediately heard voices. Raised voices.

They were coming from the corridor, down near Thaddeus's office.

"—those useless gorillas of yours left the place in a shambles!" Dr. Deal was saying. "And I want to know why!"

"You're saying you *don't* know?" It was Adolf who answered. Cadel worked this out when, having crossed the foyer from the fire stairs, he poked his head cautiously around a corner. There, in the corridor, were Thaddeus, Dr. Deal, and a short, wiry man with a gray crew cut, wearing battle fatigues. Cadel recognized this man from a photograph in the Axis Institute handbook. It was Adolf.

In the handbook, of course, he hadn't been wearing camouflage colors.

"No, I do not!" cried Dr. Deal. "I do *not* know why I'm being persecuted!"

"You expect us to believe that?" said Adolf.

"Now, gentlemen." As Thaddeus began to speak, Cadel pulled

back. He didn't want to risk being seen. Edging away from the corner, he heard Thaddeus plead for calm. "There's no need to shout."

"No need?" exclaimed Dr. Deal. "I came here to find out why this moronic mercenary thinks it necessary to subject me to his clumsy attentions—"

"I will tell you why!" the Führer interrupted. "I came here to tell Dr. Roth; I'll tell you, too!"

"Gentlemen, *please.*" Thaddeus spoke sharply. "If you want to discuss this, do it in my office. Not out here."

"Yes!" said the Führer. "We should discuss this envelope! We should discuss Tracey Lane!"

"*Adolf.* I told you. *Not out here.*"

Cadel shuddered. He had never heard that note in Thaddeus's voice before and never wanted to hear it again. When the door of the psychologist's office slammed shut, he toyed with the idea of pressing his ear against it, before finally deciding not to. Taking a risk like that was unjustified. He knew what would be said in Thaddeus's office. Adolf would accuse Dr. Deal of asking Tracey to deliver the envelope. Dr. Deal would deny having done so. Thaddeus might want to know why Dr. Deal hadn't simply come to him with his suspicions about Terry; had the recording of Terry's phone call been acquired through questionable means? Through a police phone-tapping operation, for example? Dr. Deal, if so accused, would repeat angrily that he had *nothing to do* with the recording. He didn't know where the envelope had come from. He didn't know what Tracey was up to.

Cadel doubted that Adolf would believe Dr. Deal. The meeting would come to nothing, he was sure. And whatever Dr. Deal did next, Cadel would know about it from the Führer's surveillance reports. If, that is, Dr. Vee ever shifted his enormous bulk out of Hardware Heaven. Cadel was beginning to worry that he would be there all day.

But Cadel's worries were unfounded. Upon returning to his computer, he discovered that Dr. Vee had gone. Only Com remained in Hardware Heaven, tap-tap-tapping away. It was a great relief. Cadel was at last able to jump on board the spy sweep, and jump off again when it reached Adolf's files. He scanned them feverishly, anxious to see the surveillance reports.

So far, they were pretty uninteresting. Brendan's condition was unchanged. Terry had stayed with him all night. Tracey had gone out to a party the previous evening and come home at three A.M.; she was still in bed. Cadel had been a good boy and was now at the institute. Luther was currently engaged in making an inventory of the Yarramundi ammunition stocks.

It was among Adolf's e-mails that Cadel found more-rewarding material. Luther had e-mailed the Führer, demanding an explanation for the "flies on his tail." Clearly, he had worked out that something was going on. So what would happen when Adolf left Thaddeus's office? Would he return to Yarramundi and confront the enraged Luther there? It was possible. It was even probable. But when Cadel tried to calculate the exact probability, he found himself hampered by his own lack of data. He didn't really know enough about any of these people: Adolf, Luther, Dr. Deal. He knew Thaddeus well enough to conclude that he would very likely refuse to give Adolf authorization for a campus-wide yellow alert. But the others? With them, he was plucking numbers from a deep, black void, wearing a blindfold.

Cadel turned to the Maestro's files. He saw that Max had closed all of his accounts, but found nothing to indicate what his next move might be: no e-mails to Thaddeus, no official complaints about Art lodged with the Führer. Cadel did find an alert circulated by one of the Maestro's banks, on its internal network. The bank was informing its staff that "a fraud had been committed" against at least one customer. The perpetrator was described as being about sixty years old and five feet, seven inches in height, very nearsighted, with a slim build, gray hair, crooked teeth, and "an educated way of speaking."

So Art must have removed the money in person. A risky procedure, to be sure, but necessary for someone without much expertise in the field of computers.

Reading the description of the man who had passed himself off as Max, Cadel was convinced that the Maestro must now know exactly who had stolen his money. Who else could the mysterious thief be, if not Art? Even his crooked teeth had been mentioned.

It seemed strange that Max hadn't informed Thaddeus of this latest development. Unless he had used his phone, instead of his e-mail? That was possible. Cadel decided to see if he could dig up some of Max's phone records, but first he returned to the Führer's surveillance reports. It had been at least ninety minutes since he'd last checked them.

URGENT, he read. *Subject IJ2n tracked from work to house of subject IM3r. On-site approx. 1 hour. At 10:52 a.m. left site alone, highly agitated. Is now at DARLINGHURST POLICE STATION. New orders required ASAP. Please respond. URGENT.*

Cadel swallowed.

What on earth was going on?

FORTY-FOUR

Subject IJ2n was the code name for Dr. Deal. Subject IM3r was the code name for Tracey. Dr. Deal had gone to Tracey's house, stayed an hour, then rushed off to Darlinghurst police station.

Why?

Numbly, Cadel considered the possibility that Dr. Deal was about to spill the beans about everything: Thaddeus, Dr. Darkkon, the Axis Institute . . . everything. Perhaps the lawyer was scared. Scared because his house had been searched. Scared because someone was following him. Scared of being "sorted out" by Luther Lasco. (An unexpected heart attack, perhaps? An unfortunate accident in his own spa bath?) Nothing that the police might do to Dr. Deal could ever be as bad as a Luther Lasco solution.

While Cadel tried to work out what was happening, he kept checking the surveillance reports. There was no news after ten minutes. No news after fifteen, or twenty-five. Another hour passed before the next message came through from the team following Tracey.

Re: Subject IM3r. Police have arrived at house with ambulance. Crime-scene tapes erected. Query: Further directions? Looks bad.

A little later came another message.

URGENT. Subject IJ2n still on-site. Police team dispatched. Please advise.

Cadel was doing frantic calculations in his head, but it was pointless; he didn't have enough data to work with. Obviously, Dr. Deal had gone straight to Tracey's house because the Führer believed that she had delivered the envelope. Any man in Dr. Deal's position would have wanted to know what the hell she was up to. Unless there was another reason? It suddenly occurred to Cadel that Dr. Deal might not have known about Tracey's relationship with Terry. Other people had known (Carla, for example), so Cadel had assumed—he had *assumed*, like an idiot!—that the lawyer would know, too. Especially since Terry knew all about Dr. Deal.

But Cadel had never laid eyes on any written proof that Dr. Deal did know about Tracey and Terry. What if he hadn't? What if he had been told about Terry, for the first time, in Thaddeus's office? What if he had gone to Tracey's house with rage in his heart, discovered the truth, and decided to seek revenge by spilling his guts to the police?

Cadel considered this scenario from every angle, but he wasn't convinced. He couldn't imagine Dr. Deal doing any such thing. And the numbers certainly made no sense, when he was trying to calculate probabilities. On the other hand, if Dr. Deal feared that he was being framed by Luther and Thaddeus and Adolf—wouldn't that be enough to send him running for help?

Finally, after two more hours, a report was filed that removed all doubt.

Re: Subject IM3r. Corpse removed from subject's house in body bag. Forensic activity. Media attending. Subject IM3r deceased?

Tracey was dead.

Cadel squeaked, and covered his mouth with his hand. Com looked up. He directed an inquiring glance at Cadel.

"I–I've got a headache," Cadel stammered. This seemed to satisfy Com, who returned to his program. Cadel, however, couldn't face his computer again.

He shut the whole thing down with trembling fingers. Then he headed blindly for the door. He had to get out. He had to-to—

To what?

They were watching him. It was important to keep that in mind. He couldn't do anything peculiar—anything that might alert Thaddeus.

368

Not while he was under surveillance. Crying and moaning, wringing his hands—they were out of the question. If he didn't control himself, swallow his sobs, blink away his tears, then Thaddeus would hear of it. Thaddeus would hear and wonder.

There must be a place, he thought despairingly, as he stepped into the elevator. Somewhere I can hide . . .

And then he remembered.

He was shuffling across the lawn, making for the front gate, when someone called his name. "Cadel! *Cadel!*" The voice rang out like a siren, but he kept going. He had to. Gazo was bound to say something stupid, and the electronic sensors were everywhere. Cadel picked up his pace as Gazo's heavy steps began to close the gap between them. *Thump, thump, thump!* When Cadel swiped his key-card, the gates opened automatically. Wall-mounted cameras were trained on his small, hunched figure.

The gates were closing behind him when Gazo slipped through them, narrowly avoiding a nasty accident.

"Gazo! For god's sake!"

"Didn't you hear me?"

"I heard you." Cadel darted across the street; he wanted to put as much space as possible between himself and the institute. Before Gazo opened his big mouth and ruined everything. "What is it?"

"Wait! Cadel! I'm not allowed out here!"

Cadel stopped. His quick eye noted everything in the immediate area: the man staring from a shop doorway; the car with tinted windows parked under a plane tree; the black metal box attached to the institute wall, near the gates. When Gazo reached him, another car passed them both, so quickly that Cadel couldn't see inside it.

"Then why don't you go back?" he asked loudly, before lowering his voice and adding, "We can't talk, Gazo, it's not safe. No, *don't* look around, just go back. Please."

"Can I give you a lift?"

"What?"

"Wherever you're going, I can give you a lift."

To Cadel's horror, Gazo actually winked behind his headpiece. Cadel hoped that no one watching them had noticed this conspiratorial little gesture.

"You mean in Abraham's car?" asked Cadel.

"It's a great car," Gazo replied. "I drove it all over the place yesterday."

"I can't get in that car with you. Not if you're driving."

"No, no! It's all right!" Gazo was beaming. "I can drive with me suit on! Headpiece and all!"

"Really?"

"Really. I already tried."

Cadel hesitated. Perhaps, in Abraham's car . . .

But no. It was probably bugged by now. The Grunts would have noticed that Cadel had got into it yesterday. He couldn't take any risks.

"No thanks, Gazo."

"But—"

"Go back inside. You're not allowed out here. You're attracting attention."

"Cadel?" Gazo was looking at him closely. "What's wrong?"

"I've got a headache," Cadel snapped, and turned away. He felt bad, but he couldn't talk. He was about to crack. Hurrying toward the station, he put all his energy into controlling the muscles of his face. He tried to empty his mind, so that stray thoughts of Sonja or Tracey didn't make him cry.

On the train, he read advertisements. He listened to a conversation about someone's aunt, who had found romance in a nursing home while visiting her aged mother. When he finally reached his stop, he really *did* have a headache. It pounded away at his skull as if demanding to be released. Cadel wondered if all the tears trapped inside his head were beginning to split it open.

It was a twenty-five-minute walk from the station to Crampton. Stumbling down the quiet, leafy suburban streets, Cadel kept his eyes peeled. Several cars passed him, as did an old man walking a dog. A plumber's van drove up to someone's house and parked. A woman pushed a stroller down one street, with a real baby inside.

Surely Adolf couldn't be hiring real babies?

The school, when Cadel reached it, was deserted. On a Saturday afternoon, there weren't even any sports teams around. Cadel marched quickly across the empty playground. Using one of his Crampton keys, he entered the eastern block, then the science staff room. He couldn't risk the math staff room, because Mrs. Brezeck frequented it and Thaddeus might have bugged it as a result. But the science staff room would be safe.

Having locked himself in, he crawled under a desk. Then he curled himself into a ball and began to cry.

He didn't know what to do. Everything was out of control. Tracey was dead. *Dead.* Had Dr. Deal actually *killed* her? There, in her house? Or had he found her like that? Perhaps he had found her like that and panicked. Perhaps he had gone to the police because he assumed that Luther had killed Tracey, and he was afraid that the same thing would happen to him.

But what if he really had killed her? A sudden, vivid picture leaped into Cadel's head: a picture of Dr. Deal punching him in the face. Had Dr. Deal done the same thing to Tracey? Because he thought she was trying to frame him? Because he was jealous of Terry? Cadel didn't know. He didn't have the data. Dr. Deal, Tracey, Brendan, Art—he didn't know any of these people well enough to predict their actions, not really. He had misjudged some crucial conjunction, and made a complete mess of everything. Someone had been *killed*! Because of *him*! And now the whole scenario was collapsing. Events were playing out in a way that he had never anticipated.

He wiped his face, his chest heaving. What was he going to do? He had unleashed a tornado. Pressed a red button. He was frightened to look at the Axis network again, in case he saw something or someone else disintegrating in front of his eyes. First Brendan. Now Tracey.

Next Dr. Deal would go—Luther would get him for sure. And Art? What about Art? What if Max *did* catch him? If that happened, Cadel would be responsible for yet another death. He wouldn't have wanted it, but he would have caused it, as directly as he had caused Tracey's.

He remembered rating the probability of Max catching Art. Breaking the probability down into a complex number. Measuring it against other numbers. Why had he never thought? Why had it never occurred to him that he would actually be *killing someone*? He was as bad as the rest of them. As bad as Luther. What would Sonja say? How could he tell her? How *would* he tell her? He wanted to talk to her so much, but he couldn't; he didn't dare.

"What am I going to do?" he sobbed. "What am I going to *do*?"

He couldn't escape—not yet. Brendan and Dr. Deal might be out of the picture, but he couldn't be sure about Art. As for Alias, he knew more about Cadel's Ariel disguise than anyone, and therefore would have to be dealt with, but Cadel didn't trust himself to fashion a risk-free plan of attack. Not after making so many terrible mistakes.

"I don't know what to do," he whimpered.

He felt so ashamed. So small and lonely and miserable. More than anything else, he wanted someone to hug him and tell him that he didn't have to worry. Around him, the empty staff room was quiet and sunlit. There were snapshots pinned on a bulletin board, along with a duty roster, an ad for a sofa bed, a cartoon, a postcard from Surfers Paradise. The mugs beside the electric jug were covered in hand-painted flowers and funny slogans. A back pillow had been left propped on one chair, and a red cardigan was draped over another. Everywhere lay science textbooks, unmarked exams, broken laboratory equipment.

Gradually, these things began to affect Cadel. He began to calm down, soothed by the warm light, the happy photographs, the deeply *ordinary* quality of his surroundings. He realized how wonderful it was to sit in a room that wasn't bugged, scorched, or oozing with strange liquids. At the institute, he realized, his nerves were always taut; there was never a moment when he didn't run the risk of being spied on,

372

attacked, taunted, or ambushed by some appalling sight or smell. Here, everything was peaceful. Nothing really bad, he decided, could ever happen in this room.

He got up and blew his nose. There was a mirror sitting on one of the desks; in it, he saw his face, which was smeared and blotchy. His eyes were bloodshot. His hair was a mess.

He couldn't go out looking like this. The Grunts were bound to report it: *Subject highly agitated.* He would have to wash his face. Comb his hair. Wait until his eyes weren't so puffy.

He found a comb in a drawer and water in the electric jug. He also found another photograph—a family shot. In it, Mr. Jankovic was sitting in a rowboat with his family: a wife, two children, and a golden retriever. They were all laughing, even the golden retriever. Cadel looked at it and caught his breath. He thought: *I could have had that. I could have had that if my father hadn't interfered. I could have had a proper family.* Real *parents.*

Suddenly he didn't feel like crying anymore. All the confusion, the fear, the despair—it all trickled away, leaving something cold and hard like a stone in his gut. He thought resentfully: *This is my father's doing. I didn't start it, but I'm going to end it. I'll take the whole bloody lot down with me. Whatever happens, I'm going to make that bastard suffer for what he's done.*

And then he saw the cell phone, half hidden by a confiscated Frisbee. It was sitting directly beneath the postcard on the bulletin board. Right beside a plastic-covered library book.

The idea was there, waiting for him. If someone had written it down, it could not have been more obvious.

FORTY-FIVE

Cadel didn't return to the institute. The thought of it made him sick. Instead, he went straight home, where James Guisnel and his partner—alias Mr. and Mrs. Piggott—were comparing schedules. They sat at the dining-room table, with a bottle of red wine standing open between them.

"Hello!" Lanna trilled. "So you're back, are you?"

"Where have you been?" Stuart demanded gruffly, and Cadel snorted.

"As if you didn't know," he growled.

"Eh? What's that?"

"Nothing."

"Beef Stroganoff tonight, Cadel," Lanna interrupted, trying to maintain a cheerful tone. "Your favorite."

Cadel muttered something and escaped to his bedroom. He wondered why the Piggotts were at home. Who had ordered them to be there, and for what reason? Was it simply a coincidence? Even on weekends, Stuart was usually away. Attending to his *real* life, no doubt.

Cadel tried to imagine what that life might be like, and failed. He couldn't picture Stuart at the beach, or in a shop. The guy was like a cardboard cutout—a cartoon. On reflection, Cadel realized that James Guisnel hadn't done a very convincing job of Stuart Piggott. Either he was a lousy actor or Dr. Darkkon had requested that Cadel be raised by a man with all the warmth and humor of a scarecrow.

After all, a hopeless adoptive father would ensure that Cadel bonded to his *real* father—not to mention his therapist. Thaddeus would have worked it all out. The whole business would have been carefully planned. Cadel could just see Thaddeus calculating the exact amount of rejection and isolation that Cadel would need to turn him into a freak.

The thought made him so angry, he had to stuff it into his mental trash can and pound the lid down over it. No point fretting about that now. He had other matters to attend to.

Cadel poked listlessly at his computer keyboard until dinnertime, turning things over and over in his head. At least he was going to speak to Sonja—that was something. From Crampton, using the abandoned cell phone in the science staff room, he had called Sonja's local library. He had asked Beatrice to pass on a message to Sonja: *Be at the Memorial Pool tomorrow from two to four. I'll call you there.* Cadel had it all worked out. He had seen from the Surfers Paradise postcard that Mr. Prowse was away for two weeks. He knew where Mr. Prowse lived, of course; he knew where all the Crampton teachers lived. He would go to Mr. Prowse's house tomorrow and call Sonja from there. With his knowledge of locks, it shouldn't be hard to find a way in. And if they had an alarm system—well, he would simply disable it.

"Cadel! Dinnertime!"

Cadel groaned. He could hardly bear the prospect of dining alone with the Piggotts. Fortunately, Stuart always watched the news while he ate. It saved him from having to make conversation. And while Lanna sometimes attempted to chat with Cadel, Stuart usually shushed her when an important story (about share prices, for instance) appeared on the television screen.

That evening was no different. When Cadel reached the dining room, he saw that the news had been switched on. It was clearly visible through the archway that divided the dining room from the vast, sweeping landscape of the living room, with all its glass walls and hectares of polished wood. Stuart was already gobbling down his beef Stroganoff, his gaze fixed on a very dull item about some sort of political scandal. Cadel sat down. He unfolded his white linen napkin and placed it on his lap.

"So. Cadel," said Lanna brightly. "How was your day?"

"Good," Cadel replied.

"You went to the institute?"

"Yes."

"I hope you ate a decent lunch."

"Yes."

"Have you checked your weight lately? It seems to me that you're thinner than usual. Though of course you might have shot up a bit—that's what generally happens with you."

Tracey Lane, the television suddenly announced, catching Cadel's attention. *Ms. Lane, a former channel-seven newsreader and travel-show presenter, was found dead in her eastern suburbs home early this afternoon . . .*

"Hey!" exclaimed Stuart. "Isn't that—didn't she work for the institute?"

"Of course she did!" said Lanna. "We met her there! Oh my *god,* Stuart!"

Cadel said nothing. He simply stared at the screen, listening hard. There was mention of a "suspect in custody," but no names were provided. Lanna made a horrified noise.

"Oh dear," she shrilled. "This is awful!"

"Shhh!" said Stuart.

But there wasn't much more to the story. Tracey had been beaten to death. An ambulance was shown, receiving into its depths her shrouded form. A "glamour shot" was also displayed; in it, Tracey was gazing soulfully at the camera, her blond hair carefully set, her face gleaming with makeup.

Cadel looked away, blinking fiercely. A "suspect in custody." Could that be Dr. Deal?

"I don't understand," said Lanna. "Are they saying they *have* the person who did it?"

"That's right." Stuart spoke impatiently. "Weren't you listening?"

"How appalling." Lanna addressed Cadel, who was fiddling with his beef Stroganoff, eyes downcast. "That lovely woman! Cadel, are you all right?"

Cadel nodded.

"Are you sure? You look so pale."

Again, Cadel nodded. He also closed his eyes. *Just shut up*, he thought. *Let's not go through this farce.*

"Leave him alone," Stuart growled. "Let him eat."

"But it's got to be a shock, Stuart. They should be bringing counselors onto the campus. Talking things through. Did you see any counselors today, Cadel?"

"Lanna, for god's sake, it's the *weekend*," Stuart snapped. "Nobody's *there* on the weekend."

"Cadel is."

Stuart snorted. Lanna turned back to Cadel. "Would you like me to call Thaddeus?" she asked. "Would you like to talk to him?"

"No," said Cadel.

"Are you sure?"

"Yes."

"Well, I think I'll call him, anyway," said Lanna. "They should be offering free counseling to all the staff and students. It's very important in situations like this. You need *professionals* to deal with the trauma."

"What trauma?" said Stuart. "He hardly knew the woman."

"Death touches us *all*, Stuart. It shakes up a person's sense of security. Thaddeus should know that. He should be calling up every student and seeing if they're all right. As a qualified psychologist, he should be on top of this. He should be proactive about reaching out."

Proactive. Suddenly Cadel couldn't take it anymore.

"If you're that unhappy with the institute," he snarled, "why don't I just leave?"

Mr. and Mrs. Piggott stared at him. Cadel watched their faces, his own a complete blank. *That's right,* he thought. *Deal with that, why don't you?*

"Leave the institute?" Lanna seemed at a loss. "Well, I—I—" She glanced at her husband, whose head sank down between his bulky shoulders as he thrust out his jaw ominously.

"You start something, you finish it," he rasped. "I've bloody paid your tuition, Cadel."

"Oh Stuart, he's just teasing." Lanna spoke lightly, but Cadel caught a flash of something in her eye: something hard and sharp. "He loves the institute, don't you, Cadel? He's just trying to get us all worked up, naughty thing." She wagged her finger playfully in Cadel's face. "If you don't like it, why are you spending so much time there?"

Cadel would have liked to say: *Because I don't have a choice.* But he couldn't. He had already gone too far.

He fell silent, just as another murder was announced on the news. The body of a man had been found dumped on the side of a road in Alexandria, at one o'clock that afternoon. He had been shot twice in the chest by a gun that was discovered beside the body. Occupants of a nearby hotel had heard the shots and had seen a car driving away from the crime scene. The car was later abandoned in Punchbowl.

It belonged to the murdered man, who was believed to have connections with "the notorious Max Fanciullo." *Mr. Fanciullo's former activities in organized crime,* the newsreader declared, *have long been the subject of investigation both in Australia and overseas. And next—sports with Steve. Good news for the Wallabies, eh, Steve?*

There was a long silence in the dining room, during which only the television spoke. Stuart said nothing. He didn't have to; Maestro Max had never used the name "Fanciullo" in any Axis Institute literature. Cadel, however, knew the name quite well. He had been fishing around in Max's computer files, after all. He knew a lot about Max.

What he didn't know was the identity of the man who had been killed. Who, among all of Max's "connections," could have been shot and thrown out of his own car?

Cadel laid down his fork and left the table.

He had a ghastly, panic-stricken feeling that the dead man might be a certain nearsighted forgery teacher.

The Axis Institute was finished. In Cadel's opinion, it couldn't go on—not with Tracey Lane dead, and Dr. Deal arrested. There would be inquiries. Investigations. Especially if Art was the man left dumped on the side of a road. Two employees of the same place had both been murdered: How could that not look suspicious?

Lying in bed, Cadel tried to put himself in Thaddeus's shoes. It was difficult, because Thaddeus was such an enigmatic sort of person, but Cadel did his best. He knew how convincing Thaddeus could be—how benign and reassuring. Thaddeus would no doubt blame Tracey's death on an "unfortunate domestic dispute." A crime of passion, perhaps. He would hold to that explanation no matter what Dr. Deal might say. In fact, Cadel wasn't sure what Dr. Deal *had* said. There were two reasons why the lawyer would have gone to the police: Either he'd wanted to confess everything about Axis or he'd wanted protection from Luther. Cadel considered both these possibilities. He was sure that if Dr. Deal had killed Tracey, he hadn't done it on purpose. No doubt he had beaten her up in a rage and killed her accidentally. No doubt his bloody fingerprints were everywhere. So what had been his options?

Perhaps, in days past, he would have asked the institute for help— before the incident of the envelope had placed him under suspicion. His talk with Adolf must have changed everything. It must have filled him with fear. Cadel didn't know how afraid the lawyer had been. *Very* afraid, to judge from his actions. Only someone terrified of Luther Lasco would have turned himself in to the police.

Of course, there was one other possibility. If Dr. Deal *was* a murderer, he might have been genuinely appalled by what he had done to

Tracey Lane. He might have believed that he deserved to be punished. Cadel couldn't discount this motive. After all, what did he really know about Dr. Deal? About anybody, in fact?

Nothing. All his calculations had been based on a big fat nothing.

So what should he do? Take flight at once? No, he decided—not yet. Not before destroying all his computers. Not before he had made sure about Art and taken care of Alias. If the Axis Institute shut down, then Alias might take care of himself; surely he would destroy all his records and disappear. But Cadel couldn't count on it. Not at this stage. It would be another day or so before he had enough data to make an informed decision about the fate of Axis.

Meanwhile, he would have to lie low. Proceed as usual. Attract no attention. Thaddeus would be very busy trying to maintain control and clean up all the mess. He wouldn't be able to spare much time for Cadel.

I'll go in tomorrow, thought Cadel. *The way I normally would. I'll pretend that it's business as usual while I check the network. Then, when I've got more data, I'll decide what to do.*

Having come to this conclusion, he promptly fell asleep. But it was a restless sleep. He dreamed of a small room with no windows; he dreamed that he was being chased through a forest at night. He also dreamed of Thaddeus and woke with a start, his heart pounding furiously. For a moment he was confused; he had an impression that Thaddeus was sitting beside him, in the darkness, watching him as he slept. When he reached out, however, there was no one. No one in the room.

So he fell asleep again.

At seven o'clock he was up and dressed and picking at a light breakfast. Not wanting to disturb the Piggotts (whose bedroom door was closed), he tiptoed around, wincing at the slap of the fridge door, the clink of cup against saucer, the clatter of cereal spilling into a bowl. The last thing he wanted was to be questioned by the Piggotts about his plans for the day.

At eight o'clock he left the house. By nine he was at the institute, admitting himself through the great iron gates. It had been raining all night, and the grounds were soggy; the seminary building seemed to brood beneath a lowering sky. There were only two cars in the lot, and one of them was Abraham's. Cadel's thoughts turned briefly to Gazo. He was concerned about Gazo. Without the institute, what would Gazo do?

Cadel saw no one on his way up to Hardware Heaven. The corridors and stairwells were empty. To his surprise, however, the lights were all blazing in the computer room—because Com was already there. Cadel wondered, not for the first time, if Com had stayed at the institute all night.

"Hi," he said, not expecting an answer. Com didn't so much as twitch an eyebrow. So Cadel went to his own machine and turned it on. Wearily, he tunneled his way into Dr. Vee's spy sweep, yawning and rubbing his eyes as he pushed through an endless series of locks and firewalls. He was very tired. He felt almost numb; hours of tension had worn the edge off his fear and despair.

I just don't care anymore, he thought.

But that was nonsense. Because as soon as he hit the unexpected, he sat up straight. He caught his breath. He leaned forward, peering at the screen. Had he missed something? Done something wrong?

No—it was blocked. The whole channel was down. For the first time, he simply could not get into the Führer's files.

"Dammit," he muttered, under his breath. At first he thought that something must be wrong with the spy sweep. Because he couldn't get into the Yarramundi security system, either. As Cadel ranged around the network, growing more and more nervous, he saw that the problem seemed to be with the Yarramundi data. None of it could be reached. None at all.

He was trying to isolate the problem, when he became aware of an irritating noise. Somewhere, far beyond the confines of Hardware Heaven, a telephone was ringing. And ringing. And ringing. Cadel ignored it at first. Only when he was toying with the idea of targeting the Yarramundi network through someone else's computer did it occur to him: The phone wasn't one phone. It was one phone after another. Slowly, room by room, the ringing was growing louder, as if someone was calling first one number, then the next, then the next, in a futile attempt to make contact with any member of staff who might be around.

Cadel listened. Sure enough, he heard the ringing stop briefly before starting again. It was quite close now. Unless he was mistaken, it was coming from Dr. Vee's office, which lay just beyond the stairwell.

Cadel counted the rings. Nine. Twelve. Fourteen. Then the noise stopped, for the space of about ten seconds.

Br-r-r-ing! Br-r-r-ing!

Though Cadel had been expecting it, he nevertheless jumped when the phone across the room began to trill. Com, of course, didn't move a muscle. He probably didn't even notice all the commotion.

Cadel got up. He was almost in a daze as he approached Dr. Vee's desk and lifted a sticky receiver from a nest of dirty tissues. He could smell eucalyptus oil.

"Hello?" he said.

"Oh god! Thank god! Who's that?"

"Uh—Cadel Darkkon." The voice on the other end of the line sounded frantic. Breathless. "Who am I speaking to?"

"Is Vee there? Is anyone *there*? My god, I need help! You must tell Vee—tell somebody—it's a bloodbath here!"

"What?"

"I don't know what to do! Thaddeus must come . . . oh god!"

Cadel gripped the receiver tightly. "What's happened?" he quavered. "Who is this?"

"I'm at Yarramundi. Tell somebody—tell them I'm here, it's an emergency, there's been—I don't know, some kind of explosion. The seals are down, the power's off."

"But what's *happened*?"

"Something bloody disastrous, that's what! There's no response from the guardhouse, there are cars out here but the intercom is down—it smells like a bloody blast furnace. Tell someone to *get out here now!*"

"Wait—hang on—there's nobody here." Cadel tried to smother his rising sense of panic. "It's Sunday morning. They're all at home."

Then Cadel heard a telltale noise. He turned, and his heart did a backflip.

Dr. Vee was walking through the door.

FORTY-SIX

"Oh—wait!" Cadel gasped. "Here's Dr. Vee! He's just come in!" Cadel thrust the receiver at the Virus. "It's someone calling from Yarramundi," he explained. "Something's wrong."

The Virus heaved an exasperated sigh. He was laden with heavy plastic bags, one of which seemed to be full of rattling pill bottles. His nose was so badly blocked that his voice sounded odd—all snubbed and sodden.

"What dow?" he groaned, as he dropped his load onto his desk. Then he took the receiver. "Yeah? Id's be . . . eh? You what?"

Cadel waited, gnawing at his fingernails. He saw Dr. Vee's face settling into a look of intense concentration, the muscles knotting, the jaw tightening. His eyes swiveled around to meet Cadel's, but not as if he had any message to convey. "Right . . . right . . . okay," he grunted. "Yeah, I'll find Thaddeus. Yeah. Chrisd, really? Okay." At last he signed off, putting the receiver down very gently. For a moment he and Cadel looked at each other.

"I know Thaddeus's cell phone number," Cadel said at last.

"So do I," the Virus retorted. His expression was grave; there were no more giggles. No more smirks.

"Who was it?" asked Cadel.

"Dobody impordand." Dr. Vee wiped his nose. "You waid here," he went on. "Dode boove. I'll be back."

For such a large, unwieldy person, he disappeared very quickly. Through the glass panels in the door, Cadel saw him cross the stairwell and dive into his office. Realizing that the coast was now clear, Cadel returned to his computer. He had left it connected to the spy sweep, so he had to pull out fast, before anyone noticed.

"What's wrong?" croaked a small, toneless voice. It was Com. Cadel looked up in surprise.

"Oh—well—I don't know. Exactly," he replied. "There's been some sort of accident. At Yarramundi. Some sort of explosion, or—or . . ." He trailed off, swallowing hard. But Com seemed unimpressed. He simply grunted and returned to his work.

Cadel decided to try Luther's phone. Just to make sure. To his dismay, he couldn't get through. A recorded voice informed him that the number he had tried to reach was "currently out of order."

"Cadel!" It was the Virus. He slapped open the door and leaned into the room. "Thaddeus wants you hobe."

"Home?"

"I just spoge to Thaddeus. He wants you to go hobe."

"But—"

"*Dow*, Cadel."

Clunk! The door swung shut again as Dr. Vee withdrew. Hurriedly, Cadel packed his bag. His hands were shaking; something, he knew, must be very, very wrong. On his way out, he stopped beside Com and tapped his classmate's shoulder.

"I've been ordered to go," he said.

"Hnn?"

"I've been told to go home. You might want to think about going home yourself." Cadel's voice was as unsteady as his hands. "It might not be very safe around here."

Com stared at Cadel as if he were mad. Then he turned back to his computer screen.

Cadel shrugged.

"Suit yourself," he muttered. He was already outside, halfway to the front gate, when he remembered Gazo. Should Gazo be warned? Would it be *safe* to knock on his door? Cadel was wary of displaying too much concern for Gazo. He wasn't supposed to have any friends—not according to Dr. Darkkon.

Maybe I can ask Gazo for a lift, Cadel thought, his pace slowing. There'd be nothing suspicious about that, would there?

And then he saw a very odd sight.

Beyond the high iron gate, two men were waving at him. He didn't recognize either of them. One was tall, with a big belly and gray hair. One was shorter, stocky and dark. They both wore suits.

Frowning, Cadel approached them cautiously.

"Hey, kid," said the big one, when Cadel was close enough to hear. "Is this the Axis Institute?"

Cadel nodded.

"There's no sign," the smaller one observed. He was quite young, with enormous brown eyes and glossy black hair. "We weren't sure if we had the right place."

"Are you a student here?" his companion inquired, whereupon Cadel nodded again. The two men exchanged glances.

"Well, we're police officers," said the smaller one, "and we're looking for a Mr. Paul Souvry. His mother said he works here—is that right?"

Cadel blinked. Paul Souvry was a name that Alias often used.

Why would the police be looking for *Alias*?

"What do you want with Mr. Souvry?" he finally asked, opening his eyes very wide. "What's he done?"

"That's what we have to find out." The big policeman had a relaxed, genial air about him. "You look pretty young to be studying here. How old are you, anyway?"

"Fifteen," Cadel lied.

"Yeah? I thought this place was a college, not a school."

Cadel eyed the two men, who would have towered over him if the bars of the gate hadn't intervened. "I'm on an escalated-learning program," he mumbled, uncertain of what he should do. How could he possibly leave without letting them in? Would he get into trouble if he did?

More importantly, did he *want* to let them in?

"An escalated-learning program," the younger policeman repeated. "That's pretty cool."

"Isn't this place supposed to be for problem kids?" asked his companion. "You don't look like a problem kid to me."

Cadel peered up at him warily from beneath a fringe of curls. "My problem is that I'm very intelligent," he said, and both men laughed.

"Yeah, that must be a problem," said the younger one.

"So what's your name then, Brainiac?" the older one wanted to know, and Cadel stiffened.

"Why?" he said.

"Well, we can't just keep on saying 'kid,' can we?"

"You haven't told me *your* names," Cadel pointed out.

"Haven't we? I'm sorry." The big one was teasing Cadel in a way that Cadel had always found annoying. Some people simply could not take him seriously, because he was so small. "I'm Bob, and this is Lou," the big man went on. "And we're looking for Mr. Souvry. Have you seen him this morning?"

"No," Cadel replied.

"Is he in there?"

"I don't know."

"Can you let us in, then? So we can have a look? His mum said he was at work."

Cadel hesitated. He glanced up at one of the cameras affixed to the gatepost. Lou followed his gaze.

"I don't know," Cadel said at last, confused by all these references to Alias's mum. As far as he knew, Alias didn't *have* a mum. According to Adolf's files, she had died more than ten years before. "I'd have to ask."

"Ask who?" Though Bob had the wide girth, cheerful voice, and pleasant manner of a department-store Santa Claus, there was something watchful about his eyes. "You mean there's someone in there we can talk to?"

"I don't know," Cadel replied, backing away. "I'll have to see."

"Kid, wait—"

"I don't want to get in trouble," Cadel explained, and turned on his heel.

"Hang on! What's your name? You didn't tell us!"

"Galileo!" Cadel shouted over his shoulder. Then he hurried back into the seminary building.

He was confused and nervous. Why were the police searching for Alias? Would it have done any good to talk to them? No, he decided— of course not. Not with all that surveillance equipment around. He couldn't afford to look suspicious. And letting the police into the institute would have looked highly suspicious.

Most of the staff offices were on the same floor as Hardware Heaven. Alias had been assigned a room between Art's and Dr. Deal's. When Cadel reached it, he saw with a start that the locks on Art's door had all been destroyed. One was punched out, one ripped apart, and one melted. He stood staring at them, his fist poised to knock.

Could this be Max's work?

"Cadel!" It was the Virus, emerging from his own office. "Whad the hell are you dooig? I thought I dold you to go hobe."

"The locks . . ."

"Whad?"

"Look. The locks."

Dr. Vee waddled over, frowning. He peered at the damage and sucked air through his teeth. Cautiously, he pushed the door open.

Art's room was a mess. Normally, he kept it very neat, but now there were papers strewn over the floor, drawers upended, coffee cups smashed. The stuffing had even been ripped out of the chairs.

Dr. Vee hissed again.

"There are police outside," Cadel informed him hesitantly. "They're looking for Alias."

Dr. Vee's head swung around. "'Alias'?" he echoed.

"I thought I should warn him, if he's around," Cadel went on, shrinking away from the Virus's hard stare. "I didn't think I should let them in, without asking—"

"Whad did they say?"

"They said . . ." Cadel tried to remember. "They said they wanted to talk to him. They said his mother told them he was here."

"His *buther*?" said Dr. Vee, his face contorted into an expression of utter bewilderment before it suddenly cleared. At the same moment, a neuron sparked somewhere in Cadel's head.

Of course! That hadn't been Alias's mother. That had been Alias himself. No doubt the police had arrived at his house and he had sent them off on a wild-goose chase. While he made his escape. Disguised as his own mother.

"All ride," growled Dr. Vee. "All ride, I'll dake care of id. You go."

"But how can I? If I leave, I'll let them in."

"Take the back gade." Dr. Vee was referring to the gate that led out of the parking lot. "Here," he said, fishing around in his shirt pocket. "You can borrow this parking permit—just swibe id when you ged there."

"But I've got a key-card—"

"Won't worg. You deed one of these."

"Oh!" Cadel recognized the piece of plastic that Dr. Vee was waving at him. He had seen it in the glove box of Abraham's Ford Cortina. "It's okay," he said, with a flash of inspiration. "I can get a lift. Gazo can give me a lift."

"Whadever," said the Virus. "Just ged *hobe*, for god's sake, or Thaddeus will ead me alive."

"Is he here, now?"

"Here? Of course nod! He's headig for Yarramundi! Cadel—"

"I know. I know. I'm going." Cadel dashed off down the corridor, which led to the dormitory wing. This had been shoved onto the back of the seminary building sometime in the nineteen sixties; it was a shabby structure, full of sprayed cement and leaking windows and ancient light fixtures. While Dr. Darkkon had poured money into the business side of the institute, he hadn't worried much about the comfort of boarders, especially when those boarders were so terribly destructive. They were always smashing glass and setting fires and kicking holes in doors and yanking electrical wiring out of wall sockets. Cadel hadn't been surprised, on first entering the dorms, to discover that they were grim and dreary and furnished with pieces of Salvation Army junk.

On this occasion—his second visit—he noted the number of empty rooms, open doors, and scorch marks. The whole place smelled of moldy carpet. Gazo's room was labeled. His name was scrawled on the door in marker pen.

"Gazo," said Cadel, rapping one finger against this name. "Are you there? It's me! Cadel!"

There was a *thump* from behind the door. Then Cadel heard Gazo's voice. "Cadel? Is that you?"

"Yes! I need a lift! Can you help me?"

"Oh—uh—hang on . . ."

More thumps. Cadel was forced to wait several minutes before the door was finally yanked open, to reveal the room beyond. Cadel had never seen Gazo's room before. He looked curiously at the single bed, draped in a grimy chenille cover; at the untidy desk, which was made out of concrete bricks and wooden planks; at the milk crates overflowing with dirty clothes, newspapers, old towels, and dog-eared textbooks. A rather nasty smell was hanging in the air.

"I had to get me suit on," Gazo panted. "Sorry."

"That's okay," said Cadel. "Can you give me a lift home?"

"Now?"

Cadel nodded.

Gazo looked pleased. "Sure," he said.

With Abraham's parking permit clutched in his soiled white glove assembly, Gazo locked up his room and followed Cadel down to the parking lot. They didn't see anyone on the way. Nevertheless, Cadel said nothing, and Gazo followed his lead. Outside, the air was damp; though it wasn't raining, the pavements gleamed with moisture. The Ford Cortina was beaded with droplets.

"You'll afta tell me the way," Gazo remarked, as he pulled open the driver's door. (Its lock, Cadel noticed, had not been repaired.) "Where do you live?"

"North Shore," Cadel replied. He climbed into the passenger seat next to Gazo and sat clutching his backpack while Gazo fiddled with various wires. He couldn't see the front gate from the parking lot. He couldn't see what the police were doing.

He couldn't see any Grunts around, either.

"Right," said Gazo, raising his voice over the sound of the engine, which had suddenly roared into life. "North Shore it is." Though the Ford was a heap of junk, Gazo drove it surprisingly well, swinging out of the lot and guiding it through the back gate much more efficiently than Abraham ever had. He even seemed to know the road rules.

Cadel looked at him with growing respect.

"You *can* drive," said Cadel.

"Course." Gazo returned his look. "What's wrong? Are you sick or somefink?"

Cadel stared out the window. "Haven't you heard?" he said.

"Eh?"

"Tracey's dead. Tracey Lane. Didn't you know?"

"You what?" Gazo said stupidly. He jerked at the gearshift, which made a clunking noise.

"Dr. Deal's in police custody," Cadel continued, in a toneless voice. "The police were at the gate this morning, asking for Alias. And something's wrong at Yarramundi. Something's exploded."

"Exploded?"

"Or leaked. Or brought the whole place down. I don't know what's happened. There's a lot of people missing. It's a real mess."

"Christ," Gazo murmured. He drove along in silence for a while before asking the question that Cadel had been dreading.

"Do you think," he said, "it's because we—"

"Don't ask me," Cadel interrupted. He emphasized the word *ask* rather than the word *me* in the hope that Gazo would get the message. They couldn't talk about the envelope; the car might be bugged. "I don't know what's going on."

"Where's Thaddeus? Has someone called him?"

"The Virus did. Thaddeus is heading for Yarramundi right now."

"Oh."

There was another long pause. Gazo seemed to be thinking. Cadel told him what road to take, and he followed the directions automatically. At last, Cadel cleared his throat.

"I think something's happened to Luther," he said. "And Adolf." He fixed his compelling stare on Gazo, who must have caught it out of the corner of his eye, because he shifted uneasily. "God knows what's happened to all the computer files," Cadel added. "We'll find out soon enough, I suppose. My guess is that they've been blown up."

"Really?"

"Things are a bit chaotic," Cadel went on, gazing intently at Gazo. "If I were you, I'd keep a low profile. A *very* low profile. In fact . . ." Cadel hesitated. Should he or shouldn't he? But it was a fairly harmless suggestion, under the circumstances. "I'd keep on my toes. In case you have to leave in a hurry."

They stopped at a traffic light. Gazo turned to look at Cadel through his mask. Beyond him, the car beside them was full of staring faces. Cadel could lip-read the child in the backseat, who was pointing at Gazo. "A spaceman!" he was saying. "A spaceman, mummy!"

"You fink it's gonna get that bad?" Gazo said quietly. Studying his half-concealed face, Cadel realized, with a surge of relief, that he understood what Cadel was trying to say. Thank god!

392

"I don't know," said Cadel. "I'm just warning you. Be prepared. Things could get sticky." Sticky enough to allow Gazo a means of escape. If Luther was dead, and Adolf's files were destroyed, then Gazo might have a chance. "The light's changed, by the way."

Gazo grunted, and the car lurched forward. They were over the Harbor Bridge now, and heading north.

"But what'll I do if I can't live at the institute?" Gazo asked carefully. "I mean, what should I do?"

"Get a job at a dump," Cadel suggested. "A sewage plant. Someplace like that." Someplace smelly.

"But they wouldn't hire me."

"Yes, they would. You went to forgery class. I bet you could forge the right references." Cadel watched Gazo turning things over in his head. "And you've got this car, remember," Cadel added. "This car must be worth something."

"The car. Yeah. But—"

"I'd get rid of it, if I were you," Cadel added. He hoped that Gazo understood. He thought he probably did, judging from the glance that flashed across the car. Abraham's Ford could be traced. If Gazo kept it, he would be risking discovery.

"Right," said Gazo, and nodded.

"Turn here. First left. It's quicker."

They didn't talk again until they had reached the tall green hedge and the stone gateposts that marked the entrance to Cadel's house. Gazo parked but didn't switch off the engine. He turned in his seat and looked Cadel full in the face.

"What are you gonna do?" he asked gravely. "If the institute shuts down?"

"Oh, *I'll* be all right," said Cadel. "I'm the crown prince, remember?"

"Are you sure? Because—"

"I'm sure." Cadel spoke firmly. "Bye, Gazo." He didn't want to extend this conversation, which was already perilously close to being

393

emotional. As he extracted himself from the car, however, he added, "Thaddeus will probably sort things out. But just in case he doesn't— well, take care."

"Cadel . . ."

"What?" Cadel was becoming impatient. "What is it?"

"I could hang around, if you want me to." Gazo's tone was hesitant. "Maybe, if fings do get sticky, you shouldn't be on your own."

"I'll be fine." Cadel realized that Gazo was still at a complete loss. He didn't know what to do with himself. "I told you. Thanks for the lift, Gazo."

"I'll give you a call, okay?"

"Better not." What did the silly fool think he was doing? "Bye, now."

"Wait!" Gazo put out one gloved hand. "Wait. Cadel, I can't just go off like this . . ."

"Why not?"

"Well . . . I mean . . ." Behind his mask, Gazo was turning red. He seemed flustered. "No offense, but you're just a little kid. You shouldn't be on your own. Not wiv all this stuff going down."

"What are you talking about?" Cadel was genuinely astonished. "I told you, I'm fine."

"Yeah, but—"

"Please, Gazo. The best thing you can do is disappear. I mean it." Slamming the door, Cadel lifted his hand. "Bye!" he said.

For a few seconds, Gazo didn't move. Then slowly, reluctantly, he pulled away from the curb. With a rattle and cough, the old Ford veered onto the road again. Cadel watched it disappear around a corner. When he was sure that it had gone, he trudged up the driveway between walls of camellia bushes, toward the house. He noticed that Mrs. Ang's car was parked near the front door. *Good*, he thought. *Maybe she'll get me a hot lunch.*

"Mrs. Ang!" he called, wiping his feet on the mat. There was no reply. He unlocked the front door and pushed it open, his eyes adjust-ing to the dimness beyond. He could smell something funny.

"Mrs. Ang?"

The hand came out of nowhere. Cadel didn't have time to scream. He felt as if he was about to suffocate.

And then he fell.

FORTY-SEVEN

Cadel woke up vomiting.

He hadn't fully regained consciousness, and already he was retching and heaving, hanging over the edge of whatever he was lying on. A bed, perhaps? No—a mattress on the floor. He felt horribly sick. And his head ached.

"Ah, Jesus," said a disgusted voice.

"Clean him up," said another.

"He's puked all over the sheets—"

"Then get some more! Chris'sake, whassa matter wit you?"

Cadel drifted off again. He was vaguely aware of being moved and wiped. He groaned because his head was hurting. But it seemed like a long while later that he finally became conscious of a smell like disinfectant, and then a scratchy feeling beneath his cheek, and a weight on his legs. . . .

He opened his sticky eyes. The pain in his head, which had been lying dormant, abruptly sprang to life; it was like having an ice pick thrust through his skull. He rolled over, moaning, and realized that he still felt nauseous. Yes, he was going to throw up. When he raised himself on one elbow, the feeling grew worse. But there was a bucket. Someone had put a bucket beside the mattress.

He almost burst a blood vessel, bringing up what was left in his stomach. There wasn't much. As he hawked and strained, a large person appeared beside him. Cadel saw two shiny black shoes. A pair of trouser cuffs. A hairy hand, reaching down.

"You finished?" the man asked.

Cadel nodded, and was pulled back onto the bed. Through a haze of pain, he saw a broad, dark back and a bald head retreating.

"My head hurts," he croaked. "Please . . ."

"I'll get you some aspirin."

The aspirin arrived some time later. Cadel had dropped off to sleep again and was roused by someone flicking his cheek.

"Here." The same hairy hand offered him a glass of cloudy water. "I dissolved 'em."

Cadel sat up. He drank the contents of the glass, which the man beside him held to his lips. The man was vaguely familiar. Cadel tried to remember where he had seen that broken nose before.

"What happened?" he said faintly. "I feel so sick . . ."

"Drugs," came the blunt reply. Before Cadel could properly absorb this information, his companion had disappeared. A door slammed. Cadel fell back onto his pillow, holding his head.

Every heartbeat was hammering a bolt of pain into his temples. But beneath that steady rhythm, his brain was beginning to work. He knew that face. Of course he did.

It belonged to one of Max's bodyguards.

A pang of fear shot through him. He uncovered his eyes and surveyed his surroundings anxiously. He was lying in a concrete room. There was a toilet in the room, and a basin. Also a mattress and a heater. Exposed pipes. The glass of water had been taken away.

There was no window. The walls were streaked with rusty stains, and the door was made of metal.

Cadel closed his eyes again, massaging his forehead. He tried to think. He had walked into his house, and—what? Someone had jumped him. Stuck something over his face. A rag soaked in chloroform? But that wouldn't have knocked him out for very long. And where had Adolf's Grunts been? Why hadn't they saved him?

Cautiously, Cadel opened his eyes again. The light was on. He slowly sat up, wincing with every movement. His mouth was dry, and he smelled of vomit. Some of his hair was plastered to his cheek. He was examining his arms for needle marks when the door creaked open.

Maestro Max stood on the threshold, wearing a silk suit under his beautifully tailored overcoat. He closed the door softly behind him and walked with a heavy tread to the toilet. The lid was down. Removing a laundered handkerchief from his breast pocket, he gave the lid a bit of a wipe before lowering his bulk onto it.

He sat with a hand on each knee, his smooth jaw shining in the electric light.

For a long while, he and Cadel simply stared at each other.

At last the Maestro sighed. "So," he said. "You ain't gonna ask me nuttin?"

Cadel remained silent. He couldn't have spoken; his voice wouldn't have worked.

"No questions?" the Maestro continued. "No? Okay. What about I ask *you* some questions?" His morose brown gaze held Cadel's. "Like, for instance—you tink I'm stoopid? You and your papa?"

Swallowing, Cadel shook his head.

"You didn't tink I'd work it out, huh?" said Max, and leaned forward. "Listen to me—I *always* knew. Right from the start, I was wondering: What's dis all about? Uh? You get all your competitors, dey come together in the same place. What for? To raise an army? I don't tink so. To wipe 'em out? Maybe. To get 'em to wipe each *udder* out? Even better." The Maestro settled back again. Every movement was slow and deliberate, almost as if he was tired. "At foist I figured: Okay, Carla's dead, big deal. Coulda happened to anyone. Then I get ripped off. No problem. One little ass-wipe, what's it matter? So I go after 'im. What happens? My guy ends up dead. A little boid in the police department tells me de gun was bought yesterday, by someone called Paul Souvry. I'm tinking: What de hell? I'm looking for Art, and Alias bought de gun? Den I hear Tracey's been wiped. Barry Deakin's turned himself in. My guys are checking Art's office, middla last night, and dey see Terry loading up a van. Dey see one of Adolf's teams jump 'im. Haul 'im off to Yarramundi. Next ting I hear, dat whole place has gone up. Luther's been fighting wit Adolf, and dey've brought the whole goddamn building down. Now Adolf's gone. Luther, too. Might be dead, might be on the run. Who knows? Carla's dead. Tracey's dead. And Terry—he was in dere with the rest of 'em. So where is he now? Deal's as good as dead. Art's disappeared. What am I supposed to believe? It was all self-inflicted? I don't tink so."

Cadel simply stared, his arms wrapped around his chest. He was hardly breathing.

"I'm starting to tink: Someting's going on," the Maestro observed, wearily. "I'm starting to tink: Who's left? I am, but, hey, it's nuttin to do with me, right?"

Cadel wondered what the time was. He glanced at his wrist but his watch wasn't there anymore.

"I figured it was probably all wired up," said Max, following the direction of Cadel's gaze. "So I trew it under a train. If you wanna know, it's 6:15. Sunday night."

While Cadel kept his expression blank, his heart missed a beat. Sunday night! But he had promised Sonja. He had summoned her to the pool.

She would think that he had stood her up!

"Den I talked to Vee," Max went on. "Tracked him down dis evening. Turns out, he's as confused as I am. Says you've been hacking into all de computers for months, but when he told Thaddeus, Thaddeus didn't do a goddamn ting about it." Watching Cadel, Max must have seen his color change, or his breathing alter. A mournful smile tugged at the corner of his mouth. "Didn't know dat, uh? Guess not. Anyway, I let Vee go. It was a trade-off. He gave me his information; I gave him back his pinky finger. Man like dat—he's too useful to waste. Bit like you, Cadel."

399

All at once, Max rose. He began to walk toward the mattress. Cadel shied away, his heart pounding furiously.

"See, I figured it all out," the Maestro declared in a conversational tone. "Like I said, I'm not stoopid. You're Darkkon's son. You're Roth's blue-eyed boy. You're part of de whole setup. Somehow, you and your papa—and dat asshole Roth—you've been setting us all up. Getting us to do each udder in, while you sit back and let it happen."

"No," Cadel squeaked, shaking his head. "No, you're wrong."

"I don't tink so." Max loomed over the bed, blinking lazily down at Cadel in a way that terrified him. "I tink dey sent you in because you're such a goddamn little choirboy. Who's gonna suspect you? Nobody. Nobody except me."

"No!" Cadel cried. "You're making a mistake! It's all been a mistake! This has nothing to do with you—"

"Oh, sure." Max bent down until his grave and tranquil eyes were level with Cadel's. He smelled of cigars. "Kid, you might be able to fool everyone else, batting dose baby blues, but you're not fooling me. I know what dis is all about. And I know how to cover my back." He straightened. "As long as I got *you*, I'm safe. Because if Darkkon lifts one finger against me, he's gonna start getting little bits of you in de mail."

Cadel pressed his lips together, trying to stop them from shaking. Max must have seen this, because he smiled suddenly. It was the most bloodcurdling smile that Cadel had ever seen.

"Enjoy batting dose eyes while you can," he said, and turned toward the door. "Eh! Tommy!"

Immediately, the door opened. Baldie looked in.

"Yeah?"

"Kid's probably hungry," said Max. "Get 'im a drink—someting to eat."

"Okay."

The bald head withdrew.

Max regarded Cadel in a melancholy fashion. "Kid like you—you gotta lotta potential," he sighed. "Why'd you trow it all away?"

He shook his head sadly. Then he left the room.

Clank! Clunk!

The door swung shut and the locks clamped down.

FORTY-EIGHT

Cadel couldn't believe it.

He couldn't believe that this was happening. He couldn't believe that he had never even remotely anticipated anything so awful. Where had he gone wrong? Why hadn't he calculated the probabilities?

Because he hadn't collected enough data—that was why. The institute was a big and complicated place. He had tried to cobble together estimates without mastering the raw facts. He had rushed into things because he was desperate to leave. And now? Now he was paying for sloppy preparation.

He hadn't meant to bring down the whole institute. His intentions had been far more modest. If his plan had been successful—if only a handful of staff had been affected—then Max would never have panicked. And Cadel would never have ended up locked in this . . . this *dungeon*.

He looked around, wondering where he was. Underground, almost certainly. The whole place had a musty underground smell to it. And he had caught a brief glimpse of the area outside the door, had seen a flight of stairs going up. Some of the plumbing that ran around the walls was old and disconnected; it looked as if there had been a shower, or something similar, to match the toilet and basin still huddled against one wall. Could he be lying in an old bathroom? Or in an old locker room, perhaps?

Click! Clunk! As Cadel looked around, the door swung open. In came the bald man with the broken nose (Tommy, Max had called him) carrying a packet of chips and a small carton of fruit juice. He threw them on the floor and left, before Cadel could say anything.

Cadel didn't feel like eating. But he drank the juice, wondering if he could use the small, plastic straw that came with it. One end of the straw had been sharpened, so that he could poke it through the foil seal in the top of the box. Poking it through a seal, however, was different from poking it into somebody's eye—the only place where it would do any damage.

Cadel doubted that he would ever get anywhere near Tommy's eye. For one thing, he was about half the man's height. He doubted that he would be able to reach that far before being batted away like a pesky mosquito. And if he did poke Tommy in the eye, what then? It was hardly the kind of injury that would prevent Tommy from using his large, hairy fists or his enormous feet.

No, he would have to think of something else.

His headache had dulled a little, thanks to the aspirin, so he was able to study his surroundings without hurting his eyes, noting every little feature. The ceiling was high; he would never be able to reach that lightbulb, even if he stood on the mattress. The taps on the sink had been removed. The heater was an electric oil-heater, plugged into the wall. Hmm. If he was to dismantle that heater . . .

But he didn't have anything to dismantle it *with*. That was the problem. They had taken everything: his bag, his keys, his watch—even his shoes. The mattress was made of foam rubber, so it didn't have any inner springs. The old-fashioned toilet cistern was placed high on the wall, out of Cadel's reach, and it didn't have a chain hanging from it— just a frayed piece of string.

Max had obviously been very careful.

Cadel fell back onto his pillow. He felt ill and tired. His brain wasn't working as well as usual. Think, he chided himself. Think, think, think! You're supposed to be a genius, so prove it!

But his mind kept wandering. Even as he scanned the pipes, he found himself wondering why Thaddeus hadn't come to his rescue.

Why, for example, hadn't Adolf's surveillance Grunts stopped Max? Because they had been pulled off Cadel's tail when things started happening at Yarramundi? Because Max had killed them? Because they had been keeping an eye on Cadel, not his house, and didn't realize that Max had been waiting for him in there?

Perhaps Thaddeus didn't even know that Cadel was missing yet. He'd know soon, though. Max was using Cadel to protect himself. *Leave me alone, or the boy gets it.*

Would Max decide to send Thaddeus a little piece of proof? A finger, perhaps? A toe? To show that he was serious?

As soon as this possibility occurred to Cadel, he leaped off the mattress and hurried over to the exposed plumbing. Several pipes emerged from the wall, wandered along it a little way (dividing several times as they did so), and then plunged back into the concrete, vanishing from sight. All of them had been painted over, like the rest of the room, but the paint was flaking. When Cadel tried to pull one of them off the wall, bits of dry paint fluttered onto his sweater and caked under his fingernails.

He tugged and jerked, but nothing much happened. While the pipe did rattle and move slightly, parts of it seemed fused to the wall. Perhaps the layers of old paint were acting like a weld. Or perhaps there were brackets, rusting into the concrete, which held the pipe in place.

If only he had something hard, like a hammer. But then, if he had a hammer, he wouldn't need a piece of pipe. He could hit Tommy with the hammer.

Cadel wrenched at the pipe as hard as he could and managed only to hurt himself. When he sucked the injured finger, he got a mouthful of dry paint. Knowing that the paint was probably full of poisonous lead, he quickly spat it out. And then he noticed something.

Where he'd scraped the paint away, the exposed metal wasn't grayish galvanized iron. It was greenish copper.

Copper.

From that point on, Cadel ceased to notice his headache. His mind began to work; his gaze hopped from the pipe to the heater and back again. He made a mental list of what was available in the room: a chip bag, a pillow, a duvet, a mattress, a small juice carton. And there were his clothes, of course. His sweater was made of wool (curse it), and his pants of cotton, but his shirt was polyester. And his socks were mostly nylon.

Glancing at the door, he wondered if anyone was watching him. He couldn't see a window, or even a peephole. Nor could he see any evidence of cameras—no wiring, no cable ducts. There was just the one electrical socket, with a heater plugged into it.

The heater's cord was a long one. Moreover, it was insulated, not by plastic but by old-fashioned textile, which was frayed in some places. Of course, the wires inside would be plastic-coated, but Cadel was still pleased. He ticked a mental box before returning to the mattress and making a feeble attempt to pull it toward the heater. Having dragged it across the floor a short distance, he pretended to give up. Instead, he went back to the heater, which he turned off at the power point. Then he pushed the heater closer to the mattress and untangled its knotted electric cord, surreptitiously wrapping the cord around a copper pipe. By digging his fingernails into the fabric insulation wrapped around the cord, he managed to tear some of it away, exposing the multicolored wires underneath. But that wouldn't be enough.

The trick was to wind the cord as tightly as possible, stretching it dangerously and damaging the plastic insulation, to ensure that every wire was clamped against metal. He had to act quickly, too, because someone might be watching. With a final tug, he dropped the cord and turned the heater back on. Then he scrambled back under his duvet, where, concealed by its heavy folds, he picked away at its stitching—*and* at the stitching of his pillow. He wanted to get at the stuffing, which was probably made of polyester. Fluffy, flammable polyester. There was his mattress, as well: The foam might burn, or at least melt.

He didn't know how long it took him to rip open the duvet. Without a watch, he couldn't be sure. Fifteen minutes? Twenty minutes?

The pillow took longer, because the workmanship was better. As for the mattress, that was a real test. He yanked and gnawed away at it for ages. At last, having done as much as he dared, he opened the chip bag and ate about a third of its contents. He didn't want to eat it all, though by now he was quite hungry. He couldn't afford to waste all that oil by stuffing it down his throat.

Not once did he allow his gaze to linger on the power cord. Sometimes he would glance around the room, and on these occasions, he would check the spot where the cord was coiled around the copper pipe. He made sure, however, that he paid more attention to the toilet, or the door, or the light fixture. Anywhere but that nasty little time bomb, which didn't have a fuse.

For all his calculations, he was uncertain when the short would occur—if, indeed, it occurred at all. He wasn't even sure what time it was. How long had it been since Max's visit? Two hours, perhaps? A little more? Time was irrelevant here in his dungeon. It could be the middle of the night, for all he knew.

Sonja could have been waiting for hours and hours. Waiting and hoping . . .

Finally, he had to go to the toilet. He didn't have a choice. The toilet flushed when he pulled the dangling string; almost immediately afterward, Tommy stuck his head into the room.

"You all right?" he rasped, as Cadel fumbled desperately with the zipper on his fly. "You been sick?"

"No, I—"

"Pissing?"

"Yes."

"Okay."

"Wait!" cried Cadel, because Tommy was shutting the door. "I'm thirsty! Can I have a drink? I've finished the first one."

In reply, another box of juice sailed into the room, hitting the floor at the same instant the locks clicked into place. Obviously, there was a pile of juice boxes right outside the door. A pile of chips, too, probably. Cadel wondered if they were intending to feed him nothing but chips and juice.

Then he smelled it.

He looked around before he could stop himself. Sure enough, the cord was turning brown. An oily drift of smoke was followed by a small, hot, orange flicker. . . .

Cadel dashed for his pillow. He plucked out a wad of polyester fluff, which he placed on the melting insulation. The fluff caught alight immediately. Cadel dropped it on the ground. He emptied the rest of the pillowcase, allowing the drifts of fluff to pile up and start burning. He added the contents of the duvet, slowly, so as not to smother any shooting flames. To his disappointment, the duvet stuffing didn't burn as well as the pillow stuffing. (Could it have been treated with fire retardant?) When he added the chips, however, he got a better result. The pillowcase, too, was threadbare enough to burn well. But his socks were so sweaty, they didn't have quite the effect that he'd expected.

He began to tear up the duvet cover, coughing as the smoke tickled his throat and stung his eyes. The smell was awful. The fumes were probably dangerous. By the time he threw his shirt onto the fire, it was good and hot, though the fabric burned slowly, emitting a lot of smoke. Paint flakes helped, as did the chip bag, which was slick with oil. The mattress stuffing, however, was hard to tear up. Cadel struggled with it furiously before finally peeling back the cover and pushing a corner of the foam into the flames. To his surprise, it went up like barbecue bricks. What sort of people manufactured a mattress stuffing that caught fire so quickly? The mattress cover, on the other hand, wouldn't cooperate at all. When Cadel held it to the flames, it was barely singed. So he discarded it.

"Help!" he cried. He had to hurry—he didn't have much fuel. He was just heading for the door, coughing furiously, when a sharp *crack* startled him. Turning, he saw an awe-inspiring sight.

The heater was ablaze.

Evidently, there must have been a faulty weld in the heater—an oil leak, in other words. Cadel was just beginning to calculate probabilities (would the machine actually explode?) when he heard the sound of a key in a lock.

"What's going on?" a gruff voice demanded.

Cadel collapsed to the floor, gasping and retching. The room was already full of the most vile-smelling smoke; behind him, the heater's metal sheath was making alarming noises. Suddenly, the light went off.

"What the hell—," exclaimed Tommy, as he stepped into the room. By now, Cadel was lying facedown on the floor. Tommy stooped down to touch him. "Are you all right?" the big man coughed. "Oh, for Chris'sake . . ."

"What's going on?" a distant voice called, and Cadel's heart skipped a beat. There was another one! Damn it!

"Get the extinguisher!" yelled Tommy, coughing.

"What?"

"Get the extinguisher!" As the fire crackled, fed by a draft from the open door, Tommy hauled Cadel out of the room and dropped him onto the floor outside. Cadel kept his eyes shut, and his mouth open. He heard feet thundering down the stairs beside him.

"Here!" someone panted.

"Give it to me," snapped Tommy.

"What the hell?"

"How do you work this thing?"

Cadel lifted his eyelid a fraction. Two pairs of legs were lined up in front of him. He saw one advance, disappearing back into the smoky dungeon. The other pair seemed to hesitate. It stopped in the doorway.

"What are you—*cough, cough*—doing?" the owner of these legs demanded.

"It doesn't work!" his mate replied.

"Pull the pin!"

"I did!"

"No, not like that, like this. Here . . ."

As soon as the second pair of legs followed the first, Cadel lurched to his feet. He flew up the stairs, desperately gulping down tainted air, and reached the top to find himself in an enormous room. A vast, cavernous space. In the split second available to him, Cadel caught a glimpse of windows high up near a lofty ceiling . . . a gigantic piece of machinery, bolted to the floor . . . double doors, with an EXIT sign over them . . . a switchbox . . . a fire alarm . . . a hard hat . . . a pair of plastic chairs . . . a table with playing cards on it . . . a steel thermos and two mugs . . .

But someone had heard his fleeing footsteps.

"Hey!"

A large weight was pounding up the stairs. Cadel hardly had time to think. He dashed to the table, grabbed the thermos, and bolted across the room to the fire alarm. Then he smashed the glass with the thermos and slapped at the alarm button.

A high-pitched siren began to sound. It was deafening.

"Little *shit!*" screamed Tommy's mate, charging Cadel like a rabid rhinoceros. Cadel ducked and dodged the man's flailing fist. Screaming, "Help! Help!" he ran toward the exit, slipped, recovered, and threw himself onto the double doors. As he yanked at the handle, someone grabbed his hair from behind and pulled.

He shrieked.

"It's locked, ya moron!" Tommy's mate roared, stamping hard on Cadel's bare foot.

The pain was excruciating. Cadel sank to his knees, writhing in agony.

"What are you doing?" Tommy demanded, from nearby—Cadel wasn't sure where. "Don't hurt him, are you crazy?"

"I was just—"

"Shut off that goddamn alarm!"

Even now, Cadel could smell smoke. He was lying on the floor, groaning and holding his foot, his ears ringing. He wore nothing but a pair of brown cords.

Someone grabbed his arm and hoisted him upright.

"It's your own stupid fault, kid," said Tommy grimly. "Con, will you *shut off* that *alarm?*"

"I'm trying to!" came the frantic reply, pitched loud over the siren's wail. "Tell me how!"

"Oh, for Chris'sake . . ."

"We gotta get out of here!"

Tommy turned to Cadel, giving him a shake.

"Can *you* turn this off?" he growled. Through tear-filled eyes, Cadel saw that Tommy's own eyes were bloodshot. His nose and cheeks were purple. His scars stood out vividly on his flushed, bald head.

He looked terrifying.

"Tommy, we gotta go!" Con insisted. *"Now."*

"You'll pay for this, you little shit," said Tommy. His hand moved from Cadel's arm and grabbed a handful of curly dark hair. "You better keep quiet," he warned, thrusting his face into Cadel's, "or I'll cut out your tongue."

Thump! Thump! Thump!

It was the sound of a knock on the big, double doors.

Tommy froze, still clutching Cadel's hair.

"Hello!" said a woman's muffled voice. "Is anybody there?"

Tommy gestured to Con. Then he pointed at something else—the opposite wall. Now that the pain in his foot was subsiding, Cadel could see that he was in some sort of factory or warehouse. An abandoned print-shop, perhaps? And there was another exit. A back way out.

Tommy was pointing at the back way.

"Oh my god," cried the woman's voice. "Smell it. Can you smell it?"

"Smoke," said another voice—the trembling voice of an elderly man.

"There *is* a fire. You'd better phone the fire department."

They must have been standing right outside the double doors, because someone began to jiggle the handle. But these particular doors were locked. Tommy started to move away, dragging Cadel with him.

As he did so, Cadel realized why the woman's voice sounded vaguely familiar.

It belonged to Wilfreda. He was sure of it.

"It's locked," she yelled, straining to be heard over the keening alarm. Con unlocked the rear exit door and pushed it open cautiously. He had drawn a gun from somewhere beneath his jacket.

Tommy tucked Cadel under his arm, as if carrying a bunch of spinach or a stuffed toy. Cadel was too frightened and confused to put up any kind of fight. He could hardly even see, through his tears. He was aware of passing over a threshold into the night air; of Con, up ahead, fumbling with the lock of a dark-colored car, its shiny finish reflecting the golden glow of a streetlight; of Tommy stopping suddenly, with a jerk.

A shot rang out. Con spun away from the dark car's open door and crumpled to the pavement. Then Cadel hit the ground, too—dropped like a stone.

"Ooof!" he said.

But someone swung him up again almost before he knew what had happened. Struggling feebly, he was half carried, half dragged toward another car. When he protested, he was told to calm down.

"It's all right," said a strange voice. "You're safe now."

Next thing, he was climbing onto leather-upholstered seats. Someone was offering him a sweatshirt and saying, "Here. You must be cold." Clutching the sweatshirt dazedly, he peered into the night. There were *three* cars, all told, and twice as many people—shadowy figures Cadel didn't recognize. Beyond them he could just make out a narrow alley between high brick walls. The asphalt looked slick and sticky. Everyone was talking in muted accents, though the alarm was still wailing. Cadel heard a car door slam before a large form suddenly heaved itself into the driver's seat in front of him.

It was Wilfreda.

"Hello," she said, looking back. Her face was in shadow, so he couldn't make out her expression. *Whump!* went her door.

He gaped at her, unable to speak.

"It's all right now," she informed him, turning her ignition key. "No need to worry anymore."

Around them, the other cars were also starting their engines. One began to move, gathering speed quickly.

But Wilfreda seemed to be waiting for something—or someone.

Cadel found out who, when Thaddeus Roth slid into the backseat, next to him.

"All right, Wilfreda," the psychologist said calmly. "Let's go."

FORTY-NINE

Cadel's guts seemed to dissolve. He experienced an overwhelming sense of relief and gratitude, even though, at the same time, a warning bell was sounding in his brain. As their car split away from the convoy, purring off down a side street, Cadel stared up at the familiar beaky nose and hollow cheeks. The gleam of the streetlights, as they whizzed past, wove a flickering pattern on one side of the psychologist's face.

"Th-Thaddeus," he stammered.

"Put that top on, Cadel," Thaddeus replied quietly. "You don't want to get cold."

Obediently, Cadel pulled the sweatshirt down over his head. It was far too big for him. Thaddeus began to roll the sleeves up, with neat, practiced movements.

"How did you know where I was?" asked Cadel faintly.

"Give me a little credit, dear boy."

"They jumped me at the house—"

"Yes. Gazo told me."

"*Gazo* told you?"

"I don't know what you've done to that fellow, Cadel, but he's positively smitten." Thaddeus sounded amused. "Apparently, after he dropped you off at the Piggotts', he had second thoughts. Went back to check on you, he said. Found the remains of the housekeeper. Came tearing out to Yarramundi to raise the alarm. Knew I was there, for some reason." A ghost of a chuckle. "Not a tool that *I* would have chosen, but he's proven to be of some use."

"It was Max," said Cadel, rambling a bit. "He was scared."

"I'm aware of that."

"What happened? I thought I was being followed . . ."

"Grunts will be Grunts," said Thaddeus in chillingly flat tones. "It comes of sending a moron to do a man's work. They parked outside your house and watched you go in. When Max arrived to pick you up, they let him walk right up to their car, the idiots. Didn't think he was any kind of threat. Naturally, they got a couple of shots between the eyes as a result." Thaddeus placed a gentle hand on Cadel's curls before declaring, without expression, "At least they got what they deserved."

Cadel wasn't shocked. He didn't have the energy. Instead he began to shiver; he couldn't seem to stop. He felt the weight of Thaddeus's hand leave his head and an arm tighten around his shoulders.

"You're all right," said Thaddeus.

"I'm c-c-cold."

"It's the shock." Thaddeus struggled out of his jacket, which he draped around Cadel's hunched form. "Here. Is that better?"

"I used my shirt for the fire," Cadel went on, his words and thoughts both strangely sluggish. "I lit a fire . . ."

"But of course you did. I'd have expected nothing less."

After that, Cadel subsided. He even dozed off. When he woke up, he found himself draped across the psychologist's lap. The car was still moving.

"Where are we?" he mumbled, struggling upright.

"Nearly there," said Thaddeus.

"Nearly where?"

"Nearly at my house."

Something clenched inside Cadel's stomach. He squinted out of the window but saw only darkness. Then all at once the car swerved. It left the smooth asphalt and bounced onto something rough. Cadel could hear gravel crackling under the tires.

They were on a curved driveway. Cadel saw it spotlit by their headlights, which also swept across low bushes, flicked past tree trunks, and finally came to rest on a large, two-story house with a lot of shining windows. The engine died. Thaddeus opened the door beside him.

"You can get out now, Cadel," he said.

Clumsily, Cadel struggled out of the car after Thaddeus. As soon as his bare feet touched the gravel, he became aware of a salty smell and a rhythmic hissing noise.

"What's that sound?" he gasped.

"The sea," said Thaddeus.

Cadel froze. The sea! Why were they at the sea? He looked around in sudden fear, unable to penetrate the darkness encroaching on all sides. Were they at the edge of a *cliff*?

He took a step backward.

"Cadel, Cadel." Thaddeus leaned toward him, placing one long, thin hand against his cheek. "What's wrong? You're not afraid of me, are you?" And he laughed a soft laugh that made Cadel's skin crawl.

"I—I want to go home," Cadel whimpered.

"Home?" Thaddeus straightened; his hand dropped. "What home? Oh, you mean that silly-looking house where James Guisnel and Sue Croft live? I'm afraid that's out of bounds for the moment, Cadel. Until we clean up the mess. Mrs. Ang was there, you see. When Max's men paid their little visit."

Mrs. Ang? *James Guisnel?* Cadel couldn't cope anymore. He began to shake again. How did Thaddeus know that he knew about James Guisnel?

"Let's go in now." Thaddeus closed his long fingers around Cadel's arm. "We need to warm you up. And you could do with a bath as well, I think."

Nudged forward, Cadel limped toward the house. Thaddeus, however, noticed his uneven gait at once.

"What is it?" the psychologist said sharply. "Did they hurt you?"

"It's my foot . . ."

"*Vadi!*" Thaddeus called, and the front door opened. Silhouetted against the dazzle of a chandelier was a slim, broad-shouldered figure in a tailcoat. It moved toward them down several flights of steps, which appeared to be chiseled into solid bedrock.

"Vadi, this is Cadel," Thaddeus said, as the mysterious figure stopped in front of them. "I want you to carry him inside. Wilfreda! Where are you?"

"I'm here," said a voice in the shadows.

"Get a room ready, will you?"

"Yes, sir."

Cadel was scooped up by the man in the tailcoat, who turned out to be young and stony-faced, with dusky skin and long, dark eyes that struck Cadel as being slightly peculiar. Cadel got a good look at him as soon as they entered the house, which was lit up like a Christmas tree; he saw that the peculiarity lay not so much in the man's eyes but in his eyelids. It was something about the way he blinked.

The blinks were so rapid, however, that Cadel couldn't put his finger on why they disturbed him.

"In here," said Thaddeus, gesturing. "Put him on the couch."

Vadi obeyed. As he was carried along, Cadel had a confused impression of large spaces, vivid tapestries, and gleaming marble floors. He was finally deposited in a downstairs room that contained a fur rug, a stone wall with a fireplace embedded in it, and hectares of floor-to-ceiling windows. Beyond the windows lay nothing but darkness. Cadel could see himself reflected in one of the huge expanses of glass, along with the bronze sculptures and wing chairs and bright paintings that surrounded him.

"Go and run a bath, will you, Vadi?" said Thaddeus.

"Yes, sir."

"I'll just take a look at this foot."

While Cadel fell back into the well-stuffed cushions of a massive built-in sofa, Thaddeus knelt beside him and took his swollen foot carefully in one bony hand.

"Can you move it?" asked Thaddeus.

"Yes."

"Wiggle your toes."

Cadel obeyed. Then Thaddeus pressed his thumbs against ankle and instep until Cadel yelped.

"You've got a bruised bone," said the psychologist. "Or maybe even a hairline fracture. But there's nothing much you can do about that, except take it easy." He dropped the foot. "Ice won't help much at this late stage, though a painkiller might. You can take one after your bath." He smiled as he regarded Cadel, a glint in his eye. "I don't know what clothes I'm going to put you in. Do you know, Cadel, I never cease to get a little shock every time I see you? It's because you're so small. How can someone so small wreak such havoc? I find it endlessly surprising."

He rose and parked himself on the couch next to Cadel, crossing his legs.

"I suppose the first thing I'd better do is apologize," he went on. "If I'd been a little quicker, this wouldn't have happened. I was caught up at Yarramundi. Well, I don't have to tell *you* about that."

A pause. Thaddeus seemed to expect a comment from Cadel, but Cadel just stared mutely.

"As far as I can make out," Thaddeus finally said, "it all happened because Adolf lost his cool. Had this idea in his head that there was a dangerous conspiracy brewing. He put a tail on Luther and of course Luther spotted it. Made him antsy. And then after the business with Tracey, the police questioned Terry, and *he* got a bit nervous. Decided to clear out a lot of the stuff in the labs. Called Luther about it, naturally. Wanted to dump some of the stuff on him. Well, it's Luther's area of expertise, isn't it? Disposing of bodies." Thaddeus surveyed Cadel with hooded eyes, waiting. Cadel, however, had nothing to say. "Poor Terry wasn't security conscious," Thaddeus continued. "Didn't realize that he was being watched. When the Grunts saw what he was doing, they jumped him. I don't know exactly what Adolf thought Terry was up to. Something suspicious, at any rate. So he hauled the poor fellow off to Yarramundi to be interrogated, and used his car as a decoy. Drove it to Luther's house, got Luther to come down, and ambushed him. Am I right so far?"

"I—I don't know," Cadel stammered.

"Don't you? I find that hard to believe. Personally, I've put it together from some of the security tapes, and what I've been told by one or two of the Grunts who've surfaced. Oh yes—they haven't fared well. The ones who captured Luther didn't make it far. He escaped, and left them in pieces. Then he got into the armory, and there was an all-out battle between Luther and Adolf. I don't know who escaped and who's left in the rubble. Not yet. Adolf, Terry, Luther: They've all vanished. A really elegant solution." Thaddeus leaned forward. "How did you do it, Cadel?" he asked.

Cadel caught his breath. "I—I didn't," he gasped.

"My dear boy, you don't have to lie to me. I've been keeping very close tabs on you. I know you've been surfing the Axis network. I know you planted Max's account details in Brendan's computer files. And Brendan—that was masterly. What did you *do* to him, Cadel?"

Cadel's lips began to tremble. His eyes filled with tears. "I don't *know*," he squeaked.

"Of course you do. *And* you know all about that recording of Terry's phone call. Not to mention Alias." Thaddeus shook his head. "The way you arranged it so that Art would buy a gun using one of Alias's aliases—because he didn't want anyone to trace him—and then leave the same gun at the scene of the shooting, meaning that Max would think Alias had killed one of his hired thugs and go after *both* of them—Alias *and* Art. I'm speechless. Really. You're a genius, Cadel."

"I had nothing to do with that," Cadel croaked. "Honestly." He was overwhelmed by the sheer size of what he'd done. By accident. Not that it had all been an accident, but he had never intended to *kill* anybody. Didn't Thaddeus understand that?

It seemed not. The psychologist reached out and laid a hand on Cadel's arm.

"Cadel," he said softly, "do you think I care? I'm not angry with you. I'm proud of you. You *wiped out the institute,* Cadel. It's astonishing." His smile grew until it was a wolfish grin. "Not that I wasn't expecting it. I had a feeling, somehow. And when you found out about the Piggotts—well, it was inevitable. A very natural reaction."

"How—how—"

"How did I know you'd found out? Oh, you said something to James at one point. He asked you how you'd spent your day, and you answered—what was it? Something along the lines of 'as if you didn't know.' Of course, it was bound to happen. I warned Phineas, over and over again. I said to him, 'The penny's going to drop one day. And when it does, you'd better watch out, because he's going to feel betrayed, Phineas. After so many years living with those monsters.' It was never *my* idea, Cadel. I wanted you with me. But Phineas had this idea in his head—he didn't want you getting too attached to me. He didn't want you getting too attached to anyone. I told him it would backfire in the end. Needless to say, though, our friend didn't listen. He very rarely does." Thaddeus's smiled faded, to be replaced by a grim look. "Which is why he's where he is now."

Cadel blinked.

"It was the same with the Axis Institute." Thaddeus spoke quietly. He was staring at the stone wall, his long fingers coiled around Cadel's arm, his tone distracted. "All along, I've thought it an absurd proposition. Destined for disaster. Though it did occur to me, early on, that you might find it a challenge. So I sat back and waited for you to bring it down. Which you did, in a matter of months. You passed the test with flying colors." His gaze returned to Cadel, bright and black and piercing. "You are greater than Phineas ever was, or ever will be," he said. "You're a miracle. I was afraid that, in the Piggotts' care, you wouldn't reach your full potential. But I have to admit, I underestimated you. I don't believe you would have done any better even if I *had* taken you in."

Cadel was completely lost. It was all too much to absorb. Besides, he was very tired. And his foot was hurting.

"So—so Dad won't be mad at me?" he mumbled, snatching at the most important detail.

"Oh, I don't think we'll be telling Phineas, Cadel. After all, the institute was his baby. He won't be too pleased when he discovers what happened. And if he was to find out that *you* were responsible—no, I think it will be our little secret." Though utterly still, Thaddeus gave an impression of tautness, as if he was poised to spring. "What do you say? Hmmm? Do you want to tell Phineas?"

Cadel stared into the psychologist's narrowed eyes. He sensed that something important was being decided, but he was too tired to work out what it might be.

"No," he said. "I guess not."

Thaddeus looked away. At that moment, the rap of knuckles against wood announced Vadi's return. He stood in the doorway, a towel draped over one arm.

"Ah," said Thaddeus. "You've run the bath?"

"Yes, sir."

"Good, good." Thaddeus turned back to Cadel. "Can you manage the climb by yourself, dear boy? Or would you like Vadi to carry you?"

Cadel didn't like the look of Vadi. Apart from the eyelids (what *was* it about those eyelids that bugged him so much?), there was also Vadi's skin. It seemed to have an almost silvery sheen to it, under the glow of the electric lights.

"I'll do it," Cadel said. "I can walk."

"Are you sure?"

"I can do it! Really!"

"Very well." Thaddeus turned back to the silent Vadi. "You might go and make a cup of cocoa," he drawled. "And tell Wilfreda I want to see her. As soon as Cadel's settled."

Vadi bowed. Then he left. When he had gone, Thaddeus asked, "What do you think of him?"

"Think of who?" Cadel was still in a daze.

"Vadi. What do you think of him?" As Cadel stared, in utter confusion, Thaddeus dipped his head apologetically. "Of course, you're not in a fit state to realize," he conceded.

"Realize what?"

"Vadi's 'aquagenic.' One of your father's more interesting finds." Thaddeus rose, and stooped to help Cadel up. "In one way, he's an evolutionary throwback. Human beings are descended from amphibians, of course, and there's still a lot of the amphibian in us. Vadi's genes are simply more amphibian than most." He frowned at Cadel, who had wriggled away from his supporting hand. "What's the matter?"

"I don't need any help!" Cadel just wanted to get away—away from Vadi. Away from Thaddeus. "I can walk by myself! I know what I'm capable of!"

Thaddeus smiled.

"Do you think so, Cadel?" he murmured. "Personally, I doubt that you really understand the scope of your powers."

And he watched Cadel go, with an intensity that was more frightening than any spoken threat.

FIFTY

Cadel's bath was waiting at the top of the staircase, in the most luxurious bathroom that he had ever seen. It was made entirely of marble; there was a gilt-framed mirror, and a headless Greek statue in an alcove, and about twenty towels of every imaginable size. The sunken bath itself was so big that two steps led down into it.

"Is there anything else you need, sir?" Vadi inquired, hovering on the threshold. Cadel eyed him nervously. He looked almost normal, and yet . . . why was he wearing such a high collar?

Surely he didn't have *gills*?

"No," Cadel replied, in a shaky voice.

"If you think of anything, just call," said Vadi, gesturing at an intercom panel with a phone attached. "Your bedroom is next door."

"Okay."

"It's a very great honor to meet you at last," Vadi added gravely; and before Cadel could recover from his surprise, the young man withdrew, closing the door gently behind him.

Cadel hesitated. He was feeling so groggy that he actually had to think about what to do next. Clothes off, of course. Into the bath. The water was scented and just the right temperature; Cadel sighed as the warm, fragrant liquid engulfed his bruised body. He almost fell asleep in it. Afterward, he dried himself on the largest towel that he had ever seen, which he removed from a heated towel rail. Even the mirror over the vanity was heated, to prevent it from steaming up.

A pair of men's summer pajamas had been laid out for him. (They were far too big.) He made use of the toothbrush and toothpaste that had also been provided. When he finally, cautiously, pushed open the door, Vadi was waiting for him in the corridor outside.

"This way, sir," he said.

After the bathroom, Cadel was expecting something even more luxurious in the bedroom: a four-poster bed, perhaps? An alabaster fireplace? A gilded ceiling? To his surprise, the bedroom was furnished quite simply. It had creamy walls, creamy curtains, and a creamy bed. The lamps were made entirely of blown glass. The only painting was a strange, dreamlike landscape, which, on closer inspection, wasn't really a landscape at all, but an abstract collection of colors.

The clock on the bedside table said 2:15 A.M.

"Would you like a hot drink, sir?" Vadi queried. "I've heated up some cocoa."

"No, thanks."

"Anything to eat, or to read?"

Cadel shook his head. He simply wanted Vadi out of his room. This was unfair, he realized, but the whole aquagenic thing made him uneasy. He didn't know what to say, or where to look. He had a horrible feeling that the guy might smell sort of *fishy*.

One whiff of fish, and Cadel would vomit. He knew that. Besides, he had seen something else on the bedside table, standing between the lamp and the clock. It was a photograph in a silver frame.

He snatched it up and was staring at it, mesmerized, when Vadi left the room.

The woman in the photograph was Cadel's mother. She had to be—there was no other explanation. Her eyes were exactly the same as his. She was smiling, and even her teeth were the same. She wore a pale yellow top, and the wind was blowing her hair back. She looked young, and happy, and pretty, and . . . and nice. Really nice.

Not like a junkie at all.

Cadel lowered himself onto the bed, still gazing at the photograph. Suddenly, it was all too much: the chloroform, Max, the fire, the foot, the long drive through the night, and now this. On top of everything else. His mother, laughing up at him from a silver frame.

Tears spilled down his cheeks.

Oh, Mum, he thought, squeezing his eyes shut. *What am I going to do? Why aren't you here to help me?*

"Cadel?"

It was Thaddeus. He had entered the room as silently as mist.

Cadel looked up. "Why did you do this?" he asked in a hard, accusing tone.

"Do what?"

"Put this here! This is my mother!"

"Yes."

"She looks just like me!"

"Thank god," said Thaddeus. "Or Darkkon might have suspected that you weren't his child."

For several seconds, Cadel didn't understand what Thaddeus had just said. It was the psychologist's taut expression that caused him to backtrack—to review the words that he had, at first, ignored.

Darkkon might have suspected that you weren't his child.

What was that supposed to mean?

"Huh?" he said, gaping like a fish.

"It's time you knew," Thaddeus explained quietly, his dark eyes glittering in the soft light. "You're *my* son, Cadel."

Cadel's mind went blank. He just sat there, slack-jawed. He couldn't move. He couldn't speak.

No one said anything for a long, long time.

Finally, Cadel bleated, "Wh-what?"

"You're my son." Thaddeus's pale face was flushed. "I'm your real father."

"No, you're not."

"Yes, I am. I'm sorry, but it's true. Your mother and I . . ." For the first time, Thaddeus faltered. He scratched his nose and looked away. "She was so sweet. So *young.* She had no idea what she was getting herself into. He treated her like a pet parakeet, and she turned to me for help . . ."

"No!" Cadel cawed.

"Listen—"

"You're *lying*!" Cadel felt hot. He felt ill. It was as if the whole world had turned upside down.

When Thaddeus approached him, he pulled back. So Thaddeus sat down on an upholstered armchair nearby.

"Phineas didn't trust her, you see," the psychologist continued quietly. "Even in the beginning, when she loved him, he used to lock her up. Put things in her food to make her sick, so she couldn't leave the house. He was paranoid. He thought she was bound to betray him, because she was so young and beautiful, and he was so old and ugly." Thaddeus cracked a mirthless half smile. "Well, he got his wish. He was proven right. In the end, she was so miserable that she turned to me. And then she had you. And when that happened, Phineas got tests done. DNA tests. Because he still didn't trust her." The smile died. "You're my son, Cadel. There's no doubt about it."

Cadel shook his head. "No," he mumbled.

"Phineas never found out, of course."

"No!" Cadel covered his ears. But Thaddeus leaned forward and gently unclamped one of Cadel's hands.

Cadel pulled away from him.

"The irony is, while he didn't trust *her*, he trusted me wholeheartedly," the psychologist explained. "He asked me to arrange the tests. Naturally, I faked the results. He was convinced that you were his child. In the end, though, it didn't help your mother. He still destroyed her."

"This isn't true," Cadel gasped.

"I'm afraid it is. He became obsessed with the idea that she was going to leave him, so he had her killed." Thaddeus took off his glasses and wearily rubbed his eyes. "If I'd known what he was planning, I would have stopped it, of course. But he arranged it himself. Pretended

425

that she'd left him. I think he was ashamed to admit what he'd done, even to me."

"But—"

"I know what I told you," Thaddeus interrupted, replacing his glasses in order to peer intently into Cadel's face. "I told you I'd caught up with the culprits. Well, I did. And I had my revenge. What Darkkon doesn't realize is that I traced your mother's killers back to him. He doesn't know that I know."

Cadel swallowed. His hands dropped slowly from his ears to his knees. He couldn't have been more dazed if Thaddeus had hit him on the head with a truncheon. Nothing made sense anymore. *Everything* was a lie.

What if Thaddeus was lying to him even now?

"You might be asking yourself: Why didn't I revenge myself on Darkkon as well?" Thaddeus went on, still watching Cadel intently. "The answer is that I did. I was the source of the anonymous tip that landed him in jail. If I'd had him killed, the whole empire would have broken up, because at that stage *he* was in control—not me. Without him, everyone would have been at each other's throats, fighting over the spoils. I wouldn't have been able to stop it, because I didn't know who everyone was, or what they were doing. That can't happen anymore. Even if Darkkon dies, it won't matter, because I have it all in hand now. I'm running this operation, Cadel. He thinks I'm doing it for him. But I'm doing it for *you*."

Cadel found that he was staring at Thaddeus. He couldn't help himself. The psychologist's voice, always smooth and reassuring, had a hypnotic effect.

"You're his heir, Cadel, and he's dying." Thaddeus placed a hand on Cadel's. "He has cancer. He hasn't told you—he hasn't told *me*—because he thinks he'll beat it, but he won't. He's an old man. A very old man. When he dies, you'll get everything. Which won't mean much, unless you have me to help you. I know every tax shelter and shell company and payoff recipient in this whole empire. Without me, it would

426

fall apart. You'd never keep it together by yourself—not yet. If we pool our resources, we can go further than Darkkon ever did."

The crispness of Thaddeus's tone dispersed the fog in Cadel's head. He began to think again. He realized that he was in a very, very dangerous position. One wrong move, one wrong word, and he might cause offense.

Thaddeus seemed to be offering him . . . what? The keys to the kingdom? Cadel didn't want the kingdom. It would mean more skulking around. More endless surveillance. More Thaddeus, watching his every move.

He just wanted to be free.

Thaddeus misread his hesitation.

"I'll be honest with you, Cadel—this wasn't only for your sake. It was for mine, as well," he admitted, squeezing Cadel's hand tightly. "GenoME won't move without Darkkon's say-so. Neither will any of the franchises. When you succeed him, however, they'll obey you. They'll have to, as long as I'm backing you up. It's not going to work without both of us. I knew that from the beginning. There was a certain amount of self-interest involved." Thaddeus gave a short, shaky laugh. "Frankly, I always knew that Darkkon would dig his own grave. He's mad, you see. Brilliant, but mad. All these insane plans for the future of the world. I mean, it's delusional. I always knew that if I positioned myself properly, I'd be able to take over when he finally dropped out of the race. It was just a matter of . . . well, making myself indispensable."

Cadel gazed at Thaddeus with blank eyes. Something about his grave expression caused Thaddeus discomfort. After shifting in his seat, the psychologist suddenly launched himself out of it, releasing Cadel's hand and pacing the floor. Cadel had never seen him so disturbed.

"If you want proof," the psychologist said, dragging his fingers through his hair, "you're welcome to it. You can arrange your own paternity test. Pick a firm out of the phone book—I don't mind. I'd be delighted. I *want* you to know. I want you to convince yourself that I'm your father." He stopped abruptly and clutched the back of the armchair with both hands. "Darkkon could never have produced something like you," he insisted, with subdued fierceness. "All his crazy ideas have left him muddleheaded. You're not like that. You're a clear thinker. Logical. You don't let yourself get distracted by emotional commitments to idiotic worldviews. You're like me, only greater. A miracle. I might have made a difference, in my time, but *you* are my crowning achievement."

Cadel dropped his gaze, unnerved to have caught a glimpse of Thaddeus's heart. The glimpse left him shaken. All at once, he realized that he was being told the truth. Thaddeus *was* his father. It was written all over the psychologist's hawklike features.

But what did that mean, exactly?

How should it make him feel?

"Do you believe me, Cadel?" Thaddeus was trying to sound calm. "I know that I've told you not to believe anyone about anything, but—"

"I believe you," Cadel interrupted. An anxious Thaddeus made him uneasy. He wanted to put the psychologist's mind at rest.

"Is that the truth? Look at me, Cadel."

Reluctantly, Cadel obeyed. The two of them regarded each other, until a ghost of a smile touched Thaddeus's mouth.

"I can't always tell," he confessed. "It's not something you ought to know, but with that face of yours, I can't always tell if you're lying or not. Are you?"

"No."

"You've every right," Thaddeus conceded, recovering himself. He straightened, released the back of the chair, and allowed his smile to develop into something more confident. "I don't expect you to act out of sentiment. If you did, I would have failed. But consider this, Cadel: When you discover that I'm your father—and you will discover it, I assure you—then you may feel inclined to tell Dr. Darkkon. That would be a mistake. You should have no illusions about him. He will not be grateful. He will try to destroy you—and me. Now, I can protect myself. But you?" Thaddeus shook his head, without taking his eyes off Cadel. "You'll gain nothing from revealing the truth to Darkkon. You'll ruin everything, for both of us." Placing his elbows on the back of the armchair, Thaddeus clasped his hands together and raised his eyebrows. "Do you understand?" he finished.

Cadel understood, all right.

"Yes," he said.

"Good." Thaddeus looked at the picture of Cadel's mother, which lay on the bed. "You can keep that," he added. "I would have given it to you before, but . . . well, you were very young. I didn't want you questioning Darkkon. He would have told you all kinds of lies, and then if I'd tried to correct them, in private, your resentment might have shown."

"He did tell me lies," Cadel pointed out dully. "He told me she ran away."

"Yes. Well. I'm sorry about that."

"*Did* she run away, or didn't she?"

"She might have, given time." Thaddeus seemed to be searching for the right words. "She would have taken you with her, though. She would never have left you, Cadel. She loved you."

"She did?"

"Oh yes."

Cadel wondered if this was the truth. He realized that Thaddeus had succeeded in teaching him at least one thing—namely, to doubt everything that he was told.

"It's very late, Cadel. You should go to bed. Sleep on it."

"But what happens now?"

"We'll discuss that in the morning. You've had a hard time. You need your sleep." For a moment, Cadel was sure that Thaddeus intended to pull back the covers on his bed—perhaps even tuck him in. But something about Cadel's body language must have made Thaddeus change his mind.

So he headed for the door instead.

"Good night, dear boy," he murmured. "Sweet dreams. I'll see you tomorrow."

He left the room as silently as he had entered it. Cadel, who was exhausted, pulled down his own covers before climbing into bed.

Sweet dreams, he thought. What a laugh.

He would have started turning things over in his head, given half the chance. But he couldn't. He couldn't even stay awake.

He fell asleep before he had managed to turn off the bedside lamp.

FIFTY-ONE

Cadel woke at midday, after sleeping like a dead man. Sunlight was streaming into his room. His corduroy trousers were laid out for him, neatly washed and pressed; beside them were a blue sweatshirt and a vinyl jacket. A pair of gleaming white sneakers was sitting on the floor. Everything, except the cords, was brand-spanking-new, and slightly too big for him.

As he dressed, Cadel tried to plan his next move. He had to get away. He had to return to the Piggotts' house, grab his forged documents (as well as his Ariel disguise), and go. Just go. With Art and Alias dead—with Brendan out of the picture—he could safely disguise himself as Ariel. He could bury himself in some out-of-the-way place, forge more documents, dye his hair, change his name, pretend to be sixteen, get a job in a fast-food outlet. . . .

He suddenly thought of Sonja. What about Sonja? How could he contact her? Through the Internet, obviously. Through many far-flung re-mailers. He could stay ahead of Thaddeus, *and* Dr. Vee, if he just kept moving. And perhaps, after a few years, he might have changed so much (with the help of a little plastic surgery?) that he could actually approach her again.

Cadel realized that he was starting to stray into fantasyland. The important thing, the hardest thing, would be to get away in the first place. Once he'd done that, he could afford to concentrate on his long-term future—which wouldn't include Thaddeus.

The previous night, Cadel had been confused. Now his mind was clear, but he hadn't changed it. Thaddeus might be his father, or he might not. Whatever he was, it made no difference to Cadel. It was irrelevant. Cadel still wanted nothing more to do with him. Thaddeus was a brilliant man—a man whom Cadel still admired, despite himself. But Thaddeus couldn't be trusted. Not one iota.

Limping to the window, Cadel pulled the filmy curtain aside. Beyond it, the sun was blazing. He had to squint, and lift his hand to shield his eyes, before he could see what lay spread out at his feet. It was the sea, dark and serene under a cloudless sky. Far off, on the horizon, he could just make out the shape of a large ship—a tanker, perhaps. To his right, if he craned his neck, he could see headlands folding back like bedcovers. To his left, he thought he spied a beach.

Where *was* he?

Below him, waves crashed against an unseen cliff face. There was a terraced area, planted with hardy shrubs, and a patio wet with salt spray. *Good place to get rid of a body,* Cadel thought, and shuddered. He *had* to get out.

After dressing, he cautiously sidled into the corridor that bisected the top floor of this startling house. Would he be lucky enough to escape detection? Would he be able to walk straight downstairs and out the front door? For an instant his heart leaped; then he heard a voice from the bottom of the staircase.

"Good morning, sir." It was Vadi. "How is your foot this morning?"

Cadel cursed silently to himself. It was obvious that Vadi had been appointed to watch over him. There would be no slipping out of *this* house. Not while Vadi was around.

Not, at least, until Cadel had a better grasp of the building's layout and security systems.

"Uh—my foot's fine," said Cadel. In fact, it was still sore, but not nearly as painful as it had been the previous night. "Where did the shoes come from?"

"I went shopping," Vadi replied, enigmatically. "Would you care for something to eat, sir?"

"Um . . ." Cadel hesitated. He felt squeamish about accepting food from Vadi. An image of worms and oysters flashed into his mind. But he suddenly realized that he was famished. "Maybe . . . toast?"

"Of course, sir." Vadi was still dressed in his tailcoat, which looked a little odd in the harsh light of day. "Anything else? An omelette, perhaps? With bacon?"

"Well . . . yes. Okay."

"Mushrooms? Fried tomatoes?"

"No thanks." Cadel didn't like mushrooms. And he preferred his tomatoes cold. "Where's the bathroom again?"

"Directly to your left," Vadi replied. He went away to order the omelette but was back by the time Cadel had finished in the bathroom. Cadel then followed him into a downstairs room that overlooked the spray-lashed terrace. On a pale marble floor stood a long wooden table and six chairs. The table was laid with a white linen cloth, a damask napkin, silver cutlery, a crystal glass, and a jug of orange juice. There was also a folded newspaper lying beside the jug.

It was like being in a hotel, Cadel decided, intimidated somewhat by the silence, the high ceiling, and the immense, enfolding view that he could see through a wall of windows.

Vadi waited behind a chair until Cadel had sat down on it. Then he pushed the chair toward the table and disappeared.

Cadel looked at the newspaper.

He wondered if it was there for a reason. Was he supposed to pick it up? Read a certain story about a dead man, or a mysterious explosion, or a warehouse fire? He wasn't sure. Above him, from the vaulted ceiling, dangled a lamp made of wrought iron. Behind him, a strange modern tapestry, all blurred lines and muddy colors, hung from another piece of wrought iron: a twisted black bar with frayed, clawlike ends. In front of him, the endless ocean made him feel very small.

433

"Ah. Cadel." All at once Thaddeus appeared, as if he had walked through a secret hatchway. "How are you this morning? Or this afternoon, I *should* say." He glanced at his watch. "At least you've managed to catch up on your sleep. How's the foot?"

"Fine," said Cadel. He realized, with a sinking heart, that his bruised bone (or whatever it was) would undoubtedly hinder him when he tried to escape. It wouldn't be easy running away with a dud foot.

"Is Vadi attending to you?" asked Thaddeus.

"Yes."

"Do you like the view? Impressive, isn't it?"

"I guess." Cadel glanced at the window. "Where are we, anyway? The south coast? Somewhere like that?"

"Somewhere like that."

Cadel waited, but Thaddeus didn't elaborate. He only smiled. So Cadel continued.

"Is this your house?" he asked.

"Not exactly. It belongs to a man called Ivan. Very good citizen. Pays his taxes. Never makes himself conspicuous. The sort of person it's impossible to locate, when all's said and done."

"Oh," said Cadel. So Thaddeus lived here under an assumed name. It made sense. "Who else lives here?"

"Vadi. Wilfreda. She cooks. He cleans."

"That's all?"

"That's all."

"So you don't . . ." Cadel paused, wondering how to phrase his next question. "You don't have a family?" he concluded, at which point Thaddeus narrowed his eyes.

"Of course I have a family," he rejoined. "You are my family, Cadel."

"Oh. Right." For a moment, Cadel had forgotten. "I mean, any *other* family."

"No. I told you. Your mother is dead." Thaddeus, who had been standing near the door, crossed the room and sat next to Cadel. He was wearing a silk waistcoat over a soft linen shirt. His sleeves were rolled

434

up. "We have to discuss our plans, Cadel, before you talk to Phineas again. Axis is finished, as you know. The police are swarming all over it now, though I've tried very hard to contain the damage. Unfortunately, while Vee has erased all the files, and we've sealed off Yarramundi, I can't do much about our troublesome Dr. Deal. God knows what he's told the police by now. Even if I disposed of him today, it wouldn't guarantee our safety. He could have spilled his guts the minute he gave himself up. That's why we have to pull out."

Thaddeus looked around as Vadi entered the room, bearing a tray. On the tray were a toast rack, a small bowl full of marmalade, and an omelette arranged on a plate under curls of bacon and tufts of parsley. Vadi unloaded the tray with swift, deft movements. Thaddeus asked him for coffee.

"Yes, sir."

"Black. It's for me."

"Yes, sir."

Vadi withdrew. Cadel attacked the omelette with enthusiasm. He almost forgot that Thaddeus was watching him.

"Fortunately, Deal doesn't know you as Cadel Piggott," Thaddeus remarked. "Nobody at the institute did except Adolf and some of the Grunts. They had to know for security reasons, but I thought it best to keep your whereabouts a secret otherwise. In case some of your fellow students got any ideas into their heads."

"But it was on my security card," Cadel pointed out. "My name *and* my address." Suddenly a vivid picture flashed into his mind. He saw himself trying to persuade Sonja that he was really Cadel Piggott. Waving the card at her.

So *that* was how she'd found him! She'd seen his address!

"Yes, but who saw your security card except the scanners?" Thaddeus wanted to know. "You didn't show it around, did you, Cadel? You were told not to."

"I didn't." Cadel opened his eyes very wide, his jaws working. "I didn't show it to a single person." *On campus,* he added to himself.

"Then we've got a good head start," said Thaddeus. "We can disappear much more easily. You might have to change your name for a while—"

"Disappear?" Cadel interrupted, spraying food everywhere. He swallowed quickly. "What do you mean?"

"We can't hang around, dear boy. What with the doctor, and the chaos at Yarramundi, there'll be a feeding frenzy very soon. Police and media and I don't know what else. Phineas will understand."

"But—but—"

"But what?" Thaddeus folded his arms and studied Cadel's expression. "Surely you agree with me?"

"But I have to get back home! I mean, to the North Shore!" Cadel knew that his voice was too loud, too urgent, and tried to lower it. Without much success. "There's stuff I need."

"What stuff?"

"Stuff. Work."

"That Brezeck business is immaterial now. You won't be around to persecute any longer."

"It's not that! It's—it's my program! All my calculations . . ." Actually, it was Cadel's forged documents. His disguise. They had to be retrieved or he was doomed. *"Please,* Thaddeus!"

"Take it easy. I'll send someone to get them."

"No, no! They're hidden! It has to be me! Anyone else will just wreck them!"

There was a tense silence. Thaddeus threw back his head and looked down his long nose at Cadel. Cadel clenched his fists and tried not to sweat. Instead, he concentrated on replicating the kind of sulky, mulish countenance that he had often seen at school—the face of a child who's been denied a fancy new toy, or a trip to the beach.

"Well," said Thaddeus, at last, "I suppose that house is pretty safe at this stage. Barry doesn't know the address, or your alias. The rest of them who *did* know are out of the picture—except Vee, and he's no threat. All right, you can go."

"Thanks," said Cadel.

"I can't come myself," Thaddeus apologized, checking his watch again. "I have a lot to do. In fact, I probably won't be here when you get back. But don't worry, I won't have forgotten you."

"It's okay," said Cadel, through a mouthful of omelette.

"You realize that this is all *your* fault, young man." Thaddeus flashed his canine teeth as he rose. "If it wasn't for you, we wouldn't be in this mess. I hope you're suitably contrite."

Contrite? Puzzled, Cadel stared up at Thaddeus, who had never before uttered anything that even remotely resembled the words "you ought to be ashamed of yourself." In response, Thaddeus laughed out loud.

"My dear boy," he said, ruffling Cadel's hair, "don't look so alarmed. There's no need for you to be contrite about *anything*. As a matter of fact, I'd be very upset if you were."

Then he strode from the room.

A few minutes later, Vadi returned with the coffee. When Cadel told him that Thaddeus had already gone, the young man looked slightly sick.

It was this change of expression that convinced Cadel once and for all. He had to get out. While Thaddeus might be all smiles at the moment, he was still dangerous. There was no telling what he might do if crossed.

As Cadel ate his breakfast, he considered his situation. He was sitting on a headland, but he didn't know which headland. How far was he from the nearest community? He had a vision of himself slogging along a bleak seaside road, as exposed and vulnerable as a newly shorn lamb in a paddock. He would be escaping on foot, and Thaddeus had a car. Probably more than one, in fact. Cadel wouldn't stand a chance.

So it would be pointless trying to escape from here. Once he'd picked up his documents and his disguise, *then* he would slip away from Vadi. Perhaps on the drive back to this house? A pit stop at a gas station? Cadel could ask to use the bathroom, don his disguise, sneak out, and hitch a lift with another customer. A truck driver, perhaps. He seemed to recall that truck drivers were usually eager to pick up young female hitchhikers. Especially young female hitchhikers who had been dumped by their boyfriends. "I can't let him see me," Cadel would say. "Please, I've got to get away!"

Perhaps, if he whispered, no one would notice that he didn't have a girl's voice.

After breakfast, he accompanied Vadi to a sleek gray BMW parked near the front steps. Outside, the light was dazzling. It flooded a scene of great beauty, which nevertheless made Cadel's heart sink. How far away they were from everything! The house, a modern structure made of glass and steel and stone, was sitting right on the point of a wooded headland. Behind it rose a hill covered in gum trees, through which threaded a winding road. The road led straight to Thaddeus's front door, switching from asphalt to gravel where it formed a circle at the base of the steps that led up to the house. There was no garden wall that Cadel could see—just the road appearing out of the bush. Between the bush and the house was a lawn, a fountain, a handful of trees, and a collection of heathery shrubs. Seagulls wheeled overhead.

"Where are we?" Cadel asked when Vadi was comfortably installed in the driver's seat.

"Curramulla," said Vadi, turning a key in the ignition. As they followed the curving road up into the trees, Cadel racked his brain. Curramulla? It didn't ring a bell.

Only when they had traveled for about five minutes, and passed through an automatic gate in a high brick wall, did Cadel begin to understand. He saw the brass letters by the gate and realized that Curramulla was the name of the *house*. The house and all the land attached to it, which must have cost a fortune.

Cadel wondered if Thaddeus owned any other headlands around the place. Or any islands, perhaps? Someone like Thaddeus could only live in very isolated spots, away from prying eyes. Where he could come and go without being noticed by sticky-beak neighbors.

After leaving Curramulla, Vadi and Cadel drove for a long time on a rather featureless highway, littered with turnoffs. Cadel didn't recognize many of the names, though one or two of them seemed familiar. Vadi was heading north, at any rate. The young man drove in silence, his dark eyes fixed on the road ahead. Cadel noticed the webbing between his fingers; it reached almost to the lower knuckles. He wondered about Vadi's feet: Were they also webbed? But Cadel didn't let his gaze linger on Vadi's webbed fingers, or his pinched nostrils, or his oily skin. In fact, he made a point of keeping his face turned away from his companion. There were plans to be made, after all. Cadel didn't want to reveal himself while he plotted and schemed. The slightest change of expression could be dangerous.

Then he saw the turnoff to Wollongong and began to get a sense of where Thaddeus was living.

"Oh!" he said. "We *are* far away."

Vadi said nothing. But that didn't matter: Cadel knew where he was now. He settled in for a long drive—much longer than he'd anticipated—calculating that they wouldn't reach the North Shore until at least three o'clock, or even later. If he managed to escape during the trip back to Curramulla, then he might find himself still wandering around when night fell. Would that be a good thing or bad? Probably bad. While the darkness would make him harder to find, it would also be dangerous for an unaccompanied girl.

He thought he might go interstate, to begin with. Not by air; airline databases were too vulnerable. No, he would hitch a lift. Or buy a train ticket. Something like that.

He was still weighing up his options when he dozed off, waking with a start to the sound of a nearby horn. Blearily, he gazed around. They were on the Pacific Highway, crawling through Chatswood.

"Jeez," he mumbled, and checked the car clock. "It must have been that chloroform."

Vadi didn't reply.

"Ugh," said Cadel. His mouth was dry. "I'm really thirsty."

"There's lemonade in the glove box," Vadi informed him. To Cadel's surprise, the lemonade was homemade. It had been poured into a stainless-steel thermos, and was very, very good.

Cadel sipped it quietly until they were farther up the highway. Then he instructed Vadi to "turn off here."

"It's all right, sir," Vadi replied. "I know the way."

He did, too. He guided the big, purring car through a maze of peaceful suburban streets until he reached the Piggotts' house, which could not be seen behind its hedge. The sight of that hedge filled Cadel with a complicated mixture of anger, fear, and nostalgia. He reached for his door handle.

"Wait," said Vadi, and punched the horn several times. Obediently, Cadel waited. At last Stuart Piggott appeared, lumbering down the driveway onto the road. He raised his hand in greeting.

Cadel suddenly felt sick.

"Okay, sir." Vadi nodded at him. "Dr. Roth has instructed me to keep watch here until you're done."

"Th-thanks," Cadel stammered. Slowly, he got out of the car. Slowly, he approached Stuart Piggott—or James Guisnel—who gestured toward the unseen house.

"Any help you need, just ask," James said calmly. "Sue's inside."

For a moment, Cadel was speechless. He gazed up into the fat, red face with loathing. Thaddeus had never mentioned the Piggotts! He had never said that *they* would still be here!

Cadel turned abruptly and began to trudge up the driveway. But when he heard the crunch of James's tread behind him, he stopped.

"You can stay here," he croaked.

"But—"

"Stay here." He whirled around, his face working. "I don't need *your* help!"

How he hated them both! It must have shown in his expression, because James pursed his lips and shrugged. There was obviously no point arguing. Cadel left him there at the mailbox. *I should have spat at the bastard,* Cadel thought. *I should have punched him in his big, fat belly.* Sweating and panting, his teeth clenched, Cadel marched toward the house without once looking back. Upon reaching the front door, he kicked it open with such force that it almost sprang back into his face. Then he headed toward his bedroom.

"Cadel?" A familiar voice hailed him from the kitchen. "Is that you?"

Mrs. Piggott. Sue whatever-her-name-was. Cadel didn't even want to look at her.

"Piss off," he hissed, without turning his head.

"Cadel—"

"Get out of here!" He rounded on her, the hot blood rushing to his cheeks. "I don't want to see you! You make me sick! *Get the hell out of here,* you piece of slime!"

"Just doing our jobs," the woman responded coolly. In the shadowy vestibule, it was hard to see her face. "No need to get personal."

"No need to get . . . ?" Cadel was gasping for breath. *No need to get personal?* She was supposed to have been his *mother,* for god's sake! "That's been your motto all along, hasn't it?" he cried. "'No need to get personal!' Funny way to bring up a kid, don't you think?"

Sue shrugged. Cadel, almost retching with disgust, stumbled down the hallway. She was right behind him when he reached his bedroom door.

"I told you to get lost," he spat.

"I'm not supposed to leave you alone."

"You *what?*" He couldn't believe what he was hearing. "All you ever *did* was leave me alone!"

"I—"

"Get the hell out of here! *Get out!* Or I'll tell Thaddeus you hit me!"

The woman recoiled. It was as if Cadel had hit *her.* Cadel threw himself over the threshold and slammed the door in her face. Then he locked it. He was nearly in tears by this time, but he told himself that it was all right. Thaddeus wouldn't suspect anything. It was natural to feel the way he did about the Piggotts. It was natural to hate them after being forced to endure them for so many years.

But he would have to pull himself together. This was no time to lose his cool.

He glanced around the room, which hadn't changed a bit. Everything was in its proper place, including the computer. He had lost his backpack—Max had taken it—but that didn't matter. He kept another on the top shelf of his wardrobe. Once he had dragged it down, he turned on the computer and pretended to download information. Meanwhile, between commands, he rifled through his wardrobe. Pulled out an innocent-looking T-shirt. A pair of leather shoes. The jacket with the forged documents concealed in its lining.

His Indian skirt and makeup were concealed inside a folded sweater. Knowing that his movements were probably being monitored, he had to remove this garment from under his bed and place it in his backpack without allowing any stray bits of hem to show. He had just accomplished this tricky maneuver to his satisfaction when he heard Vadi's horn again: three short, sharp blasts in the distance.

There was a shriek from somewhere nearby.

Cadel, who had been kneeling, rose to his feet. Footsteps pounded down the corridor.

"Cadel!" Sue cried. She began to jiggle the knob on his bedroom door. "Quick! Come on!"

Cadel hesitated.

"*Cadel!*"

"What?"

"Open this *door*! They're *coming*!"

And then the shots rang out.

FIFTY-TWO

Cadel had twice before heard gunshots, at the Axis Institute. He recognized them instantly.

Out in the hall, Sue cursed him.

"Quick!" she shrieked. *"Goddammit!"*

She began to kick at the door. Cadel stood frozen. He didn't know what to do. He heard her gabbling away between kicks—*Tory, this is Pepper. We're clocked, repeat, clocked*—and realized that she must be talking into a cell phone, or a two-way radio.

What did "clocked" mean? Spotted? Pinned down?

"Cadel!" Sue yelled, and all at once there was an enormous *crash* from the direction of the living room. Cadel heard the sound of hurried footsteps. Raised voices. Another shot, closer this time . . .

Cadel dived under the bed. He was scared out of his wits—too scared even to think. He curled himself into a tiny ball, holding his breath, as the terrifying noises continued. Lots of yelling. A heavy tread that seemed to shake the foundations. Glass breaking. Doors banging.

Please, God, Cadel prayed to himself, *please, God, save me. Please don't hurt me. Don't let them find me.*

Thump. His own door had just repelled a large weight.

"Hello?" A voice was raised, outside in the hall. A male voice with an American accent. Cadel didn't recognize it. "This is the police! Is anyone in there?"

Cadel swallowed. *The police?*

But it might not be. A little warning sounded inside his head. *It might be something to do with Max. That's an American accent, after all.*

"Hello?" the male voice repeated, and there followed a short, muttered conversation. Then the whole room seemed to explode. Cadel couldn't help squeaking; the vibration ran straight up his spine and made his ears ring. He cowered. He trembled. He tried to disappear.

As his door slammed against the wall, he realized what had happened. Someone had shot out the lock.

"Check the wardrobe," one man ordered. Cadel couldn't see him through the hanging folds of handwoven bedspread, but he could feel the weight of each heavy boot hitting the floor. He was certain that anyone in the room must have picked up the pounding of his own heart. He tensed every muscle. He tried to stop breathing . . .

Light hit his face.

The game was up.

"Ah." A pair of small gray eyes. A long jaw. A gun muzzle. "Here he is. Under here." The gun was whisked away, as the man with gray eyes dropped to one knee. "It's all right, Cadel," he said. "I'm a friend of Sonja."

Nothing but that particular name would have pierced Cadel's cocoon of fear. Sonja. A friend of *Sonja*?

"You can come out," the man continued, trying to soften the gruffness of his tone. "I won't hurt you. My name's Kale Platz, and I work for the U.S. government."

Dazedly, Cadel watched Kale flash his identification. It looked convincing—though what wouldn't have? No fancy shield by itself would have lured Cadel out from under that bed.

Only Sonja's name did the trick.

"That's it," said Kale, retreating to give Cadel some space. Wriggling slowly into the light, dragging his backpack behind him, Cadel disturbed a lot of dust. He started sneezing. To his surprise, Kale passed him a handkerchief.

"You okay?" the American inquired. "Not hurt?"

Cadel shook his head, wiping his eyes. "You—you know Sonja?" he stammered.

"That's right." Kale, who had holstered his pistol, touched Cadel lightly on the back. He was small and slim and dressed in a black suit with a narrow gray tie. His complexion was sallow. His mousy hair was cut very close to his skull. "Let's get out of here, eh?"

"They've brought a car up," Kale's companion remarked, glancing out the window.

"Good," said Kale.

"But how?" Cadel allowed himself to be led down the corridor, too urgently in need of an answer to worry about where he was being taken. "*How* do you know Sonja?"

"Well, now, that's complicated." Kale hesitated in the vestibule. *"Hey, Nick?"* he called, to someone outside. *"We all clear?"*

"Yeah!" came the reply.

"Okay. Go."

Before Cadel could say anything else, there was a flurry of activity. He found himself suddenly hemmed in by six big men in suits and uniforms. Three were wearing helmets. He was swept out the front door, down the stairs, and into a dark blue car that was parked in the driveway.

Not until he had landed on the backseat of this car did he catch a glimpse of his adoptive mother. She lay flat on her face in a bed of annuals, with her hands cuffed behind her back and an armed man standing over her.

"Hey!" said Cadel, as Kale Platz slid into the seat beside him. "Hey, what are you going to do with her?"

"Her?" Kale didn't sound very concerned. "She's under arrest. She assaulted a police officer." He leaned forward and addressed the driver of the car. "Okay. Let's go."

The car began to move. Craning back over his shoulder, Cadel saw camellia hedges closing in behind them, blocking the Piggotts' house from view. He tried to count the police officers scattered around, but the car was moving too fast. Then they were on the road, and there were more cars, and more people, and someone was winding yellow crime-scene tape around telephone poles and tree trunks. Cadel saw, on the footpath, a shrouded human shape.

He gasped.

"Who—who—?"

"Nobody you know," Kale interrupted grimly. "A police officer."

By this time, however, Cadel was on his knees, peering out the back window. He had seen the gray BMW. It was empty. Its windshield was shattered.

But Cadel's car was gathering speed, and the BMW rapidly dwindled in size before disappearing behind a screen of fir trees.

"Where's Vadi?" Cadel demanded. "He was in the gray car—"

"He got away," said Kale. "But we'll find him. Sit down. Keep your head low."

"How do you know Sonja?" Cadel was still confused, but there was one thing, at least, that he had to find out. "Tell me!"

"I spoke to her," Kale replied. "I got the whole story. She was worried about you."

"She was?" said Cadel.

"I'm not surprised." The driver of the car was a policeman. He seemed to be chewing gum. He had an Australian accent. "Just look at the size of this kid."

"Good things come in small packages," Kale rejoined enigmatically.

"But how do you *know* her?" Cadel exclaimed.

"She contacted us," said Kale. "You were supposed to phone her on Sunday, and you didn't, so she figured you must be in trouble."

"I was."

"Yeah. Well. She's not stupid, is she? Poor kid. Anyway, she mightn't have attracted much attention if she hadn't mentioned the name Darkkon. Because of the Darkkon alert."

"The what?" said Cadel.

"We know who you are, mate." The driver glanced into his rearview mirror; Cadel saw his eyes reflected there. "You're his son, right?"

"Let's not talk about that now," said Kale without expression.

"But I *want* to talk about it!" Cadel was becoming agitated. What did it all mean? What was happening? "What's the Darkkon alert? Is it an international hot button, or something? Do you have to ring a special number if someone mentions the name Darkkon?"

The driver snorted, as if he was trying to swallow a laugh. Kale regarded Cadel thoughtfully.

"If a crime has been committed anywhere in the world and there appears to be a Darkkon connection, then my office is informed," he finally said. "I flew in yesterday."

"Because of Sonja?" asked Cadel.

"Because of the lawyer. Guy who murdered his girlfriend. He's scared to death of Darkkon, goes straight to the nearest lockup and spills his guts in exchange for protection. That was on Friday. Took a bit of time for word to filter through. Then your friend Sonja starts talking about someone called Cadel Darkkon, son of Phineas. At first we thought it might be a hoax. But Barry Deakin confirmed."

"And Sonja had my address," Cadel murmured, the scenario unfolding in his head. "And you've been staking the place out, waiting to see if I came back."

"That's right."

Cadel didn't know whether to laugh or cry. Sonja had been worried! About *him*! He hugged the knowledge close, letting it warm his chilled heart.

"Listen, Cadel," the American went on. He spoke quietly. Dryly. "Sonja says you've had enough of your dad. She says you've been trying to dodge him. Is that right?"

Cadel nodded. He was hardly listening, being preoccupied with his own thoughts. Sonja! Where was she? Did she know that he was all right?

"Well, we can help you there," Kale went on. "We've had enough of your dad ourselves. This Axis Institute cesspit—we're only just getting a grip on it, but it's the kind of thing I'm talking about. The kind of thing we could do without." A pause. "Cadel?" He prodded Cadel's arm. "Are you listening?"

"Uh—yeah."

"You went there, didn't you? You attended the Axis Institute?"

Again, Cadel nodded.

"We'll track down the other students," Kale assured him. "Find out what they can tell us. They've mostly dispersed, but we'll track 'em down. Meanwhile, what we *really* want to know is if you'd like to help us out." The small gray eyes were strangely compelling. "Your dad might be serving time, but his operation's still grinding on because of one man. His second-in-command. Guy called Prosper English. You know him?"

Cadel shook his head.

"Sure?"

"I don't know anyone by that name."

"What about Thaddeus Roth?" said Kale, and Cadel whipped around to face him. "That's the name Prosper's been using lately. Thaddeus Roth. You know Roth?"

"He knows Roth," said the driver, who had been using his rearview mirror again. "He's scared of Roth; look at him."

"The more you can tell us about Roth, the better," Kale remarked. "He's the one we need."

Cadel swallowed. Talk about Thaddeus? To the police?

He would be throwing his life away.

"If—if I tell you about Thaddeus, can I go?" he queried.

"'Go'?" Kale repeated.

"Somewhere. Out of the way. Where no one can find me."

Kale pursed his lips. They were very thin.

"I guess we can help you do that," he said at last, slowly. "Billet you with a foster family. But not until we've cleaned up Darkkon's whole

448

outfit. Think about it. Until that organization is dismantled, you're a sitting duck. Your father's going to want you back. You're not only his son—you know too much about how he operates. How Prosper operates. We've gotta make sure you're safe; we can't let you run around on your own until the coast is clear."

"But I can disguise myself!" Cadel insisted. "I can! I'm really good at that! I'll have a whole different identity!"

"Sure, sure." Kale was peering out the window. "When we know it's safe."

"But—"

"Anyway, you're a minor. You need a social worker, legal representation, some kind of official status . . ." Kale shook his head. "I've got to tell you, Cadel, you're the invisible kid. We can't find any birth records, adoption records, nothing. We didn't even know you existed." Kale studied Cadel with a kind of subdued intensity. Cadel had rarely experienced such a sharp and searching regard—except from Thaddeus. "I've gotta say, you don't resemble your father any," the American murmured.

All at once, darkness fell. They had plunged into some kind of underground garage.

Cadel, who hadn't been paying any attention to their route, jumped like a rabbit.

"It's okay," said Kale, in soothing accents. "This is a secure facility."

"And it's where we get out," the driver announced. "How you feeling, Cadel?"

"I—I don't know."

"It'll be over soon," Kale assured him. "No more Darkkon. No more Prosper English. Just sit tight, and let us do the worrying."

FIFTY-THREE

It didn't take Cadel long to work out that he had been brought to a police station. It was a very big police station—a police *headquarters*, in fact—which seemed to contain several floors full of offices and corridors and laboratories. Everything had a slightly worn and grubby appearance. The gray carpet was stained and frayed, and many of the vertical blinds were broken.

Cadel waited in someone's office for half an hour. After that, he was put in a drab, putty-colored room with a nice young police officer called Bronwyn who gave him a can of Coke and a plate of chocolate cookies. Bronwyn, who had a big warm smile, asked him what his favorite TV shows were. When he replied that he didn't watch much TV, she asked him what he did instead.

"Stuff," Cadel muttered.

"Where do you go to school?"

"I don't."

"You should. How old are you? Twelve? Thirteen?"

"I've graduated," said Cadel.

"Oh," said Bronwyn.

"What's happening? Why am I here? Don't they want to know about Thaddeus?"

"There's a lot going on at the moment." Bronwyn smiled encouragingly. She had large brown eyes and full cheeks. She was quite pretty. "They're looking for a social worker at the moment. You can't be interviewed unless there's someone present to take care of your interests.

We have to make sure everything's done right. Just give them a few more minutes."

Munching a cookie, Cadel reviewed his situation. It wasn't good. On the one hand, he was out of Thaddeus's clutches. But now he was stuck inside a police station, which wasn't exactly the safest place in the world. Suppose Thaddeus had agents working for the police? Even if he didn't, a "secure facility" like this one would be the obvious place to look. Kale had been right. Dr. Darkkon would want his son back. He would stop at nothing to penetrate the police defenses. In fact . . .

Cadel's chewing slowed as his mind began to work more smoothly. It occurred to him that if Thaddeus—or Prosper—was Kale's number-one target, then Cadel would be the perfect bait. Who but Thaddeus would be given the job of rescuing Darkkon's son? No doubt the police were hoping to lure Thaddeus out of hiding by dangling Cadel in front of his nose.

Well, that wasn't going to happen. It didn't *need* to happen. Cadel lifted his gaze to the ceiling; he noted the sprinkler system, the air-conditioning ducts, the flickering fluorescent lights. He got up and drifted to the window, which commanded a view of inner-city treetops, chimneys, and apartment blocks. He judged himself to be on the second floor. Below him, the building stood in a small area of paved yard, with no fence or wall separating it from the street. Security must all be in the foyer.

Pressing his nose against the glass, he could see one half of the street that bordered the building's western side. There were several corrugated garage doors with NO PARKING AT ALL TIMES splashed on them in fading paint. There was a little kebab shop, a Laundromat, a row of blank-faced row houses with no front yards; and down the street a bit, near a busy intersection, a bus shelter. A bus shelter *and* a taxi stand.

Cadel wondered where Sonja was at that very moment. He wondered what she was thinking. He would never know if he stayed around here. Even if Thaddeus *didn't* get to him, Cadel would be kept apart. Monitored. Followed. It would be like the Axis Institute all over again;

he shuddered at the thought. They would stick him in safe houses, smother him with police protection, and forbid him to go anywhere dangerous.

Like Weatherwood House, for example. Thaddeus had sent agents to Weatherwood House already. There was nothing to stop him from sending them again, if he was desperate.

Cadel's brain clicked through its calculations while his gaze roamed around the room. His backpack was on the floor. It contained all that he needed. He knew exactly where he was—in the dead center of a large and crowded city full of bolt holes. What's more, there was a taxi stand not far away, and a railway station not far beyond that. He checked the time: twenty to five. It would be getting dark soon.

After about five minutes, he turned to look at Bronwyn, who had subsided into a blank-eyed reverie.

"I know where Prosper English lives," he said.

Bronwyn blinked, then shook herself.

"What's that, sweetie?" she asked.

"I know where Prosper English lives," Cadel repeated. "The man you're all looking for. I slept at his house last night. Doesn't anyone want to hear about it?"

"Uh—well—yeah. Of course." Bronwyn was beginning to look flustered. She tucked a loose strand of hair behind her ear. "But I'm not the one to tell. Especially when you're by yourself, like this—"

"He lives in a house on a headland. A house called Curramulla," Cadel continued. "It's about forty-five minutes south of Wollongong— I'm not sure where, exactly. It's supposed to belong to a man called Ivan. I don't know the second name." Cadel regarded Bronwyn calmly with his guileless blue gaze. "Don't you think you'd better tell someone?" he said.

"Probably. Yes. Um . . ."

"I need to go to the bathroom," Cadel added.

"Right. Okay." Bronwyn rose. "I tell you what—you follow me. I'll show you where to go, and while you're in the toilet, I'll get somebody. All right?"

"All right."

"You don't have to take that." Cadel had just picked up his backpack. "You can leave it here."

"No," said Cadel, clutching the backpack to his chest.

"It'll be safe."

"How do *you* know?" Cadel snapped. His hands were sweaty, but his voice didn't tremble. "I'm not leaving this anywhere."

"Why not?" Bronwyn had paused, with her hand on the doorknob. "What's in it?"

"My *stuff*," Cadel retorted, as rudely as possible.

"Can I have a look?"

"Why?"

"Because I wouldn't want you trying to kill yourself or anything." Bronwyn spoke matter-of-factly, but Cadel was appalled. It must have shown on his face, because Bronwyn smiled.

"*Kill* myself?" Cadel cried. "I don't want to kill myself!"

"Or anyone else?"

"No!" Something about Bronwyn's expression—the detached, quizzical look in her eye—upset Cadel. "I'm not like my father! You're not being fair! I wouldn't kill anyone . . ." He trailed off suddenly, as he recalled that he *had* killed someone. Several people, in fact. Though he hadn't meant to.

The memory brought tears to his eyes; he felt dirty and ashamed and frightened. What would happen when the police found out about *that*? Would they send him to a juvenile correctional center? Would the name Darkkon protect him *there*? Not without Thaddeus, it wouldn't.

He had to get away.

"It's not my fault," he said thickly. "I mean, I didn't—you—you don't understand."

"Calm down," Bronwyn crooned, patting his shoulder. "It's all right."

"Here! Take a look!" He thrust the backpack under her nose, praying that she wouldn't unwrap the sweater at the bottom of the bag. "Do you *see* any guns? Do you *see* any knives? I hate all this! I just want to be normal!"

He pulled out the T-shirt. The jacket. He dropped them on the floor. Bronwyn held up her hand apologetically as she glanced into the bag.

"It's okay," she said. "Calm down. I believe you."

"Well, don't *look* at me like that."

"I won't."

"It's not *my* fault I've got a maniac for a father!"

"No, no. Of course not."

As Cadel knelt down to retrieve his jacket, Bronwyn crouched beside him. She stuffed his T-shirt into his bag. She smelled of flowers.

Cadel suddenly thought, with a pang, *I wish I didn't have to trick her.* But he had no choice.

"Okay," said Bronwyn, straightening up. "Let's go."

She led him out of the room and down a corridor until she reached a door marked with a male and a female figure. On the way, they passed a bank of elevators, a kitchen alcove, six office doors, and one labeled FIRE STAIRS. Cadel made a mental note of the fire stairs. He saw several uniformed police officers drinking coffee, or hurrying along with colored files tucked under their arms. Every one of them stared at him curiously.

He must have looked out of place, with his grubby old backpack. Unless they had been told about him?

"Here," said Bronwyn, stopping in front of the restrooms. "This do you?"

"Thanks," Cadel replied.

He plunged through the door, which opened into a very small vestibule. On the right was the ladies'; on the left was the men's. Cadel tapped on the right-hand door.

There was no reply.

When he pushed it open, he found himself in a bathroom containing three stalls and three sinks. He immediately locked himself in one of the stalls and started to change. He took off all his clothes except his underwear. He put on the Indian-cotton skirt, the leather shoes, and the T-shirt that he'd packed, as well as the sweater in which he'd wrapped his makeup. He pulled a shoestring out of his brand-new sneakers and tied his hair back. Then he shrugged on the jacket that was lined with forged documents.

His discarded clothes went into the bag, which he decided not to take with him. Instead, he stuffed it into the big plastic garbage bin under the hand dryer. He used the mirror over the sinks while donning his makeup, acutely conscious that anyone might walk in at any minute. But he had to be thorough—even the mascara had to go on. He looked a lot different with mascara in his lashes.

Time was slipping away. Cadel wondered if Bronwyn had gone to fetch one of her superiors. He wondered if—more importantly—she had returned. But just as he reached the door of the ladies', he heard the outer door squeak open.

"Cadel?" said a voice.

It was Bronwyn's.

Cadel stopped, his heart in his mouth. Then his mind began to race, leaping ahead of the action, whirring fiercely through the probabilities. She would go to the door of the men's. She would knock. She would enter.

"Cadel?"

He heard the knock. He heard the door of the men's squeak. When it flapped shut behind her, he waited an exactly calculated three seconds (to give her time to reach the stalls) before sliding into the vestibule and out into the hallway.

There was no one waiting there. Just as well, because somebody like Kale Platz might have seen through his disguise. But there *were* people around—in an office, in the kitchen alcove—so Cadel didn't rush. He didn't run. He walked briskly to the fire stairs and calmly through the door.

Only *then* did he run.

He knew that he didn't have much time. Bronwyn would check the ladies', then sound the alarm. This thought had barely entered his head when he hit the second-to-last flight and caught a glimpse of his destination. Ground floor.

The stairs kept going, down into the underground garage. But Cadel wasn't heading for the garage. He was heading for the street, and—lo and behold!—there was a street exit! Not just a foyer exit, but a street exit as well!

It hadn't been locked from the inside. Someone was following the fire regulations. Cadel slammed through it, then stood still for a split second, panting hard.

There was a brick planter in front of him, full of low bushes that fenced the building off from the street. Across the road was a kebab shop, a Laundromat . . . of course!

The taxi stand!

Cadel hurled himself across the road, dodging a motorbike. He didn't look back. He didn't want to know if anyone was chasing him. He focused all his energy on the intersection, the bus shelter, and the taxi stand, which, if his eyes weren't misleading him, had a taxi parked in it.

Cadel scurried toward the taxi, desperately afraid that someone might reach it before he did. That man, for instance—the one in the leather jacket—but no. That man walked right past. Cadel nearly knocked into him, dodged his leather-clad elbow at the last possible instant, and began to wave at the taxi. He didn't think to check whether its FOR HIRE sign was illuminated.

He just yanked open a door and threw himself into the backseat.

"Miss!" the cab driver was saying. "Miss, I'm on my lunch break—"

"Blacktown!" Cadel gasped, wildly plucking a distant suburb out of his head. He knew, from his long study of the Sydney Rail network, that from Blacktown he could catch a train to Lithgow, and from Lithgow a bus to the country—Bathurst, perhaps . . .

Then the driver's words sank in.

"I'll—I'll pay double," he stammered, forgetting to disguise his voice. "Triple! Look, I've got the money—"

"*Cadel?*"

He almost choked. The driver turned. There was a *click* as the central locking system engaged.

Wilfreda was sitting in the front seat, wearing a black wig under a knitted beret.

"Christ!" she exclaimed, and the engine roared to life. Cadel couldn't believe it. His mind went blank.

The taxi burned rubber swinging into the street. Wilfreda scrambled for her phone. She jabbed at a single key and started to gabble, driving one-handed.

"Rudy!" she said. "It's me! I need backup; I've had to leave. Yes, the whole team. No, and I can't! Because I've got *cargo*! Of course I know what I'm doing!"

She stamped on the brake. Cadel banged his nose on the headrest in front of him. "Sorry," said Wilfreda. She opened a window, and yelled at the man in the leather jacket who had passed Cadel not a minute before. "Get in!" she cried. "Quick!"

He didn't protest. Cadel heard the door locks again, but before he could pull at a handle, the man in the leather jacket was beside him.

"What the hell?" gasped the man.

"Cargo!" Wilfreda growled, hitting the accelerator once more. Cadel's head snapped back.

"Who's this?" The man was staring at Cadel. He was unshaven, with floppy black hair and cold eyes.

"Guess," said Wilfreda.

"It's not—it can't be—"

"It is."

"Bloody hell!"

"There's Nikolai."

Nikolai was a fat, bald, elderly man in shirtsleeves, slouched on a foldout tin chair that had been placed in front of a row house. He was nursing a string of blue worry beads, and he struggled to his feet when he saw the taxi come to a halt on the other side of the road.

At Wilfreda's signal, he waddled across to her.

"In," she said.

Next thing, both of Cadel's escape routes were cut off. On one side of him sat the man in the leather jacket; on the other sat a big, fat, snorting old man who looked vaguely familiar . . .

Suddenly Cadel remembered him. From the train to Strathfield. He'd been slumped in one corner, snoozing.

"By all that's holy," Nikolai said, as the taxi surged forward again, "Cadel Darkkon."

"He walked straight out of that goddamn police station," Wilfreda exclaimed. "All by himself."

"I'm not surprised," said Nikolai. "Dressed up like that."

"But *you* recognized him."

"I was trained to." Nikolai pulled a pair of sunglasses out of his breast pocket. "You should wear these," he advised, passing them to Cadel. "Your eyes always give you away."

Numbly, Cadel put on the sunglasses. He didn't know what to do. What was he going to do? How had this *happened*?

"I wasn't expecting *you*, Cadel," Wilfreda remarked, almost as if she'd read his mind. "Christ, I was here on another job entirely."

"We all were," said the man in the leather jacket. "What are you going to do about *that*, now?"

"This has priority." Wilfreda glanced up into the rearview mirror; for a moment, Cadel saw her eyes. "Do you know they've got Barry Deakin holed up in there?" she asked him.

Cadel stared at her, mutely.

"Well, they do," she continued. "*That's* who we were after. Thaddeus hadn't even tracked you down. I only just got the alert about you myself. I was on standby while he checked his sources." She chuckled. "God, he's going to be pleased."

"What happened to the others?" asked the man in the leather jacket. He was staring morosely at Cadel. "What happened to Sue Croft? She was with you, wasn't she?"

"Leave it, Busy." Wilfreda's voice was cold. "Watch the road. It could be a decoy. They didn't *let* you go, did they, Cadel?"

Cadel swallowed.

"No," he said hoarsely. "At least—I don't think so . . ."

"How'd you do it, then? How'd you get out?"

"I—I went to the toilet. Changed my clothes. Sneaked down the fire stairs." Feeling the tears rush to his eyes, Cadel clamped his mouth shut. All that work for nothing!

"What a stroke of luck," said Wilfreda. "Still, we'd better switch cars. I'll just take care of it."

"And use the Stage One car?" Busy protested. "What about Rudy's team? What if *they* need to switch?"

"I told you. Cadel has priority."

Cadel couldn't think straight. He was putting all his energy into fighting back his tears. It was a disaster, a total disaster. They had seen his disguise; he could never use it again. All he had now were his documents, and what use were they if he couldn't use his disguise?

Then he remembered. He had told Bronwyn about Curramulla.

Was that where they were going now?

"I'm—I'm thirsty," he said, grasping at straws.

"Sorry, Cadel. Can't stop now. Got to put some distance between us and them." Wilfreda glanced into the mirror again. "Maybe later. After we've switched cars." Once again, she picked up her phone.

Cadel subsided. He sat trying to focus, but all he could think was: *Thaddeus will know. If the police turn up at Curramulla, Thaddeus will* know *who told them about it.*

Wilfreda was driving carefully. She didn't exceed the speed limit and was as brief as possible with her phone calls. Cadel wondered if there was any way he might get her to run into the back of somebody else's car, but dismissed the idea at once. If it was a minor accident, Wilfreda wouldn't stop. And if it was major, what chance would he have to get out, wedged as he was between two bodyguards? No—his best chance would be when they switched cars.

He would demand to go to the bathroom. Pee all over Busy's fancy boots if he had to. The important thing was to stay alert.

They drove for about twenty minutes, then plunged into a suburb of old brick bungalows, dodging and weaving through a network of almost identical streets. At last they reached a plain house with an attached garage. Wilfreda headed straight for the garage. Its blue door ascended as they approached.

Within seconds it was rolling down again behind them.

"Wait," said Wilfreda, her gaze on the rearview mirror. "Wait, wait . . . now!"

Everyone moved with bewildering speed. The moment the garage door closed, Cadel was jerked out of the car and hustled to the back of the filthy old garage, where another door led to a paved backyard. "I need to go!" he exclaimed, but nobody seemed to hear. They all charged straight past a rotary clothesline into a corrugated iron shed, where a second car was waiting. This was a red Daihatsu four-wheel drive.

When Wilfreda tried to push Cadel into the backseat, he jammed his hands against the doorframe.

"Wait!" he said. "I need to—"

"Later," Wilfreda snapped. "In a minute."

Her grim expression subdued Cadel. So did the brisk, professional behavior of her companions. Everything seemed to have been planned and practiced. There wasn't a single wasted gesture or fumbled step. Within minutes they were out of one car, into the other, and on the road again.

Something about the smooth execution of this maneuver frightened Cadel. It indicated what he would be up against if he tried to run away. He decided to wait a little. Until they had been driving for a while and had relaxed their guard.

Unfortunately, however, his companions never relaxed their guard. During the next half hour, no one spoke or even stopped watching the road. When Cadel finally, desperately, requested a pit stop, Wilfreda took a detour through another suburb and parked, not at a busy gas station but beside a deserted sports field. Here, a portable toilet stood on the edge of a barren waste of boggy ground. There wasn't anything much around, not even a tree or a bush. It was getting dark, but not dark enough. If Cadel *did* climb out a window, he would be spotted long before he could reach any kind of cover. And there was no one in sight to ask for help.

"Make it quick," said Wilfreda, parking beside the portable toilet block. "Nikolai, go in with him."

The place stank. The stall doors wouldn't lock. There wasn't even any toilet paper. And Nikolai stood right by the door to Cadel's cubicle, holding it shut. Waiting.

Listening.

Cadel had to admit defeat. He did what he had to do before returning glumly to the car. *It's all right,* he told himself. You have to grab opportunities *when they happen.*

Once again, he found himself penned in by Busy and Nikolai. Busy had BO, and Nikolai's breath smelled of garlic. It was enough to make anyone sick.

This gave Cadel an idea.

"I feel sick," he said, when they were drawing close to Wollongong.

"You *what?*" said Wilfreda.

"I feel sick. Carsick. I have to sit in front, with the window down."

"For Chris'sake," Wilfreda muttered.

"That's not wise," Nikolai remarked. "He won't be properly covered."

"Are you going to spew?" Busy asked Cadel. "You'd better not spew on *me.*"

"Here," said Wilfreda, emptying her handbag and passing it over. "If you're going to spew, spew in that. I'm not stopping. Not again."

"But I feel *sick*," Cadel whined. "It's smelly back here! I need fresh air!"

"Climb in the front, then. Quickly."

"Wilfreda—"

"Shut up, Nikolai! I don't want him spewing in the car!"

Cadel saw his chance. As he clumsily hauled himself through the space between the two front seats, he fell. Deliberately. He grabbed the gearshift as he thrust his knee at it, pushing it forward into PARK.

Then everything went crazy.

FIFTY-FOUR

"Cadel?"

"He's awake, look."

"Oh, Christ. Thank God. *Cadel.*"

It was Wilfreda. She wasn't driving anymore. The car was motionless.

Cadel's head hurt.

"We've got to get out of here." Nikolai sounded worried. "Someone's stopping."

"Cadel. Look at me. Say something. Can you hear me?"

"Yeah," Cadel slurred. He could hear Wilfreda, and see her, too. What had happened? He remembered a cracking pain and a flash of light.

He must have hit his head on something. The windshield?

Looking past Wilfreda's wig, which had been partially dislodged, Cadel saw that the windshield wasn't broken. Though there *was* a smear of blood on it. His own blood?

He realized that he was lying across the front seat, his bare legs crumpled against the dashboard.

"Can you move?" said Wilfreda.

"Uh . . ."

"Are you okay?" a breathless voice inquired. It was coming from far away. From outside the car. "What happened? Oh my god—"

"It's all right," said Nikolai coolly. "We're all fine."

"But—"

"She knocked the gearshift," Nikolai explained, while Cadel struggled to rearrange his legs and sit up. He felt a bit dizzy and his wrist hurt. He couldn't put any weight on it.

"Ouch!" he croaked.

"Do you want me to call an ambulance?" Someone was peering in through the front passenger's window—a young man with a beard. He was barely visible in the murky light.

"We're fine," said Wilfreda. "We'll take care of it."

"Are you sure? Because—"

"I'm sure. Thanks." The Daihatsu's engine was still running. Wilfreda hauled at its wheel and began to guide the car back onto the road. The bearded young man had to jump aside.

Something clanked as they bounced over a ditch and across the gravel-strewn shoulder. But nothing fell off.

"He's got a bloody cell phone," said Nikolai, looking back. "He's reading our license."

"It's okay." Wilfreda was scrabbling around for her cell phone. "Just look after Cadel."

"How can I?"

"Get him in the back with you, stupid! Make sure he lies down!"

"Ow-augh!" Busy suddenly groaned. "My *neck*."

"Shut up!" snapped Wilfreda.

Cadel was beginning to understand what had happened. They had swerved off the road but hadn't hit anything. Someone behind them had pulled over to help. Wilfreda had left the scene as quickly as possible.

And Cadel had lost his chance, too dazed to manage an escape attempt.

Even now, he wasn't quite himself.

"I'm going to be sick," he moaned, and vomited onto the floor.

"Oh, *Christ*," said Wilfreda into her cell. "Hello? Who's that? Lennox? Oh. Well, I need a pickup *now*. I'm in a dead car and I've got cargo. Forget that, it's solved. It's *sorted*. Yes! Well, use the bloody

464

pickup, then. Just *get up here with it*! I don't know, behind Yorkie's? Okay. Okay, good." She signed off with a curse. "What a shambles. No-body seems to know what the hell is going on."

Cadel allowed himself to be dragged, awkwardly, into the backseat. He had lost Nikolai's sunglasses. He felt something trickling down his forehead: blood, perhaps? Nikolai pressed a handkerchief to the wound.

"Lie down," he ordered. "Stretch out. Put your head here."

"Is he hurt bad?" Busy wanted to know. "If he is, we're dead."

"Shut up!" spat Wilfreda. "He's fine! He'll be fine!"

"He was out," said Nikolai gravely. "Out cold. That's not good."

"He was out for five seconds. That's nothing."

"You should call a doctor."

"I will. When we get there."

Wilfreda pulled off the road and parked.

Cadel's mind was beginning to clear. He understood that they were waiting for another car—a car that wouldn't attract unwelcome atten-tion on the highway. With his head cradled in Nikolai's lap, Cadel couldn't see where they were waiting, except that it was dark. Nikolai refused to let him sit up.

"Not until you must," said Nikolai.

"But I feel all right," Cadel protested. "I feel better—"

"No more risks. Not now."

"You've caused enough trouble," Busy interjected in bitter accents. "Can't you just do what you're told?"

Cadel decided not to argue the point with his companions. He was lucky; it hadn't even crossed their minds that he had nudged the gear-shift on purpose. If he was obedient, the possibility might never occur to them.

So he lay quietly, trying to plan ahead. After about half an hour of tense silence, he heard a vehicle pull up somewhere nearby. Wilfreda murmured something under her breath. There was a fusillade of slam-ming doors. Nikolai said, "Can you get up? Cadel?"

"I—I don't know." Cadel had decided to fake severe injury. It was, he thought, a way of tipping the balance in his favor. If he looked ill enough, they might underestimate him. "I feel dizzy."

"Wilfreda? Did you hear that?"

"I heard," said Wilfreda shortly. She sounded to Cadel as if she was outside the car. "You'd better carry him. Busy? Help Nikolai."

"I can't," whined Busy. "My neck . . ."

"Oh, for Chris'sake! Len, you do it."

Through half-closed eyes, Cadel saw a wiry little man with a crooked nose and a huge Adam's apple thrust his bald head into the car. He took hold of Cadel's legs, and he and Nikolai awkwardly transferred Cadel from the red Daihatsu to the elevated cabin of a white utility truck. As they did so, Cadel took in his surroundings from beneath drooping eyelids. He couldn't see much, in the evening dimness. He thought there might be a fence on one side of him, and a eucalyptus sapling on the other. Beyond the eucalyptus was a kind of shadowy dip—a culvert?—and beyond it a two-story building studded with glowing security lights. A faded sign on this building said BRAKES—WHEEL ALIGNMENT—SPARE PARTS.

"Where are *we* supposed to sit?" Busy demanded, gazing at the truck.

"You're not," said Wilfreda. "There's no room. I'll take the pickup. The rest of you can make your own way back."

"*What?*"

"Yorkie might let you borrow one of his cars," Wilfreda went on, climbing into the truck, beside Cadel. "Or you can steal one."

"But—"

"My advice is to get rid of that Daihatsu quick-smart."

Cadel almost felt sorry for the three men standing in the cloud of dust that was left behind as Wilfreda drove away. Almost, but not quite. He was too worried about his own immediate plans to concern himself with theirs. Although he was now sitting right beside a door, that door was much higher off the ground than the taxi's doors had been. Jumping out at a red light would therefore be rather more dangerous. After his disastrous attempt to disable the Daihatsu, he wondered if he should risk tangling with another moving vehicle.

Probably not.

So he concentrated on looking sick. It wasn't hard. His head still hurt where he'd bumped it, and he thought that he'd probably sprained his wrist. Slumped against the passenger-side window, he moaned occasionally, and let his lips go dry. Once or twice, Wilfreda addressed him.

"Cadel? You still with me? Hang in there, kid."

"I want to lie down."

"You will. In a minute. We're not far away."

She was right. It didn't seem all that long before they passed through the gates to Curramulla and were bumping along Thaddeus's private road. When they reached the house, Wilfreda pulled up right next to the front steps.

Cadel saw the car immediately. Abraham's car.

Gazo's car.

It was parked under one of the windows, which blazed with light. The whole house was lit up, keeping the night at bay.

"What—what—?" Cadel stammered. He couldn't believe it. *Abraham's car?*

"Dammit," Wilfreda muttered. "Where is everyone? Cadel? We're home."

Cadel tried not to wince. Home? What a terrible thought! "That car," he said. "Why—why is it here?"

"Huh? Oh." Wilfreda shot the Cortina a careless glance. "Your friend brought it when he rescued Vadi."

"When he *what?*" Cadel couldn't believe his ears.

"Come on. Out."

"But what happened?" As Wilfreda hopped from her seat and came around to his side of the truck, Cadel pressed her for an explanation. "Are you talking about Gazo? The guy in the space suit?"

467

"That's the one."

"But—"

"He was watching your house, apparently." Wilfreda opened the car door and helped Cadel down. "Don't ask me why. Worried about you, he said. Maybe Dr. Roth didn't tell him you were all right—he has a lot on his mind, has Dr. Roth."

"So—so Gazo was there when the police raided us?"

"Vadi spotted him. Vadi had to move fast, with the cops swarming around. He jumped into your friend's car. Made him come back here." Wilfreda peered into Cadel's face. "You feeling better now?"

"Not really." Remembering that he was supposed to be concussed, Cadel hung off Wilfreda, dragging his feet as they slowly climbed the stairs to the front door. His mind was whirring. If Gazo was around— why, he had an ally! Unless he had underestimated Gazo. Perhaps Wilfreda had lied. Perhaps Gazo, too, was one of Thaddeus's creatures.

"I'll take you straight up to your bedroom," Wilfreda gasped. "Then I'll get some help. *Hello?* Dammit."

No one answered her hail. So she unlocked the door and entered the house, which, though well lit, was apparently unoccupied. Cadel's heart began to beat more quickly. If she left him here and went to get help . . . why, he could walk straight out again! Walk straight out and *take the truck*!

He had never driven a pickup before—he had never even driven a *car* before—but he knew all about it, in theory. He understood engines better than most people. Surely it couldn't be too hard?

"Here," said Wilfreda, having heaved him upstairs and into his bedroom. The bed had been remade. The photograph of Cadel's mother was still sitting between the lamp and the clock. Wilfreda turned on the lamp. She let Cadel fall onto a luxurious stack of pillows propped against the headboard. She pulled off his shoes, hoisting up his long skirt to do so. "Now just lie still," she said. "There's bound to be someone around here somewhere—this place is supposed to have twenty-four-seven security. I shouldn't be long."

And she disappeared.

Cadel waited until the sound of her footsteps had faded into silence. Then he got up and put his shoes back on. Their rubbery soles squeaked a little against the parquet floor of the hallway, but not enough to concern him too much. Every few steps he would stop and listen, but he couldn't hear anything except the distant pulse of the tide, and the ticking of a nearby clock. The only thing moving was a gauze curtain, which fluttered in a sea breeze at the end of the corridor.

Coast's clear, Cadel thought, then swallowed. Shaking with nervous tension, he began to tiptoe down the sweeping staircase.

He was almost at the bottom when the living-room door burst open and Thaddeus Roth emerged.

FIFTY-FIVE

Thaddeus saw Cadel and froze. For a moment they stared at each other.

Then Thaddeus staggered.

"Elspeth?" he hissed. "But you're dead! I saw you—"

He stopped suddenly, but it was too late.

Cadel already knew.

"You killed her," he gasped.

"Cadel?"

"You killed my mother." It was all so clear. Cadel had seen Thaddeus's expression. He had heard the anger and the fear and the hatred in Thaddeus's voice.

"Cadel, my god!" The psychologist stepped forward. "You *escaped?"*

"Get away from me!"

"Listen, Cadel—"

Cadel turned and bolted up the stairs. He intended to lock himself in his bedroom. But Thaddeus had longer legs than he did.

Cadel didn't even make it to the first landing.

"Wait! Cadel!"

"Let go!" Almost crazed with fear and revulsion, Cadel lashed out. He strained against the psychologist's grip. "I hate you! *I hate you!"*

"Cadel—"

"I know what happened!" cried Cadel. He kicked and clawed, exploding against the months and months of endless surveillance, the lying, the manipulation. "You were afraid, so you killed her! You *scum*! You *murderer*! You've made me a *murderer*!"

"Shh. Calm down."

"You *shit!*" Cadel spat, tears of rage and sorrow spilling from his eyes. "You *lying scumbag!* You lied to me, *Prosper!*"

The psychologist blinked, then stared. He opened his mouth. Before he could speak, however, someone else did.

"Hey."

It was Gazo. He was standing at the foot of the stairs, and he wasn't wearing his headpiece. For the first time ever, Cadel found himself gazing at Gazo's entire head. It was long and bony, perched on top of a long, skinny giraffe's neck. His close-cropped hair was a murky brown, and his ears stuck out like wings.

"Are you all right, Cadel?" he asked, frowning. Startled by his appearance, Thaddeus had loosened his grasp on Cadel—who took advantage of this fact by wrenching free and stumbling down the staircase.

The psychologist, however, had very quick reflexes. His hand shot out and grabbed Cadel's collar.

"Wait," he said.

"Let go!" Cadel gasped. He was nearly choking. "Gazo! Help!"

Vaguely, Cadel was aware of Gazo's anxious voice, bidding Thaddeus to let his friend go. Thaddeus, who had flung one arm around Cadel's wriggling body, snapped, "Get out of here! Now!" Then everything became confused. With the psychologist's arm clamped across his chest, Cadel felt as if he was suffocating. He bucked against it—the pressure fell away, but still he couldn't breathe. There was a terrible smell and his vision failed.

When he came to, it was dark. He was no longer on the staircase. He was no longer *inside.* And though he felt someone's arms around him, dragging him along, they didn't belong to Thaddeus.

He moved against them feebly.

"It's all right," Vadi gasped into his ear. "Calm down."

Cadel suddenly realized where they were. They were in front of the house, and there was Wilfreda's truck, and there was Gazo's car, and there . . .

There was Gazo. Lying facedown on the dirt, in a pool of light that spilled from one of the windows.

"Gazo!" Cadel croaked.

"It's all right," Vadi repeated. He was slowly mounting the steps to the front door, his arms hooked under Cadel's. "It was a vicious smell, but I can hold my breath longer than any other man on earth. Long enough to swing a poker."

"Gazo . . ."

"I'll take care of him, never fear. But we have to be quick." Staggering through the door, he raised his voice. "Sir! Dr. Roth!"

"Here," came the feeble reply. It sounded as sick as Cadel felt. Now he was in the living room, and there was Thaddeus, collapsed across one of his stylish chairs, green-faced.

"Sir, are you all right?" Vadi queried.

"I'll live."

"He was trying to take the boy," Vadi continued, dropping Cadel onto the sofa. "I knocked him out."

"Well done," said Thaddeus, shutting his eyes. Cadel knew just how he felt. Nauseous. Dizzy.

But better than before. Definitely better.

"Sir, I have to report that there are cars converging on the other side of the wall."

"Cars?"

"Police cars."

Thaddeus hissed. He looked up and caught Cadel's eye.

Cadel glanced away. All at once he was very, very frightened.

"Sir, I think they're staking the place out," Vadi went on. "What should I do?"

"They're coming from inland, not from the sea," Thaddeus replied. He straightened and swallowed; the color was returning to his face.

"We need to get to the boathouse quickly. Where's Wilfreda? She must be here. She brought Cadel."

"Sir, I don't know. I just got back from my sweep—"

"I have next to no staff," Thaddeus muttered. "They're all in Sydney, looking for Cadel. Dammit. *Dammit.*"

"Sir, what about that problem out in front? I don't think he's dead. Should I finish him off first?"

"No!" Cadel squawked, and the two men stared at him, long and hard. Then the psychologist's eyes narrowed. "You do that, Vadi," he said in the calmest of tones. "He knows far too much, wherever his loyalties lie. Can't have the *polizei* stumbling over him, can we?"

"No sir."

"Quick as you can, then meet us at the boathouse."

Vadi moved. So did Cadel. He launched himself out of the deep, dense cushions of the sofa, missed his footing, and hit the floor. By the time he'd scrambled up again, Vadi was holding his arm.

Cadel pulled free, but his head was swimming. He never made it to the front door. Vadi intercepted him.

"Cadel," said Thaddeus. Turning, Cadel saw that the psychologist had pulled out a small silver handgun. Staring down its barrel, Cadel froze. He felt, rather than saw, Vadi's surprise.

"Sir?"

"Go. *Now.* I'll take care of Cadel."

Hypnotized by the gleaming gun, Cadel didn't even hear Vadi's retreating footsteps, or the sound of the front door closing. He just stood, paralyzed. Slowly, Thaddeus rose from his seat, the gun steady in his hand. Slowly he approached Cadel.

"Right," he said. "Let me just point out, Cadel, that we have no time to waste on family skeletons and the like. Once we're in the clear, we can thrash out all your rejection issues at leisure. Until then, you'll oblige me by holding your tongue." He laid one hand on Cadel's shoulder. "Is that understood?"

473

Cadel nodded, speechless. He could hardly see; his eyes were full of tears. Somewhere outside, Vadi was killing Gazo. Gazo, who had come to Cadel's rescue. Cadel wanted to throw back his head and howl.

Instead, he allowed Thaddeus to steer him into the hallway, toward the back of the house. He was feeling much better now. So was Thaddeus, obviously, though he coughed a couple of times. They were moving at a brisk pace. As they passed the staircase, someone addressed them from the first landing.

"Dr. Roth?" It was Wilfreda.

"Where the hell have you been?" Thaddeus snapped.

"I'm sorry, sir, I was just—"

"We're getting out. Now."

"What?"

"They're coming by land, so we'll have to go by sea. I'll need your help, Wilfreda."

"Yes, sir, of course."

"Are you armed?"

"Uh—"

"Never mind. We can't linger. Come on."

Thaddeus didn't wait for Wilfreda to clatter down the stairs. He forged ahead, past a number of rooms opening off the hallway, until he reached the back door. He didn't fling it open, though. Instead, he peered through one of the panes of glass that flanked it, cautiously lifting the edge of a blind.

Suddenly a voice assailed them. It was a male voice, electronically magnified.

"Attention! This is the Australian Federal Police! I am Detective Sergeant Ken Pearce! If there is anyone in the house, will you please come out and show yourself!"

"The police!" Behind them, Wilfreda stopped in her tracks. "How—"

"There is no way out!" Detective Sergeant Ken Pearce continued.

"The house is surrounded, but we will not fire on you! If you're in there, Mr. Ivan Bleski, or anyone associated with him, will you please show yourself!"

"Look out the window!" Thaddeus ordered. He had his hands full; one was pointing the gun, the other was clutching the back of Cadel's neck. "Is it clear out the back?"

Wilfreda took up his station at the window, twitching at its blind. "I can't see," she complained, in an unsteady voice. "It's too dark." She looked to Thaddeus for guidance, her face taut, her gaze questioning.

"Attention, inhabitants of Curramulla! We will not hurt you! This is the Australian Federal Police . . ."

Somewhere several phones rang at once.

"That's them," said Thaddeus. He was frowning. "I'll have to answer or they'll start coming in. They'll think the place is empty." He cracked a mirthless half smile. "Which it practically is."

"How did they find us?" Wilfreda croaked.

"I don't know. But I can guess." To Cadel's immense fright, Thaddeus squeezed the back of his neck. "Lights off, Wilfreda. Yes, those. All of them." Wilfreda slapped at a bank of light switches positioned by the back door, and most of the lights were extinguished. Now Cadel could see only the shiny highlights on Thaddeus's nose and cheekbones, along with the gleam of his silver gun barrel. "Get down to the safe room," Thaddeus continued, addressing Wilfreda, "and bring up . . . let's see . . . bring up three gas masks and all the T-4 canisters. We'll fire 'em from the *back,* then make for the boat. Wind's an easterly. In the dark, we might just pull this off. And get the night goggles, too."

"But—"

"Do it! I'll keep them occupied. I'll be in the butler's pantry."

"But even in the dark, with the gas, once we're out there—"

"Once we're out there, we'll have a hostage," Thaddeus said calmly, gesturing at Cadel with the barrel of his gun.

Wilfreda gaped.

"Him?" she said.

"Him."

"But isn't that kind of dangerous? For him, I mean—"

"Wilfreda." Thaddeus spoke with barely controlled impatience. "Who do you think *told* them about this place?"

There was a brief silence. During it, the phones stopped ringing, before immediately starting up again. Wilfreda peered at Cadel.

"For Chris'sake . . . ," she breathed.

"No time to lose, Wilfreda."

"No. Right."

Wilfreda turned and hurried through a door under the stairs.

FIFTY-SIX

Thaddeus pulled Cadel through another door, which led into the murky dining room. But they didn't stop there. Instead, they moved straight across the floor and darted into a small, enclosed, windowless room, which dazzled Cadel when Thaddeus switched on the light. For the room was lined with shelves, all of them bearing bright glass, shining silver, jewel-like bottles. There was a phone on the wall.

Thaddeus released Cadel's neck. He pushed his son against one row of shelves, so roughly that a wineglass was dislodged, falling to the floor with a crash. Thaddeus then placed the barrel of his gun directly between Cadel's eyes.

Staring into them, his own gaze unreadable, Thaddeus picked up the wall-mounted receiver with his free hand.

"H-hello?" he quavered.

His voice, nervous and weak and unsteady with age, was at odds with his expression. It sounded like the voice that Cadel had heard outside the warehouse when he was still in Tommy's custody. (No doubt Thaddeus had been with Wilfreda, beyond the double doors.) For a while the psychologist stood listening. Cadel could hear another voice jabbering away at the other end of the line.

Cadel himself was so terrified that he couldn't think straight. The gun had driven almost every other consideration from his head. As for Thaddeus's expression, it was unlike anything that he had ever experienced before.

It was so cold, so empty, that it was practically devoid of life.

"I don't know what you mean!" Thaddeus wailed. "My name is Walter Felton, I'm *renting* from Mr. Bleski! No, he's not here! There's only me and my wife and my grandson! What? He's ten years old . . ." Thaddeus suddenly winked at Cadel. The wink was so obscenely, shockingly frivolous that it was like a slap in the face and brought tears rushing to Cadel's eyes. But he blinked them away and swallowed.

"Are you sure? Can you prove it?" Thaddeus went on in a querulous tone. "What do you mean? I can't leave my wife! She's not well! She has a bad heart . . . What's that? Phyllis? Oh my god . . . oh my god, look what you've done! Phyllis! *Phyllis!*"

Thaddeus slammed the cordless receiver against a tabletop, returned it to his ear for a moment and listened. Then he closed the connection.

"Right," he said, tucking the phone into his back pocket. "That should hold them for a minute or so. Come on—we have to watch the access points."

He nudged Cadel through the door ahead of him. They retraced their steps until they were once more just below the staircase in the center of the house. From there, Thaddeus had a view of both the back and front doors.

"This place is a joke," he remarked softly, still holding his gun to Cadel's head. He was standing straight behind Cadel, who couldn't see his eyes. "It's got more holes than a sieve. Mind you, I never thought I'd be using it as a bloody *redoubt*. Well—I never thought anyone would find me here. Just shows you, doesn't it? I must be getting slow in my old age."

Cadel said nothing. He didn't know what to say. Staring blindly at the hall table in front of him, he felt Thaddeus tug the shoelace out of his tangled curls.

"What on earth is this getup?" the psychologist inquired. "Were you *trying* to look like your mother?"

Cadel shook his head, still unable to speak.

"Well, you do. It was the skirt that really threw me. She was a hippy at heart—she always used to wear those god-awful Indian things . . ." He trailed off, and Cadel felt the gun barrel quiver against his scalp. "I couldn't help it, Cadel," Thaddeus continued, so quietly that he was barely audible. "She was insane. She thought we could sit down and thrash it out, the three of us—her, me, and Darkkon. Apparently it never crossed her mind that he was a maniac. You don't betray Phineas Darkkon, not if you want to stay alive. I knew he'd have us all killed. You, too, because you weren't his son." Thaddeus sighed. "I couldn't risk that," he said. "Don't you see? I had to choose. I had to lose one of you or all of us."

At that instant, while he stared at the arrangement of coral branches on the hall table, something clicked inside Cadel's head. His eyes widened. He caught his breath and slowly turned around, ignoring the gun that hovered at eye level. He gazed up at Thaddeus.

Someone knocked on the front door.

"Mr. Felton?" said a vaguely familiar voice. "Are you there?"

Thaddeus sucked in air through his teeth. He looked over at the door beneath the stairs. Though fleeting, this glance was enough— enough to give Cadel a head start.

He made a run for it.

"Cadel!" cried Thaddeus.

"Mr. Felton?"

No shot rang out. Cadel hadn't been expecting one. He reached the front door and would have hauled it open.

But before he could do so, Thaddeus was beside him, gun in hand.

"Take one more step," Thaddeus whispered, pressing the gun against Cadel's temple, "and I'll blast your brains out."

Cadel froze. Then he swallowed. Then, without moving his head, he let his eyes slip sideways until they found Thaddeus.

He and Thaddeus surveyed each other for a long, tense moment. The psychologist's hand was rock steady.

Cadel took a deep breath.

"No, you won't," he said, and drew the latch. *"I'm coming outside!"* he called. *"Don't shoot me!"*

"Cadel?" The familiar voice was now directly on the other side of the door. Cadel recognized it as belonging to Kale Platz. "Cadel Darkkon, is that you?"

"Yes! And I'm coming out!"

There was a scuffle of boots, suggesting that the people on the front steps were taking cover. Thaddeus cocked his gun. Cadel flinched but didn't yield.

Slowly, he turned the doorknob. Slowly, he pulled open the door.

He caught a glimpse of Thaddeus's crooked smile, as the silver gun was lowered.

Then he walked out into a blaze of spotlights.

"Hands in the air, Cadel. That's the way. Just a few more steps . . ."

Blinded by the glare, Cadel allowed himself to be yanked, jerked, and patted down. He realized that tears were streaming down his face. Someone gave him a tissue. A hand on his shoulder steered him quickly away from the house while Kale fired questions at him. "Who's in there? How many people? Have they got weapons? Guns?"

"Where's Gazo?" gasped Cadel.

"What?"

"He was out here." Wiping his cheeks, Cadel looked back at the house, which was bathed in light. The police had brought their own lights with them. He heard a helicopter and peered up into the night sky. "Didn't you see him? He was on the ground . . ."

"Guy in the white outfit, you mean?" said Kale, and someone behind him remarked, "Oh, we picked *him* up. He's with the other one— the one in the tailcoat. *They* won't be going anywhere in a hurry."

"You mean—Gazo's alive?"

"He's breathing," Kale rejoined, and his hand tightened on Cadel's shoulder. "Look at me, Cadel. That's it."

"He's my friend!" Cadel cried. "You mustn't hurt him! He was trying to help me!"

"Well, we'll sort that out later. In the meantime, I need *your* help. Are you listening?"

"But is he hurt?"

"Cadel. Listen to me." The American's tone was stern. "Who's in there? How many are left?"

"Thad—Prosper is in there."

"Prosper *English*? He's *in* there?"

"Don't hurt him." Cadel was frantic. "Don't shoot him."

"Who else? Who's with him?"

"I don't know. Wilfreda . . ."

"Get this kid out of here," an Australian voice commanded. "Get him right out of the way. It's too dangerous."

"But if we need to negotiate—"

"This kid's nonnegotiable. *Where's Jenny? Bring her over!*"

Cadel was helped into a car. He was vaguely aware of a whole ring of cars out at the edge of the lawn. Milling bodies looked identical in the poor light. The soothing, rhythmic sound of the ocean seemed at odds with the urgent voices and flurries of movement.

There were dozens of people around. Thirty at least, that Cadel could see. And distant shouts told him that there were even more, hidden away in the shadows.

Nearby, a muttered argument was going on between a man and a woman.

"But sir—"

"Jenny, will you *get in*?"

"But I'm on the squad—"

"He's a kid. He'll feel more comfortable with you. So get in. That's an *order.*"

Someone buckled Cadel's seat belt. Someone else slid into the car, next to him. The woman—Jenny—threw herself into the front passenger seat. Doors slammed. The engine roared.

"You'll be all right, son," declared the man beside Cadel. It was Kale Platz. "We're just making sure you're out of harm's way."

"What are you going to do?" Cadel's voice cracked. "You're not going to kill him?"

"We won't kill anyone if we can help it. You should know that—we're the good guys."

"It wasn't my fault . . ."

"Shhh. Take it easy."

"I just—I just wanted to get away! From everything! I'm sorry! I'm very sorry!"

"We can talk about that later."

"I just want to be *normal*!"

"Oh, Christ," Kale muttered. He placed an unexpected hand on Cadel's forearm and squeezed it. The car plunged down the winding dirt road, illuminating gum trees on its way. Cadel heard whistles blasting somewhere back near the house. He cried and cried. He felt as if his heart was breaking, but he didn't know why.

At last they stopped. They were near the big gate in the high brick wall. Three more cars were parked in the same spot.

"You want some chewing gum?" Kale inquired, offering a piece to Cadel. Then, somewhere on his person, a two-way radio crackled to life.

A distorted voice announced that, back at the house, Prosper English had surrendered.

He had suddenly walked out of the front door with his hands up.

FIFTY-SEVEN

To: Il Primo
From: Stormer

Hi there, Sonja!

It's me—Cadel. I guess you thought you wouldn't be hearing from me ever again. Maybe you were hoping that you wouldn't. I can understand if that's how you feel. It's all been a big mess.

But I wanted you to know how grateful I am for what you did. If it hadn't been for you, things might not have turned out so well. Not that everything's GREAT—I'm not allowed to see you, for one thing—but at least I'm alive.

The reason I didn't call when I promised to last week is that I was kidnapped. Were you told? Probably not. I was kidnapped, then I was rescued, then the police found me, then I escaped, and then I had a bit of bad luck. Well, a lot of bad luck, really. Remember how I said I wanted to find a hiding place and get on with my life? Well, that's not going to happen anymore. I blew it.

Maybe I didn't deserve to succeed.

It's amazing how much they've managed to keep out of the news. There was a lot of stuff about Prosper English—did you see it?—but almost nothing about me. Just the odd mention. I guess it's because I'm underage, and they don't want a media circus. That's what my lawyer said: "The last thing we want is a media circus." They're worried about me. I don't think they know what to do with me, for one thing. They've got me holed up in a big house (I can't tell you where—security reasons) while they work out who the hell I am. You see, officially, I don't exist. My birth was never registered in America. I was smuggled into Australia. They don't know where I belong, or who I belong to. I'm a bit worried that I'm going to be kicked out of the country, actually. After all, who wants the trouble? On the one hand, someone might try to kill me. On the other hand, I might try to escape again. I told them I wouldn't, but it's no good. Some of them don't trust me, and probably never will. (I blew that, too.) The ones who do trust me think I'm a sad, twisted little kid. (They're not far wrong, I suppose.) There's only one guy—an American—who's keeping his opinions to himself. He's always debriefing me, trying to find out how much I know about Dr. Darkkon's empire. I hardly know anything, but I'm not sure if he believes me or not. He always seems to, and then he always comes back with more questions. My social worker, a really nice woman, is constantly complaining about that. They have a lot of fights over me. I hate it.

I hate the whole place.

Maybe I won't be here for much longer, though. I hope not. I'd rather not stay floating in limbo for the next four years while they work out what they're doing. I'd like to go to university—a real university. Not like the Axis Institute. I guess you've heard about the Axis Institute. I went there, did they tell you? It wasn't very nice. But then, I wasn't very nice, either, so maybe it was the best place for me. I've done some terrible things, Sonja. I might even have to pay for them—I don't know yet. There's a lot of talk about that. At least I've started to make things right, though. I just signed a legal document that will change the lives of a lot of kids at my old school (I hope). By doing so, I wanted to convince everyone that I could do better. That I could be better. Most of all, I wanted to convince myself.

The trouble is, I'm still a minor. Which means that I don't have control over where I live, or everything I do. Next thing they'll probably make me a ward of the state (if there's any state that even wants me) and I'll end up in some kind of foster home, or something. I wish I was eighteen. If I was, I'd be able to make some of my own decisions.

I'm getting an idea of what it must be like for you.

But I shouldn't complain. The thing I have to do is, I have to look at this whole situation in a positive way. I have to regard it as an opportunity. So what if I'm in limbo? It will give me a chance to work out what I'm going to do with my life. Before this, someone else always made the decisions for me when it came to the future. Now I'm on my own. Phineas Darkkon can't get at me. Prosper English can't get at me. I suppose, in a way, I am free. Though freedom isn't quite what I expected.

In case you haven't been told, Prosper English was my therapist. They've got him locked up somewhere for questioning, and one of these days there might be a trial, though I wouldn't count on it. He's very clever. The latest I heard, he's saying that he was just renting the house that he was found in and didn't know about the secret room full of arms and ammunition. He even has the lawyers all tied up in some kind of argument about search warrants. Also, I've got a feeling that he's covered his tracks pretty well when it comes to the Axis Institute. Kale—the American—keeps coming to me with more and more questions about what Prosper did, as if no one can find any solid proof. It's a bit of a worry. Because if they have to rely on witnesses, they're in trouble. All kinds of things can happen to witnesses.

As for me, I'll probably have to testify against Prosper. God. I mean, I'd do it. I would. But I really don't want to. I really, really don't. He'd be in the same courtroom. I'd have to look him in the eye. I haven't seen him at all since he was arrested, and I'm hoping that Kale won't ask me to go and talk to him in the hope that Prosper will "open up." It would be so hard. You don't understand what Prosper's like—no one does. It's very complicated. He's different from other people. He's even different from Phineas. Despite everything he's done, I can't hate him. I try to, but I can't.

I guess I'm hoping that I'm a bit like Prosper, in that one respect. I'm hoping that, despite everything I've done, you can't hate me. Because you're my best friend. My only other friend—well, he's gone now. The police arrested him, but he escaped. He has this special skill that they didn't know about—not until it was too late. I don't know where he is, and I don't expect I'll see him again. Maybe I'll have more friends in the future (I'm working on it), but that won't change how I feel about you.

I don't expect you to reply—not really. But if you can just read this letter, and the ones that come after it, at least you'll know what I'm doing. How I'm going. And maybe, in a little while, I might hear from you again. When you realize that I'm not completely bad.

You see, I have this vision in my head. It's of you and me playing chess in a park somewhere. You don't know how important that picture is to me. I think about it a lot of the time, for some reason: playing chess in a park. For the whole afternoon. As the shadows lengthen and everyone slowly goes home except us.

Maybe it means something, though I don't know what.

I guess I'm not so smart after all.

To: Stormer
From: Il Primo

$$53 - 178.5 - 73 - 12.01 - 92$$

Coming soon...

GENIUS SQUAD

Sometimes when it comes to fighting evil,
one genius isn't enough.

AXIS INSTITUTE

CHANCELLOR: *Thaddeus Roth*

SCHOOL OF DECEPTION

PROFESSOR: *Thaddeus Roth*

CLASS:	TAUGHT BY:
Basic Lying ~~Coping Skills~~*	Thaddeus Roth
Pure Evil ~~Pragmatic Philosophy~~*	Max de Litto *aka the Maestro*
Forgery ~~Cultural Appreciation~~*	Art East
Loopholes ~~Law~~*	Barry Deakin *aka Dr. Deal*
Disguise ~~Personal Presentation~~*	Alias
Infiltration ~~Computer Science~~	Dr. Ulysses Vee *aka the Virus*
Manipulation ~~Psychology~~	Thaddeus Roth
Misinformation ~~Media Studies~~	Tracey Lane
Embezzlement ~~Accounting~~	Brendan Graham